MURDER
ON THE
TITANIC

A NOVEL BY JIM WALKER

BROADMAN
& HOLMAN
PUBLISHERS

Nashville, Tennessee

0-8054-0198-9

Published by Broadman & Holman Publishers, Nashville, Tennessee
Acquisitions and Development Editor: Vicki Crumpton
Page Design: Anderson Thomas Design
Page Compositer: TF Designs

Dewey Decimal Classification: F
Subject Heading: MYSTERY FICTION \ TITANIC—FICTION
Library of Congress Card Catalog Number: 97-42332

Published in association with the literary agency of
Alive Communications, Inc.,
1465 Kelly Johnson Blvd., Suite 320,
Colorado Springs, CO 80902

Library of Congress Cataloging-in-Publication Data
Walker, Jim.
    Murder on the Titanic
        p. cm.
    ISBN 0-8054-0198-9
    1. Titanic (Steamship)—Fiction.   I. Title.
        PS3573.A425334M871998
    813'.54—dc21—dc21

                                                            97-42332
                                                            CIP

2 3 4 5   02 01 00 99 98

This book is dedicated to the gallant men of the Titanic
who stood aside for those they loved
and paid the ultimate price.

It is also dedicated to my best friend,
the one who stood by me and made this possible.

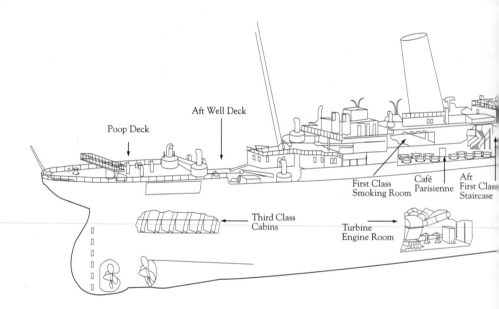

Poop Deck

Aft Well Deck

First Class
Smoking Room

Café
Parisienne

Aft
First Class
Staircase

Third Class
Cabins

Turbine
Engine Room

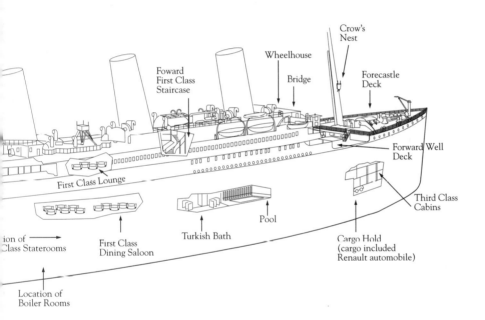

Crow's
Nest

Wheelhouse

Bridge

Forecastle
Deck

Foward
First Class
Staircase

Forward Well
Deck

First Class Lounge

Third Class
Cabins

ion of
Class Staterooms

First Class
Dining Saloon

Turkish Bath

Pool

Cargo Hold
(cargo included
Renault automobile)

Location of
Boiler Rooms

The *Titanic*

AUTHOR'S NOTES

This book is a work of fiction. I use historical characters and the actual events surrounding the *Titanic* tragedy to tell the story. In many cases, I lifted references noted in the hearings that followed the disaster. At times, I use quotations from the press of the day. I have also taken the opportunity to advance several theories that spotlight events that led to the sinking, at least one of which may have prevented the great loss of life.

While attempting to portray the history, I tell the story of a number of fictional characters. The actions of these characters and their interaction with historical people are entirely a product of my imagination. The reader should draw no conclusions about people of history from what I have written.

The ultimate lesson of the *Titanic*, from my own viewpoint, is the overconfidence we place on human endeavor. It is seemingly our greatest desire to live our lives in such a way that we never need to depend on God. In our modern lifestyles, He is the beloved distant one.

It is my hope that in reading this book, we will all realize how much we need Him and how little we can count on our ability to remove ourselves from His power.

THE MAIN CHARACTERS:

Morgan Fairfield: Morgan is a recent graduate from Oxford. A wealthy orphan, Morgan is embarrassed by what he sees as the lifestyle of the rich. An American by birth, he has decided to go to New York and accept a newspaper job. Even though he loves Margaret Hastings, he believes he must first go and prove himself before he can ask for her hand in marriage. Morgan is responsible to a fault and bound by a code of honor.

Margaret Hastings: Margaret is an attractive only child to a landed member of the House of Lords. She has known and loved Morgan since old enough to remember. She is a free spirit and a tireless worker for the cause of women's suffrage. Margaret was heartbroken when Morgan informed her of his decision to make a name for himself before he could hope to ask for her hand in marriage. In an attempt to get on with her life and forget Morgan, Margaret has become engaged to Peter Wilksbury.

Peter Wilksbury: Peter has recently become engaged to Margaret Hastings to the great delight of both their families. Peter is a gentleman who is enchanted by Margaret's friends and political views. He views Margaret's attachment to Morgan as nothing more than a schoolyard crush that crosses social classes.

Hunter Kennedy: Hunter Kennedy is a semisuccessful actor. His father is a minister, and Hunter is living a life apart from God and the upbringing of his childhood. Hunter lives life on the edge and sees no point to anything that doesn't involve a good time. He is in love with Kitty Webb and highly resentful of her relationship with Benjamin Guggenheim. His main reason for being aboard the *Titanic* is to confront Bruce Ismay.

Months before, his young sister was killed by a hit-and-run automobile. He has evidence in hand that Ismay was driving the car.

Bruce Ismay: Bruce Ismay is the director of the White Star Line. He is conceited, competitive, and determined to undermine any authority but his own. Ismay works hard at ensuring that the *Titanic* will operate at peak performance on its race across the icy waters of the North Atlantic. He also has a terrible secret that he will pay any price to hide, the death of Hunter Kennedy's sister. *Note: Bruce Ismay is a historical character.*

Benjamin Guggenheim: Guggenheim is an American millionaire in what he sees as a loveless marriage. He has been traveling throughout Europe on business but also in the company of his mistress, Kitty Webb. He is sensitive to the proper way of concealing their affair but sees his passage on the *Titanic* as an enjoyable thing and the last stop for him and Kitty until they once again must conceal their relationship in New York. *Note: Benjamin Guggenheim is a historical character.*

Kitty Webb: Kitty is the mistress of the American millionaire Benjamin Guggenheim. She is a beautiful woman whom he pulled from the chorus line in a New York City musical. She knows the man is married but has a seemingly devil-may-care attitude about the position this leaves her in. Her attitude about life in general is jaded, and she looks with contempt on what she views as out-of-date morality. She does not want to return to her life on the stage and has grown accustomed to relying on her beauty and charm to gain the material comfort she seeks. Her former lover is Hunter Kennedy. She treats him with disdain but fears his knowledge of her past life and suspects that he may try to extract revenge for his broken heart. *Note: Kitty Webb is a historical character.*

Donald Delaney: Donald Delaney is a successful novelist. He has become wealthy with a series of successful novels and is a freewheeling drinker and gambler. He is daring and brash and with a background that has deep roots in the Irish rebellion. He has ties to the IRA and makes no effort to conceal his contempt for the English government. Delaney is deaf due to a near miss with a terrorist bomb of his own making. He does read lips very well.

Jack Kelly: Jack is an old man in third-class steerage. The man is a grandfather traveling to America with his two grandchildren. He is a boatbuilder of wooden fishing boats and a former Royal Marine. Jack Kelly knows the only way to keep the *Titanic* afloat long enough for it to be assisted by rescue vessels. His only problem as a steerage-class passenger and a builder of wooden boats, is getting people to listen to him.

Mrs. Gloria Thompson: Mrs. Thompson is a young widow. She has suffered grief with the passing of her husband three years ago. She befriends Margaret and tries to steer her away from a loveless marriage. With her wealth, she has grown used to discouraging men who want her for her money. She has given much thought to the quality of one's life and passes on to Margaret the idea that love is from God in its power and passion and that it rightfully belongs to only one man living on the earth.

Mr. Hoffman: Hoffman is a man aboard the *Titanic* with his two small children. He is using a fictitious name and actually is Michael Navratil, who has kidnapped the two children in an attempt at revenge on his estranged wife. He makes every attempt to conceal his real identity and refuses to become involved with the murder investigation, even though he may be the only witness. *Note: Michael Navratil is a historical figure.*

Fitzgerald: Fitzgerald is a steward to the first-class passengers. He is an agent for the cause of Irish independence and will use his position to do anything he can to advance the cause.

Hans Reinhold: Hans is the valet to Benjamin Guggenheim. He is a towering hulk of a man who has great loyalty to his employer. Hans is also good with a sword, practicing with his saber on a daily basis. He suspects that Hunter has cheated Guggenheim at cards and distrusts Hunter's motives in disclosing the past relationship Hunter has had with Kitty Webb.

Joseph Boxhall: Boxhall is the fourth officer on the *Titanic*. He is keeping the charts of the *Titanic* and carefully makes notes of the sightings of ice being radioed to them by other ships in the vicinity. Unlike many of the other officers, Boxhall is highly concerned with the route he is being forced to chart. He is cautious and a very capable officer. *Note: Joseph Boxhall is a historical figure.*

Major Archie Butt: Major Butt is a friend and the military attaché of President Taft. He is aboard the *Titanic* to receive secret papers from the Pope that may prevent a war. Taft is in a close race with former President Theodore Roosevelt. Butt knows that these papers may very well spell the difference between the president's winning and losing the primary elections of 1912. *Note: Major Archie Butt is a historical figure.*

Howie O'Conner: O'Conner is a third-class passenger who keeps to himself and sleeps in the bow of the *Titanic* where the single men are berthed. He is an operative of the IRA and reports to Delaney. Fitzgerald supplies him with a steward jacket and passkeys, which allow him to move freely among first-class passengers. He has orders to try to use the explosives he has carried aboard the ship to seriously damage or sink the *Titanic*.

MONDAY,
APRIL 15, 1912,
2:24 A.M.

PROLOGUE

The water surged over the sinking bow of the great ship, sending sheets of icy brine over the forecastle. Morgan leaned over the railing. He had forced Margaret into her life jacket and into a life-boat, and that gave him some comfort. The boats below were being rowed away, and already he could see that the oarsmen were keeping their distance from the swimmers in the water. The shouts and screams of the men went unanswered.

He climbed over the rail and watched the approaching flood. The sea was dark and still, and in the distance he could see only a few stars as they winked at him over the dim ice field. He stepped off, his arms spin-ning in wide circles.

As he plunged into the bottomless pool, the frigid seawater whirled him around. His drop from the deck carried him under for what seemed like an eternity. He thrashed his arms in the inky blackness and blinked back the salty water, choking on the sudden stinging sensation in his lungs. He kicked furiously, fighting the feeling of bursting lungs. He reached up with his arms and strained to find the surface.

Bursting to the surface of the bone-chilling sea, he gasped, first waggling his arms at the night sky and then kicking to put as much distance as he could between him and the sinking vessel. He knew that the suction of the great ship might well carry him back under when it went down for the final time. He was determined not to let that happen, at least not while he had breath left in his body.

The shock of the cold made Morgan feel like a thousand knives were being jabbed into his body. In a way, it was a good feeling. He was alive; when the pain stopped, he'd be in the process of dying. He stroked in the direction of the distant lifeboats. He couldn't understand why they were rowing away. All around, he watched as men struggled against what would be an all too quick death with arms flailing and cries cut short by the sudden shock of the cold.

The *Titanic* rose in the water, its stern lifting. It began a slow spin like an enormous ballerina poised on the stage before taking a final bow. A massive black hulk of dead and dying steel, it hung suspended in history. The sound of creaking thunder came from the bowels of the upright ship. Enormous engines and boilers tore loose from their anchors in the belly of the ship and cascaded in an avalanche of iron and steel. Lights blinked in the starry sky, winking at the darkness in a last gasp of life.

The band on deck had been playing "Nearer My God to Thee," a plaintive but prophetic cry. The Almighty Creator of this great ocean seemed to be standing silently by, waiting for hundreds, perhaps thousands, of arrivals at His heavenly doorstep. Morgan's faith had been strong in college but never before tested. He gasped a prayer and stroked one frigid push after another against the coal-black sea.

Morgan watched as men, women, and children dropped helplessly into the heaving sea, their screams floating out over the dark water, their dying cries the evidence that they had lived. The shouts and screams were a symphony of death that seemingly fell on deaf ears of the people in the faraway lifeboats. Escaping gas and steam surged up from below, giving the impression of a pot of bubbling stew. Breaking steel and belching air drowned out the piteous cries of the last-minute leapers.

The great ship seemed to break in two as it hung upright in the air. Morgan watched the heavy stern drop as the bow slid into the icy Atlantic like a knife through a plum pudding.

Kicking with the mound of suddenly displaced water, Morgan spotted the Irish mother he had seen cowering on the deck with her baby only moments before. She had been a steerage passenger and had on her life jacket. They would no doubt recover her body. The young woman had red hair with rivulets of wet curls falling down the sides of her face and polka-dot freckles pasted to her chalky face. She clutched her whimpering baby in her arms. Her eyes were closed as he swam by her, and only the baby looked in his direction.

The sight of the woman brought back the picture of what must have been his mother's lot. It seemed that his fate was to be just like that of the parents he'd never known. They'd both drowned in a boating accident off Newport, Rhode Island, twenty-two years ago. The only face he could remember from his childhood was that of Lilly, his childhood nurse. Only days ago, he'd spontaneously purchased a bouquet of fresh irises to give to her after docking in New York. He'd soon discovered that they were too fragile to survive the five-day voyage and now it seemed neither would he.

Morgan raked through his mind as if to discover what his parents actually looked like in flesh and blood; he tried in vain to recall a touch of family love. How did they smell? What perfume did his mother wear? What was the aroma of his father's pipe tobacco? Nothing ever came to him, nothing at all. *If I am dying, shouldn't there be some flash of memory?* he wondered. Their pose in an ornate brass-framed photograph gave him his only impression of whose loins he'd sprung from. That and the wrinkled, yellowed newspaper articles about their lives and their deaths that his aunt had saved.

He kicked against the water and surged forward, slithering through the sea in his best Australian crawl. If he were about to die, it would not be for lack of effort. He knew the identity of a murderer, and even if the murderer didn't survive, Morgan had to find a way to pass the story on to someone who would. He also had to find Margaret. She was safely aboard one of the lifeboats. He had seen to that. It had taken Morgan so long to discover just how much he loved her, and he longed to tell her once more before dying. She loved him, and he couldn't bear the thought of dying with the only love he had ever known of Margaret something from his childhood. He also wanted her to know Morgan Fairfield, the real Morgan Fairfield.

WEDNESDAY,
APRIL 10, 1912,
6:15 A.M.

CHAPTER 1

The sky was slate gray. A brisk breeze rippled the budding maple leaves. Morgan paused on the steps of the old hotel to watch the sea birds twist in the wind in lazy swirls. He hadn't slept well in the too soft bed. The mattress was old like the rest of the place, which was filled with worn settees and overstuffed chairs. He patted his coat pocket for the notebook and the pen given to him by a school chum. No reporter, even one taking on his first job, would be without his tools of the trade.

Morgan watched two men pass, one shabbily dressed in a brown coat and the other in a vanilla-ice-cream-colored suit. He stepped out from the stone doorway and followed them slowly, swinging his silver-tipped cane over his shoulder. His gray day coat along with the cane distinguished him as a gentleman.

He would hurry to the Carlsford to eat and to read the morning paper before his Uncle John and Aunt Dottie arrived. His uncle's forced chatter would make eating breakfast and reading a virtual impossibility. Plus, Morgan knew he'd have to put up with the man's nagging over this decision to work at the *Herald* in New York. Anything outside the world of finance seemed like a waste of time to Uncle John.

He quickened his pace. The porter had assured him that his trunks and bags would be delivered to the ship and be waiting for him. He hoped so. They contained everything in the world he truly owned and a few items he didn't.

The red cobblestone sidewalk wound along the narrow street and passed brownstone buildings that once belonged to sea captains. These places, their windows turned to the White Star docks, had brightly painted boxes filled with blooming flowers. Many had been turned into lodgings and taverns. A few lonely women, still sheltered there, looked out the doors at passersby.

The street seemed to be deserted, except for a hansom cab that rolled by at a hurried pace and two men who sauntered ahead of him. The cab distracted the man in the shabby brown coat, and he turned his head to watch it pass as the pair rounded the corner ahead. The clamor of the heavy hooves caused them not to notice Morgan as he brought up the rear.

Morgan absently mused that the portly man's cream-colored suit seemed totally out of place for England in the chilly spring. Clutched tenuously under his arm was a beaten leather satchel. The satchel obviously had a leather shoulder strap that would have allowed him to swing it comfortably, but he nervously ignored it, preferring to crowd it under his left armpit.

Rounding the corner, Morgan quickly noticed that the two men had disappeared. The suddenly empty, eerily quiet street flanked by alleyways and closed doors made the hair on the back of his neck stand up. *Odd,* he mused. *There is no place they could have gone.* He picked up his pace. Then he heard the sound of a scuffle from the alley just ahead. He started to run.

When he reached the alley, he stopped dead in his tracks. The man in the brown coat was crouching over the prone figure in the vanilla suit. He wrenched the leather carrying case, finally prying it from the man's grasp. He then reached into the man's inner coat pocket and took out a leather ticket case.

"Here, here!" Morgan yelled. His heart beat fast in his chest, like a rabbit running through the moors. "What seems to be going on?"

The thief got to his feet and flashed a knife in Morgan's direction. Morgan glanced at the man on the ground. A deep wound was blossoming crimson just below his chest and spreading rapidly over his belly. The sight of the blood made Morgan suddenly queasy.

Morgan felt frozen in time. The man with the knife sized him up with the cold stare of a trapped wild animal. Morgan instinctively knew he had only one flimsy advantage against a knife. He forced thoughts of fear from his head. Pulling himself to his full height of six-feet-two, he stepped forward. "See here, you leave this man alone." He croaked out the words, trying his best to sound brave.

The man with the knife was a full head shorter. He sneered, his pencil-thin mustache barely visible on his stubbly unshaven face. "Back, boy, go on," he growled.

Reminds me of a cur dog that one would find on the street, Morgan thought. The idea sounded brave in his head, even if he didn't believe it. *Call his bluff, and he'll light out with his tail between his legs—I hope.*

Morgan inched forward.

Suddenly, the thief darted forward with the knife.

Morgan dodged his lumbering attempt. With that, the man turned and ran.

Ripping the scarf from around his neck, Morgan crouched down and pressed it into the older man's bleeding abdomen. The man had a neatly trimmed, gray mustache and a dimple in his chin much like Morgan's. His gray hair was parted on the side, and his large brown eyes were the color of walnuts. Panting and now feeling somewhat desperate, Morgan tried his best to try to console the man. "You will be all right, sir. I'll get help."

The man sputtered and spat, drops of blood spotting the corners of his mouth. "Never mind me, go get my case. Please, sir, if there's an ounce of decency in you, don't let him have those papers."

"No, you need help and right away." Morgan daubed nervously at the gushing wound. Truthfully, Morgan had little desire to chase the man with the knife. He was already in a cold sweat.

The man coughed and shuttered at the very conjecture of help. "Do as I say! Never you mind me. Those papers are of utmost importance." He got more agitated and desperate in his plea. "My life is nothing compared to them. You're a young man, now go, boy, go now!"

Morgan got to his feet and backed away. A feeling of renewed terror shot through him. Fencing in school was the closest he'd come to combat. But facing a man who would do anything to kill him was quite another.

The man shouted at him again. "You must go now, boy. Those papers are of more value than my life, yours, or a thousand others."

Turning slowly, Morgan ran off in the direction of the fleeing felon. *Maybe he's had time to get away,* his mind pondered as he ran. *This is really a police matter.* If the truth be known, he had little desire in finding the man, only in showing the attempt. His mind rose in a desperate prayer. *Please, Lord, help me now.*

Coming to a T in the alley and looking both ways, he decided to go to the left in the direction he'd come from. The doors were all shut that led out to the alley, and trash bins dotted the rough brick pavement.

Rickety stairs sloped along the sides of the buildings. A man would never make it up those things. Their worn treads wouldn't bear up under the weight of more than a child. It was obvious that the owners of these houses had made little effort at retaining paint on these sides of the structures and even less at maintaining cleanliness. Morgan continued to run, slowing down on occasion as he came to large trash bins that might conceal a man in hiding.

Suddenly, the sound of the man's feet slamming up against a wooden wall echoed through the alley. Morgan's heart knocked against his chest as he rounded the corner and saw him. He was attempting to jump and latch on to the upper edge of a picketed wooden wall between two buildings. It was just out of reach, especially since he insisted on keeping one hand tightly clutched to the leather satchel. Morgan thought it would have made an amusing sight had he not known the treachery possible in this man.

"Stop, thief!" Morgan yelled. He shouted in the vain hope that some tenant would open a window or door and lend assistance. Better still, he hoped someone might summon the police. "Thief!" Morgan screamed, "Murderer!"

The man dropped to the alley. Swinging around, he once again took a menacing stance. "Stay out of my way," he yelled. Pointing the knife in Morgan's direction, he rushed forward.

Morgan had spent hours in training with both foil and saber. It was the gentlemanly sport for a boy in school. In spite of his serious nature with books, Morgan had developed quite the reputation among his classmates. With his long legs and strapping build, he'd been marked in school early on as an athlete. Raising his outstretched cane, he parried more out of instinct than bravery. His teacher would have been quite proud. The wooden slash caught the man's wrist and dispatched the knife.

Shock swept across the thief's face. His eyes widened, and his mouth dropped open. The sudden action of this mere boy came as a total surprise.

The quick success astonished Morgan. Suddenly emboldened, he swung the cane furiously, slashing the man across the shoulders and face. Morgan became an animal, too. Adrenaline shot through him as he rapped the man in the jaw.

Dropping the leather case, the man raised his hands and arms to fend off the blows. Stumbling backward, he seized a large, empty water barrel. Holding it above his face and head to ward off Morgan's continued blows, he heaved it.

The container landed hard on Morgan's shoulder. Slightly dazed, he staggered backward but stayed on his feet.

The thief crouched low against the wall and moved to the side like a crab, keeping his hands and arms above his head.

Morgan stepped toward him and continued his rain of terror-filled blows. As each one landed, grunts and cries of pain were mixed with furious howls. The sounds the man made would have been terrifying if Morgan hadn't already been overwhelmed with desperation and panic. He followed each blow with yet a harder one, as if he were driving a stubborn nail that simply refused to take its place in a wall.

The man inched his way to the left, now on all fours. He cleared the narrow passage and crawled out into the alley. Growling like a whipped cur, he dove for the relative safety of the space he perceived to be beyond the hammering. Scampering to his feet, he ran down the alley with reckless abandon.

Morgan stopped and watched the man run. He had no intention of giving chase. His heart beat like a bird in a tight cage, its flutters followed by collisions against the wiry bars. Gasping for breath, Morgan bent over, bowed his head, and rested his hands on his thighs. *Whatever have I done?* he wondered.

Swiveling his head around, Morgan spotted the scratched and weathered satchel. He picked it up and knocked the dirt from its surface.

T he man's eyes were half-closed, but he brightened when he saw Morgan trotting back with the case. Morgan laid the satchel in his lap. "Here you are. I retrieved your bag, but the man got away."

In the distance the shrill sound of a police whistle ripped through the morning air. Someone had obviously alerted them. *It's about time*, Morgan thought.

The man on the ground took little comfort in that thought. He only clutched the pouch closer and lifted his brown calflike eyes toward Morgan. The man's eyes reminded Morgan of his own. "Are you English?" he asked.

Morgan thought the man's question quite odd. "Actually, I'm American," Morgan replied. "I was educated here in England but born in the United States. I'm sailing on the *Titanic* today."

"Excellent," the man coughed. The cleft in his chin quivered. "Then you must complete my mission."

"Your mission? And what is that?"

He shoved the satchel in Morgan's direction. "This must go to an American officer aboard the *Titanic*, Major Archibald Butt, and failing that you must take it to the War Department in Washington." He clutched Morgan's hand with a firm grip. The man's steely grip was surprising, considering his condition. "Tell no one about this, you understand?"

What choice do I have? Morgan wondered. *Lord, help me here!* He nodded from pure bewilderment.

"Lives depend upon this reaching our . . . War Department. It can prevent . . . a great war . . .," he gulped, ". . . looms in front of the whole world. Do you understand, sir?"

The man was obviously weakening, his speech faltering. Morgan put the satchel to one side.

"Yes, but you'll be fine. Help is almost here." Morgan looked down the alley and to the street, wondering why that policeman was taking so long.

"As far as the authorities are concerned"—the man spit up blood—"this attaché case belongs to you."

"What about you?"

"I . . . too . . . was to sail on the *Titanic* t-today, but that man took my tickets and money. I won't be needing them anyway."

"The police will be here soon, and we'll get an ambulance for you."

He tightened his grip on Morgan's wrist. His eyes cleared for just a moment. "You don't understand. I am of no importance. Only those papers in my bag matter now. Tell no one." His face was now ashen. Blood trickled from one corner of his mouth. "Only do as I ask," he gasped almost angrily.

Two constables suddenly rounded the corner, one continuing to blow his whistle. "What, what's this?" the first asked.

"This man needs help now, " Morgan said, almost exasperated.

The policeman with the whistle backed out to the street and, waving his arms, continued to signal for assistance.

The policeman crouching over the man applied more pressure to the bleeding wound. "Is this your scarf, sir?" he asked, eyeing Morgan suspiciously.

Morgan's mind raced. He realized they might easily mistake him for the culprit.

"I saw the man who did this. And that is my scarf, but you can keep it now."

The bleeding man looked plaintively at the constable. "This young man tried to help me." He winced and once again grabbed Morgan's wrist. "And what is your name young man?" he asked.

"Morgan Fairfield. Morgan Montague Fairfield."

"Of the Rhode Island Fairfields?" he asked, his eyes widening with interest.

"Yes, sir."

The man's eyes raked over Morgan, seemingly studying each and every feature. Reaching out, he lightly touched the dimple in Morgan's chin. He swallowed, blood gurgling in his throat. "Thank you, Morgan Montague Fairfield." The mention of Morgan's name made his grip tighten all the more. He coughed, spitting up blood.

Just then the ambulance chugged its way down the narrow street. Morgan stepped back as two attendants saw to the now unconscious man. When he was loaded aboard the lorry, a shrill blast of the siren accompanied his departure.

It took Morgan the better part of a half-hour to answer all of the constable's questions. Morgan wrung his hands.

"You may need to come to Scotland Yard for further questioning," the constable said.

"I'm afraid that will be quite impossible," Morgan replied. "I sail on the *Titanic* today."

The policeman backed away, eyeing Morgan up and down. "If we have further questions, we may have to come aboard and find you then."

Morgan straightened his jacket, pulling the cuffs down over his sleeves. "I'd really like to help you catch the man who did this. I don't know any more than what I've already described to you, however."

The constable jotted down a few more hasty notes, obviously listing Morgan's location as the *Titanic*. Putting the pad away, he nodded. "I suppose that will have to be all for now. But as I say, if we do need more, we will come and find you." He paused, considering his words. "The bloke may even be aboard the ship with the man's tickets."

"I would hope not, but on second thought you might be quite right."

"So you see, you may be required to identify the man."

"Let's hope that's not necessary," Morgan stammered, his stomach rumbling, reminding him he still had to hurry to breakfast. He thought it funny how a rousing brush with death should make a man even hungrier. "Let's also hope that man recuperates enough to tell you anything you might need to know."

With gas escaping his heavily mustached lip, the constable stifled a laugh. "I shouldn't hold out any hope of that. I'd wager he never makes it off the lorry."

Morgan shivered at the thought. The man's blood still stained his hands. There was even some on his sleeve. "Dead?" Morgan's face drooped.

"I'm afraid so, sir."

Oh, Lord, that's dreadful, he thought. "I certainly hope you're wrong." Deflated, Morgan turned to continue his walk.

"Sir, hold on a moment."

Morgan stopped in his tracks.

"Are you forgetting something?"

Morgan looked bewildered.

"Your satchel."

"Oh, yes," Morgan summoned a nervous smile. "I can't forget that."

Morgan's knees wobbled all the way to the restaurant, but he felt that the walking did him good. He sucked the crisp air down in huge gulps, never before imagining himself to be a hero. The thought of chasing down an armed robber had never occurred to him.

He did have every reason to see himself as a future crusading reporter but that was as far as his dreams had dared to take him. To report the news was one thing and to be the subject of it, quite another. He knew that never again did he want to imagine his name being attached to a policeman's blotter or mixed into the headlines of a newspaper. He wanted to make headlines, but not that way.

A short while later he was seated at a table, wolfing down a breakfast of tomatoes and bacon.

"Morgan, my boy."

His uncle, John Baxter, was a walrus of a man with a mustache that seemed to suit his ample girth and an air of self-importance that he carried like an ornament on his gold fob chain.

Regardless of his constant effort to be his own man, each time someone called out his name, he was hammered with the reminder of the family to which he belonged. His pedigree seemed indelibly stamped on his forehead.

Morgan had been named in his father's futile hope of pleasing his great-uncle, J. Pierpont Morgan. Morgan's occasional acquaintance with the old financier had always left him with an odd feeling. Occasionally the old man's glare would warm when he saw him and a faint smile would budge up from under his bulbous, pock-marked nose. His eyes were lifeless doll eyes, with all of his thinking locked up inside him and none of it escaping his lips. This, of course, was when he wasn't bearing down on some underling who he perceived as about to cost him money. Then all the bowels of his passion would rush forth like Noah's great flood. The perception of impending loss was never a difficult matter to accomplish as each and every event of every day in America seemed to be something that either cost or made J. Pierpont Morgan money.

When the old man had fastened his glare on Morgan, he knew at once who the boy was, where he had come from, and even seemed to sense what he was to become. Since the age of ten, Morgan had always made it a point never to discuss the matter of wealth in his presence. Following the untimely death of his parents, Morgan had always had the distinct impression that the old man saw him as someone who would one day become a liability, which he was determined to never be. Whatever it took and for however long it took, Morgan was determined to make his own way in the world by self-effort and not by some accident of family heritage.

J. P. Morgan owned the White Star Line. He had been scheduled to take the maiden voyage to New York but at the last minute had canceled. That bit of news brought great relief to Morgan, even if it did lessen the importance of the voyage to others. It would make Morgan's trip much more comfortable.

"Morgan, there you are, my boy."

John and Aunt Dottie Baxter had schooled Morgan in England and had provided him with the direction necessary to make him a proper gentleman. A conversation with John Baxter, however, was out of the question. He always knew everyone in any room and trotted out salutations or orders to suit whatever thought blinked across his brain.

Waving a leather packet over his head like a general about to sound a charge, Baxter rounded the tables of the Carlsford, bearing down on Morgan's late breakfast. His Aunt Dottie brought up the rear, as usual. "I have your C-deck tickets, first-class, befitting your status."

Morgan got to his feet out of respect for Aunt Dottie and motioned to the empty chairs. She stood in front of one, but Baxter didn't think to seat her. He was much too busy to sit and chat and that made her too busy as well. "Second-class is quite sufficient for a cub reporter," Morgan reacted.

Morgan knew the remark would send the man into a flurry of unspoken thoughts, a few of which would break the surface in disgust. It was a reaction he'd often delighted in producing. On a morning where he had suffered from fear and actual battle, he needed the security of familiar emotions. His uncle had always wanted him in banking as a mortgage broker, but the idea of turning widows out of their homes had never appealed to Morgan. He wanted to see the world and write about what he saw.

"Pshaw! That rag! The *Herald* gave you that position out of spite for me. They only want to exploit your connections and your family for the next piece of dirt they can fling on the unsuspecting public for a nickel."

Dottie clutched Baxter's arm and dug her nails in. "Now, John, we're not here for that." There was a plea in her words, one she'd never been prepared to enforce in the entirety of her life. She was a sweet woman, but Morgan had always viewed her as one might see a decorative doormat.

Morgan knew that if the facts were known, he'd have been only too happy to write about the exploitations of the upper class. It would have taken no trouble at all to drudge up the dirt that awkwardly fell from the faces of the families belonging to his various schoolmates. He thought them to be a brood that saw him still as an outsider. The only solace he could take was in his constant practice of rising righteously above them.

Morgan took no comfort in strong drink, while they, for the most part, didn't feel that an evening was complete without slipping under the table from the effects of an empty row of bottles. He read his Bible, rather than simply marking the tally sheet at chapel, and he knew he actually had pure thoughts seep now and again into his educated mind. All of his strongest accomplishments were matters of creative industry and that of a soul constantly searching for the right motive. While he pretended humility, Morgan knew that deep down he was quite proud of a level he felt he possessed that they could never hope to accomplish. It was a blemish but one he was prepared to live with.

Baxter laid the leather-cased passage ticket on the table. "You can begin your quest for true humility when you disembark in America, the perfect place for such an enterprise, I'm sure. You will, however, travel first-class on the *Titanic*. It is our graduation gift to you, and it cost us over two thousand pounds." Morgan knew the man never let any favor go without the price tag attached to it.

Baxter suddenly tipped his hat to a man who strolled by. "Nice to see you, Benjamin. Are you traveling on the *Titanic* today?"

The man, complete with silk hat and a white starched shirt never broke stride. He gave a simple nod while continuing a pompous promenade with a striking beauty on his arm. Her hat appeared for all the world to have an entire bird perched on its cobalt broad brim, and her slender figure was wound with a spiral of meandering pearls climbing up a folding curtain of azure fabric. Across her dainty neck was hung one of the largest sapphires Morgan had ever seen. She appeared to be a creature made entirely of cut glass—lovely to look at and expensive to taste from.

Morgan could quickly tell that Baxter was displeased at not meriting even a word in the man's walk out the door. He inwardly applauded the audacity of the passing stranger. He knew not many could avoid his uncle. Baxter watched the two of them as they floated from the room. "That, my boy, is Benjamin Guggenheim."

He bent his head in an aside of disappointment to Dottie. "I shouldn't have asked if he were traveling on the *Titanic*. Of course he is. Now he'll think me foolish."

He blushed slightly at the notion that Morgan had seen him admit to this social faux pas. Then in a pompous air of moral superiority, he threw back his shoulders and offered a matter of social gossip.

"I shouldn't think his wife will be greeting him on the docks of New York. The woman he's with is a Miss Kitty Webb, his mistress. Kitty. Imagine that! What a name for a person to have. Of course, given the fact that he pulled her from a chorus line, I presume it to be most appropriate."

Morgan smiled, more at the expression of discomfort on Aunt Dottie's face than anything else. The name *Dottie* had never seemed to be a social tag that struck the members of elite society with awe.

"Your captain on this ship is a man of vast experience, and I've taken the liberty of placing you at his table on the third night of your itinerary. You'd do well to meet anyone of status and importance while you're on this voyage. People travel first-class to meet people who travel first-class."

WEDNESDAY,
APRIL 10, 1912,
7:12 A.M.

CHAPTER 2

J oseph Boxhall stood on the bridge and watched the loading of the forward hold through the window. He jerked his cuffs into their proper position on his wrists. Cupping his fingers around a mug of hot tea, he blew softly at the steam. He ran one finger under his collar where it chafed his skin. He had shaved closely this morning, and his stiff white collar bit into his neck with its sharply starched edges. He was broad shouldered and well aware of the dashing figure he cut in the blue serge uniform. He absently brushed lint from between two rows of brass buttons running up his chest.

Pulling out the rolled map, he spread it on the chart table, placing his cup on one corner and weighting the other corners with his cap and two paperweights. He couldn't help admiring his cap. He had polished the bill last night, and it gleamed in the morning light.

As the fourth officer, one of his responsibilities was to chart the course of the ship, a solitary duty he warmed to. Mixing with passengers was not something he enjoyed, especially those coming aboard the *Titanic*. He saw himself as a sailor, not a butler. Today, he was dressed in his best blues. He would be the helmsman for the morning, and for that reason alone he had taken the time to polish the brass buttons on his coat.

"Morning, Boxhall."

He turned at the familiar deep voice of Captain E. J. Smith. The man was a legend among officers of the White Star Line, and Boxhall felt himself lucky to be able to simply watch him cross the bridge. His barrel chest filled out his elaborate captain's tunic, and the full gray beard he sported made him the embodiment of a captain at sea. Boxhall had seen Smith's icy-blue gaze alone quiet a room full of rowdy sailors. Now those same eyes locked on Boxhall, bringing him to attention.

"Good morning, sir."

Boxhall glanced quickly at the large Afghan hound at the captain's side. Aristocratic and obedient, the dog seldom was far from Smith's trouser leg. The hound was large and well groomed, and Boxhall felt him to be the perfect companion to the captain. The two of them had a mutual sense of command about them.

"Is the loading of the cargo going well?"

"Quite well, sir."

The hound fell into step with Smith as he walked over to the large window and peered out as the hands swung cargo onto the forward deck. Turning back, he looked at Boxhall standing over the map. "I see you're working on our course."

"Yes, sir. I thought you'd want to avoid any possible ice fields, and so I have us swinging somewhat south."

Smith grunted. "It will add time."

"Yes, sir, but I can't imagine any complaints from the passengers."

"Just one."

"You mean Mr. Ismay?"

"Precisely."

"We can maintain full steam if we sail the southerly route," said Boxhall, gliding his finger across the map.

"I'm quite certain Ismay will have us at twenty-two knots no matter what our course. Harland and Wolff has made certain that our bow can stand up to any floating ice, a matter that Ismay and the board of directors never tire of reminding me." He brushed his mustache aside. "We will follow your course unless otherwise directed. If that does happen, you make sure it's recorded in the log."

"Aye, sir."

Corporate sailoring had never appealed to Boxhall. His father, a man raised on the sea, had always looked to the best interest of the vessel with seldom a thought to headlines or corporate image. It was the type of mentality that seemed to be lost on the directors of the White Star Line, however, and Boxhall well knew it.

The port door to the bridge opened, and a rather informally dressed man with baggy pants, white shirt, and suspenders stepped inside. He fussed momentarily with his thinning blond hair and then stuck out his hand. "Jack Phillips, gentleman." He shook Boxhall's hand. "Mr. Bride and I are to be your Marconi wireless operators."

"Joseph Boxhall, fourth officer." Boxhall shook his hand. "This is Captain Smith."

"Is your equipment operational?" Smith asked.

"Yes, sir," the man grinned, "and the very latest it is, too. We have a one and one-half kilowatt apparatus, one of the most powerful afloat."

"What is the range of this contraption of yours?" Smith asked.

Phillips threw back his shoulders, obviously taking great pride in explaining one of the wonders of the modern world to two seagoing dinosaurs. "We are capable of reaching a distance of four hundred miles by day and treble that by night."

"Quite impressive," Boxhall said.

Smith turned to once again watch the loading of the cargo. It was plain to see he quickly lost interest in things he didn't fully understand.

"Well, I'll leave you gentlemen to your duties," Phillips said. He turned and stepped out the door, sliding it shut.

"Business aboard ship," Smith muttered.

"Yes, sir, but we only give them room and board. I think the arrangement allows us a thirty-word-per-day average for matters of ship's safety."

"Another measure of little need."

"Aye, sir."

9:40 A.M.

Berth 44 was a wild confusion of activity. The *Titanic* was due to sail on the noontide, and from the looks of things, there was not a moment to spare.

The *Titanic* filled up not only the dock but the horizon and sky as well. Its black hull and sparkling white superstructure stretched out on the river like the Alps would rest on and dominate a cow pasture. There simply was no room in the eye for another sight. She was overwhelming. Morgan felt like a wide-eyed child with his mouth gaping open.

He stood next to a large gentleman at the bottom of the rear ramp, doing his best to imitate some of the man's self-assured demeanor.

The man gave off the appearance of an oversized emperor penguin, regal but tottering on undersized feet, but so well-dressed that Morgan fussed with his buttons and cuffs in a self-conscious flutter. The man's black bowler sat gingerly on his head, and his pin-striped trousers were set off by gray spats that hugged his shiny black shoes. With a reporter's eye for detail, Morgan noted that his cutaway coat was the appropriate black, and that a diamond stud on his blue necktie sparkled in the morning light.

The man was lost in thought, watching the ladies on the arms of gentlemen as they climbed up the ramp. He lit a cigar, seemingly oblivious to Morgan's inspection.

A *banker*, Morgan decided. Just then, the man spoke, "Quite a sight, what?"

For a second Morgan was worried he'd spoken his thoughts aloud. "Yes, indeed, sir," stammered Morgan, blushing slightly.

The man coughed a puff of cigar smoke through his oversize gray mustache. "At my age, watching the women brings me a feeling of composure." The man pointed with his cigar in the direction of the first-class passengers boarding.

Morgan smiled. Composure was the last thought in his mind.

The man's close-cropped beard would have been wild and woolly had he not made sure it was combed and waxed. His cheeks were tangled with spiderwebs of red capillaries and flushed with a blush that gave him the appearance of a recent slap. Morgan suspected, however, that this was the result of strong drink and not an offended woman. "My name is Billy Carter," the man said. "I'm a vice president with Lloyd's. We're insuring this vessel."

Transferring the cane to his left hand, the one holding the satchel, Morgan politely extended his hand. "Morgan Fairfield's my name. You must be concerned about this voyage, what with all the money you have tied up here."

"No, indeed." He spat out the words with a smirk in his voice. "The *Titanic* was built by Harland and Wolff of Belfast, the best shipyard in the world. At over 46,000 tons, it is the largest ship afloat. It is 882 feet 9 inches long and 92 feet 6 inches beam. If stood on end, it would dwarf the world's tallest buildings. My boy, this is a triple-screw steamer with the middle propeller measuring 16 feet across and the other two measuring over 23 feet in diameter. It has 29 coal-fired boilers capable of giving us a speed of over 23 knots. You will notice there is no smoke from the fourth stack. That is simply there for appearance's sake."

"That's impressive." Morgan thought Carter's ability to rattle off figures was even more impressive. Numbers had always seemed devastating to Morgan.

"It's extraordinary. And this ship is also perfectly safe, even for a floating palace. Do you see that blue ensign flying from the bridge up there?"

Morgan craned his neck to look up at the top of the white steel castle high above. "Yes."

"That flag signifies the presence of Captain E. J. Smith. The man has over forty years' experience on the open sea. He made a number of courageous runs during the Boer War and was awarded the Transport medal. He was also made an honorary Commander in the Royal Navy, which allows him to fly that banner. We will be safe with him at the helm, my boy."

"I'm certain we will be." *Impossible to argue, anyway,* Morgan thought.

"This is the finest ship ever built and has the safety measures of this century that shipbuilders of the past could only have dreamed about. I saw Thomas Andrews, the man who designed the *Titanic*, earlier this morning. He is a brilliant man and one who has personally seen to every detail. Watertight compartments are built into the hull. Young man, not even God could sink this ship."

Morgan's mouth dropped open. He wasn't sure if it was because of what he'd been told about the size and strength of the ship itself or the boast that seemed uncomfortably blasphemous. Clamping his jaws shut, Morgan nervously cleared his throat. "I'm certain Pharaoh's army felt the same way about their invincibility."

The man blew cigar smoke in Morgan's direction. "A Bible student I see. Well, good for you. I can assure you, however, the chariots of the Egyptians were no match in comparison to the hull of this ship."

The screeching of steel caused them both to snap their heads around. The train bearing the second- and third-class passengers was just pulling in from Waterloo station. Even before the train came to a complete stop, the teeming mob piled down from the bright red cars. They dashed and rambled across the street and made their way to the aft ramp. There were large numbers of Scandinavians, a tribute to the ticketing agents the White Star Line maintained in that region. Most held what was called a "first available ship" ticket, and on this morning the first available ship was the *Titanic*.

Morgan watched them assemble by families, some of which were large. Several of the women from the northern climates had strawlike hair that was twisted and knotted into buns. A number of them seemed to be wearing all of their clothes. He watched as two women waddled toward the docks wearing three dresses each. It must have saved them the space in their limited baggage for clocks and silverware. They checked in with the ship's officer, who stood on the dock and ambled up the ramp that led to the third-class quarters.

The Scandinavians had no monopoly on large families. Two British families checked in with the officer.

"Are you going aboard?" Morgan asked.

"Directly," he said, "As soon as I see my automobile loaded."

Carter pointed to a bright red Renault on the dock. Morgan watched the deckhands strap padded halyards underneath the expensive automobile. The seamen signaled to the men on deck, and both Morgan and Carter looked on in amazement as the vehicle began to swing in midair.

"I do so hate to be subjected to New York carriages, don't you agree?" Carter smiled.

"I'm sure I don't know," Morgan said.

Morgan watched the ornate motorcar swing over the heads of the steerage-class passengers. He felt inexplicably sad. There was something about this class to which he belonged that bothered him. Perhaps it was the calloused nature with which they overlooked poverty entirely. Or maybe it was how easily cars, clothes, and privilege substituted for real meaning in their lives. After all, being an orphan with a trust fund had been little comfort to Morgan. Bank accounts and bond funds couldn't hug or reassure him. They had no warmth. There was no guidance. Morgan craved more as a child, and as a man the most he could hope for was to find his own way and to ignore them as best he could.

"I should go along and find my stateroom," Morgan said.

"Mmm," Carter grunted. "Yes, you do that. Perhaps I will see you at dinner." He turned away, having already forgotten Morgan had ever been there.

Morgan made his way up the ramp along with the straggling swells to C deck. The officer on deck was all business. He held a notebook with names presumably in it.

His white collar was uncomfortably high on his neck with a black tie that set off the blue officer's suit and cap. "Good morning, sir. I'm Charles Lightoller, second officer."

"Morgan Fairfield's the name."

"Ah, here you are." He made a mark in his notebook, relieving himself of one more responsibility. "I have you in C-73. Fitzgerald is your steward there. He will take very good care of you and see to any needs that you may have."

"Hey there, we're neighbors."

A young man in a bright-green serge suit appeared suddenly. His bushy, bright-red hair caught Morgan's eye first. His ice-blue eyes twinkled with laughter. He stuck his hand around Lightoller's elbow. "I'm Hunter Kennedy. Welcome to the palace of the haughty."

Morgan thought instantly that he was going to like this chap. "Pleased to meet you." Grinning like fools, they shook hands.

Grabbing Morgan's arm, Hunter hustled him past Lightoller and toward the edge of the railing. Lightoller brushed his elbow and rolled his eyes as the pair danced away.

"Have you ever seen such a sight? The way people are spiffed up, you'd think we're at the world's largest state funeral." Hunter grinned.

"Yes, everyone does seem to be in evening wear."

Hunter leaned back and looked Morgan over. "I can see you gave little thought to pretentiousness."

Morgan ran his hands down the worn lapels of the day coat, self-consciously covering the blood spots on his cuffs. Had the remark come from anyone else, he might have been a bit defensive. As it was, he merely chuckled. "Why should I suffer to impress total strangers? Besides, I've had quite the day."

Hunter slapped Morgan's back with a thud. "Quite right, my man. You are quite right, indeed."

Morgan gasped. Hunter instantly noticed Morgan's sudden stare at the three people walking up the boarding ramp. A fetching blonde walked arm in arm with a tall, handsome man and an attractive older woman.

"Quite the beauty that one," Hunter said. "But from the look on that chap's face, he's not a casual acquaintance."

Margaret. Morgan tumbled her name over in his head. He'd heard of her engagement over a month ago. He thought he was past it, but seeing her walk up the ramp with another man was agony for him. She was slight but well proportioned. She glowed in a bright yellow dress that melted into her shoulder-length golden hair.

"Of course," Hunter muttered, "the fun is in the chase."

Morgan could only nod stupidly at Hunter's misguided observation. He couldn't take his eyes off her. Her generous mouth was matched with a slight chin and a straight, diminutive nose. Margaret's fierce brown eyes seemed to laugh and twinkle with intense, intelligent combativeness. Seeing her brought more to mind than the desire for her at the moment. It carried with it the innocent memories of his entire childhood, the times they'd played together and climbed the trees around her home.

"Maybe there is someone you'd like to impress after all," Hunter smirked.

Morgan turned away from the threesome. "Why don't we walk up and take a look at the bow?" he said, already stepping off in that direction.

Hunter grinned and moved slowly, stroking his chin. "You know them, don't you?"

"Yes, I do. Now shall we take that walk?"

They moved up the rail, taking care not to draw any undue attention.

"Who are they?" he demanded.

Morgan was startled at the audacity of the man he barely knew. "No one I'd care to discuss, thank you," he said icily.

Hunter seemed oblivious to Morgan's irritation. "You know, old man, regardless of the size of this ship, you're likely to see them a number of times. You shouldn't let it bother you. I have two people aboard here that strike a fire in my eyes. The truth be known, I look forward to seeing them, if only to gloat."

Morgan smiled at the genuine innocence behind the man's words. Hunter reminded him of a good-natured, oversize puppy of sorts. "And who would that be?"

"One is a young woman, as you might suspect. The other is a treacherous snake in the grass whom I intend to sue."

"Is he with her?"

"Mercy, no! She has better taste than that, much better taste in fact. I rather doubt that I shall be running into them in the same party."

He clasped his hand around Morgan's shoulder, pulling him closer. "So you see, I have double your fears, and it doesn't raise an ounce of perspiration."

Morgan then turned to look and watched as the young woman cast a quick glance in their direction. It was only a quick look, with her head immediately going down.

"They're going down to the first-class lounge," Hunter said, "so I think it will be safe if you want to take an inspection of your room." The grin on his face was disarming. It was almost as if he could read Morgan's mind. "You might even want to change into more gentlemanly attire."

They soon found themselves facing the brightly polished door which led to C-73. "I'm across the hall in C-74. We'll have jolly good fun."

Twisting the brass doorknob, Morgan stood in the doorway in amaze-ment, surprised at his carefully laid-out belongings. The steward had unpacked his baggage and taken care to lay his evening clothes on the bed. He was used to nice furniture, but this azure-blue carpet looked too plush to be stepped on. The gold seashells dotting the corner of each patch made the carpet seem like precious artwork to be admired. The electric brass sconces shaded in green glass warmed the cherry veneer of the room.

They stepped in, and Hunter plopped himself down on the sofa and clamped his feet on an oval table. "Quite the place, what?"

"Yes, it is." Morgan was startled at how casually Hunter treated lux-ury.

The straight, wingback sofa was about as uncomfortable looking as anything he'd ever laid eyes on. Upholstered in embroidered silver leaf on a dark blue background, it seemed suited more for effect than func-tion. From the look of Hunter Kennedy, however, he appeared to be a man who could make himself appear cozy on a bed of nails. His lanky legs stretched out, and he propped his feet on the coffee table.

Morgan sat the leather satchel down on the bed alongside the opened bags. The bed was a cherry sleigh that looked like a crib for adults. The sides offered protection from falling off in a sudden strike of high waves, and the cream-colored bedspread ran up to four oversize goose-down pillows.

A brass lamp with an ornate cut-glass shade hung over the bed. The lamp had a brass chain and ball hanging down, and Morgan decided that any tugging on the fixture should be kept to a minimum.

"Do you think you'll be able to surrender to the sandman in here?" Hunter asked. "Or should we look under the mattress for any peas that might be lurking about?"

"I'm certain I'll be quite comfortable."

"This must have set you back quite a farthing?"

"The stateroom is a gift from my aunt and uncle."

"They must be wealthy birds," said Hunter bluntly.

"He is the president of the Commonwealth Bank and yes, they have far too much money for their own good." Morgan chuckled. He wasn't used to warming up to people this fast. It delighted him and worried him at the same time.

Hunter leaned his head back and laughed. "That would be a lovely feeling for once. Living a life without the clawing and scratching would be a good frame of mind, don't you think?"

Morgan decided right away that Hunter was a delight. Direct and disarming. Morgan liked his quick mind. "I don't think so. Somehow the clawing and scratching is what makes a man alive. Possibility is always more invigorating than probability."

"I like you," Hunter said. "A man of the people with rich relations."

Margaret and her mother watched as two children raced through the lounge. They both had long, curly black hair with eyes that would have shone in the dark. Had it not been for the short pants and suspenders that each of them wore, they could have no doubt passed for girls. Of course, she had never seen girls run in a public place. Only little boys would do such a thing. She bent down and caught the smaller of the two. "Here now, you must not run inside."

The child looked up at her with a cherubic face that would have melted butter. Margaret stroked her fingers through his hair. "Where is your mother?" she asked.

Just then a man, obviously the boys' father, marched into the room and surveyed it. Spotting Margaret, he marched in her direction.

"Please excuse my children," he said. "They are excited by the ship."

Margaret stood erect, and the younger boy skirted around her dress, making every attempt to keep out of his father's line of sight. "I'm Margaret Hastings," she said, "and this is my mother."

The man bowed at the waist. He was dark in complexion and wore a tan suit. "My name is Hoffman," he said, "and I hope they didn't disturb you."

"Not in the least," she said. "I enjoy children at play."

She watched as Peter returned with the older of the two children. "And this is my fiancé, Peter Wilksbury," she said.

"Pleased to meet you," the man said, nodding at Peter. "I must see the boys punished."

"They're just children," Margaret blurted out. "I'm as excited as they are." She smiled. "If it weren't for this dress of mine I might be running as well."

April Hastings was not so easily forgiving. "Let the man tend to his own children, dear. If you were to run through here, I might just as well punish you."

The man grabbed both children by the wrists and pulled them toward him. "I'll see to them now."

They watched as the man spun the children around and pointed them toward the door.

Margaret bit her lip, quelling the urge to race after the man and protect the boys. Softhearted to a fault, she'd somehow make it a point to check up on them later. "I wonder where their mother is?" Margaret said.

"No doubt lying down, as I should be," April responded.

"Of course, Mother. You go right ahead. I'll join you directly."

April lifted her skirt and made her way to the door.

"Strange," Margaret mused, "He doesn't look like a Hoffman."

"No. More Italian than German, I'd say," Peter offered.

She turned away and nervously paced back and forth between the crystal chandeliers. The lounge was comfortable looking with writing tables studded around the room and palatial leather chairs and couches. Peter watched her as she studied the overhanging glass. She was trying very hard not to make eye contact with him, and staring at the fixtures above seemed to be the best of the alternatives.

He stepped toward her and, taking her arm, patted her hand. "What's wrong, darling? Are you nervous about the trip?"

"Yes, I am, a little."

"Or is it something else?"

Margaret was a terrible liar, and his warm, loving concern made it worse. The last thing she wanted to do was cause Peter any pain. But she couldn't keep this from him. "I saw him on deck. He's on the *Titanic*," she blurted.

"Who's here, darling?"

"Morgan. Morgan Fairfield."

Peter dropped his gaze to the floor. "I see."

She laced her fingers through his. "No, I don't think you do. That is over with me. I was a girl, and Morgan was a nice boy."

"My dear, the roots of a mangrove swamp grow together as they sprout. Later they become inseparable." He looked into Margaret's eyes as if searching for an unspoken truth in them.

She wanted very badly to deny any attachment she felt for Morgan. Not seeing him for over a year had helped, but just the glance on the deck outside had brought the old feelings back and she knew it. She squeezed Peter's hand, and her lip quivered slightly. "Perhaps it's time to form new roots, Peter."

WEDNESDAY,
APRIL 10, 1912,
10:15 A.M.

CHAPTER 3

Hunter was totally at home anywhere, even in Morgan's room. Still, Morgan couldn't find it in himself to even relax enough to sit down. Suddenly a man stepped into the room behind him. He cleared his throat to catch Morgan's attention. "Excuse me, Mr. Fairfield. I am Fitzgerald, your steward."

Morgan swung around to look him over. Fitzgerald held himself in a way that seemed to demand an inspection.

"Pleased to meet you, sir," said Morgan.

The man was tall and thin. His highly polished bald head was set off with dark eyes, a carefully trimmed mustache, and eyebrows that resembled bramble bushes on the moors. His white waistcoat and starched shirt were the perfect picture of efficiency, and the black bow tie and trousers the perfect complement to the uniform.

Morgan felt tacky again. Being surrounded by elegant and fastidious dressers was starting to annoy him.

Fitzgerald handed over an envelope on a silver tray. "I have here a special welcome letter from your host, Mr. Bruce Ismay, the president of the White Star Line."

Morgan noticed the man's hands, indeed, his most striking feature. They appeared to be made from rugged alabaster, freshly cut from the mines and washed with bleach. His fingers were thin lines of stone chiseled from the quarry, washed but not polished, accustomed to work but white as a sheet. *Scary hands*, Morgan thought, *and cold*.

"Thank you." Morgan picked up the envelope from the tray, grateful he didn't have to touch those hands and test his theory.

"I took the liberty of finding and laying out your evening clothes, Mr. Fairfield. I hope you find the accommodations to your liking."

"I do, indeed."

"You have only to ring the bell on your desk there and I will be most happy to give you anything you might need. Would you like a guided tour of the ship?"

"I don't think that will be necessary. I like to explore things on my own." The man seemed displeased but resigned. Morgan wondered what he did. Just sit in some room below deck waiting for a ring? *Poor chap*, Morgan mused, *must be dull*.

"As you wish. Then if you'll not be needing me further—"

"No, please, you can go."

He bowed slightly at the waist and turning, left the room, closing the door after him.

"Those kind of servants make my spine crawl," Hunter said.

"Why is that?"

"They are just too proper, no character, no personality. They make you feel that they will always know more than you do and that it's your privilege to have them at your beck and call."

Morgan chuckled. "Perhaps in this case, it would be my privilege."

"And you got your letter from Ismay." He said the words with a sneer on his lips.

"You know Mr. Ismay?"

"He's the chap I intend to sue, although I would prefer to see him in jail."

"Why is that?"

He waved the question off. "I will explain later, in some detail if you like. Somehow I can't bear the thought of him or of relating the story without an entire bottle of port in me."

Hunter sat back on the sofa, feigning a look of ease. Pushing his feet back onto the table, he once again assumed the position of a man who could never be deeply disturbed, though now Morgan knew better. "I will tell you about the girl in my life, if you tell me about the one we saw on the ramp."

"I'm afraid there is little to tell."

"Balderdash! From the look that came over you, I'd say you were a man terminally smitten."

Morgan was again amazed and somewhat uncomfortable with Hunter's ability to cut to the heart of a matter. "We grew up together as children," he said. "We've been conspiring our marriage vows since I was twelve and she was eight."

"And?"

"The man you saw her with is her fiancé, the quite proper Peter Wilksbury."

Hunter stroked his chin. "So, she tossed you over, did she?"

"Actually, it was my doing," Morgan said sheepishly as he sat on the bed.

"Why, in the name of all that's holy, would you do a thing like that?"

"Her father is a member of the House of Lords, one of the landed gentry, and while I do have my trust fund, I've achieved little on my own."

Hunter stifled a chuckle and shook his head. "You just couldn't bear the thought of reaching for the top branches to pick off the sweetest fruit."

"Something like that. Now what of your girl?" Morgan asked the question in an attempt to change the subject.

"My story is somewhat different." Hunter reached into his coat pocket and drew out a silver cigarette case. Morgan could see that it was not just a functional device but a thing of beauty. It was trimmed in gold and had an inlaid gold fleur-de-lis displayed prominently on the cover. He held it out to Morgan. "Would you like one of these, old man, Egyptian tobacco?"

Morgan waved it off. "No, thank you. I don't smoke."

Hunter shrugged. He picked out a white stick and snapped the case closed. Drumming it on the top of the lid, he beat a rhythmic sound on the polished silver. Taking out a lighter, he flicked it to life and waved it over the edge of the cigarette, puffing out a cloud of smoke. "Kitty and I come from the same class and the same profession."

Morgan watched Hunter rub the top of the shiny inlaid gold.

"Then what is the problem?"

"The difficulty is the fact that between the two of us, I'm the only one who knows his place." He slipped the silver cigarette case back into his pocket. "She has resorted to using that natural beauty of hers to land an extremely wealthy married man. It isn't the immorality of the thing that grates on me, however. It's the way she's turned her back on me. She treats me like someone else's attendant and not like a former lover."

Morgan could see the flushed expression on Hunter's face at the very notion. A man's pride is such a sensitive thing, and in that way he and Morgan both had a lot in common when it came to love. Morgan turned to save Hunter face and fussed at putting away his shirts and trousers in the oak dresser. "And what do you do?" he asked Hunter.

"Well, I've seldom been a man of leisure at a fancy school. I'm an actor." He grinned and raised his voice. "I pretend for a living." His eyes sparkled with pleasure.

Morgan chuckled. "I enjoy the theater and try to go whenever I can. Where have I seen you?"

"I was in *Charley's Aunt*. Played the part of Jack Chesney."

Morgan nodded in admiration. "I saw that. Loved it." Morgan paused and looked him over, studying him for some memory he might have of the man in the footlights. He broke into a wide smile. "I do remember you. You were wonderful. I laughed hysterically, but not until later that night."

Hunter arched his eyebrows at the notion. "You didn't laugh until later. Why not, pray tell?"

"Had I been with friends, I would have died in my seat, but I was with my aunt and uncle."

"The banker?"

"Yes, and addicted to proper demeanor. As it was, I snickered a few times, and when I got a stare from the humorless woman in front of me, my uncle snapped me a glance that put me in my place. I hate my place."

"Your place sounds like no fun at all." Hunter cocked an eyebrow.

"It is a horror. So much of what is proper is wrapped up with not doing anything. If one doesn't laugh too loudly, speak out of turn, use the wrong spoon for soup, pass gas, or stare, then one can be a proper gentleman. To the best of my knowledge, the finest gentlemen in London lie buried in Westminster Abbey. They do absolutely nothing."

Hunter roared loudly at the notion. "You're a caution, old man. Perhaps you should consider becoming a critic of the theater."

"I have a position waiting for me in New York with the *Herald*. I have a feeling they will want me to cover the social set, however."

"Egad."

"Yes, the worst of all worlds. It just may kill me out of sheer boredom. If it hadn't gotten my foot in the door with the appointment, I might have retched."

"I should think so."

The beaten satchel on the bed reminded Morgan of the morning's escapade. Contrary to all that he had been told by the man who lay dying, his curiosity was overwhelming. Despite Hunter's presence, or maybe because of it, he undid the straps. Maybe with Hunter in the room, he could resist the temptation to carefully peruse the contents.

"They have a saltwater swimming pool aboard, I hear," Hunter said, as he studied his nails. "I love to swim, don't you?"

"Yes, I do." Morgan pulled out what were the only personal effects of the man in the alley, leaving a wax-sealed packet of papers inside.

Hunter rattled on, oblivious to Morgan's perusal of a total stranger's satchel. "The gymnasium has rowing machines and all sorts of machinery I'd love to try. Perhaps we should do so on our way to Cherbourg. I understand many of our most wealthy passengers will be embarking there. It will be a fine sight to see yet another funeral."

"Yes, quite right," Morgan muttered absently. He sifted through some of the man's personal effects, and what he saw looking back at him left him startled. It was a photograph, and in spite of its dated nature, he knew at once who it was. Gasping, he clasped his hand over his open mouth.

Hunter jumped to his feet. Like any good actor, he was quick to notice a change in character. "What is it, old boy? You look like you've seen a ghost."

Morgan gulped. "Not a ghost, just someone I've known all my life."

"Why wouldn't you carry a photo of someone you've known all your life?"

Morgan sat down on the bed, shaking visibly. "This isn't my bag."

"Whose is it?" Hunter looked genuinely confused.

"It's a long story, and I really shouldn't say. The circumstances were really quite morbid."

Hunter broke out into a sly smile. "This does sound interesting, old man. Don't leave old Hunter here out in the dark."

"The less you know, the better it might be for you."

Morgan knew at once that he should have known better than to say that. Perhaps the shock still running through him clouded his judgment. Or maybe he needed someone to talk to.

In any event, Hunter was a man who obviously loved challenge. Morgan could see that plainly. The very idea of danger to a man like Hunter was like *sic 'em* to a dog. Reaching back, Hunter pulled over one of the chairs that surrounded the small card table near the bed. He swung his leg over it, leaned on the back, and pointed in Morgan's direction.

"Say on, old man. Now you have me hooked for sure."

Morgan stared at this Hunter Kennedy, a man he'd never met before. He knew nothing about him, although he knew he liked him instantly with his disarming candor and a face that beamed with life. If, as the constable hinted, the thief was onboard the *Titanic*, Morgan would be in enough danger all by himself without dragging someone else into it. Haltingly, he went through the story of the morning.

Hunter was riveted to every word. Morgan could almost hear the other man's mind working over the details and possibilities.

When Morgan finished, Hunter let out a whistle and shook his head. "If what that man said was true, you might well be the most important person aboard this ship."

Morgan clasped his hand tightly around the satchel. "Not hardly, but this might be the most consequential piece of luggage."

"You say the bloke you chased off in the alley took the old man's boat ticket?"

"Yes, and his money as well. From the looks of him, I'd take him to be a common thief. He probably sold the ticket."

Hunter leaned forward, the legs of the chair pivoting. "Look, old man, I don't want to burst your soap bubble. I know you've been in school, but I live in London. I see thieves all the time. A thief is a thief, not a murderer. The black heart you met up with had a good reason to stab that man, and I wouldn't say it was for money."

Morgan looked at the satchel, thinking the same thing as Hunter.

"That's right," Hunter said, once again reading Morgan's mind. "Whatever it is you're carrying there, he wants it bad enough to kill for it."

"And he's—"

"Precisely. He's in all likelihood right here on this ship, looking for you and that satchel even as we speak." He paused for a moment, letting the words soak in. "But you haven't told me about the photograph."

Morgan dropped his gaze to where it sat cupped in his hand. "It's a portrait of a woman I've known all my life, my nurse as a child, Lilly."

Kitty Webb had taken to a sofa in their suite and watched as the maid Gwen hung up her dresses. Benjamin Guggenheim never traveled without a full complement of servants. Help, even on a ship like the *Titanic*, was not to be trusted in Guggenheim's book. His valet, Hans, had taken his coat and draped it over his arm for pressing before it was put away. Hans was large by normal standards, over six feet tall and more than two hundred pounds. Kitty saw him as more of a bodyguard than a valet. His square jaw and close-cropped blond hair could have served as a poster for the German nation. When he looked at Kitty, his blue-sapphire eyes seemed to bore right through her. They were of the same class. Kitty knew that, and in their own way they both served the needs of Benjamin Guggenheim.

"That will be fine, Hans," Guggenheim said. "You can take that and be back in two hours."

"Yes, sir." The man clicked his heels together and, spinning around, marched out the door.

Guggenheim sat down at the desk and, taking out pen and paper, began to write.

Gwen busied herself performing her daily laundry work on Guggenheim's pocket money. She had taken out a bottle of polish and was rubbing coins to a beautiful shine. Long ago, Kitty had learned that there was money and then there was Guggenheim money. One must never confuse the two. Gwen rubbed each coin and placed them carefully on a silver tray.

Kitty watched as Gwen finished with the coins and then picked up the stack of currency. Taking an iron, she laid the bills out on an ironing board and started pressing them. When she had finished, Benjamin Guggenheim would have the prettiest money a man ever pulled out of his pocket.

Kitty still saw the silly exercise as an excess that was totally unnecessary. She had, however, long since learned not to question the man who made her life a fairyland. Benjamin Guggenheim may have been ruthless when it came to business but with her he was a gentle giant.

He turned from his desk to face her. "What's wrong, my sweet? Are you concerned about our docking in New York?"

"There will be reporters."

"Have no fear of that," he said, waving his beefy paw in the air. "I'm preparing a series of wires right now. I'll have Hans send them when we come within range of Cape Race. I will have a tug take us into New York, so you need not fear that crush of people on the dock. I'm also taking the liberty of having a suite prepared for you at the Waldorf." He grinned. "You can spend all the time you like patrolling Fifth Avenue and shopping to your little heart's delight." Guggenheim took great pleasure in spoiling her.

"I just want to see you, Benjamin." Kitty smiled softly, gazing adoringly across the room at him.

"And you shall, my dear, each and every day."

Kitty crossed her legs and watched as Benjamin admired her ankles. "I love traveling with you, Benjamin. I felt so very free in Europe. There was no one to point at us, and people treated me like your wife."

Guggenheim looked over at Gwen, still laboring on the ironing board. "That will be enough for now," he said.

Gwen swung around, slightly embarrassed at hearing what little she had. She curtsied. "Certainly, sir. May I go now, sir?"

Guggenheim waved limply in the direction of the door and she hurried out, giving Kitty a passing glance as she rushed by.

"Some day you will be my wife," he said matter-of-factly.

Kitty turned her head to the window.

"I've told you many times that I must wait until my children are older. Divorce is bad enough without the picture of young children clinging to their mother's skirts. My friends know all about you and so does my wife. They just want to avoid the public humiliation that accompanies such a thing."

He slid out of the chair and walked over to her. Placing his hand under her chin, he lifted it slightly. "You know that you have my heart. Can you not wait a while longer for the rest of me?"

"And what if it does become a public scandal?"

"I know of no one who would do such a thing."

Kitty looked up into his eyes. She knew that no doubt he was right. No one in polite society would cause such a stir. She also knew that even though Benjamin Guggenheim knew of no such troublemaker, she did. Hunter Kennedy was the man, and the thought of seeing him again sent shivers up her spine.

10:30 A.M.

Morgan sat on the duck-feather mattress for a long time. The second that Hunter had closed the door, he'd torn the man's satchel apart hoping to find some explanation for the faded photograph.

Lilly's face was as familiar to him as his own, even though this picture was at least twenty years old. She'd been his nurse and constant companion as a child. Even when he became a young man and an adult she'd remained far closer to him than his aunt and uncle. In fact, he knew Lilly could always see right through him. She seldom had to imagine what he was thinking. It was as if his thoughts had begun in her mind and tracked their way into his own.

The writing on the back of the picture only fueled his reporter's curiosity, "To George, my love will be with you always, Lilly." He'd never thought of Lilly having a life of her own. He chuckled at the childlike arrogance of such a thing. With a man's eyes he had traced the features of the handsome young woman in the portrait. Thick hair the color of crushed pecans fell to her shoulders. Her small chin was held high, and the lighting of the picture emphasized her chiseled cheekbones. Lilly might have seemed cold and unapproachable if not for the slightest hint of a smile on her perfectly shaped lips and the sparkle of her warm-brown eyes.

"Lilly, we will have to have a long chat about this when I see you," he said aloud to the picture and smiled. Oddly, the thought of Lilly having loved and been loved was reassuring. He kept trying to recall in detail the features of the man on the ground. But all he could conjure was the look of astonishment when Morgan had told him he was a Newport Fairfield.

He must have known Lilly was in their employ. *Of course. That was why in spite of the pain he'd clutched my sleeve,* Morgan thought. *Maybe he was even planning on meeting her when we docked.* Morgan could see the man had been one given to his duty. That much had been obvious. *He was just like a man Lilly would choose, a man of principle and duty. What will I tell her?* Morgan thought. *The odds that he survived the stabbing were next to none. I'll eventually have to tell Lilly the whole story.* He took comfort in the fact that he had at least four more days onboard ship to figure out just what the story was.

There was a note referring to a Major Archibald Butt. It simply read, "Must see." Morgan knew he would have to take a closer look at the papers later. Right now, he had to change and join Hunter in the smoking room.

He didn't smoke and was sure that fact alone would amuse Hunter. Being a gentleman, a cigar crammed inside one's cheek after dinner or on a special occasion was considered somewhat a part of one's necessary apparel. Morgan could never see the sense of it. The smoke gagged him, and while he did enjoy hot soup or tea, the feeling of fiery escaping gases inside his mouth held no particular enchantment for him, even if it was a testament to his gender and social status. He would meet Hunter there, however, and stifle his chokes with good-natured laughs.

A short while later he strolled onto the deck in his new togs. The blue blazer and tan slacks were set off by the colors of his school tie. It gave him a sense of belonging, one which he rarely felt.

The *Titanic* would be pushed out into the river in less than an hour, and already the decks were crowded with people in their best bon-voyage regalia. Ladies' hats rippled in the cool breeze, and gentlemen pointed their chins up in defiance. *England would be proud,* Morgan thought. The interior of the ship would be practically deserted as everyone would want to be seen on deck. It would give him some time with Hunter, and that he looked forward to. Besides, the smoking room would be free of women. He wasn't sure he could face Margaret. Not just yet.

Morgan turned her name over in his mind as he wound up the grand staircase, *Margaret Hastings, Margaret Hastings.* Often as a boy her name had brought many a smile to his face, and now it was something that caused his heart to sink.

He spotted Hunter right away. Even through the thick blue haze of the smoking room, the man was hard to miss. He had his arm around a chap as they both puffed cigars and laughed. At least Hunter was laughing. It was a deep, rolling baritone that sounded like a boulder stumbling down a grassy hill—a softness in the grass of the thing, but a hardness in its intent.

Morgan found Hunter to be dangerously magnificent, and he'd known him only an hour. Hunter was capable of saying or doing almost anything, and Morgan knew that made him entertaining to any bystander while, at the same time, threatening to a friend. The man was indeed an actor, and Morgan wondered if he knew when the performance part of his life was over and real life began.

The smoking room reeked of masculinity. Its polished wooden walls gleamed with a buttery hue; the red leather chairs and numerous fireplace mantels all made for a setting where one might casually lean or sit and still appear the perfect gentleman. The place had windows that allowed the light to curl around the billows of smoke. *At least I can see the spring air,* Morgan thought, *even if I can't breathe it in here.*

"Morgan, old man, there you are." Hunter grinned, the cigar protruding from a set of perfect gleaming white teeth. "I thought I was going to have to come and tumble you out of that soft bed of yours. I have someone here you must meet."

He turned the middle-aged man around that he'd been making small talk with. "Allow me to present Colonel John J. Astor."

Morgan stuck out his hand. "Morgan Fairfield." He knew perfectly well who John Jacob Astor was and also knew he enjoyed the title of Colonel. Robber barons and landlords always enjoyed whatever military title they might extract from politicians. Morgan also knew of Astor's extensive honeymoon in Europe. His second wife was a slip of a nineteen-year-old girl. They had escaped the perils of the New York press and the society news of his divorce and remarriage by traveling to the continent. The man did cut a striking figure with a high, stiffly starched collar and a thick tie that looked like a silk pillow sitting on his chest.

Astor touched his neatly trimmed mustache and narrowed his eyes at Morgan. "Are you of the Fairfields of Newport?"

"Yes, sir, I am," he acknowledged for the second time today.

"Your parents' death was a great loss to us all."

Morgan nodded. The extended sympathy he was always shown by members of New York's society had always been a two-edged sword. No one felt their deaths more keenly than Morgan, but for some reason he had the feeling he would always be known as the unfortunate orphan, no matter what his age.

"Your family must be quite proud of you, I'd wager," Astor said. "I understand your great-uncle J. P. owns the White Star Line."

Again the mention of his name flagged Morgan to be heaped in with his mogul great-uncle. There was no way of escaping it. "It is quite the ship," he replied flatly.

Astor smiled. "And I'm sure if there's money to be made, J. P. Morgan will have a position in the venture."

"Morgan here is the literary sort," Hunter chimed in.

"Ah, an aspiring writer."

"Actually, he's starting out by working for a New York newspaper, the *Herald* I believe."

It was plain to see that the thought of any newsprint, the *Herald* especially, sent defensive shock waves through Astor. Instantly, he drew his shoulders back and straightened himself to full height.

Morgan did his best to soften the blow. "I won't begin until I reach New York. Even then, they'll most likely have me covering garden parties in Rhode Island."

"You really must try one of these cigars," Hunter interrupted, sensing a definite shift in Astor's demeanor. "They're Havana made, and I understand the ship has brought eight thousand of them aboard."

"Eight thousand?" Morgan waved the brown tube of weed away. Just the thought made him ill, and right then he could have sworn that at least half that number were lit and billowing smoke right now.

Astor bent over and crushed his out on a silver ashtray. "We sail soon," he said. "I must be up on deck and see to my wife."

It was only then that Morgan noticed the valet who was obviously traveling with him. The tall man watched every move Astor made and took the millionaire's coat off the rack at the very idea Astor would be stepping outside.

"It's been a delight to meet you," Astor said. He looked through Morgan with the words rather than at him.

"The pleasure is all mine." Morgan nodded his head respectfully. He watched as Astor took the coat from his man and the two of them paraded through the doors.

Hunter laughed. "Somehow I thought he'd react that way when he found out you were employed by the *Herald*."

"You take great delight in making people uncomfortable, don't you?"

"I enjoy making an impression wherever I go," Hunter chuckled. "It's what I do. The stage is a place where the players create the mood in an audience. The people take their seats with a blank slate, and we scrawl feelings where none existed before."

"But this is not a stage, Hunter. This is life."

Hunter lifted his chin and proudly said his line as if in a dress rehearsal. "The world is a stage."

Morgan had to smile at Hunter with that remark. *He wants to entertain and be entertained*, Morgan thought. "Well, it is never a dull stage or world with you, old boy." Morgan slapped Hunter's shoulder. "You're quite the—" He froze in mid-thought.

"What is it?"

"Outside, on deck." Morgan pointed to the glass doors of the smoking room. "The man I saw in the alley this morning."

"The thief?"

"The thief and the murderer."

"Are you sure?"

WEDNESDAY,
APRIL 10, 1912,
11:25 A.M.

CHAPTER 4

Morgan hurried to the door and opened it with Hunter crowding him from behind. Winding his way through the throng was the man with the brown coat.

"Perhaps we should go and get one of the ship's officers," Hunter suggested.

"And if I'm wrong, I should look like a blasted fool."

Morgan made his way out the door and did his best to elbow his way through the crowd of wavers and those merely waiting to be seen. Hunter kept up, clawing along at Morgan's heels. "Is it just the coat?"

Morgan mumbled over his shoulder. "He was about the same size and with a dark complexion. I'm sure he was the man."

Morgan was embarrassed and felt like an absolute buffoon as he broke up conversations and crowded his way between people while they waved to those on shore. He knew they must have thought him desperate to reach a far off privy, too locked in thought for common courtesy or any attention whatsoever. It occurred to Morgan then that he had no idea what to do if he caught up with the man. He was without his walking stick. If he did find the man, he'd be defenseless against a knife.

He hurried past the lifeboats, glancing around them for some sign of the man. *Useless things,* he thought. *A ship like the* Titanic *would never need them. The man might be anywhere,* Morgan thought. With the glare of polished wood and the bubbling throng in their brightly colored attire, he had lost sight of him.

"Should I circle around the other side?" Hunter questioned. Hunter was tenacious, if nothing else.

"No, stay with me. If I do find him, I want you by my side."

"Jolly good," he snickered, "I find a friend, and he tries to have me butchered."

Morgan's eye caught a scene on the dock below. A half-dozen of the "black gang," as the stokers and firemen were called, were running to scramble aboard. They had obviously gone ashore for a last pint and no doubt lingered too long. The gangplank was up, however, and the officer on the dock wanted no part of the scruffy bunch. The men began to curse their bad luck, but the officer simply turned and strode away.

Morgan ran smack into Peter Wilksbury coming out of the first-class passageway with Margaret on his arm.

"Here, here," Peter said.

"Morgan," Margaret stammered.

Morgan knew there was no way he could simply brush past them, not and continue to live on this earth. At that moment he would much rather have faced the thief. "Pardon me." He faced them sheepishly. "I didn't see you."

"Obviously not," Peter chuckled. "Nice to see you Morgan."

"What are you doing here?" Margaret asked, skipping the courtesies.

"I'm on my way to America," Morgan stated the obvious. Now he did feel the fool. "I took that position with the New York *Herald* we spoke about some time ago."

"Aren't you going to introduce me?" Hunter interjected, bobbing up from behind. Morgan wasn't sure if he was trying to diminish the anxiety of the moment or simply add to it.

Morgan backed away, allowing Hunter to step forward. "Hunter Kennedy," Morgan said, "Allow me to present Peter Wilksbury and Margaret Hastings."

"Pleased to meet you, Kennedy," Peter said, shaking Hunter's hand.

Hunter watched Peter's thick, wavy-blond hair as it blew in the breeze. The nip of the wind added color to the man's smooth cheeks, and Peter's riveting gray eyes made him a handsome man, indeed. "Charmed," Hunter replied. He released Peter's grip, and, taking Margaret's hand, he brushed his chin to her knuckles.

"Delighted to meet you, Mr. Kennedy." Margaret dipped sweetly and smiled.

"And what takes you two in the direction of the United States?" Hunter asked.

"We are having a bridal shower with relatives in America," Peter said. He patted Margaret's hand. "Plus, we both thought the trip would be a lark."

"I'm quite certain it will be," Hunter said.

Morgan's eyes were fastened on Margaret. Just seeing her so close and smelling her perfume seemed to send him into a trance. She looked back at him, fearing to turn away and almost daring him to continue his stare. He obliged her, and the silence of the moment grew too much for even Hunter to bear. He quickly spoke up.

"Morgan and I were determined to give the ship here a quick inspection before sailing."

"All too quickly, it would seem," Peter added, smiling.

The man had always annoyed Morgan. For as long as Morgan had known him, Peter Wilksbury's only duties had seemed to be parading around his father's estate with a shotgun under his arm, shooting quail, and waiting for the old man to die. Morgan looked into his eyes and felt badly about his harsh attitude. He knew so very little about the man, and right then Peter's smile seemed genuine, even under these uncomfortable circumstances.

"And where is your mother?" Morgan asked Margaret. Small talk with Peter was impossible.

"She's resting in our cabin. Crowds do seem to strain her."

"I can understand that," Morgan replied lamely.

"The three of you are together then?" Hunter asked.

Morgan rolled his eyes. He could have shot Hunter right on the spot. Margaret Hastings was a proper lady, and the idea of her accompanying a man on a trip alone would have been unthinkable, even if the man was her fiancé. Morgan could also never see April Hastings agreeing to share her cabin with anyone from the opposite sex. It was doubtful to him that she had ever maintained a room with Margaret's father. The Hastingses had relations like proper English gentry, with him announcing his intentions well in advance and her reluctantly agreeing with the insistence that all the lights be put out. The very thought of it sent ice rushing into Morgan's veins.

"No, indeed," Margaret blushed. "Peter has his own cabin."

Peter could only stare at Hunter, still aghast at the audacity of the man.

"Of course." Hunter grinned with a smile bordering on a smirk. "How very droll to do otherwise."

He winked at Morgan. For his part, Morgan was wondering if throwing Hunter overboard right then would be a forgivable sin considering the situation.

Several small boys had large chunks of ice and were scooting them around the deck with their feet. The small group was forced to move aside and make way for the young hooligans. The ship had loaded tons of ice for the voyage, and these industrious chaps had found good use for the scraps.

They raced by, pushing the blocks with their polished shoes. "Boys do love to play," Morgan said.

Peter took Margaret's hand and rubbed it slightly. "Yes, but eventually they become men, one would hope. Perhaps you gentlemen could join us for dinner," Peter went on. "It might be great fun."

"Perhaps we shall," Hunter replied.

"Capital!" Peter exclaimed. He leaned toward Margaret. "Shall we continue and see the tugboats push us off?"

"Yes, indeed," she said, smiling up at him.

"Then perhaps we will see you gentlemen at a later time," Peter said.

"Oh, I'm certain of that," Hunter replied.

For Morgan, the moment had been an excruciating debacle, but it was plain to see that Hunter didn't see it that way.

"What a fortuitous thing that was, eh, what?"

"Yes, quite." Morgan dripped the words off his tongue with fiery sarcasm.

Hunter put his arm around Morgan. "Listen, old man, difficult things are best to be done straight off. No dallying about. Get right at it."

"I suppose you're right. Still, I won't be having dinner with them."

"You most certainly will," Hunter chided him. "And I'll be right there with you. To fail to show would be an admission of cowardice, and you may be many things, my boy, but a coward you're not." Hunter watched the couple walk to the railing. "Besides, he didn't seem like such a bad bloke."

"No, I suppose not. If he was I could honestly dislike him. Unfortunately, he seems genuinely fond of her."

"Any man agreeing to dinner with his intended's last love has to have some visceral fortitude, I'd wager."

"It would seem so."

"Perhaps she's made a wise choice," suggested Hunter somberly, studying Morgan for whatever effect his words might have.

Morgan turned his head and forced himself to watch them at the rail as Peter slipped his arm around Margaret's waist. "I hope so," he said. "She deserves the very best. I just don't look forward to dinner. You don't know Margaret's mother. April Hastings can slice a man in half with a look."

He looked away from the couple, concentrating on the vivid-blue, cloudless sky. The pain coursing through him was so strong he'd swear Hunter could see it.

"All the better to see her then. You will be splendid." Hunter stifled a laugh. "Who knows, perhaps you can even convince the *Herald* to allow you to cover their bridal shower."

Morgan laughed. "And if you get any friendlier, perhaps you could convince Peter to make me his best man."

He forced his mind back to the man in the brown coat. It helped the pain to subside, but he could see that the chase was off. That was plain to see. Hunter and Morgan simply continued their walk around the deck in the hope that the man they were pursuing would magically appear.

They sauntered through the renowned Café Parisien, one of the high points in all the brochures for the *Titanic*. Wicker furniture and lattice-work with silk ferns climbing up the trellises gave the place the illusion of a sidewalk café in Paris. It boasted genuine French waiters, although the attraction of these haughty, rude European food servers was beyond Morgan.

They walked out the other side and into an area painted white that contained a set of spiral iron stairs. Pushing their way out the doors, they walked onto the rear deck of second class. An officer nodded. He was there to prevent second- and third-class passengers from coming into first class, not the reverse. Stairs on the weather deck led to the well deck and third-class steerage areas below.

A well-built but older man with white hair and bushy snow-white eyebrows sat on the top step. Below him, two children were playing. He lifted his head, and his soft blue eyes sized up the two of them. "Er you gents lost? This leads to steerage."

Morgan could see the man measure both him and Hunter for first-class dandies bent on a bit of slumming. "It might be more fun down there," he said. Morgan stuck out his hand. "I'm Morgan Fairfield, and my friend here is Hunter Kennedy."

"Pleased to meet you." He got to his feet, shaking his limbs to life. The man was like a gaunt greyhound, all bones and muscle. The lines that cut across his face were deep with life, and his eyes sparkled with curiosity.

He stuck out a gnarled hand with broken fingers, his knuckles swollen to twice their size. "I'm Jack Kelly, on my way to America with my grandchildren."

Morgan shook his hand, as did Hunter.

"What takes you to the United States?" Hunter asked.

"My son and his wife are getting settled there and I'm bringing up the rear with the children. I'm a boatbuilder by trade, and I'm hoping to find work when I get there."

The man looked strong enough to build a boat in spite of his age. Most men couldn't build a boat fit for a child's bath, but this man's look of determination said otherwise.

"Then you must be enjoying your look about this ship," Hunter said.

Kelly raked his hand over his stubbly chin. "There ain't much for a man to see down yonder where we are. We're like squirrels in a cage."

"Perhaps we can help you with that," Morgan said. "When we take our tour, we'll just come down and get you."

"You'd do that?"

"Why not?"

A smile cracked across the old man's lips. "I do hanker to take a look-see. That be the honest truth of it."

"Then you shall," Hunter exclaimed.

"Did you see a man come down here before us?" Morgan asked.

"I seen lots of men."

"This one was in a brown coat," Hunter offered.

"What did he look like?"

"Dark complexion," Morgan said.

The man wrapped his fingers around his pointed chin and stroked his chin with his index finger.

"Kind of a short swarthy fellow with dark eyes and a thin mustache?"

"Yes, that's the man," Morgan replied.

"Saw him come by a few minutes ago, a wog he was."

Hunter looked over at Morgan. "He's got that first-class ticket, but he might be harder to spot among the third-class passengers."

"Now, why would that be?" Kelly asked. "You reckon us all to be Italians below deck here?"

"No." Hunter shot the man an apologetic reply.

It was the first time Morgan had seen Hunter embarrassed by his words, and it was something he was going to let Hunter get out of himself.

"It's just, well, what I mean was with all the people down there, it might be a better chance of our man staying lost," Hunter replied.

Kelly nodded, but Morgan could tell he only believed part of what Hunter had said. That made him a smart man. "And he wants to stay lost?" asked Kelly.

"It's a long story," Morgan said. "We just need to find him."

"Then you boys just follow me. I wouldn't want any of the riffraff down here to jostle fine gentlemen like yourselves."

They tagged along behind the man as he descended the stairs. Morgan now felt out of place with his blazer and tie. It would seem that wherever he went, he was destined to be the object of attention and amusement.

Minutes later, Hunter and Morgan stood on the aft well deck. They craned their necks around in the hope of spotting their prey. "You asked if we thought you all to be Italians down here," Morgan said. "Did the man appear to be Italian?"

"I seen plenty of them types in my lifetime, and I'd peg him for an Italian." Kelly focused on Hunter, but he was still too embarrassed to attempt a witty comeback. Kelly craned his neck around, surveying the crowded deck space. "Do you see him?"

The sound of several detonations boomed from port. The reports sounded like gunshots and snapped the men's heads around.

"Look at that!" Kelly said, "Blimey!"

The propellers on the *Titanic* were the size of a two-story building. Her wash, combined with a displacement of thirty-five feet, was enough to swell the estuary. Two smaller liners were tied up at pier 38, the *Oceanic* and the *New York*. Both ships were less than half the size of the *Titanic*. Both vessels had been grounded by the coal strike. As the *Titanic* passed them, the water level swelled and then dropped, tossing the empty vessels around like corks in a washing machine.

The strain on the hawsers of the *New York* grew to the point where they snapped one by one, giving off the sound of pistol shots. It swung free, and its stern glided into the path of the *Titanic*. Both Morgan and Hunter watched in horror, fully expecting a collision.

The shudder of the *Titanic*'s great engines told them at once that the captain had thrown her into reverse. Still, a ship of this size was obviously one that few men were used to controlling. It simply took too long to change course, even at the reduced speeds of the harbor.

They watched as a heroic tug darted toward the *New York* and, throwing her a line, pulled furiously to move her out of the way. The throng of people on the deck swarmed to the rail and watched to see how close they were coming to disaster. Moments later, the *Titanic* eased by, seemingly with only inches to spare.

Kelly swung his head around and looked off in the direction of the bridge. "I'd say that captain of ours has much to learn about handling a vessel of this size."

"Captain Smith is a man of great experience," Morgan said, parroting his earlier encounter with Carter.

"Let me tell you, son, no man alive knows how to handle a ship of this size. That's why we have maiden voyages like this one. No one has ever seen what a ship of this dimension is like under steam in the open sea. I'd say those boys up there have a lot to learn."

Both Hunter and Morgan blinked at each other in amazement. It was obvious that Kelly was a man who knew his boats and that the *Titanic* was the largest afloat.

"This could be an interesting trip, indeed," Hunter said.

"Let's hope it's not too interesting," Kelly shot back.

Morgan froze. There on the stairs above stood the man. He was climbing to the door that led to second-class, and he stopped for one brief moment to look back. They would have been hard for anyone to miss, and the man didn't. He stood in place looking both Hunter and Morgan over carefully. Then for one brief moment, his eyes fastened on Morgan alone.

Fourth Officer Boxhall spun the wheel hard to port. Steering any boat, let alone one the size of the *Titanic*, was unlike steering anything else that had movement. A man had to turn the wheel to port to head the vessel in a starboard direction. He had barked out orders to send the telegraph to the engine room; an order of "full astern" and the ringing of the bells on the device told him that the order had been carried out.

Captain Smith leaned out the port window and watched the near miss to their left. Boxhall didn't have the luxury of seeing the results of his orders. Certain catastrophe would have to be felt from where he stood. It could never be seen.

Second Officer Lightoller scampered back from the wing deck off the bridge. He had the best view of the near miss, and his face was white as a sheet. "I think the tug got her," he said. "I'd say, though, that we missed it by no more than a few feet."

Boxhall's knees shook, but his chiseled face was drawn and cold sober. There had been no way to predict the snapping of the *New York's* mooring lines. The engines of the *Titanic* were just too powerful for the narrow channel and much too unpredictable.

Smith stepped back from the wing window and stuck his hands in his pockets, staring straight ahead. Boxhall hated the thought of the man's silence more than anything else. The incident would have to be written up, and no doubt an inquiry would be held by the Board of Trade. The thought sent shivers up his spine. The *Titanic* was untested and therefore simply too unpredictable in a near collision. He knew that, but would they?

Lightoller removed his cap, mopping his brow with a white handker-chief. Boxhall could feel the man's eyes on him. "I say, old man, that was close. A meter more and you'd have had your ticket punched for certain."

"Joseph did well." Captain Smith spoke in his low tone without emotion and without taking his eyes off the bow.

Boxhall swung the wheel to starboard to correct the ship's direction. He bit his lower lip, still feeling a great deal of unexpressed anxiety. "All ahead slow," he shouted.

The sailor manning the telegraph cranked the device, sending out a ringing sound.

The time it took for a vessel of this size to respond to orders was something that frightened Boxhall. He'd seen it firsthand and never wanted to see it again. The helm responded slowly at best, and even when it did, the sheer size and turning radius of the ship made a change of direction cumbersome and exceedingly slow. The *Titanic* was unlike any other ship afloat. There was no way an officer or a helmsman could possibly know what she was like. Nothing could prepare a man except experience, and right now that was a commodity sorely lacking in the *Titanic's* crew. Boxhall knew he could admit it because he had felt it. He was not so sure any other officer could, however.

Lightoller did his best to ease the tension on the bridge. "One thing is for certain. We have the worst of it behind us. We won't be running into ships where we're going. We don't dock at either Cherbourg or Queenstown, and after that there's nothing but open ocean."

He walked up to Boxhall and rammed his fist lightly into the man's shoulder. "Just steer us clear of shipping, old boy, and we'll do fine."

"I'll try to do just that." Boxhall spoke the words grimly.

"Shipping and icc," Lightoller added.

WEDNESDAY,
APRIL 10, 1912,
12:35 P.M.

CHAPTER 5

For some time Morgan and Hunter followed the thief through crowds milling about in the second-class dining room. They lost him outside the smoking room. Inside, the large room was deserted. Small, marble-top tables were surrounded by red-velvet chairs in swooping, Queen Anne-style carved woodwork. An open-beamed ceiling gave off the shine of freshly poured honey, and a large window was latticed with polished wood and surrounded by stained glass. The room was bathed in a soft amber glow. Morgan couldn't imagine what it must be like with men smoking their cigars, a cave, perhaps, with the growling of masculine laughter.

The emptiness of the room was haunting. The man was nowhere to be seen, and it was plain to see that Hunter was grateful.

"It appears our man has given us the slip," he said.

"It seems so."

"But at least we know he's aboard."

He stopped and looked Morgan in the eye. There was a sudden seriousness to him. "I fear that the hunted may soon become the hunter."

"What do you mean?" Morgan asked.

"He knows you're here. You have the satchel he wanted so badly, and you know his identity. I should think it would be to his advantage to find and dispose of you before we reach New York."

The thought sent a sudden chill up Morgan's neck because he knew Hunter was right. Oddly, however, the feeling excited him. He'd felt this way before, motivated and energized by a feeling that logically should have made him apprehensive. Maybe it was moving beyond the safe, predictable boundaries of the world he grew up in. He wanted adventure. He craved experience that went beyond which fork to begin a meal with.

"Then I should find him first," Morgan said, feigning bravery. "And think of the story this will give me to write as my first assignment for the *Herald*. Maybe I can avoid those garden parties yet." Morgan's rationale seemed to fire his bravado even though he knew full well he felt like the white mouse chasing the cat.

Hunter smiled and braced himself like a warrior. "We should find him first, old man." The emphasis on the *we* made Morgan feel more confident, even though he already knew Hunter could be quite the actor when it suited his purposes. Of course, Morgan still wasn't sure he knew when the man was pretending and when he was genuine.

"Are you serious?" Morgan asked.

"Serious about what?"

"You said 'we should find him.' I seem to be dragging you into something that isn't any of your concern."

"Of course I mean it, old man. You don't think I'd let a friend of mine prowl the ship for a killer alone, do you?"

"He does have a knife. Of that, I'm quite certain."

"Then we must arm ourselves."

"With what?"

Hunter laughed. "I'd suggest we pocket the butter knives at dinner."

The thought brought a smile to Morgan's face and erased some of the tension he was feeling. Hunter's blue eyes danced with mischief, the corners sharpening. He raised his arm in the stance of a swordsman, leaving

Morgan only to imagine the short stubby butter knife poised in his fingers.

"We just need to be chipper. I won't have little things like a murderer aboard ship or your sullied little romance spoil this magnificent voyage. Buck up, old man," Hunter quipped.

Morgan knew full well that Hunter was playing with him, trying to relieve his anxiety. He was beginning to love the man as much for his attitude as anything else. *We are a pair,* Morgan thought. Hunter's way of coping with stress was to be cavalier and outrageous, suggesting they deal with treachery as one would manage ants at a picnic. Somehow, though, to Morgan at the moment it seemed more useful than his own option of worrying and fretting. "All right, buck up it is. But we'll keep a sharp eye. Watch each other's back. Agreed?"

"Indeed, we shall." It was plain to see that Hunter was still intent on being dramatically absurd. "Let's get out of here, old man." He ducked his head, narrowed his eyes, and crept to the door, pretending to survey the empty smoking room.

"We will look and play," Hunter mocked, peering around the corner and into the hall. "We will look and eat." He whirled back to face Morgan so quickly that they almost collided with each other. "We will look and survey the feminine charms sauntering about." He clasped Morgan's shoulders and winked.

Morgan just shook his head and laughed. Nothing had prepared him for someone like the irrepressible and irreverent Hunter Kennedy.

Putting one arm around Morgan's shoulders, Hunter marched him out the door. "We shall even look and sleep, I'll wager."

"I don't think I could sleep a wink," Morgan responded. They strode down the long hall, their feet mashing the deep carpet.

"I'm quite certain you will, old boy. I've seen tonight's menu and after what they intend to ply us with and a few stiff rounds of brandy, the gentle rocking of this ship will make you sleep like a baby."

Morgan tucked his chin.

"Oh, I did forget. You are the young Christian gentleman, aren't you? The man of great resolve." He straightened himself to full height, throwing his shoulders back. "Not a drop of strong drink shall pass over these lips of mine. Eh, what?"

"Something like that."

"The man of righteous resolution, dueling the bogeymen of the world with his pen and ink."

Morgan had long ago ceased to defend his scruples, and he knew that to do so with Hunter would be pointless. He could see Hunter's rapier wit had been sharpened for use at just such an occasion. Morgan knew he had far too many inner demons to conquer without taking on the rest of the known world. "Right now," Morgan replied, "the only bogeyman I hope to find is that man with the knife."

Hunter stopped by a potted palm tree, its miniature fronds sending up fingers of prayer toward the overhead skylight. "I do hope we find him before he finds us. I always prefer to lay the ground for my own battles in a place of my own choosing."

He slapped at the largest of the leaves.

"I do think we should report this to one of the ship's officers, however," Morgan said.

"And have them take us in tow as we make the rounds of the first-class millionaires in search of a killer? Do you seriously think they would agree to that?"

"I suppose not."

Hunter pushed open the large double doors that led to the grand staircase. "The only purpose that would serve is to have them think you've taken leave of your senses. They'd be following us around with prying eyes, scrutinizing our every move and questioning each and every step we made."

"I imagine you're right," Morgan mumbled.

"Of course, I am." He stood on the landing, surveying the decorative carpet. "No, I think it best if we could identify the man first and if possible find out which room he is using. Even then, they might not believe you, but it would narrow their investigation of the matter."

"Yes, that would be best."

Turning around, Hunter motioned back to the second-class area. "Let's take another turn through here. One never knows what might be found."

They marched down the carpeted hall. The walls were a brightly painted white with brass numbers on the doors. Morgan was relieved when Hunter stopped trying to turn the knobs. One never knew when a door might pop open to their great embarrassment, or at least his.

"You haven't told me about your parents," Hunter said.

"They both drowned in a boating accident." Morgan bit his lower lip.

"Touchy subject then, what?"

"I seldom discuss it. Tell me about yours."

Hunter did a spry shuffle, accompanied by a grin that went from ear to ear. "My father was a circus performer." He leaned toward Morgan and lightly chucked the underside of his chin. "And my mother was the bearded lady." He laughed. "If I'd only inherited his acting ability and her facial follicles. I might have turned out all right then. Instead, I grow hair like my father and act like my mother. Ruddy shame, too."

They both laughed, although Morgan was unsure if the joke was with him or on him.

"I wonder sometimes if you have a serious bone in your body," Morgan said.

Hunter stopped and faced his new friend. "My father is a minister. I grew up being parented by the church."

Morgan was less dumbfounded by the circus performer story. He watched as Hunter ambled off without explanation.

They spent the next half hour wandering through the second-class section of the ship. Then, taking the spiral staircase to first class, they opened the doors and stepped into the hallway. Walking to the end of the hall, they pushed open two massive doors and found themselves in the grand staircase. This was obviously the crowning feature of the great ship. Natural light streamed through a wrought-iron-and-glass dome overhead. A sweeping balcony looped around the stairs with light reflecting off the polished oak and marble stairs. On the upper landing, a massive, carved panel contained a clock surrounded by carved figures. Hermes stood on the banister below them with lifted blazing torch.

There they spied a strange-looking chap with a clipboard. The man was strange only in what he seemed to be doing. He was dressed in a dark suit with a high, starched collar and appeared to be all business. He held a ruler in his hand. They watched him measure a section of molding along the corner of the stairway.

"Are we shipshape?" Hunter asked, honing in on new prey.

The man had been totally absorbed in his work, but he dropped the clipboard to his side and managed a smile. "Indeed we are."

"Hunter Kennedy's the name." Hunter stuck out his hand, forcing the man to switch his pencil to the left hand, in which he already clutched his paperwork.

"Thomas Andrews. I'm the ship's architect."

"Fascinating," Hunter said. "You designed the *Titanic?*"

"Yes. I'm just inspecting it for modifications that may need to be made."

"Indeed?"

"I'm afraid this voyage will be more work for me than pleasure."

"My friend here is a reporter with the New York *Herald*. Perhaps you could give us a tour of the ship. I'm sure it would make a fabulous story. Don't you think so, Morgan?"

Morgan stuck out his hand. "Morgan Fairfield's the name."

Morgan could see Andrews turn the name over in his head. Morgan's great-uncle owned the White Star Line, and anyone employed by it might easily make the connection. He was happy to see, however, that if Andrews did make the connection he didn't let on. Andrews had the most arresting eyes, cold and gray with flecks of brown.

He studied Morgan with new interest, looking him over as if he were a building he was determined to make perfect. Andrews's smooth complexion was the texture of chilled butter. There was no color to it, and the absence of any facial hair gave him the appearance of Italian statuary. His casual smile carried hardly a wrinkle. "That would be splendid," Andrews said, shaking Morgan's hand. "I would be most pleased to take you with me on my rounds. The *Titanic* is the finest ship ever built, and any word written on it would be most appreciated, especially by someone who has seen it for himself."

"That's most kind of you, Mr. Andrews," Morgan replied.

"It's the least I can do for a gentleman of the press."

Morgan fought back the notion of complete honesty. For Morgan to tell Andrews he was on his way to be a cub reporter describing the color and cut of women's garments at garden parties would make him the butt of jokes the man might tell for years.

"I do appreciate it," Morgan said, "and I'm certain the *Herald* will as well."

"Fine. Then both of you give me your stateroom numbers, and I will make certain you are notified. Are you gentlemen swimmers?"

"Yes, I swim," Hunter replied. "But I shouldn't think we would need to be on this ship of yours."

Andrews was flustered, caught off guard by Hunter's knack of saying outrageous things in a serious tone. *Odd*, Morgan thought, smiling. He was getting somewhat used to it.

"Why, of course not," Andrews stammered. "It's just that I was on my way down to the first-class swimming pool. I thought you might like to see it."

"That would be splendid," Morgan replied, trying to rescue the man's dignity. "I swim quite well and was on my college swimming team."

"Excellent. Then you'll enjoy seeing it."

They followed Andrews out the doors to the deck, where the departure revelers were just beginning to break up and look for their cabins. Barely out to sea, Morgan had already chased a murderer and seen Margaret. He hoped the rest of the trip wouldn't be nearly so calamitous. He took his place in the lift behind Andrews and Hunter, and Andrews threw the thing into a slow downward drop.

Morgan hoped they wouldn't meet up with Margaret and Peter again. He had always been uncomfortably lost in matters of the heart.

The doors opened. Walking through what Andrews described as the Turkish bath, he pushed open the glass doors leading to the swimming pool and stood aside. Warm, wet air rushed toward them as they stepped inside the enclosure. The room was stark white, with portholes allowing light to beam down on the gently lapping water. The smell of salt would have made anyone think of strong stew. Polished wooden railings rose above the tank perched on a lattice girder of painted steel. The white tile of the pool itself was bordered along the top with a blue band of parading whales.

A sloping set of wooden stairs rose from one end of the enclosure. They were like the stairs one would find leading up from the back porch of a country home. They allowed a tired swimmer to walk out of the water without giving the appearance of a beached dolphin. Most pools simply forced one to struggle out of the water and, after hiking up on one's elbows, push himself out belly first.

"I'll allow you gentlemen to inspect it for now," Andrews said. "I need to report to Captain Smith, but I'll find you tomorrow when we leave the Irish coast. By the way, you must try the Turkish bath."

"Thank you, Mr. Andrews," Morgan said. "You've been most help-ful."

"My pleasure."

Hunter stooped and tested the water. He waggled his hand through the water like a game fish on a hook. "Quite warm, actually."

"We wouldn't want you to catch your death of cold."

Hunter stood up and shook the water off his hands. "Certainly not when I could better drown onboard ship."

Morgan frowned.

"I'm sorry, old man. I forgot."

"That's all right."

"Most unmindful of me." He reached for a towel to finish the drying of his hands. "I'd forgotten about your parents."

"I'm afraid the incident will be with me always, even though I remember nothing about it." Morgan moved to the other side of the pool.

"How old were you?"

"I was two."

"How did it happen?"

"We were on my father's small sailboat." Morgan decided to test the water himself and stooped next to it. "Father had a larger yacht but always preferred the boat because it gave him a better feel for the sea and wind."

"You say *we*. Were you with them?" Hunter stepped closer to him.

"Yes, and as near as I can determine I was the reason for their drown-ing." Morgan splashed playfully at the water. "No one will ever discuss it with me, but it's what I've been able to discover on my own."

"How can you as a two-year-old be in any way responsible?"

Morgan got to his feet, shaking his hands. He walked toward the steps, Hunter trailing behind him. "The boat was swamped by a large wave, and the three of us were thrown over. My parents were both very good swimmers, and without me they could have undoubtedly made land. But they had me and only one life preserver they could find."

Morgan absentmindedly stopped beside one of the orange life pre-servers left beside the pool for timid swimmers. It hung on a brass hook. He fingered the straps that held it in place.

"I was too small to fit in it, so they took turns holding me in it, hop-ing for rescue. My father covered me with his shirt to protect me from the sun. They treaded water through the night and finally tired and drowned after making their best attempt to tie me down."

"How awful for you, old man." Hunter slipped his arm around Morgan.

Feeling uncomfortable, Morgan stepped away. "I suppose it explains the idiotic heroic nature I seem to wear like a badge. A man tries desperately throughout his life to fulfill his father's life, and I suppose I'm merely doing my duty."

"Life is not a casual thing for you, is it?"

"Never."

"And perhaps this may explain the religious nature you carry about."

"I suppose if I didn't believe in a sovereign God, someone whose design is perfect, I should become quite an angry man. I was allowed to live for a purpose, though, and that purpose is not to simply enjoy a trust fund and sit around on lawn chairs."

"Oh, bitter aren't we?"

Morgan cast his gaze out steamed glass doors that led to the Turkish bath. "I reserve my animosity for the Atlantic, I suppose. Most people go to the beach to relax and frolic; I go there to stare at an old enemy."

"And yet, here you are crossing it."

Morgan stepped toward a painting of the ocean that hung on the wall. In it, the sea was an azure blue with white caps. Morgan studied it. "I never shall cross it again. America is my home, and when I set foot once again on its soil I will never return to England."

"Is this the reason you can't be with this Margaret?"

"Partially." Morgan whirled around. "In England with Margaret, I should always be the lapdog of her family and mine, never having my chance to carve out a life of my own. I wasn't spared those many years ago to be a creature of English gardens and verandas."

"And so, instead, you go to America to report on the social comings and goings of the idle wealth." Hunter cracked a smile.

The irony of the matter was not lost on either of them, and Morgan forced a smile in spite of himself. "It's a start, my start."

"Then perhaps you can graduate to crime in the squalor and slums," Hunter grinned.

Morgan laughed. "Yes, and perhaps that will be a step up from where I am now."

"In the meantime you can turn your investigative talents to finding a murderer here on this ship of splendor."

"Yes, an excellent place to begin." Morgan muffled a chuckle. "If I can place a good story, maybe I can avoid the wedding receptions of Rhode Island."

"In the meantime, perhaps you can investigate an ongoing crime."

"What is that?"

"A card cheat."

"And who might that be?"

"Me, old man, Hunter Kennedy the third."

"You must be daft."

He dipped his head and smirked. "Cunning, my man, simply cunning. How can you expect a struggling actor to pay for his passage if I don't take advantage of the stuffed shirts on this boat, and there's one in particular whose pockets I would love to plunder."

"Don't tell me. Let me guess. Benjamin Guggenheim."

Hunter gave out with his loud laugh. "Splendid! My boy, you will become a crime reporter yet. I merely assume that if Kitty can fleece the man by night, I can plunder his wealth by day. He was in the smoking room with several other gentlemen when you came in earlier. They seemed to be starting a game of cards, and I was hoping to steer the good Colonel Astor into it when you walked in."

"At least I spared Astor from your scheme."

"Only temporarily."

"And what if you're caught?"

"That's what makes me a good cheat—that, along with my bumbling stupidity. I simply appear incapable of even playing, let alone cheating, sober men." He raised a finger in the air. "You forget, all the world's a stage, especially a card table."

With that, Hunter produced a bottle of Gordon's Gin from his pocket. He took a mouthful of the substance, and swishing it through his mouth, spit it into the pool. Dabbing a few samples of the liquid onto his coat lapels, he proceeded to pour two-thirds of the bottle into the pool. "Now, your lesson begins old man."

Morgan could hardly believe Hunter was pouring liquor in the pristine pool. He was speechless.

Walking over to a water fountain, Hunter filled the bottle with fresh water and replaced the cap. "Always use gin for this. It's impossible to detect when gin has been cut. And when I've finished most of the bottle and appear totally snockered, that's the time I go after my mark," explained Hunter matter-of-factly.

Then he saw Morgan's wide-eyed astonishment. "Don't worry about the pool, old man. This simply adds to the therapeutic value of the water," he laughed.

"You are frightfully amazing," Morgan said.

"Now, I don't in any way expect your approval, just your passive watchful eye. You will get a performance you hadn't expected. Look at it this way. I will earn my keep here by educating men who have more money than they ought, and it will go to a very good cause. Me!"

Morgan was shocked and as uncomfortable as he'd been in quite some time. He felt like a man wandering into the ladies' lingerie department, totally out of place in a foreign land. Hunter was trampling on Morgan's scruples, and Morgan knew the man was totally aware of just how uncomfortable he was.

Still, he was determined to watch, even if he did disapprove. Perhaps it was the danger of the thing that excited him. He had to admit that just watching gave him a tremendous rush of revulsion and morbid curiosity. The reporter inside him couldn't keep away from a story, and he resolved to reserve the theologian in his bloodstream for afterward. Sermons were always best delivered after the fact.

"You can't tell me that you're not given to a smidgen of deception yourself, old man. I noticed how you avoided telling Andrews of your real job on the *Herald*."

Every man must pay, Morgan pondered. *Even sins of omission have their consequences*, he thought. "I said nothing of my employment."

"Precisely."

He pulled a deck of cards out of his pocket. "I did manage to filch an unused deck of cards from the smoking room. They may come in handy should I need another card."

"You wouldn't!"

"Indeed, I would, if the time was right." He held up his hand as if to ward Morgan off. "Spare me any of your sermons, old man. I know right from wrong as well as the next man."

"If that be the case, then why not practice it?"

Dropping the deck back into his pocket, Hunter clasped his hand around Morgan's shoulder. "Fastidious morality is something to be perfected by the upper class with trust funds. Those of us born with tin spoons in our mouths have to make do the best we can."

"I'm quite certain the gentleman with the knife holds the same convictions as you do, my friend," Morgan said. "The leap from what you propose and what he does for a living is a small one, indeed."

"There you are." Hunter pulled Morgan closer, grinning. "I knew if I tried even in the slightest, I could find a sermon on those lips of yours."

Morgan shook his head. "I'm not quite certain of God's purpose in putting us together."

"How so?"

"Were you sent to rescue me, or was I sent to rescue you?"

He laughed. Hunter was an irregular man who took great delight at putting those around him in their proper places. It was evident to Morgan that Hunter knew just where his place truly was. A short time later, Morgan found himself sheepishly following along behind the would-be card cheat like some ill-fed puppy. Hunter was Morgan's only friend aboard, and he was beginning to doubt that he'd chosen wisely.

WEDNESDAY,

APRIL 10, 1912,

2:30 P.M.

CHAPTER 6

Morgan."

The sound of Margaret's voice brought Morgan to a dead stop. He turned and spotted Margaret standing alone behind one of the boats. There was no smile on her face, but her eyes were soft.

Hunter had opened the door to the smoking room. He turned and grinned. "I say, old man, you seem to be wanted. I'll just stagger in here and take my position." He dipped his head in Margaret's direction and, putting on a deliberate totter, fumbled his way through the door.

"Is he all right?" Margaret asked.

Morgan bit his lower lip. "Oh, he's fine. Just playing the role of the court jester."

He could see by Margaret's eyes that she was uncomfortable with being seen alone with him. If Peter should wander by, or worse, her mother, Morgan knew he would have to beat a hasty retreat. He was dead certain there would have to be some lengthy explanation to follow.

"I was hoping to see you," she said. The curls that fell from under her hat bounced as she swung her head slightly to see if they were being watched.

"Is that why you're here alone?"

"I suppose it is."

"I didn't know you'd be traveling with Peter on the *Titanic*. Had I known—"

"Stop. There is no need to explain." She held out her hand, her narrow fingers spread apart. "I see no need to make this voyage uncomfortable for either of us. Morgan, I've known you all of my life, and this is the first time I've ever dreaded seeing you."

"I feel the same way."

"What's done is done for us."

"I suppose I just find it difficult to understand this sudden engagement of yours." Morgan stuck his hands in his pockets in his best brooding manner and stepped to the rail.

"My parents both think that a girl's heart is best not left unattended."

Morgan's eyes dropped away from her, looking out to sea. "Is that what you think?"

"And you left me just that way, unattended and uncared for."

Morgan looked up at her, daring to try to see what was in her heart. "So now you're marrying a man that you do not love?"

"I didn't say that I don't love him. My feelings for him are different from what I had for you, but that doesn't mean it's not love. Peter is a fine man. He will look after me in the best way he can and not leave me yearning away while he tilts with the windmills of his soul. I despise this silly masculine pride of yours, Morgan Fairfield. Sometimes you can be so pretentious and think that your own feelings are more important than anyone else's."

Morgan looked away, once again. "I just thought you would wait."

"But for how long and for what? How am I to know when you will chance upon this Holy Grail of self-discovery? You seem so very uncomfortable with what and who you are."

Morgan had to look back at her. He felt so defensive. "What I am has little to do with a mound of papers in my accountant's office or a desk my uncle has set aside for me. It lies out there in my future, a future I hoped to share with you."

"You are the man I've loved since I was old enough to discover the meaning of the word." Her words melted Morgan's heart. "I have no longings for your dreams, only for what you were when you held me in your arms."

Right then, Morgan wanted to reach out and once again take her in his arms. Her slim waist seemed to call out for an embrace. He bit his lower lip, unable to abandon what little masculine pride he had left. "That was me as a boy, Margaret. My dreams are what I'm to be as a man."

"I hate that you have left me in this position, torn between my heart and my mind."

"*Hate* is a strong word, Margaret."

Her eyes narrowed with a fierce intensity. "I can do no less. All of the feelings I have about you are strong."

Morgan looked up to see Peter Wilksbury at a distance and bearing down on them. "I should go," Morgan said.

"Yes, you should."

Morgan turned and walked into the smoking room, shaking like a leaf. His self-righteousness had always been a liability, and now the one person he had hoped would understand him had turned her back on him in anger and disgust. It set his head to spinning like a top. He wondered, *Could I have been so cruel as to never have understood Margaret's needs above my own? Am I making the biggest mistake of my life?*

Hunter stood at the bar, curling his fingers around a glass of clear liquid Morgan could only guess was the man's diluted gin. Hunter was bobbing his head to pretend drunkenness, but the brightness of his eyes shone through it all.

"Morgan, old man," he yelled, "there you are."

Morgan made his way over to the table quickly to avoid any more loud salutations on Hunter's part. *Hunter couldn't have picked a worse time to make me feel like a robber's accomplice,* he thought.

"I see you kept your promise."

"Yes." Morgan smiled at onlookers, afraid to identify himself with the man. Morgan stood at Hunter's elbow and leaned over. Almost in a mixture of a grunt and a whisper, he spoke in a low tone. "I'm here hoping to prevent you from being keelhauled or hanged from the yardarm. You forget. We're due in Cherbourg soon. They may just as well put you off."

"You just stay glued to my elbow, old man, and learn."

With Morgan in tow, Hunter lurched toward the table of well-dressed gamblers. "Is this seat taken?" he asked.

"Why, no. Please join us."

"Hunter Kennedy's the name, and my friend here is Morgan Fairfield."

Morgan knew Hunter was just using his name as part of his ticket into the game, and now, more than ever, he felt a part of his dirty scheme. "He's not the gambling sort, but if you gentlemen don't mind, I'll have him sit behind me."

"No, not at all. Please be seated, Mr. Fairfield. I'm Stanley Baxter."

The man who spoke was a man dressed in a fine dark suit and diamond stickpin. His long black mustache was well waxed.

"Allow me to introduce you," Baxter said. "The attractive lady to my left is Mrs. Molly Brown of Colorado."

She held out her hand to Hunter. "Pleased to take your money." While Molly Brown had no doubt once been attractive, Morgan could see at once that Baxter was given to superlatives. She had on a large, swooping black hat with clouds of white feathers floating on its brim, and her black lace dress was joined at the neck by a diamond choker. Her drooping jaw bubbled as she spoke. "I'm in the gold mining business."

"We shall only hope you will leave some of it with us," Hunter laughed.

"The gentleman to her left is Mr. Benjamin Guggenheim."

Hunter shook the hand of his intended prey. Morgan could see at once why his uncle had been so impressed with the man. His cold, dark eyes seemed to burrow right through a man. His broad face with lantern jaw was smooth, and his hair parted down the middle was carefully laid out with each strand in place. He gave no hint of thought as he shook Hunter's hand.

"And the green-eyed gentleman to your right is Donald Delaney, the famous Irish novelist."

Morgan was impressed. The man had received numerous awards for his books, and his latest one, *The Pilgrim Saint*, had been at the top of the best-seller list for months.

"You will have to watch him, though. He's stone deaf, but he reads lips very well."

"I read them and the eyes of a man well enough to know when he's telling a lie or running a bluff. I've been recognizing the blarney of the best of them since I was a mere child. It is good to have another man of the Emerald Isle with us."

"The pleasure is all mine," Hunter said as he shook the man's hand.

Delaney was the only man who seemed out of place at the table. Morgan counted his eccentricity as a writer to be the reason. His tweed jacket was draped over the back of the chair and his white shirt was cocked open at the neck with a blazing red tie pulled asunder. He had the appearance of a roaring drunk with his black hair scattered all over his head and his full beard matted. But Morgan could tell he was stone-cold sober. His eyes were sharp, set into his head over ledges of bushy eyebrows. They were almost jet black in appearence.

"Of course, Mr. Kennedy, I'll take your money, a son of Ireland or no."

"We'll have to see about that," Hunter slurred.

"The game is draw poker," Baxter said, "Not for the faint of heart."

Hunter reached into his coat for his wallet, but Baxter stopped him. "That's not necessary, Mr. Kennedy. We're all ladies and gentlemen here. We assume you're good for your debts. What would you like in the way of chips?"

"Ten thousand pounds worth would be sufficient for now," Hunter said.

Morgan almost gasped. Hunter was in no way good for even a tenth of that sum. It would only take a few losses for him to be upside-down financially.

"Fine." Baxter pushed a stack of chips in Hunter's direction. "Table stakes start at a hundred pounds. You can see we mean business here." With that, he shuffled and began to deal the cards.

Morgan watched carefully as Hunter began to lay down his act of drunkenness. He polished off his glass of clear liquid and, taking out the bottle of diluted gin, poured another before setting it on the table in front of him. Picking up the cards, he held them closely to his chest like a child playing a game of old maid. Morgan shuttered at the ruse.

The betting started, and soon Hunter had placed over five hundred pounds that he undoubtedly did not have into the midst of the table. "I'll only take one card," he said. "Come on, ace of spades. Come to papa."

His brash talk seemed to alarm most of the people at the table, but Morgan held to his silence.

"Ah," he said as he lifted the card and held it close. "This beloved card will cost you all another five hundred pounds." He pushed a fresh stack of chips into the center of the table.

Morgan's curiosity was aroused. He scooted close to Hunter's shoulder. Seeing him, Hunter peeled back his hand to give him a look. What Morgan saw astonished him, but he tried very hard to keep a stone-cold composure. Hunter had only a pair of fours, hardly anything that would prompt a bet of any proportion.

One by one, the players around the table threw their cards into the center and folded.

"Too rich for me," Molly Brown said.

Guggenheim laid his cards down silently.

Hunter laughed maniacally as he dragged the stack of chips toward him.

"And what did you have, Kennedy," Delaney asked.

Hunter grinned and slapped his hands together. "Sorry about that chaps, but to look would have cost you another five hundred pounds."

Morgan knew he was right, but the intense curiosity as to how Hunter played his cards was crushing. Morgan could clearly see the cold glare from Guggenheim. The man said as much with his eyes, coupled with an icy silence.

Delaney slapped Hunter squarely on the back. "That's the way to play your cards, my boy. Never let them see until they pay the dues."

Baxter passed the cards to Molly Brown, and the entire table watched as her fingers flew through the cards. She amazed Morgan especially at how adept she was with small pasteboard pieces of paper. She cut the cards with one hand, a sly smile crossing her face, and laid them in front of Delaney. He tapped them, and she picked them up and began to deal.

Morgan watched Hunter pour himself another glass of watery gin, and slurp the liquid. Hunter was doing his best to appear unable to even sit straight. Morgan felt a little queasy at the sight. Even though he was doing nothing wrong, just his presence at the table was enough to make him feel condemned to hell itself. He slowly got to his feet.

He said, "I'm afraid I'm going to have to excuse myself. I'm not feeling very well."

"Don't go just yet, old man. They haven't even started taking my money."

Morgan dropped his hand to his stomach. "It's a touch of seasickness, I'm afraid, and the cigar smoke in here isn't helping me any."

"You go right on, me boy," Delaney said. "We'll take fine care of your friend here and even better care of his money."

Morgan could see Hunter's look of disappointment. The corners of Hunter's mouth drooped, and his lower lip shot out. In Morgan's book, shame was always something to be practiced in private, but Hunter seemed to need the presence of a chum.

"My friend here is a Christian gentleman," Hunter said, "and I'm afraid our vices have made him ill."

Morgan could take the reproach. At that moment he didn't care what insults he might suffer, just so he didn't have to watch any more. "I'll be back later," he said. "I just need some fresh air."

Morgan made his way out the doors of the smoking lounge and to the deck. He knew full well that Hunter might actually survive the evening of gambling, but win or lose, he didn't want to watch.

The air was crisp and cool with a pearl-gray sky. The day had passed quickly, and soon the *Titanic* would be in Cherbourg to pick up more passengers. After that, dinner would be served. The setting sun tinted the sky with the color of torn plums, streaking its gray exterior with bright plumage. Morgan walked along the rail, taking in the sight of the whitecaps over the English Channel. The weather could be unpredictable at this time of year, but so far it was holding up.

A chain lashed the stairway on the deck leading down to second class. Morgan unhooked it and walked down the steel stairs. Somewhere on this vast ship there had to be merciful fellowship, and if Morgan were to bet on where that was, he'd have put his money on the steerage compartment.

Near the rail that led down the stairs to third class, one of the ship's officers stood beside a large chain. Undoubtedly he was there to prevent the passengers below from slaking their curiosity about what lay above them. Morgan greeted him. "Evening," he said. "Looks to be a nice sunset."

"It is pretty."

"Can you allow me to go below? I have friends in third class I'd like to find, a Mr. Kelly and his grandchildren."

"Well, I don't know. There's really not to be mingling among the passengers."

"I'm a first-class passenger, Morgan Fairfield. Surely you can let us have the run of the ship?"

The man scratched his head slightly, lifting the back of his cap up with the digging of his fingers. "Well, I suppose it will be all right."

"There's a good man. I do appreciate it."

He unhooked the chain and dropped it. Money had a way of separating all people, especially the English. Everyone in English society seemed to have a place and knew what it was. Morgan knew there could be no crossing of society's barriers, although many young men of the gentry sought their evening pleasures in the streets of White Chapel, much to his disgust. It would seem that the barriers erected by English civilization could be crossed only one way and that was at night.

Strange music floated up the stairs from the great room that served as a dining room in third class. It was the caterwauling of an accordion that in Morgan's book could only loosely be termed music. He opened the door that led below and made his way down the steps to Scotland Row. Winding through the narrow hall, he came to where the music was loudest and stepped inside.

The place was full of all manners of people. Women sat in gaggles of close conversation with children playing in their midst, and men were off to the sides laughing and smoking.

Morgan spied Jack Kelly right away. With a smile plastered on his face he sat with his back to the wall, watching his grandchildren dance to the music. Morgan could also tell by the bulge in the man's cheek that he was chewing on a wad of tobacco. Morgan was relieved about one thing. At least he wouldn't have to breathe it. He walked over in Kelly's direction. "Mr. Kelly," he said.

Kelly lifted his eyes. "My boy, what are you doing here?" Slowly, he got to his feet.

Morgan smiled. "I was just hoping to find some gaiety and laughter."

Kelly chuckled. "You've come to the right place then, me boy." He lifted up a tin cup and spit into it. He pointed to the children doing what must have passed as an Irish jig. "There's nothing like a man watching his own grandchildren dance."

Morgan nodded and watched the two youngsters. The boy must have been all of seven, and anyone would have placed the girl at four.

"My son and his missus were fine enough to allow them to stay with their old grandpa here until we saved enough for their passage. I am grateful for that."

"I suppose you are."

"I haven't seen that wog you were prowling around for since he came through this afternoon. Are you still looking for him?"

"Yes, we are."

"Did he take money from you? I would have pegged him for a thief."

"No, he attacked a man with a knife earlier this morning and stole his steamship tickets."

"Blimey! That's a rub of a thing."

"Yes, and I doubt if the man survived."

Kelly shook his head. "Well, if he comes through here, we'll hold him for sure."

"You'll have to be careful. He's armed and dangerous."

"All of life is armed and dangerous, to be sure, and there's too little of it to be giving it away to a thief."

"I also wanted you to know that we've lined up a tour by the ship's designer, a Mr. Thomas Andrews."

"Thomas Andrews of Harland and Wolff?"

"Yes, I think so."

Kelly ran his hands through his gray-flecked red hair, then furiously scratched it. "That would be pure bliss, my boy. I'd love to see this behemoth from its innards."

"I think we could arrange that."

"Have you counted the number of lifeboats aboard?" he asked.

"No, I haven't."

"I've seen those new Welin davits. They were designed to carry more than one lifeboat. They can easily handle a second set inboard, even more. They could have two more sets of boats inside of those. I guess the owners of the White Star Line are so confident they just didn't think about how many passengers they would be carrying."

"The ones I've seen are just single ones."

He blew out a stiff breath and shook his head. "I reckon they're more concerned with your view over the boat deck then they are with providing enough boats."

"They say this ship is unsinkable."

"Unsinkable ships are monuments to the stupidity of man. I build boats, but I've never built one yet that the good Lord couldn't take to Davy Jones's locker."

"Perhaps you'll think differently after our tour tomorrow."

He bowed his head and shook it once again. "I don't rightly think so. Pays to take precautions. Of course the Board of Commerce don't make no allowances for the people these vessels carry."

Morgan watched the children dance for some time and then listened to one of the men sing in a beautiful Irish tenor voice. There was no thought of pretentiousness here, just people meeting others and having a good time.The time passed quickly. Suddenly, there was a blast heard, the blast of a deep horn that must have been the signal that that the ship was nearing anchorage.

"That'll be Cherbourg," Kelly said.

"I suppose so. I had better be joining my friend. We're going to dinner together. That is, if I can pull him away from his game of cards."

Kelly got to his feet and patted Morgan's shoulder as he walked him to the door. "I am quite beholding to you for including me on your little jaunt tomorrow."

"I thought you might be interested."

"I'm pleased I came into your head on that matter."

"The pleasure is mine."

"Meanwhile, you just watch yerself, ya hear. You can never tell when that fella's gonna spring up. Like I said, pays to take precautions."

WEDNESDAY,

APRIL 10, 1912,

6:05 P.M.

CHAPTER 7

Morgan made his way up the stairs and back onto the deck, once again passing muster with the officer at the chain. The lights of Cherbourg were winking in the water like drowning stars. The thought of going back into the smoking room struck him with fear, fear of just what he might find. If Hunter had gone through with his plan to cheat at cards, Morgan thought he would be sick. He took some comfort in the fact that when he left, Hunter seemed to be winning on his own, but with the little Morgan knew about cards he knew that wouldn't last long.

He pushed open the door and stood for a moment, watching the game at a distance. Hunter was still seated at the table. They hadn't locked him up just yet, and that gave Morgan some comfort. He edged his way over to the bar where the man behind it in his white shirt, bow tie, and black beard that ran along his jaw was watching the game at a distance also.

"What can I pour for you, sir?" he asked.

"I'd like a club soda."

"Certainly." He reached for the silver bottle and pumped the foaming liquid into a tall glass filled with ice. Swinging around, he set it down on the bar.

"I see the game is going strong," Morgan said.

"Your friend appears to have had much too much to drink," he replied.

Morgan sipped from the glass. "I'm sure he has."

"Gambling requires all of a man's best faculties. It amazes me how he's done so well."

Morgan wasn't quite sure, given the glint in the man's eyes, if he was implying Hunter's game wasn't on the level. He wasn't about to press the issue, however. "Some men have all the luck."

The man wiped down the bar. "And some have too much."

Turning, Morgan walked slowly over to the game. Hunter was raking in a pile of chips from the middle of the table, laughing. He spotted Morgan and smiled broadly. "There, you are, old man. Come back to us with a better stomach?"

"I think so." Morgan timidly took his chair.

Hunter slapped his hands together and rubbed them in glee. "This is great fun," he said. "Of course, I probably won't remember it in the morning."

Guggenheim's eyes were riveted to Hunter. Rarely had Morgan seen a look of more passive hatred. Guggenheim's cold hard stare told all there was to know about how much he wanted to win the next hand.

Delaney slapped Hunter on the back. "My boy, the Irish should hold their strong drink better than you. There are some things done in a night of drunkenness that a man just doesn't want to forget, not ever."

They passed the cards to Hunter. He raked them into a pile and clumsily stacked them. Morgan could see he was doing his best to show a state of intoxication, one that both he and Morgan knew did not exist. He shuffled the cards clumsily, sending them spraying over the table. He came down on the table hard with his elbows, reaching for the spilled cards. "By jove, these things are getting slippery."

"I reckon you're the one that's getting slippery," Mrs. Brown said.

Raking the cards back into a pile, Hunter crammed them together into an imperfect fit. Trying to shuffle once again, he managed to look quite the buffoon. He passed the cards over for Delaney to cut, and the man did.

"There, now let's see if I can give them out. One for Baxter here. One for Mr. Goggenhem."

"That's Guggenheim. If you're going to take my money, you ought to get my name right."

Hunter smiled. "One for the lovely Mrs. Brown, and one for my Irish writer friend." He sat back. "There, did I do that right?"

"Yes, Mr. Kennedy," Baxter said. "Now, let's see if we can get the rest of our cards."

Slowly and deliberately, Hunter distributed the remaining four cards for each player. He then sat back and looked his over, rearranging them as best he could. Morgan knew little of gambling, but that seemed to be quite foolish.

"I like what I see," he said. "All except this one." He tossed the one card away and dealt himself another.

The group shook their heads but ignored Hunter's mistake in dealing himself first. They obviously thought he was drunk.

"I'll take two," Baxter said.

"Three for me," Mrs. Brown replied.

"Let me have two," Delaney said.

"I'll bet one hundred pounds," Baxter said.

Guggenheim smiled and pushed chips into the middle. "I'll see that bet and raise you one thousand pounds."

"I'll call that," Molly Brown said, pushing her chips forward.

"Too rich for me," Delaney replied.

Hunter stared at his cards and then at Baxter and Guggenheim. He stroked his jaw, widening his eyes. "I'm going to make this short," he said. "We'll have to change for dinner soon, and we might as well eat hearty." He rifled through his stack of chips and pushed a large stack forward. "I'm going to see your thousand pounds, Goggenhem, and raise you five thousand pounds. Let's see what you do with that."

"I'm out," Baxter said, tossing his cards to the table.

Guggenheim pushed two stacks of chips forward. He got up from his chair and leaned over the table to look Hunter in the face. "That's Guggenheim, and I'm seeing your bet and raising you ten thousand pounds."

The table hushed. It was plain to see that this duel had boiled down to a turn of the cards and that Guggenheim was intent on seeing Hunter's hand.

Hunter laughed. "You're a determined sort, aren't you?"

"Yes, I am."

"All right," Hunter said, "You win."

Guggenheim reached for the chips but Hunter stopped him cold with a shout. "Hold on. I said you win. You get to lose more money, but you haven't won this hand just yet."

Leaning back, Hunter pushed more chips into the middle. "There you are. Here's ten thousand pounds to see my hand. Show me yours, and I'll show you mine," he snickered.

Guggenheim fanned out his cards on the table. "Here you are, Mr. Kennedy, four sevens."

Hunter sank back in his chair and once again looked over his cards. Guggenheim broke out into a broad smile and leaned forward. "And now, let's see yours, Mr. Kennedy."

Hunter smiled and laid his cards down one at a time. "This one doesn't count," he said, "a queen of hearts. But these," he turned the cards over slowly, laying each one side by side: one, two, three, and four nines. "I'd say my four nines beat your four sevens, Goggenhem."

Guggenheim shot to his feet.

"Now, let's see," Hunter said, "I believe you owe me sixteen thousand one hundred pounds."

"I'll have my man come around to your cabin and settle this before dinner." Guggenheim turned and left the table, signaling his valet to follow.

"See that you do, Goggenhem. We wouldn't want you known as a welsher, now would we?"

Guggenheim's valet had his eyes riveted on Hunter. The man was massive in size, almost six-feet-three or more and well over two hundred pounds. His hair was close cut and black, and he had a black handlebar mustache. His face was beefy in appearance and he had eyes that looked like two pieces of coal, black and dull, as they looked Hunter over carefully.

The blast of the ship's horn and the slowing of the engines told everyone that they were coming into Cherbourg. Hunter collected his cash from the others and haltingly got to his feet. "My friends, it's been a sheer pleasure spending my time with you all. I trust we can do this again. I'm sure it will make the voyage go much quicker. This part certainly has for me."

Morgan walked out with him onto the deck, and they both watched the ship drop anchor. The chains that held the heavy anchors slid noisily into the dark water. Gangplanks were pushed into position, and several ferryboats chugged into position to rendezvous with the *Titanic*. Their lights blinked and inside them Morgan and Hunter could see the well-dressed passengers staring out the windows at the floating palace.

"Don't even tell me what you did in there," Morgan said. "I don't want to know."

"I did just what I wanted to do. Did you see the look on that man when I kept calling him *Goggenhem?*" Hunter chuckled. "I think he was much more concerned about the loss of face than the loss of money."

"I saw it, but I didn't like it." He shook his head. The idea of Morgan talking to Hunter about the morality of what had just occurred was one that he knew was useless. The man had no scruples when it came to taking a millionaire's money, and when mixed with the motive of revenge any sermon from Morgan would be a waste of time.

They watched from the rail as the ferries from Cherbourg pulled closer. The lights of the small boats twinkled against the dark sea, their backwash churning the dark water into foaming, chugging rooster tails.

Hunter took out a thick, black cigar. He was obviously feeling his oats and the delight of taking Guggenheim's money. He grinned somewhat sheepishly at Morgan as he bit off the end of the stogie. In spite of his self-satisfaction, he seemed uncomfortable with Morgan's honest disapproval. Leaning over, he spit it over the rail. Then taking out a lighter, he sparked a flame, running it over the unlit tip. "Old man, we are going to have a high time on this trip," he puffed. "I can feel the luck creeping through my bones even now. This makes losing Kitty to that man feel just a might better." He blew smoke into the crisp air.

Leaning back against the rail, he stretched out. Suddenly, he grabbed Morgan and shoved him to the deck. Both of them hit the polished wood as a large metal box clanged to the rail where they'd been standing.

"What was that?" Morgan asked, his heart racing.

Hunter got to his feet and spat the remains of the smashed cigar from his mouth. He beat out the sparks that had settled into his coat lapels and reaching down, pulled Morgan up. "I saw a man on the boat deck shoving it over."

"Was it—"

"I couldn't tell," he interrupted, "Let's go see."

They both ran inside, taking the grand stairs two at a time. They raced by strolling couples, almost knocking them aside, leaving a trail of "here, here's," and "bloody-rude hooligans" in their wake. Morgan's heart beat faster. He was running to find a man who had tried to kill him. They must find the killer, or surely he would find them first.

They bounded through the double doors that led to the boat deck. Small groups of people congregated at various locations, each straining to see the new passengers coming aboard from Cherbourg.

"You go along starboard, and I'll circle to port."

Morgan nodded his head.

"You be careful now, old man," Hunter said. "You're the one he was aiming for."

Morgan felt his stomach twist at the reminder. It was one thing to know it himself, but to hear Hunter voice the truth gave it a steely reality. He moved off toward the bow of the ship. Cautiously, he inspected the boats that hung over the davits. His heart was pounding, like a trapped bird beating against a windowpane. Morgan felt very vulnerable, being not only unarmed but the one the killer was looking for.

It came to Morgan that he might not have been the target at the rail. *Maybe Hunter was the intended victim after all*, Morgan thought. From what he'd seen of Guggenheim's valet, they just might meet up with him instead. Hunter's paying the money wasn't what mattered to that man; what mattered was the hatred seen in his eyes. He didn't dare to hope for either case.

Finding the stairs that led to the top of the wheelhouse, Morgan stopped and looked at the shadowy top of the ship. *Perhaps the man tried to climb*, Morgan thought. *The sight of someone running through the ship itself might have attracted too much attention.* Putting his hand on the rail, he slowly climbed the metal ladder. If the man had tried to climb to the top of the ship, he could be anywhere among the smokestacks and superstructure.

Pulling himself on top, Morgan surveyed the deserted deck. The polished wood glistened eerily. The gold forward smokestack was held in place by a net of guylines. It was massive. A row of houses could fit inside one. Morgan stepped over to it, placed his hand on the smokestack, and looked up. It was warm to the touch. A shower of sparks belched up from it, forming a cloud of moving fireflies high above.

The deck was dotted with smaller white funnels that ran up from the interior of the ship. Morgan wove between them, drawn like a moth to a boxlike structure pouring light heavenward. He peered over the edge of the well of light and saw the heads of passengers strolling up and down the grand staircase. This was the skylight over the most regal, elegant part of the *Titanic*.

All alone in the chilly night air, Morgan felt again the pang of an outsider looking in. Twinkling crystal chandeliers glowed, as did the ladies in their colorful gowns. He could see the pairs mingling and chatting, nodding and smiling. But all he could hear from where he stood was the lapping of the sea against the side of the *Titanic*.

His momentary fantasy was shattered by the sound of scraping feet. The unmistakable noise was behind the second smokestack, the sound of a man taking the stairs to the open deck amidships. They were deliberate steps, that of a careful man. *Maybe, he's one of the crew,* he hoped.

Moving to the side of the second smokestack, Morgan spotted a pry bar strapped to its side. He pulled it loose, gripping it with both hands. The feel of the iron in his hands gave him some comfort. He could go up against a man with a knife if he had something to defend himself with. He knew he just had to make sure the man wasn't lying in wait in the shadow of some funnel. Hunter was below, walking around the deck.

Carefully, he circled the smokestack, ducking the wires that held the anchor in place. This would be a most inopportune place for him to try to swing the pry bar.

He came to the stairs that led to the upper deck amidships. Crouching down, he peered into the gloom. He could see a figure moving stealthily below on the deck. The man passed under the compass platform and then disappeared.

Morgan carefully climbed down the stairs. He took great care not to have the metal bar come in contact with the metal of the stairway. There was no sense in alerting the man to the fact that he, too, was armed.

Stepping to the bottom of the stairs, Morgan moved off into the darkness of the deck, straining to see anything that moved. Swinging wide of the funnels that dotted the deck, he came to the platform that held the third smokestack. He ducked under the suspension wires and slowly crept forward.

Narrowing his eyes, Morgan could make out a shadowy figure climbing over the structure leading to smokestack number four. Morgan already had been told that the fourth smoke stack was simply there for looks. There was no smoke coming from it and no boilers underneath.

He hurried forward. If the culprit found the stairs leading to the deck below, Morgan knew he might never find him. One way or another, Morgan was determined to prove that he couldn't be ambushed without the man paying a price. He had to stop him, if only to put the fear of God into him.

Hurrying to catch up, Morgan climbed over the white structure and stepped down onto the steel grate that covered the aft staircase skylight. Scooting his feet forward, he took care not to slip and test the strength of the glass below. To slip here would not only be hazardous, it would subject him to an embarrassment he might never recover from, to say nothing about injury.

Morgan deftly slipped off the housing and onto the deck below. Making his way to the white blockhouse that gave anchor to the fourth funnel, he climbed the stairs. He could clearly hear the man's steps now, his footsteps ringing on metal. He just couldn't tell from which direction they were coming.

He glanced up and just noticed the man was climbing up a ladder on the outside of the false smokestack.

"Stop!" Morgan cried out in the darkness. "Who are you?"

The man froze. He leaned back away from the ladder and looked down, like a bird of prey would survey a dying rabbit. Morgan couldn't make out his features but could see him watching. The man started back on his climb to the top.

Morgan slipped the bar into his belt. He gripped the metal ladder and swung himself upward. The bar pressed into his stomach and slipped a notch with each step. One move in any direction, and he'd have to use a hand to steady it.

Morgan climbed quickly, moving his feet steadily up the ladder. The night sky was magnificent. This felt like the top of the world. Heights had seldom bothered Morgan. If that had been true, he would have been quite petrified. The *Titanic* was at a dead stop to allow the Cherbourg passengers to board. The thought raced through Morgan's mind, however, that any minute now that procedure would be finished and the captain would give orders to get under way. The top of a smokestack would be the most unfortunate of positions. He had little desire to try to maintain his grip on a ladder, keep his weapon from falling, and manage the task of hanging on to a moving ship from that far up.

Leaning back, Morgan watched the man disappear over the top of the stack. He paused and looked down. Morgan became worried. If the man had an object to drop, Morgan would be a target too rich to pass up. There was no way he could move from his place on the ladder. He had made himself an easy mark. He hoped against hope and said a silent prayer.

There must be a ladder that goes down into the darkness, Morgan thought.

Minutes later he found himself at the top of the empty smokestack. The ladder looped and continued its descent into the dark structure of the ship.

The blast from the horn of the ship sent shivers through Morgan's spine. It was an eruption of steam that signaled an end of the stop in Cherbourg. Morgan could hear the distant rumble of the engines, and from his vantage point see the boiling of the waters at the stern that meant the triple screws had begun their revolutions.

He looked over the side of the stack—total darkness. For all he knew, the man had stopped at some unseen landing and was waiting with a knife for Morgan to continue his chase.

Suddenly, the *Titanic* lurched forward. Morgan clutched the side of the ladder. Now he was in trouble. *Can I make the climb back down?* Morgan wondered. One thing he did know, he couldn't continue to hang on where he was.

Leaning his head down the stack, he called out. "You had better identify yourself."

Morgan knew that any sound of movement from inside the empty smokestack would reverberate through the empty tube. He strained to listen but heard nothing. The man was not moving. He was evidently waiting in the darkness. He had the advantage now. He was in position, and Morgan was clinging to the ladder for his very life, hoping the movement of the ship wouldn't shake him loose.

"You had better speak up and quickly," Morgan cried out.

Again, there was nothing.

I can't hang on here forever, Morgan thought, *and I won't climb down there in the darkness.* The movement of the ship turned the air cold against him; a dampness cut through to the bone. It sickened Morgan's stomach. Very seldom had he ever been seasick. Of course, the sea had never been one of his closest friends, and the height where he now found himself would have made the strongest man queasy. Morgan knew he couldn't climb back down without extracting some form of revenge, but he wasn't about to go into that dark funnel.

Suddenly he slipped. Grabbing on with his right hand, his knuckles turned white with a desperate grasp as his feet fumbled to stick on the slick steel ladder. He felt like one of the puppets he'd seen as a child: held up by who knew what, and feet scrambling underneath to look human. What the puppets had that he didn't was the pasted smile that refused to disappear with calamity. Morgan knew he must appear to be a panic-stricken child.

He gasped as his chest hit the ladder. His grip tightened. Shuffling his feet with the rungs of the ladder, he found himself semi-stable. What took possession of him then, only God knew. He carefully reached into his belt and slowly pulled out the pry bar. The sweat now forming on his hands made him doubt whether he could actually hold the thing.

He leaned over the dark funnel. "You had better speak up, and do so now." The sound of his voice boomed down the dark smokestack. Morgan listened as it traveled deep into the bowels of the ship.

There was nothing but silence, no movement on the ladder below, and not the hint of even a whisper. The man was obviously waiting him out, hoping Morgan would climb down the ladder after him or simply go away.

Holding the bar over the empty stack, Morgan released it just inches away from the ladder. It took only seconds before the sound of the man's cry of pain, a plaintive yelp like that of a dog rapped across the snout, boomed up through the stack. Morgan heard the bar continue to fall to who knows where, before it clattered to an abrupt stop somewhere in the abyss of the great ship.

"I told you," Morgan cried out. "I told you to identify yourself."

Morgan could still hear the faint whimpers of the man below. Obviously, he'd been hurt; how bad, he couldn't tell.

There was nothing but silence below. Morgan still wasn't about to climb down after the man. Frustrated, Morgan probed the space below for the solid sensation of the next rung of the ladder. With a feeling of relief, he found the steel rung and put his weight down on it. One careful step at a time brought him closer and closer to the swaying upper deck of the *Titanic*.

The lights twinkled, gleaming like lanterns hung and lit by an angelic lamplighter. From where Morgan now stood, his head in the dark night sky, clinging for life to the fourth smokestack, the lights seemed to be below him on the horizon. Looking down, he could see the choppy waves on the surface of the water. The Atlantic was black like the ink in the well of God's desk.

It took Morgan some time to slip his feet back on the deck. He stood there for a moment, refusing to release his grip on the iron rails of the stairway. Leaning his head onto the ladder, he breathed a prayer. *Thank you, Lord.*

It was sometime later when he found a stairway that took him once again to the deck. He knew he must have appeared to be somewhat drunk when Hunter saw him. He could feel himself weave over the deck, his knees ready to buckle.

Hunter's mouth dropped open. "Here, old man," he said. "Are you all right?"

"I am now." He grabbed for the railing, tightening his grip. "I think I found the man." Morgan looked back, pointing up at the fourth funnel. "I found him and I dropped a pry bar on his head down that smokestack up there."

"Blimey! Did you kill him?"

"I don't think so."

"You're more vicious than I imagined," Hunter smirked, "dropping iron bombs on people's heads."

The sound of a bugle jerked their heads around.

"That will be the signal for dinner," Hunter said. "I suggest we change for it, and you can tell me all about it."

Morgan looked back at the fourth smokestack. It would do no good to stand here and wait. The man was gone. "I don't think I could eat a bite."

WEDNESDAY,
APRIL 10, 1912,
6:50 P.M.

CHAPTER 8

onald Delaney was working on his tie when there was a knock on his compartment door. He mumbled to himself as he let the strings drop. Blinking into the mirror, he pulled his hair back into place. His black mane was shoulder length and tended to mark him for the nonconformist he was. The receding hairline was something he tried to cover by pulling a comb dipped in olive oil across his brow and feathering the remaining strands at the front of his head, over the top.

There was another knock at the door, this time louder.

He picked up the ends of his tie and once again tried to knit a knot that might look presentable.

In the mirror, Delaney saw the door open. He saw Fitzgerald in the mirror as the man stepped into the room.

The steward caught his eyes in the looking glass. "I'm sorry, I forgot about your hearing."

"What do you have for me?"

Fitzgerald produced a wire. "I got this from the wireless operator. It's from Scotland Yard and it's addressed to the captain."

Delaney took the message and opened it.

"I brought it directly to you, just like you asked. I do have to take it to the captain, however. The police may send a follow-up wire."

Delaney kept looking at the man to make out the words. He then carefully read the message. Handing back the wire to Fitzgerald, he narrowed his eyes to make his point. "See that you keep this message with you until after we sail from Queenstown."

"I don't know if I can do that."

Delaney's lower lip bunched up, pushing his black beard below his lip into a fierce bramble bush of nettles. "You will do as you're told. This is your first and last voyage on the *Titanic*, and we both know it."

Fitzgerald nodded, lowering his chin.

"Did you take care of the other matter?"

"Yes, I took one of the steward's jackets and trousers. They are hanging in the storage room in the third-class area in the bow, just as you instructed. I put them in the bag and tied the red ribbon on it. I also put the lock on it you gave me." Reaching into his pocket, he produced a brass key.

"Good."

"Will there be anything else?"

Delaney could see that the man was nervous. Fitzgerald slipped the wire back into his pocket, and his fingers twitched in the process. In his years of doing his duty, Delaney had learned one thing. It was always best to keep someone more afraid of you than any fear he might have of the enemy. That was the only way a man could be depended on.

"Yes, you can tie this blasted tie for me. I hate them with a visceral passion."

Fitzgerald reached for Delaney's tie and began to wrap it around the man's neck. The white starched shirt and expensive tie looked odd on Delaney. The man's black suit hung on him as it would a scarecrow in the field, and the wrinkles at the elbows showed that the suit had been hastily thrown into his bag. Fitzgerald finished his knot and flicked the tie to make sure it hung properly. Stepping back, he looked Delaney over. "There you are."

Delaney turned and looked in the mirror. Reaching for the glass decanter of Scotch, he poured a half glass. Swishing it around to make sure it coated the inside of the glass, he held it to his mouth and inhaled deeply through his nose. Then tipping it up, he sloshed the liquor down his throat in gulps. "One thing more."

Fitzgerald raised his head, prepared for the worst.

"Keep an eye on the man identified in the wire. At 10:00, I want to know where he is. Is that understood?"

"Perfectly, sir."

"Good. Then that will be all." Delaney could almost see the sigh of relief written all over the man. He knew Fitzgerald was dependable. If he hadn't been, he wouldn't have been called on for this. Still, with some men there was always a little bit of sheep in them when it came time for action. He'd have to watch the man.

He straightened his suit as Fitzgerald closed the door behind him. The Scotch would help him seem more relaxed and jovial. He'd need all the help he could muster if he was to pull off this nonchalant attitude he liked to exude. Reaching over, he poured himself a full glass. He tipped it up, downing the amber-color liquid. Setting the glass down, he picked up a spray of the mint leaves he'd asked for. Sticking them into his mouth, he chewed vigorously. The fresh mint would help to hide the liquor. He'd want people to see the mellow attitude as something coming from inside him, not from a bottle.

8:10 P.M.

Morgan was already dressed in his evening clothes when a playful patter sounded on his door. He was seated on the hard sofa, still seething with rage. "Come on in. It's open."

Hunter swung through the door, a smile plastered on his face. His face was freshly scrubbed and his hair curly but parted to the side, showing some care in its placement. "There you are, old man. It's time we were taking our places."

"I don't know if I'm up to it."

"Nonsense. You don't want to waste this time. You'll be seated with the lovebirds for the evening."

"Egad."

"Surely you haven't forgotten."

"First dangling from that smokestack and now this. I frankly don't know which is worse. I just don't know if I can do it." Morgan put his hand on his stomach. "I'm feeling queasy enough as it is."

"I'll be right there at your elbow. And you know me, I won't let a dull moment pass at the entire table."

"Oh." Morgan pressed his hand into his belly. "My worst fear at the moment."

Hunter put his hand on Morgan's shoulder. "Don't worry, old man. I promise, I won't make you the butt of any of my jokes. You have a free pass from Hunter Kennedy tonight. You can relax and look the hand-some gentleman that you are. You want that lady to see what she's turn-ing down, don't you?"

"Not really."

Hunter pulled Morgan to his feet, squaring his shoulders. "Well, I for one do. The thought of a woman refusing a better man is one that leaves me with shivering rage."

Morgan blinked his eyes, staring at Hunter. "I'm afraid you'll have to exorcise your own demons. Just because you bear a grudge against this Kitty woman is no reason to drag me through your pain."

Hunter spun on his heels and paced to the far end of the cabin. Mor-gan could tell the remark had struck home.

"Women should know better. How some can prefer to be used rather than loved is beyond me. Shouldn't a woman choose a family of her own rather than become a cared-for trollop?"

"For some, security now is preferable to happiness later."

"Now! Now! We live in an age where the nowness of a thing dictates its goodness."

Morgan swallowed and watched him pace. "You chose what you wanted now at that poker table, my friend."

The statement brought Hunter to a dead stop. There was a flash of anger on his face, soon followed by a smile. "Yes, my preacher friend, but you see that only proves my point."

"And what point would that be?"

"That Kitty and I are both cut from the same cloth. We understand each other." He raised his hands as if drawing a picture on the ceiling. "Two stars crossing in their paths, destined to burn in one bright glow, don't you see it?"

Morgan nodded. "I think so."

"We're both actors using our talents in the way we live life. That man she's with can't possibly understand her the way I do."

"Then you'll just have to understand why she's chosen to be with Guggenheim."

"Oh, I do, old man, believe me I do."

Morgan straightened his tie.

"Now that you have your sermon out of the way, perhaps we can go to dinner. I know how preaching is such a tonic for your soul."

Morgan laughed. "Yes, I am feeling somewhat better."

"See there, your health at my expense."

They turned to walk to the door. Hunter stopped abruptly. "You have that satchel safely put away?"

"It's in my bottom drawer in the chest."

"Fine, then let's have some fun at other people's expense for a change."

Their seat numbers had been delivered earlier in the day, along with the list of other diners sharing the same table. It was one of the benefits of being a first-class passenger, the ability to know ahead of time how one should be prepared for dinner conversation.

The dining saloon was spacious. It featured Jacobean-style alcoves and leaded windows. A large, Middle Eastern carpet filled the room, which had ample passageways between the tables to allow for ladies in full, chiffon dresses. White linen tablecloths were adorned with blue, white, and gold dinnerware with peaks of white linen napkins bedecking every plate. A glowing lamp that shimmered behind a salmon-colored shade was in the middle of each table. The glasses sparkled, and the silverware that was laid beside every plate shone brightly in the light. The walls were white with ornate carvings, and the green upholstered chairs had arms and legs that glowed with a honey-colored wooden shine.

Morgan and Hunter took their places at the end of the table, and Hunter smiled as Delaney sat down to his left. He turned and, in an aside to Morgan, spoke in a low tone. "This ought to be rich old man. Delaney here reads lips, and I should think there will be a few we'll want to have him watch most closely."

Morgan's eyes widened at the notion. Margaret and Peter were sitting at the far end of the table with April at Margaret's side. "I don't think I want to know."

"Oh, yes, you do, and if you don't, I most certainly do. You'll understand when you see the rest of our table."

Morgan watched. At the opposite end of the room and moving in their direction was Benjamin Guggenheim, with a bedazzled Kitty Webb on his arm. Her floor-length scarlet, satin dress hugged her curves. The gown rippled and caressed her body as she walked. Around her throat hung a large ruby pendant that one could see from across the room. "You didn't," Morgan gulped.

"I most certainly did."

"How did you arrange for this table seating?"

Hunter grinned. "I had to put some of that ill-gotten money to good use, didn't I?"

"You're going to make those people terribly uncomfortable."

"I'm counting on that," he said, locking eyes momentarily with Kitty as hers widened in recognition.

The men at the table rose as Guggenheim found the cards at the table with their names inscribed. He seated Kitty next to Morgan and took his place between her and April Hastings. Kitty kept her eyes riveted to the empty places across the table while Hunter snickered in a barely audible tone.

Moments later the two empty places were filled. Colonel Archibald Gracie, who had authored a book on the American Civil War took one seat. Mrs. Gloria Thompson, a wealthy young widow, took the other.

Gracie was a distinguished looking man with brown eyes and mustache. A large, obviously expensive horseshoe-shaped diamond stickpin adorned his tie. *Only Americans would wear anything so loud and garish,* Morgan thought.

Mrs. Thompson had dark, shoulder-length hair and a bright smile that showed a row of perfectly matched teeth. There was a look of appealing confidence about her, even in a gathering of strangers.

The table steward joined the gathering almost as soon as Mrs. Thompson had taken her seat. He was short, with a pencil-thin mustache and hair that parted down the middle. "Good evening, ladies and gentlemen. I am Vincent. I will be your ship's host and will see to your needs this evening." He began to pass out menus.

"I believe you will find our selections most gratifying tonight and should you desire something that you do not see listed, you have only to ask me and I will see that your needs are satisfied. Allow me first of all to make the proper introductions."

Beginning with Morgan, Vincent circled the table announcing the names of all ten people. Each of the men nodded as the names were announced, but Kitty Webb never so much as cast a glance in Hunter and Morgan's direction, and Morgan couldn't much blame her.

Morgan felt a great deal of guilt on seeing Guggenheim, and sympathy as well. He knew Hunter had no doubt cheated the man and baited him in the process. He also knew that Hunter was doing his dead-level best to arouse as much anger in Guggenheim as humanly possible. Hunter obviously felt that a man aroused would forget any caution at the poker table, and that his anger would make him a prime mark for any of Hunter's underhanded methods.

Morgan leaned over as soon as Guggenheim's name was called. He spoke in a low but unmistakably warm tone. "I am very glad to see you, Mr. Guggenheim, and delighted to meet you, Miss Webb."

Guggenheim seemed startled by Morgan's warmth. He blinked like a man finding accidental money and then smiled.

Turning around, Vincent snapped his fingers, and the table server positioned a silver tray at each end of the table. "We begin with oysters on the half shell and salmon mousseline. I will be back momentarily to take your orders." Snapping to attention, he turned on his heels and marched off in the direction of the kitchen.

The *Titanic* took pride in its service and boasted a more than adequate supply of crew per passenger. Morgan thought as he looked around the room that the ratio of servers to guests seemed to be one to one. Dark, cutaway steward jackets were everywhere.

The meal progressed, with Hunter enjoying his conversation with Delaney. The two of them seemed to be thicker than thieves, even though Hunter had lightened Delaney's purse during the afternoon's game. Hunter would dip his head and have Delaney explain what was being said across the table. The noise in the place made it such that it was almost impossible for one end of the table to hear what the other was saying.

A man like Delaney, who could read lips, was an advantage to any one with a prying eye. Hunter seemed to take a special interest in Margaret's conversation with Gloria Thompson.

Leaning over to Morgan, Hunter stifled a laugh. "I say, chap, this is rich. Are you sure you wouldn't like to hear what the old girl is saying about you?"

Morgan gritted his teeth. "No, I certainly would not. Eavesdropping has never been considered a sport with me."

Hunter went on, not to be discouraged. "All right, old man, but this is rich."

He pointed to the two women with his finger, as if talking about them was not embarrassing enough. Morgan wanted to die right on the spot.

"Margaret is telling the woman about her upcoming marriage to this Peter." Hunter snickered. "It seems this Thompson woman is quite the bold one. After some time of Margaret talking about all her plans, the woman asked her the magic question, do you love him, my dear?" Hunter chuckled. "Can you imagine asking that question with the man seated right between them?"

"Please, don't tell me anymore. I feel like a skulking Peeping Tom."

Hunter let out a hooting laugh. It brought heads around, even Kitty's.

Morgan leaned behind Hunter's chair and spoke to Delaney. He didn't have much to worry about in the way of volume, since the man couldn't hear anyway. He just mouthed the words carefully. "Would you please stop encouraging my friend in this worthless endeavor? I find it rude of him, and you are just making it all the more impossible to live with the man."

"Here, here," Hunter said. "No talking about a man behind his back."

Delaney smiled and patted Hunter on the back. "I will do me best to hold me fine Irish hothead in check. What I do with reading lips is an absolute necessity for the likes of me. I've got to maintain some sort of contact with the outside world. I'm afraid however, for those who can hear, it's no more than a simple parlor trick. It's understandable for a man to be amused by it, but like most toys for children, the novelty of the thing will soon pass."

Morgan could tell that Hunter was uncomfortable with having the conversation go on behind his back. In a sick way, that gratified him. It made him want to continue it all the more. The man deserved any reminder of what might be given him on the nature of what comprised bad social etiquette. "And how did you lose your hearing? Were you born that way?"

"Why, no, chap, I was born hearing and spent most of my life enjoying Mozart."

"Then how?"

Delaney's eyes fell to the floor. Morgan could tell the man was weighing the truth before he let the words out. "In my younger days, I was quite active in the Irish Republican Army. I had a little mishap."

"With a bomb?" Morgan asked.

"Of course, with a bomb," Hunter growled out over his shoulder.

"Yes, a rather large bomb." Delaney held up his hands and wiggled his fingers. His eyes were fastened to the movement of each digit. "It could have been worse. I could have lost my hands, and for a writer that would be the same as losing my mind."

Morgan gulped.

"The cause of freedom is the only one worth dying for, worth living for, worth killing for. When God gave breath to man, He told him to be free."

"I was always taught that submission to the powers that be is the same as submitting to God Himself."

"Protestant dribble!"

"But is it worth killing the innocent?" Morgan asked.

"There are no innocent, only the ignorant that stand in the way of freedom."

"You are quite the passionate man."

"Me boy, I am first and last a writer. That, and a son of Ireland. If you are to write anything worthy of a man taking his time to read it, there must be passion."

"I'm a writer."

"Then write about something I would want to read. Everything else is just shoveling around words on a page."

The band struck up a loud tune near where they were sitting, and Delaney blinked and turned his eyes. He raised his voice slightly. "And just what do you write about me boy?"

"I am going to New York to write for the New York *Herald.*"

"Splendid. Newspapers are the conscience of a society. Make certain your conscience doesn't die when you sit behind that writing machine."

Morgan turned back to the table. His leg of lamb and mint jelly was being served. He patted his stomach. He still wasn't quite certain it could face what he intended to put in it.

Guggenheim smiled in his direction. "You'd better eat that while it's still hot."

"I'm not sure if I've got my appetite to adjust to this ship."

Morgan watched as Kitty cut into a plate of lamb chops.

"The sea has a way of bringing out the best in a man," Guggenheim replied.

Morgan shot Hunter a quick look. He had leaned over and was continuing his contrivance with Delaney. "And the worst," Morgan replied.

"I wouldn't worry about him. These things all have a way of working themselves out," Guggenheim said.

There was a twinkle in the man's eye that Morgan didn't care for. It was almost as if Hunter was another selection on the evening's bill of fare.

WEDNESDAY,
APRIL 10, 1912,
8:40 P.M.

CHAPTER 9

The bridge was dark, except for the twinkling lights on the dial of the ship's compass. Boxhall always loved the feel of the ship's bridge at night. It was quiet, with a minimum of interruption from visiting dignitaries, and a sailor could feel like a sailor rather than a blooming tour guide.

Quartermaster Robert Hichens stood behind him and held the wheel at the column, maintaining a steady course that would put the *Titanic* off the coast of Ireland by the morning's light. The feel of the great ship was exhilarating as the bow sliced through the blackness of the English Channel. Boxhall could see the lights of France off starboard while port was shrouded in the darkness of the open sea.

"Bring it ten degrees port," Boxhall called out.

Hichens swung the wheel to his right, sending the rudder to the left and edging the ship farther into the blackness of the open sea.

The officer in command on the bridge was First Officer William Murdoch. He was someone with a hunger for command, and that ambition had made him a rising star. Boxhall knew that one of the characteristics of an officer born to command was the ability to know the exactness of a situation. There was a right way to do anything, and every other way was wrong. He watched as Murdoch lifted his smooth chin and leaned over the starboard-wing bridge rail. From there he could see the foredeck and watch the white foamy spray as the bow of the *Titanic* tore through it.

Next, Boxhall followed the man's gaze and fastened on the crow's nest where seaman Fleet was detectable only by the glowing ash of his cigarette.

Murdoch turned and walked from the wing bridge into the glassed enclosure where Boxhall stood. "Do you have our binoculars?" Murdoch asked.

"No, sir, I gave them to Fleet."

He could see the look of disgust on Murdoch's face. The man had been standing in the perfect position to see the last of France, and Boxhall could tell the notion of having a pair of binoculars to watch the sight would have been welcome.

"Do we have another pair?"

"No, sir. I'm afraid those are the only ones aboard."

"Rubbish!" Murdoch spat out the word. "We have tons of caviar and only one pair of binoculars?" he asked incredulously.

"That seems to be the case."

"Well, you make sure that when Fleet comes down he brings the binoculars to the bridge. I want them here so the ship's officers can see."

"Aye, aye, sir."

Boxhall felt sheepish about telling the lookouts they couldn't have the only pair of binoculars aboard ship, and the thought that they'd been so ill-prepared about such a small but important matter sent a shudder through him. This was the maiden voyage, and mistakes were bound to happen; still, if these matters of safety could be overlooked, what else might go wrong? God only knew.

It was a short time later when Captain Smith stepped onto the bridge. The man was wearing his white uniform. With the white full beard, Boxhall thought he was a striking figure, indeed. He'd obviously only touched his supper and perhaps had only done that so the passengers scheduled to eat at the captain's table might have their look-see at the old man.

Close behind him was Bruce Ismay, the director of the White Star Line. He brushed his handlebar mustache aside. Murdoch snapped to attention, only too pleased to be able to make a good impression on the man who held his future in the palm of his hand. For Boxhall, however, a sense of irritation and defensiveness came over him. Businessmen had no business running a ship, and from everything Boxhall had seen, this man was bent on interference.

"Good evening, sir," Murdoch said.

"As you were, Mr. Murdoch," the captain replied.

They moved over to where Boxhall stood by the compass. "Calm sea," Ismay said. It was a statement more than a question.

"Quite calm, sir."

Ismay moved up near the window to get a better look, and Smith turned on the lamp over the charts. The blackness of the sea always seemed to have a calming effect, and Boxhall hoped it would work its wonders on Ismay. Clasping his hands in the small of his back, Ismay rocked back and forth, staring at the vast water. His dinner jacket was brand new and even in the pitch-black, Boxhall could see the spit shine on his shoes.

"When do you place our arrival at Queenstown, Captain?" said Ismay, almost as if he had eyes in the back of his head to see Smith poring over the charts.

Smith raked his hand over his beard and studied their position. Ismay walked up and looked over the captain's shoulder.

"We are here," Smith said. "I would place our arrival in Queenstown at shortly before noon tomorrow."

"Capital."

Peering at the chart, Ismay frowned. "And just what is this, Captain?" he asked, pointing to the markings on the map.

"I believe that is the course Mr. Boxhall has laid out for us."

"Nonsense."

Ismay looked up sharply at Boxhall, still standing by the compass. "This course will add a day to our time, a day at least."

"It's a much safer course than the northern waters at this time of year, sir," Boxhall stammered. "We would have to reduce our speed and watch for ice."

"Utter nonsense. Captain, this ship must make all speed for New York. We have passengers aboard to whom time is money. I won't have them delayed by our timidity."

The captain stood erect and blinked both eyes. Boxhall had seen the look before. Above all else, Smith was a military man in his thinking. He was used to obeying orders and expected his to be followed as well. Boxhall knew full well that as the captain it was Smith who was in command, but it was a technicality that was obviously lost on Ismay.

"Bergs and growlers will have no effect on this vessel, Captain. I will expect your man to draw up a new course for us before we leave Queenstown."

Boxhall swallowed hard. "I can do that tonight, Captain, if you wish."

"He does," Ismay spat back. "We must arrive in New York on the sixteenth of April. I won't have us docking at night and I won't have us arriving on the seventeenth. Is that understood?"

Boxhall nodded. "Yes, sir."

"One more thing," Ismay went on. "I want any reports of ice brought directly to me. You tell our wireless operators that. Am I making myself clear?"

"Perfectly, sir," Boxhall replied.

Ismay looked over at Smith but continued speaking to Boxhall as if the captain wasn't there. "Of course, Captain Smith must be fully informed as well. He is in command."

8:55 P.M.

The belly of the *Titanic* echoed with the shouts of the black gang and the scraping sound of broad-brimmed shovels. Groans and grunts blended with the tumbling coal. Fire hissed and spat as it licked at the black rock. There was a musical quality to the boiler room, almost as if some great orchestra were playing a sweaty symphony, the unseen conductor with his flaming baton, waving it through the heavy, dark air.

To walk through the oily, dust-filled boiler room was to walk through one of the world's great industrial caverns. A taste of gritty metal hung in the air, acrid and sweet. Pink lights overhead cast a rosy hue through the steamy cave. Twenty-nine boilers were each over two stories high, and every one of them weighed nearly one hundred tons, as much as a small house.

Collins shoveled a spadeful of coal into the flames of boiler number 3. He was a member of the black gang for no halfway reason. Soot covered him from head to foot with only an occasional peek of white cotton cloth from underneath. He wiped his pug nose with the back of his hand, smearing the licorice-colored dust and revealing a streak of rosy-red flesh underneath.

His black cap was matted, and from underneath the wool where the leather lining formed a torn ring around the headband, a trickling stream of sweat meandered, creeping down his temple, onto his cheek, down his neck, and wandering down his chest to a pool forming in his navel.

He leaned on the shovel and puffed several blows.

"What ails ye, mate?"

Finnian had sailed with Collins before. Both of them had considered themselves lucky to find a berth aboard the *Titanic* and not left to starve at the docks while the coal strike went on. There had been a third one of them, however, Bickerstaff, who hadn't made it back aboard ship in time for the sailing. The stoker had gone for another quick pint ashore, and that was the last they'd seen of him. It worried Collins. Bickerstaff had always been his good-luck charm. The man had a way about him, and he loved to sing even when working. Now, without him, the work seemed more like work. His absence made a sickening knot at the base of Collins's belly.

"It ain't right."

"Whatcha talkin' 'bout?"

"Bickie not being 'ere. It jest ain't right."

Finnian slid his shovel over the steel floor, lifting and flinging a mound of coal into the sizzling flame. "It's on 'is own head, mate. We done told 'em not to go, now didn't we?"

Collins shook his head. "It jest ain't right."

"You best jest cram it out of dat dere noddin' of yourn and get on wif it."

Collins shook not only his head, but his whole body at the notion. "There's lots that ain't right 'bout this here."

Finnian leaned on his shovel and scratched his head.

Collins grew animated. He waved his arms around as if he were pointing to a maze of items on invisible shelves. "Bickie's gone. The fire's still burnin' in that coal bin, and there's a body in the hull."

"What ere ye palaverin' 'bout?"

"Ain't ya heard?"

"Naw."

Collins leaned on his shovel, pushing his dirty face close to Finnian's. "They say there was a chap who went to sleep below when the hull was being fitted at Harland. They didn't find out about it till they counted heads. By then it was jest too late. Some say they heard his tappin' with a wrench for days."

"Blimey."

"A man's got hard enough troubles without signing onto a ghost ship."

"You figger the thing's hexed?"

"It's bad luck, I tell you. Havin' a ghost under yer feet when yer tryin' to work ain't no way fer a man to go to sea. I figger Bickie found out and jest never come back."

Finnian shook his head and upper body in a spasmodic shutter. "Gives a bloke the creepers."

"That it does. I don't know if I can be doin' this thing. This is an unlucky ship, mate. We stay on here, and we're gonna be sleepin' with the man below our feet, sure as the world."

9:15 P.M.

Morgan lightly fingered his chocolate éclair. Setting it down, he wrapped his fingers around the cup of steaming tea. He held the cup up to his lips and stared at Margaret over the rim. She was beautiful. Her blond hair came down the side of her neck, stopping at the shoulder with a bounce. He noticed April looking back at him. It made the tea catch in his throat. The woman had always been polite to him, distant, but polite. Tonight, however, she seemed like the queen of ice. It was as if she could read his mind and didn't like what she was seeing. April obviously saw Peter Wilksbury as the answer to a mother's dreams, and Morgan could only guess where that left him.

Hunter took out a cigar. "Well, old man, I think I'll go into the smoking room and polish this off. Who knows," he winked, "I might even happen across a card game."

He got up and circled around behind Delaney. He made sure Morgan caught his eye. "Why don't we meet at your room later on, old man? I should think you'd want to take a more careful look at that satchel." Being away from Delaney's eye contact made him feel more bold. "I should think you'd want to find out all you could about why a man had to die for that thing."

The ranks at the table continued to dwindle as the band struck up a waltz. Gloria Thompson looked eager to escape as well. Gracie continued to bore her with how the Confederacy should have won a decisive victory at the battle of Chickamauga. It was the subject of his book, and he was making sure that the attractive widow understood every detail of the battle.

Guggenheim and Kitty had got up to dance, and Delaney wanted to drone on about the plight of the Irish. Morgan thought Gloria Thompson was an attractive and young-looking widow. He mulled over the possibility of going to her rescue. It wouldn't hurt either, given the fact that she was seated next to Margaret.

He looked Delaney in the eye. "If you'll pardon me, I think I have an errand of mercy to perform."

Delaney glanced down to where Morgan had fastened his gaze. He laughed. "Yes, my boy, I think you do, too."

Morgan got to his feet and slowly walked around the table, catching Mrs. Thompson's eye as he walked toward her. He stopped between her and Gracie. "Pardon me, Mrs. Thompson. I was wondering if you would honor me with a dance."

She smiled and nodded. "Why, of course, Mr. Fairfield. I should be delighted. Would you excuse me, Colonel?"

The man brushed aside his ample mustache. "Go right ahead, madam. We can continue this at some later time."

"That would be delightful."

Morgan pulled out her chair as she got to her feet. Taking her arm, he led her to the dance floor.

She wrapped her fingers around his and gave out a sigh. "You don't know how much I appreciate this, Mr. Fairfield."

"You can call me Morgan and, yes, I think I do. I was watching you."

"Was it that obvious?"

"Not to our military historian, I'm sure."

"Good. Men have such fragile egos. Please call me Gloria."

"I think I rescued myself as much as anyone." He laughed. "Having little desire to smoke and even less interest in the Irish Revolution, I find myself compelled to choose what I would want to do."

"You put that very well, Morgan."

The two of them began to swing around the floor. Dancing was something Morgan was quite accomplished at, even though he'd had far too little practice at it of late. He held her around the waist and, with graceful movement, they soon became one with the melody.

"Pardon me for being so forward, but it is my way. I noticed you watching Miss Hastings during dinner."

Morgan tried not to look surprised.

"She is an attractive young lady. Do you two know each other?"

"We were friends in the past."

"In the past?"

"Yes, the not-too-distant past."

"From the look in your eyes during dinner, I would say you view the history of your relationship with some regret."

"You can tell all of that?"

"Women have a sense of these things." She smiled warmly. Morgan felt no malice in her queries.

"I don't think we ended well."

"I see. And what do you think of her Mr. Peter Wilksbury?"

Morgan spun her around. Peter and Margaret had taken to the dance floor, too. "I was prepared to despise the man, but I actually like him. I think she has chosen well."

Gloria smiled. "That remains to be seen, doesn't it?"

"I think we've seen all of it we're going to see."

"These sea voyages have a way of opening the eyes as well as the heart. There seems to be something about a man and woman's first love that never leaves them. It haunts them like a ghost that rises in the night."

Morgan could tell the woman was right. Such personal observations from a stranger startled him, though. It made him wonder how transparent he truly was. He had to admit, though, that the sight of Margaret dancing with another man, even her fiancé, made his blood boil. "Does it ever go away?"

"I don't think so. My own John has been dead for three years now, and there's not a sunset I see that I don't think of him sharing it with me. It's not that I have conversations with him, at least not that anybody could hear. I just lift my heart and think about what I would say and how he would answer me."

"That must make you very sad."

"It used to. The man was so deeply a part of me that to not think of him would be to cease the act of thinking altogether."

Morgan studied Margaret. It was as if he could read her thoughts. They had always been able to do that. She had the annoying habit all through childhood of even completing his sentences before they left his lips. Gloria and Morgan danced closer to Margaret and Peter.

Suddenly, Gloria stopped and turned to Margaret. "Excuse me," she said sweetly. "Miss Hastings, I wonder if I might have the pleasure of dancing with your partner?"

Margaret seemed stunned at the very idea, but Peter broke into a broad smile. "That would be delightful," he said. "Go ahead Margaret. Why don't you dance with Morgan here, and I'll see to Mrs. Thompson."

Morgan took Margaret by the hand and led her off. "I'm sorry. This wasn't my idea."

Without a word, she placed her hand on his shoulder, and the two of them continued somewhat stiffly with the dance.

"I do hope Peter won't be put off by this," Morgan said.

"How could he be? Peter is a very secure gentleman."

"I'm happy to hear that, happy for you. I do believe the last dance I had was with you."

"Yes, but that was more than a year ago."

"I hope I haven't forgotten how."

"You're doing very nicely, as always."

"Mrs. Thompson was just telling me about her departed husband."

"She seems quite young to be a widow."

"Yes, but somehow one gets the impression that she is still married to the man."

"Really?"

"Yes. She told me a person never forgets his first love."

"Really? And have you?"

Morgan's mind raced with the question. There was a terrible chanciness to any answer he might give. As always, however, he opted on the side of total honesty. He'd been brought up by Lilly to always give the truth in its totality. If a man knew there were seven parts to the whole of a story but opted to tell only six out of the seven in order to cast the truth in a better light, it was as good as telling a lie. The truth was always the truth.

"No, Margaret, I haven't, I'm afraid. I am ashamed to admit it, what with you here aboard ship with Peter."

"Then I pity you, Morgan Fairfield."

WEDNESDAY,
APRIL 10, 1912,
10:20 P.M.

CHAPTER 10

Alone in his stateroom, Morgan licked his wounds. Leaning back on the sofa, he put his feet up on the small table and eyed the whiskey decanter placed in his room by Fitzgerald. Liquor had never appealed to him. It went against everything he held sacred about the sanctity of the mind. Still, there was something about the notion of forgetfulness that held some appeal. Right then, all he could think of was Margaret's final note of pity that ended the conversation and the dance.

There were times when a man was betrayed by his honesty. He had hoped for a better response from Margaret, although he hadn't for the life of him known how he would react had she said otherwise.

He ripped off his tie and unbuttoned the top three buttons on his stiff shirt. Running his hand over his chest, he could feel it tighten. Clasping both hands to either side of his head, he pulled straight back on his hair, flattening it against his skull. There was no driving the thought out of his mind that all was forever lost when it came to conjuring up the fading image of Margaret's love. He had taken her for granted.

At the time it had seemed to him like a natural thing for her to wait patiently for him to establish himself. He had said nothing about his thinking. To do so, to actually ask her to wait, would have been presumptuous on his part. Of course, he thought she would, nonetheless. He had envisioned his triumphant return in the glorious ink of acclaim along with the sight of Margaret throwing herself into his arms with breathless abandon.

He pulled his feet back off the table and dropped them to the floor. Putting his elbows on his knees, he leaned forward, resting his chin on his clenched fists. For a moment, the memory of Rodin's *The Thinker* raced through his head. In Morgan's case, however, it was *Thinking Too Late*. He could see clearly now how utterly stupid he had been. He would have to be a man now and buck up about the whole thing. To be a gentleman required that he look to the happiness of others, even if it meant sacrificing his own.

He settled back in the sofa, as much as possible. Pain always had a way of bringing back the pictures Lilly had told him about as a small boy. Joan of Arc had died as a saint was supposed to die, with her chin up, committing her soul to God. He admired that. She knew who she was. There was no doubt about her place on the earth and no clinging to a position that involved self-interest. The saint was someone who seldom thought of self.

Tennyson's "The Charge of the Light Brigade" was a poem he insisted Lilly read to him almost every night as a child. He could see in his mind's eye the picture of those bold men, clothed in their red tunics with sabers bare, mounted on galloping steeds. They had spurred their horses ever forward into the escalating crescendo of booming cannon with no thought of danger and no notion of self-interest. There was something about men boldly dashing toward certain death that had a certain appeal to Morgan. Perhaps it was the story of his parents and their death. For Morgan, heroism was simply a part of life. To be a hero and die sacrificially meant having a life that was lived in such a way as to make that type of death not only possible but understandable.

It was such a small thing to be shamed by a woman. There was nothing heroic about what he was feeling, no shell bursting overhead, and certainly no flaming stake. He had taken it poorly, and the notion of his poor bleeding heart made him feel childish. He would put it behind him. A quiet resolve settled into the pit of his stomach. He would do better next time.

A knock at the door snapped his head around. "Come on in. The door's open."

Hunter Kennedy stepped in, a lit cigar dangling from his mouth.

"Please put that thing out. I'm afraid I'm just not up to it."

"What's the matter old man? You still thinking of being on top of that smokestack?" Hunter stepped toward Morgan and, pulling the cigar from his mouth, reached down and crushed it out on the polished silver ashtray. Any other time Morgan would have worried about cigar ash being found in his room. It was something he just didn't do. Tonight, he didn't care.

"No. Dinner tonight gave me something else to think about."

Hunter chuckled. "My friend, that brain of yours will get you into trouble every time. You'll just have to face her and smile."

Instead of telling Hunter the embarrassing truth about his encounter with Margaret, Morgan just nodded. "Yes, I know." He lifted his chin, ever so slightly. Defiance was something he had little experience at exercising, but tonight and the rest of the voyage just might call for it. Of course, what he was really defying was his own feelings for her, and his regrets.

Hunter walked over and put his hand on Morgan's shoulder. "Love weakens a man, my friend; animosity makes a man's heart grow stronger."

"Then I should think you have little to worry about."

"You're right there." Hunter dropped his hands to his side and then put them on his waist, striking the pose of a Greek god. "That Guggenheim fellow will continue to pay in the way he does best, with his wallet. And I, dear boy," Hunter leaned forward as if to make his point all the more definite, "will reap the rewards."

Morgan knew that many a man with a broken heart had attempted to drown his sorrows with liquor. But there were other ways for a man to conceal his pain. There had been some men he had known who had joined the army. The thought of danger seemed to cancel trivial notions of unrequited romance. Hunter was somewhat the latter, and Morgan knew it. Danger was almost a tonic to him, and the rush of doing the truly risky helped to deaden the pain of rejection. No matter what the man's rationalization, the woman he loved had turned him over for another man.

"I wouldn't trifle with that man if I were you," Morgan said.

"And why not, pray tell?"

"He strikes me as someone given to revenge."

"A proper gentleman like him doesn't take revenge." Hunter grinned. "He just gets taken."

"You really don't think Benjamin Guggenheim has risen in the financial world by rolling over for the likes of you, do you?"

"I really don't think he has a choice. The man's ego won't let him."

"And it's that same ego that will bring him down on you like a ton of bricks."

"That's exactly what I'm counting on. When I get him in our next poker game, I may wind up buying this ship. The man will never be able to hold up from seeing my cards and I, I will always have the right one."

"You're daft."

Hunter tapped the side of his temple and winked. "Oh, no. I'm smart, and he is just rich."

Morgan shook his head. Hunter was overplaying his hand, and Morgan knew it. The man had managed to push all sanity out of his head for the thrill of revenge and the sudden rush of doing the wrong thing to extract it.

Hunter placed his hands on his hips and cocked his head, eyeballing the stateroom. "Yes, I should think the *Titanic* will do quite nicely. Do you think that great-uncle of yours will sell it to me?"

"I rather doubt that."

Hunter smirked. "Well, it is on its maiden voyage. Perhaps with a few more barnacles on the hull, he'll part with it."

Hunter crossed his arms and began to pace back and forth. "In a way we're all on our maiden voyage."

"Why would you say that?"

"I have left the London stage to try my hand in America, and you have left the womb of the bank that uncle of yours directs. We say goodbye to all the comforts of sameness and slide into the icy brine like the *Titanic*." He moved his hands in a swooping motion. "We are all three like babies. Our bottoms and the keel of the *Titanic* soaked to the draw-ers."

"There is a vast difference between what is expected of us and the hopes for the *Titanic*," Morgan said.

Hunter blinked his eyes, expecting an answer.

"Everyone expects the best from this ship. From everything I've read, one would think that all the hopes of the twentieth century sail with us. Everyone alive knows we can do anything in this modern time of ours—end poverty and war, abolish sickness and ignorance. In a way, all the glitter and fanfare are the notions we have about how very perfect we are." Morgan waved his hand toward the ceiling of the stateroom. "If we are perfect, then we can build the world's first perfect ship."

"And you don't think people expect the best from you?"

"No, I'm going to work in a newspaper office. My uncle expects me to fail miserably and crawl back to England. Margaret expected so little that she engaged herself to another man."

"And you gave her no reason not to."

"I suppose not. She could have waited, though."

"For what? For you to return from America with some award? If you don't know when you're successful on your own, and if you don't know how to recognize the feel of standing on your own two feet, how is she supposed to?"

Hunter sat down beside Morgan, feeling uncomfortable. Maybe it was the fact that he was right. Morgan got to his feet and took Hunter's place in pacing the room. "I suppose you're correct. I feel perfectly foolish about that."

"See? You always want to be perfect. I just want to be myself. I've given in to human nature. You want to rise above it."

"You should know better than that."

"I should?"

"Yes. A Christian has admitted his sin and his inability at self-reform. He accepts forgiveness and that means admitting guilt."

Hunter brushed a lock of hair across his forehead. "You know, old man, in spite of all your talk about being forgiven, you don't strike me as someone who thinks he needs it. You still seem bent on becoming a self-made man, and that has cost you the woman you love. You've taken all the joy, the mystery, and the romance out of living."

Hunter's words cut Morgan to the quick. It was true, and Morgan knew it. He turned to the mirror and looked himself in the face. "You're right." He shook his head and looked back at Hunter in the mirror.

Turning around, he crossed his arms over his chest. "Everything you say is right. I repented of sin and my condition long ago as a child, but I'm not sure I ever lost the notion of being the perfect man. I'm willing to change, though. I need to change."

Hunter seemed stunned. He blinked his eyes.

"But what about you?" Morgan asked.

"Me?"

"Yes. You know the truth of the gospel, but you've allowed people and the hurt you carry around inside to keep you from it." Morgan was troubled by what he said, not that it wasn't true. He knew he was reacting to the pain caused by Hunter's words and not to the needs of his friend.

"Perhaps I have." Hunter hung his head.

"There is still time to change," Morgan said, "time for the both of us."

Hunter sat back. Then he looked around the room and spotted the bottom drawer Morgan had indicated earlier. Suddenly, he wanted very much to change the subject. "Shall we take a closer look at those papers?"

"Go ahead." Morgan waved his hand at him and continued with his pacing. "I really don't care."

Hunter walked to the trunk and opened the drawer. He pulled out the beaten leather satchel. "Well, let's you and I take careful stock of what we're up against."

Setting the satchel on the table, Hunter undid the leather buckles. Morgan walked over and casually looked over his shoulder. Reaching into the case, Hunter took out the large envelope with the wax seal, laying it on the table. He shoved his hand down his pants pocket and pulled out a small silver pocket knife. Raking it under the corner of the envelope, he broke the seal. "Hmm. Let's see what we have here."

Hunter began to sift through the papers, one by one. "This is the papal seal. Let's hope we're not dealing with the canonization of a saint. I do find the righteous quite boring."

The sight of the official-looking papers peaked Morgan's curiosity. He recognized the seals of the Russian and German governments.

Hunter held up a paper with an official-looking seal on it. He waved it, smiling. "See here, a document from Serbia. Those people are nothing but a bloody boil on the belly of the Hapsburgs. Have you ever been there?"

"No, I can't say as I have."

"Nothing works in Serbia. It's the opposite of Germany. Clocks don't work; automobiles don't work; people refuse to work; and even wash towels refuse to dry." Hunter laughed. "Once when I was there, I stayed wet for four days because I couldn't get my towel to dry me off. I had to just stay in the buff and twirl about my room in the open air."

"Look at this," Morgan said. "It's a letter to President Taft, and it's signed by the Pope himself."

"Here, let me see it." Hunter looked the document over carefully.

"It's a personal letter to the American president," Morgan said.

"That's right, old man. He's not a king, but he's as good as the bloody Yanks get."

"Well, read it."

Hunter began to read aloud.

> Dear Excellency, You will find the enclosed documents contain the signatory powers of the governments of Russia, Germany, Serbia, and the Austrian Hungarian Empire. They contain the solemn pledge of said governments not to begin hostilities in Europe. It is the desire of the papal to see that you use your good office to secure a mutual pledge from the government of the United Kingdom. If such an accord can be reached, I believe we can avoid European hostilities in the coming years.

Hunter lifted his head. "And it is signed *Pope Pius X*."

Morgan blinked. His blood ran cold.

"Do you know what this means?" Hunter asked. "It means all this saber rattling we've been reading about in the papers can be put aside."

Morgan mumbled. "It also means Taft may have fewer problems in the American primary elections with Roosevelt if he can pull this off."

"That's right. This would be quite a feather in the old tub's cap, eh, what?"

"I should think so."

Hunter scraped the pile of documents back together and, trying his best to make a neat pile, picked them up, drumming their edges on the table. "We do have to ask ourselves one question."

"And what would that be?"

"Who would benefit if these papers never got to the American president?"

"It might be one of the countries who signed these documents," Hunter went on. "Maybe they've had a change of heart. Perhaps they want a war."

"Could be the British government itself," Morgan offered. "No one likes to be forced into anything."

"That's the man." Hunter slapped him on the back. "You see, you can be capable of devious thought after all."

Morgan watched as Hunter stuffed the papers back into the envelope. The nature of the kettle of fish he was in gave him the shivers. These documents were important, important enough to kill for.

"I'd say this bloke with the mustache must be a desperate man," Hunter said.

"Yes."

"I wouldn't count on him being discouraged by that little iron you dropped on his head tonight. He'll be after this satchel. You can be bloody sure of that."

"We should put it in the purser's safe."

"We'd have to give a description, and it might be too late for that tonight. Would you like me to stay with you?"

"No," Morgan replied. "I doubt if I can sleep anyway."

Hunter laughed. "Old man, you won't be able to be the handsome man who drives that lady of yours to madness if you can't eat or sleep."

"A few minutes ago I didn't think anything could take my mind off of Margaret and now—"

"Now you'll just have to think about staying alive."

10:40 P.M.

Boxhall stood behind the charts and carefully traced the route he'd been instructed to follow. He placed his cap on the corner of the chart and, using a large, stubby pencil, charted the course Ismay demanded. Boxhall frowned. He didn't much care for these waters. The winter had been unseasonably warm, and the pack ice and bergs would be strewn across their path. To make matters even more forbidding, the worst of the crossing would be at night. He knew full well that given Ismay's intentions, they would also be making full steam. The thought troubled him. This was not the time for a speed trial, no matter how many feathers such a record would put in the White Star Line's cap. He put his pencil to the map and mumbled to himself. It wasn't a habit of his, and it was a sure sign that his mind was otherwise occupied.

He set the pencil down. "There is nothing to prove here." He knew full well that they still had a coal fire blazing aboard ship. That troubled him as well. He was no metallurgist and made no claims about such knowledge, but it gave him an uneasy feeling. The heat might very well weaken the hull of the ship. No one really knew its effect. Still, it stood to reason in his mind. As a boy he had seen many times a smithy heat up metal to bend and pound it into submission. He could only imagine what effect fire and bone-chilling seas might have on the same metal plates.

Boxhall shook his head at the very idea of speed trials. Realistically they could only expect to put twenty-four of the *Titanic's* twenty-nine boilers into operation. He did some quick calculations in his mind. Even with 85 percent of her boilers in operation, the engines would give them a speed of twenty-one and a half knots, almost twenty-five land miles per hour. Top speed was estimated to be above twenty-two knots, perhaps as high as twenty-four. *Whatever the figure,* he thought, *it will be nowhere near the* Mauretania's *twenty-six-knot record. When they get all of the boilers into operation on Monday the fifteenth, they might be able to tell, but what will be the point?* He shook his head. To make matters worse, they would be bringing the ship to full speed in the midst of the ice field.

Murdoch stepped into the bridge area from the starboard wing. "Did you get those binoculars?" he asked.

"Aye, aye, sir," Boxhall replied in a rather surly tone. He reached under the table and pulled out the leather case that contained the binoculars. Reaching over, he handed them off to the first officer. "I'm just not sure what's to be gained from having them on the bridge. I should think they'd be more effective in the crow's nest."

"You actually think a common seaman needs these things?"

"I don't know why not."

Murdoch looked up at the crow's nest. There was only one man up there, and for some reason, the man had turned back to get a better look at the French coastline. Murdoch motioned with his head and seemed to enjoy making his point. "I simply fail to see those men maintaining themselves at doing what they should be doing for long stretches at a time. Perhaps for a brief time, but not for long and in the cold, too."

"Then we're all doomed."

"How so, Mr. Boxhall?"

"It's been my experience that on any ship, every man is mutually interdependent on the other. If one man fails at his duty at just the wrong time, there is little forgiveness with the open sea. We all go down, including the man derelict in his duty."

Murdoch rocked back and forth on the balls of his feet, seeming to think the matter over. Without reply, he took the field glasses from their case and held it up to his eyes. Lowering them, he muttered, "The bridge is quite high enough to see what needs to be seen, Boxhall."

"Then why have the crow's nest at all?"

He watched as Murdoch walked off back through the doors to the wing bridge. The notion of being a fourth officer was begining to weigh heavily on him. At times, working on the charts, he felt like a trained chimp with a pencil. He did the work but made no decisions.

Stepping toward the window, he looked out at the crow's nest. Fleet was now staring straight ahead into the darkness. Boxhall knew that the man's vantage point was better than anyone might hope to find on the bridge. It was only right that he have the field glasses. Only the best men were chosen for duty up in the crow's nest. They were paid more, and more was expected from them. Murdoch might have a low opinion of the common seaman, but at the core of his being, Joseph Boxhall knew that was exactly what he was, a common seaman. A common seaman waiting for his break.

THURSDAY,
APRIL 11, 1912,
11:30 A.M.

CHAPTER 11

The Irish coastline was a sight Hunter Kennedy wasn't about to miss. He stood at the rail and motioned for Morgan to come over quickly. "Here my man, over here."

Morgan stepped to where Hunter was standing near the rail, leaning out as the waves broke across the bow. "There it is, old man, Queenstown." He sighed. "Beautiful, isn't it?"

"Yes, I suppose it is."

"Of course, all is not well there."

"No, so I hear."

"And being from an Irish Protestant home myself, I've had to put up with it the whole of my life."

"That must have been difficult."

Hunter lifted his head and looked at the sky. "Amazing isn't it, that God should divide us. Personally, I could care less that a man would worship Mary and bow the knee to Pius X. What difference does that make to me?"

"Obviously, not everyone shares your sentiments."

"Ignorant shopkeepers and shipyard workers in Belfast, more often than not. They think that where they sit themselves down on a pew on Sunday would mean the difference between them having a job or going hungry. If a man can't blame his own ignorance, it becomes all the easier to blame the man standing in the pulpit."

"A man like your father?"

Hunter nodded. "Yes, a man like my father."

"That must have been hard for you."

"Being a preacher's kid is nothing to be desired. Just the thought of being made into something I never was became a burr under my shorts. I had to look the part of a saint, no matter what I felt like."

Morgan chuckled and shook his head. "Somehow, the thought of you as a saint leaves me at a loss for words."

"I should think it would." He stared at the approaching harbor. "It made me all the more determined to be anything but."

"Well, I think you've succeeded."

"Bleeding right, I have. I take my pleasure in the accumulation of sin these days. I may have started with trying to peer up the dresses of ladies and occasionally snitching change, but I've since graduated into more heinous vices. Acting and the stage can take a young innocent and make him into a hardened harbinger of depravity."

Morgan watched the man's jaw harden. It was almost as if the years of having to bear up under a calling he didn't have had come back to haunt him, like a weight dropped on his shoulders from high above. "What about the truth of what your father preached?"

"The truth?"

"Yes, the truth about Jesus and the gospel."

Hunter looked at him as if some foreign thought had been introduced, a thought he had no association with. He shook his head. "I never gave much thought to it. I suppose I was too preoccupied with what that business meant to me, rather than what was being said. To me, it was always caught up with what I was to do and what I was not to do."

"Amazing."

"What's so amazing about that?"

Morgan ran his hand over the polished rail and looked down at the water. "I suppose I've been taught so much about foreign missions and the heathen in the jungles that it never occurred to me that the heathen could be sitting in the front row of the church."

Hunter laughed. His eyes widened. "Yes, and here you have the blackguard right before you, wicked as sin itself and too proud to let on."

"I suppose you've been so preoccupied with the trappings of the truth that you've never stopped to consider the truth itself."

"My father used to say that I was blinded by Christianity and never saw Christ."

"Your father was right."

Hunter looked off in the distance. "My mother was quiet about it in front of me, but my father was always right."

"Always right?"

"Yes. We'd be walking through the countryside, and father could watch a man pruning his hedges. He'd turn to me and say in his most reverent tone, 'That man is not doing it right.' I'd want to know which way was right. His only response would be, 'The way I do it is right.' Of course, whether or not it was the right way never occurred to him. The way he did things made them right. Everything else was wrong, thoroughly wrong. Life was a black-and-white page, and I always stood among the blackest of the letters."

"That must have been very troublesome for you."

"It was at first, but after a while a man becomes numb to the pain. Then when one comes of age, it becomes easier to escape the pain by creating your own." Hunter continued to look at the harbor. "I may not be Catholic, but I know what religious pain feels like. The perpetrator is too far above you to feel any responsibility for it whatsoever. He can only watch you squirm under the gaze of his exalted righteousness."

Morgan watched the man brood. Wounds of the soul go deep, and the cure is only given with love wrapped in years of patience. "I'm sure your father must have loved you."

"For father, love was a matter of performance, and I'm afraid I never rated the first nod of approval on his part. So I gave up the entire notion."

Morgan hung his head. A man's bad reactions about his father were something he'd never been accustomed to feeling. The very word *father* had always meant *hero* to Morgan, never associated with any sort of rejection or disapproval. "I'm afraid such a thought is foreign to me."

Hunter put his arm on Morgan's shoulder. "I can believe that, old man. A lucky fellow you are, in my book. Your dad gave himself for you. My dad gave me hell to save me from it."

Since there was no dock in Queenstown large enough to berth the *Titanic*, the helmsman eased the liner off Roche's Point. The sound of the massive anchors sliding into the blue water brought every head around. Passengers and mail would have to be tendered aboard. A handful of people gathered at the rail, waiting for the launch that would carry them ashore. It was a small group, but these were the people who had evidently only wanted a passage across the Irish sea.

"Poor buggards," Hunter said. "To come so close to a great voyage and miss it."

The small group waited patiently at the rail, four men and three woman. They were dressed in traveling clothes and were not at all like the first-class passengers. The hats of the women were pulled tight to shelter them from the offshore breeze, and the men wore working-class britches and shoes without a shine. "They're all looking for hope. They think they can find work," Hunter said.

Collins jostled his way to the back of the group. He coiled a rope in his hand, doing his best to look busy. Finnian stood by his side, nervously watching the officer in charge of the landing of the launch.

"You better keep that bloke busy when we gets them people aboard," Collins growled under his breath. "I don't want him a tryin' to stop me."

"I shouldn't be a worryin' 'bout dat." Finnian darted his head back and forth, trying his best to look busy. "You'd best be figgerin' on how to keep body and soul together when ye set yer foot on shore."

"You jest let me ponder on dat."

Finnian looked nervous. Being confronted by one of the ship's officers was the last thing he wanted. A man had his future to look out for. To have a ticket punched by a man with a cap would mean no work at all, and this was all he knew how to do. He nervously scanned the deck and then looked up at the smokestacks. "I got me an idea," he said.

"What's that?"

Finnian dropped the line. "You just wait a few minutes. I'll get his attention and everybody else's, too."

Finnian made his way back to the stairs that led below. There was no explanation from Finnian, and it was all Collins could do to not try to stop him when he peeled away and hurried belowdecks.

Collins watched as the fourth officer, Boxhall, signaled for the tug to come closer. A deckhand on the tug below them threw a line, and Collins caught it and secured it with a few winding turns. Fastening it with a knot, he slid open the gangway and lowered the ladder.

Minutes later the passengers on the tug began their climb up to the deck of the *Titanic*. Seven second-class passengers came up first, each counted by Boxhall and directed to the stairway that led to second-class. Gathering on the deck of the tug was the mob of third-class passengers that made up the bulk of the new arrivals. Collins watched them move up the gangway like a swarm of lemmings bent on finding a place. They looked and moved like a mindless mob, the gangway giving under their feet with a bounce as they climbed.

Collins noted one of the last men to come aboard. The red-haired man had his hair parted down the middle and clear, cool, blue eyes. His ears stuck out like a cab with both doors open, and his freshly washed face was covered with freckles. The man was watching the passengers who had gathered at the railing on the deck above, almost as if he were searching for a particular face. Collins thought that strange. Had he not been watching the men coming up the gangplank, he wouldn't have paid any attention to the newcomer. Now, he couldn't take his eyes off the man. There was a foreboding feeling that came over him as he watched the man's eyes survey the first-class passengers above.

The last look of the man in the direction of those who stood on the deck was strange indeed. He had evidently found the man whom he'd been looking for. He broke out in a smile, his eyes twinkling. Collins turned his head around and spotted the man who had obviously caught the Irishman's attention, a tall man with a full black beard who stood at the rail of the deck. The man caught Collins's look and suddenly turned away.

Boxhall made no effort to take names. He merely counted them as they came aboard. When the last of the new passengers waddled onto the deck, he lifted his head and sang out to Murdoch, who was overseeing the action from the deck above. "I count seven second-class passengers," he yelled, "and one hundred and thirteen third-class."

Murdoch nodded and made notes on his pad of paper.

"What's our total?" Boxhall yelled.

"Thirteen hundred and twenty passengers," Murdoch yelled out, "nine hundred and nine crew."

It was then that Collins saw where Finnian had gone. High above in the number four smokestack, Finnian stuck his head out and waved. It was an odd sight, having a man signaling from the top of the dummy smokestack. The smallness of the man against the massive funnel made the size of the ship seem larger than life. In the brochures the funnels were said to be large enough for two locomotives to be placed inside one of them and still leave room at either end.

Finnian's face was black, almost unrecognizable, with white smears of flesh-colored skin gleaming out in streaks. Every head turned in the direction of the black-gang monkey high above. Men pointed and women stared.

Collins grinned. *Bloody good,* he thought. Craning his neck, he eyed the gangway that led to the tug and inched toward it. He glanced back at Boxhall as the officer stared up at Finnian.

"Come down, now!" Boxhall yelled. He cupped his hands to the side of his mouth. "Who are you?"

Collins grinned, his white teeth shining against the black face around them. Finnian was much too high to be recognized, and Boxhall squinted his eyes against the noonday sun. There would be no way for Finnian to be recognized, and Collins knew it.

"It's bad luck, I tell you." Collins overheard the man standing next to him as he pointed up at Finnian. The man was a newly boarded third-class passenger and, being from Ireland himself, Collins could see the look of superstition written all over his face. "To have a fella like that up one of dem smokers is an omen."

"How is that?" a second man asked.

"The man's black face. It's the face of death."

Collins knew this might be his only chance now. He turned and walked boldly down the gangway, just as if he were following orders, not disobeying them. The blasted thing bounced ever so slightly as he strode its length. Getting to the bottom, he stepped aboard the tug.

The deck hand on the tug gave him a queer look.

Collins held up a hand to his lips. "Shush. I'm leavin' that ship. It's a death ship."

The man gave him an odd look, then looked up at the *Titanic*. It was impressive and didn't fit at all with the way Collins described it. Collins dropped behind a set of coiled lines on the deck. The man started to speak, but once again Collins held a hand to his lips.

"Please, mate, keep yer yapper shut fer now. I ain't a gonna sail with no death ship."

1:30 P.M.

When Morgan heard the rap on his door, he got up from his writing desk and opened it. "There you are," Hunter said. He stepped into Morgan's cabin with Thomas Andrews.

"We're just leaving Queenstown," Andrews said. "I thought this might be a good time for the tour I promised."

"Quite so, eh, old man?" Hunter asked.

Reaching down, Morgan picked up his blazer and pulled it on. "Sounds jolly good."

Andrews strode across the carpeted floor and opened the porthole behind the curtain. He swung it freely back and forth as if testing the brass hinges. Lifting himself on his toes, he peered out.

"I find that only valuable for the sake of air," Morgan said.

"Hmm. I should think so. Perhaps we did set the portholes too high."

Turning, Andrews glanced about the posh suite. "Is the room comfortable?" He asked.

Morgan moved toward the sofa and rested his hand on the high back. "I don't think this was built for comfort. More for appearance, I should think."

Andrews nodded.

"Mr. Andrews here is going to take us into the belly of the beast itself."

Morgan picked up his notebook, stuffing it into his coat pocket. "Sounds like something to see."

"It is," Andrews smiled.

"We need to go to steerage first and find Kelly," Morgan said.

"Kelly?"

Hunter stepped toward the door. "Jack Kelly is a boatbuilder traveling to America with his grandchildren."

"I've never heard of him."

"He builds fishing boats," Morgan shot back.

"We promised him a look," Hunter said, "when you gave us the tour."

"Then we should find him."

Morgan held the door as Hunter and Andrews stepped into the companionway. Closing it behind them, the three men plodded off in the direction of the stairway. A short time later they reached the stairs that led down to the third-class area. The crew member at the top of the stairs lifted the chain and snapped his heels to attention. Just the sight of Thomas Andrews seemed to have the effect of the parting of the Red Sea when it came to giving them the run of the place.

The aft well deck was just outside the general room where the third-class passengers seemed to congregate. A number of the new arrivals had taken their positions near the railing and were staring off at the departing outline of their native Ireland. Morgan scrutinized the passive group. They were doing more than just witnessing the land dip into the water on the horizon. He knew that. They were watching the passing of their own lives. Morgan had felt the same way when he boarded the train from Oxford for the last time. He had not said good-bye to Oxford, it had said good-bye to him. Oxford would be there long after he was dead and buried. He was the temporary part of the equation, not Oxford.

They made their way down the stairs to the cabin area below the aft deck. Morgan knew that the single men in third-class had a cabin area near the bow of the ship. Coming all the way back to the aft of the ship for meals and conversation was a bit awkward, but for single men, it was not too bad an arrangement. The women and families were housed here, and Morgan knew right where Kelly's cabin was located. He led the way down the stairs.

Pushing the door open to the companionway, he spotted Kelly in the hall. The man was leaning back against the wall in a small, cane-backed chair. Kelly loved watching his grandchildren, and Morgan knew if he couldn't be found in a hallway where they could run, they'd be in the great room. "There you are," Morgan said. "Are you ready for your tour?"

Kelly blinked at them with bloodshot eyes. It was obvious to see he hadn't been sleeping well. Kelly's experience was with the open sea and wooden boats, not the iron and steel of a closed monolith like the *Titanic*. He dropped the chair forward on all four legs. "To be sure." Rubbing the stubble on his chin, he looked at the children. "I'll have to find some of the ladies hereabouts to watch the children."

Slowly, he got to his feet. "And is this Thomas Andrews?"

Andrews stepped forward, sticking out his hand. "Pleased to meet you, Mr. Kelly. The boys here tell me you build boats."

Kelly lifted his shoulders at the notion. His profession was obviously a matter of pride. There was manliness about being a builder of boats that gave him a lift inside, one that brightened his eyes and straightened the crook in his back. He tugged at the worn, brown sweater-vest that hung over his dirty white shirt and raised his chin. Extending his hand, he shook Andrews's. "Aye, for over fifty years now."

"I'm impressed," Andrews said.

"Are you?"

"A man who sticks with a trade and something he loves is to be admired."

"I've worked at it for a long time, first beside my father and then beside my son. Most of the time I love it. Sometimes, I hate it."

"I can understand that," Andrews said.

Kelly looked at Morgan and cocked his head slightly. The man always seemed to have a look of suspicion about him, mixed with the start of a smile.

"I haven't seen hide ner hair of that fella you was chasing. If he's been around, he ain't been down here."

"You were chasing someone?" Andrews asked.

"Morgan here thought he saw someone he recognized from shore," Hunter interjected. "He was hoping to ask the man a few questions."

"We can find him on the ship's manifest."

"That won't be necessary," Morgan said. "We'll find him."

"Or he'll find us, more likely," Hunter muttered.

Kelly took the two children by the hand. "Now, if you gentlemen will jest linger here fer a mite, I'm sure I can find a watchful eye for these two."

THURSDAY,
APRIL 11, 1912,
2:05 P.M.

CHAPTER 12

The red-haired Howie O'Conner had taken little time in finding his berth among the men. The steerage-class section that housed single men was in the bow, beside the mail room and on top of the first-class baggage compartment. *At least I'm on top of the swells's baggage*, he thought. It might be his only time he'd come in ahead of rich men's luggage.

The son of a tenant farmer, Howie was used to dealing with the rich from a distance. They could be seen. They could be envied. They just couldn't be touched. Now, of course, he made his way in the world by touching the rich. The notion put a grin on his face. Touching wasn't quite the word. He killed them quick, and he killed them easy. The Irish Republican Army had become his father and his mother all at the same time. He suckled its breasts and received instructions at its knee. He didn't question orders, not for a moment.

He had grinned at the swells on deck when he came aboard. So many rich English in one location was a matter of great temptation. Delaney had hinted there might be a way to stun the world by sinking the glamorous ship and taking everyone aboard with it. The thought about the possibility pleased him. To die such a death for freedom would be a glorious thing. The very idea that a man's last breath might take so many of the enemy with him made O'Conner's chest swell with pride. He stroked his chin, surveying the watertight bulkhead. He had brought the explosives with him, as ordered. The look of the ship was solid. There might be a way to punch a hole in it, but he had to see it for himself.

He stepped out onto the catwalk. The doors to the watertight compartments were solid. They stood on massive gears between the boiler and engine rooms. The guillotine-like blade of solid steel ran on a track that formed a solid wall when dropped. O'Conner peered into the darkness beyond the doors. The hull of the ship was on the other side. That would be the place for the bomb.

Of course, he'd have to find a spot where two of the compartments joined together. If he was to do any damage, it would take more than just the flooding of one compartment. It might take four or more, and he knew he didn't have enough in the way of explosives to do that.

He bent down and tried to push up on the door to test its size. There was no budge or give to it at all. Years of working the rocky fields of Ireland had made O'Conner strong. He shook his head at the very idea of causing enough damage to actually sink this ship. He hoped Delaney had a better idea.

The sudden movement of footsteps on the catwalk brought him to attention. He slicked his hair back, parting it down the middle. He'd have to pass for a steward in the first-class section, and when he had the jacket that would do it. A man in a steward's jacket could walk through the first-class section relatively unnoticed. His ears stuck out and his pug nose was covered with freckles. He sort of liked his boyish look. It always allowed him to get close to whomever it was he'd been sent to kill. Of course, his broad shoulders and powerful build showed he was much more than a boy, but the grin he plastered across his face always seemed to work. He seldom felt like smiling, unless he'd been drinking. But when he had to have one, he could find it. It could put any man at ease.

"And what are you doing here?"

The man appeared to be a ship's officer.

"I suppose I got myself lost. If you'll be kind enough to point me to the lockers, then I'll be a puttin' soma' me things aside."

"You'll find the steerage lockers just outside your compartment, some of them are between the beds, but you don't belong here. Didn't you see the NO PASSENGERS ALLOWED sign?"

O'Conner tipped his hat and grinned. "A man loses his way 'round here. 'Sides, I can't read very well." Turning on his heels, he made his way back up the stairs to the men's quarters. The haughtiness of the English had always galled him. They seemed to always know what was proper and took great care in making sure every man kept to his place. It gave him some smug comfort that he'd be a part in making sure the English found their place at last. He soon turned the corner that led to the lockers.

He had seen Delaney on deck and knew at once by the smile on the man's face that all was in order. The jacket would be in the locker, along with the location of the man. He'd find the attaché case and leave it in the locker, along with the steward's jacket. Nothing could be easier.

Reaching into his pocket, he pulled out a small brass key. He'd been told it would fit the lock Delaney had used to secure the jacket. He had a key, and Delaney had a key to retrieve the attaché case. The lockers were lined up in rows between the bunks. Unfortunately, dozens of locks were already hanging on the small, vented doors.

He looked down at the key. It was unmarked. It wouldn't make this job any easier. One by one he began to pass among the bunks, trying the key in the locks. Few lockers had locks on them. Howie was thankful for that. There was always a trusting attitude among the poor. Why should they steal from one another when there were plenty of rich folks, stuffed to the gills with what they'd taken from the poor Catholic folk of Ireland. There was no lock on earth that could keep the landlord out of a man's pocket.

Pushing the key into a lock, he turned it and it sprang open with a snap. Opening the locker, he pulled out the jacket and trousers. He held them up. The pants would be a mite tight, but for what he had in mind, they would work. As long as someone didn't notice his shoes, he'd seem just like any other first-class steward.

He stripped off his coat and pants, donning the clothes Delaney had left for him. Patting his pocket, he found the key to the first-class rooms and a note with the man's room number on it. He'd do what he had to do straightaway, and then he'd wait for whatever else it was Delaney had in mind.

Reaching into his bag, he pulled out the long knife he carried. He ran his fingers over the edge. It was sharp, very sharp. It would do the job nicely.

2:15 P.M.

It was obvious from the look on the man's face that he seemed to carry some unearthly affection for his ship. Each and every detail of the architecture called for a careful analysis. They stepped into the lift, and Andrews closed the iron gate, examining how the brass lock secured the door. He scribbled more notes and pushed the button that sent the contraption into motion.

The door opened, and the four of them stepped onto a landing below the grand staircase. Polished banisters gleamed with a bright amber hue. One could only have imagined the amount of work it had taken in polishing the hand-carved oak. The posts were decorated with carved pomegranates and pineapples, and at the base stood a carved figure of Hermes with a brightly lit torch in his outstretched hands.

"We are especially proud of this," Andrews said, his eyes filled with adoration.

Morgan watched Kelly survey the stairs with a mixture of admiration and disgust. Simplicity and function were obvious values for the builder of fishing boats. "And what do you think, Jack?" Morgan asked.

Kelly raked his thin fingers over his stubbly chin. "Looks like Cleopatra's barge to me. I can just hope what happened to her won't be our fate."

"What do you mean by that?" Hunter asked.

Kelly clasped his hands behind his back and rocked back and forth. "Sometimes a basket of the best-looking fruit contains a snake."

Andrews smiled. "That's my job on this maiden voyage, to find all the snakes and kill them."

Kelly turned his eyes toward the wrought-iron-and-glass skylight overhead. "I do like the sunlight, though. The boats I build have plenty of that."

"Nothing but, I'd wager," Hunter quipped.

"I should think that to an Englishman, most fishing boats would be a cooked haggis," Morgan added. They all laughed at this. The haggis was the national dish of Scotland, eaten only by the Scots. It consisted of a sheep's entrails with oats and other things added sewn up in the lining of a sheep's stomach, to an Englishman an object of awe, distaste, and lurid speculation. There was also a class distinction. Such a meal would have been far beneath the delicate sensibilities of the English.

"Yer right at that, boy," Kelly said, "but they do eat the fish."

"Let's move up to the boat deck," Andrews said. "You can see the look of the ship better from there."

A short time later they stood on the deck that carried the lifeboats. The gleaming white surfaces of the boats were sparkling in the sunlight. Hunter leaned over one of the boats and watched the faint outline of the Irish coast disappear. "Quite a sight, eh, what?"

"How many boats do you carry?" Kelly asked.

"We have fourteen, each with a capacity of sixty-five passengers," Andrews answered.

Kelly scratched at his forehead. "I make that 910 you can carry."

"You do have a head for figures," Morgan said.

"Of course we have four collapsible boats aboard as well as two emergency cutters," Andrews added. "The collapsible boats can carry 49 each, and the cutters can carry 35. That would bring our total capacity to 1,176 passengers and crew. That total is more than ten percent over what is required for a vessel of this size by the Board of Trade."

"And how many do we have aboard?" Morgan asked.

"The last word I heard was 2,229. Of course, we have taken extraordinary precautions against this ship ever floundering, as you'll see when I take you below. The purpose of the boats is to ferry passengers back and forth to waiting ships should we meet up with the rarest of circumstances."

"And what if there are no other ships nearby?" Kelly asked. "The North Atlantic can be a mighty lonely place."

"Our course has become a virtual highway, and the very idea of the *Titanic* getting into any difficulty at all is beyond thought. I can assure you, you're as safe aboard this vessel as you would be in your own mother's cradle."

Kelly chuckled. "That's little comfort to the Irish. I spent me own first year in the lower drawer of me mother's bureau."

They all laughed.

"And you say this ship is unsinkable?" Hunter asked.

"Gentlemen, when I show you our watertight compartments below you will understand that. The *Titanic* is its own lifeboat."

"Then we have nothing to worry about," Hunter responded.

"Nothing that I can think of."

"We all put such great store in our infernal machines, don't we?" Kelly observed. "A man would think they're the eighth day of God's creation."

"I'm afraid you're right," Andrews said. "Engineering has become the god of our minds."

"And if it is a god," Kelly went on, "you wouldn't need to make notes on how to improve it, now would you?"

Andrews self-consciously closed his notebook. "I suppose you're right about that, Mr. Kelly. We tend to think God created us and we're responsible for the creation of everything else."

"Makes a man wonder what will happen when the thing man creates runs up against the thing God creates," Kelly added.

Andrews looked up at the smokestacks high above them. "It does make a man wonder. I've seen the laying of the hull on this vessel, a thing of beauty given birth in a spiderweb of cranes and scaffolding. The web of iron at Harland and Wolff could have held the world's great cathedrals. Perhaps that makes us assume we can contain God as well." He continued to scan the superstructure, lost in his reverie momentarily. "Three million rivets in the hull alone—twelve hundred tons of them."

Andrews looked at the sky. "In fact, I watched Halley's Comet pass overhead through the wires of the cranes. A man thinks, when he sees such a splendid sight. You know what I thought, Mr. Kelly?

Andrews's passion-filled eyes made Morgan feel like an intruder on a conversation he had no hope of understanding.

"What, Mr. Andrews?" Kelly asked obligingly, almost as if he knew the answer already.

"I remember thinking about the awesome power of God's creation. I guess as the *Titanic*'s creator, in a way, I feel somehow closer to God."

"Aye, Mr. Andrews. I do understand. But that comet I hear will traverse the skies for your life, your children's lives, your grandchildren's lives, and forever. Can you honestly say that about the *Titanic*?"

The two men nodded.

"Hmm, boatbuilders must have a secret code." Hunter smiled as he elbowed Morgan.

Morgan knew that somehow these deep philosophic discussions bored Hunter. They bored him and made him restless to get back the attention.

"No matter what the product of our effort turns out to be," Andrews went on, "it can never duplicate the awesome splendor of God's creation."

Looking through the small crowd on the deck, Morgan spotted Donald Delaney. He nudged Hunter. "There's your friend."

Hunter gave nod to the bearded man, and the group strolled over to him.

In a quick aside to Andrews and Kelly, Morgan tried to warn them. "Delaney's totally deaf, but he does read lips well."

"Good day to you," Delaney said.

"We're taking the grand tour." Hunter raised his voice. Morgan gave out a smile. It was a natural thing for Hunter to do, but a whisper to the man would have been sufficient.

"Ah, and it's a grand day for it," Delaney replied.

"Allow me to introduce you to our friend, Jack Kelly," Morgan said. "He builds boats."

"Real boats," Kelly added, "Boats made as God intended, from good strong oak."

A smile creased Delaney's lips. "The kind that float."

"And Delaney here writes books," Morgan said.

The two Irishmen shook hands.

"Pleased to meet you, Kelly." Delaney looked off in the distance. "And you're seeing the last of our dear old Ireland."

"Not the last I should hope," Hunter said.

"One never knows," Delaney said. "Life is uncertain."

Morgan could see that Andrews, with Hunter in tow, had moved on. They were inspecting the davits the boats were hanging on while Andrews made notes. "I think we'd better keep up with our tour," he said. Nodding farewell, they walked toward the shipbuilder.

"I know that man," Kelly mumbled to Morgan.

"You should. He's a famous writer."

"He's more than that, me boy. He's a big shot in the IRA. Makes me kind of nervous with him aboard."

"Why is that?"

"So many of the English in one spot, and the upper class to boot. Makes this a tempting target, I should reckon."

"He wouldn't dare. He's on this ship, too."

Kelly laughed. "Me boy, you have little sense of the Irish craving for a nation do you? Any one of them would die a thousand deaths to take the lives of a thousand and one of the English."

Morgan turned back to take another look at Delaney. "I find that hard to believe. He seems like such a moral man."

"And me, boy, I'm quite certain he is. He'd no more steal anything from you than he would fly. A man like him hates what he feels like he has to do, but he hates the English worse." Kelly turned back to cast a glance at Delaney. "I think men like Delaney, men of high principle, hate the English most for forcing them to do what they think they have to do. They see them as a pet dog turned rabid and threatening a loved one. A man hates to shoot the animal for the sake of all the memories, but he does it all the same."

Morgan slowly shook his head. "There are some things a man never learns in the halls of Oxford."

Kelly squinted his eyes at him. "Some things a man has to learn on the docks."

"Let's hope you're wrong."

"I'm wrong about many things, but boats and the Irish, I'm seldom wrong about."

The small party made their way below as far as the lift would take them. Reaching the bottom they curled around a series of iron stairs and narrow companionways to the floor of the engine room.

"This is the turbine engine room," Andrews shouted over the deafening roar of the *Titanic*'s turbines.

The men covered their ears. "Let's leave this place," Hunter shouted back at them.

Morgan craned his neck up, spotting a set of stairs that seemed to go upward for a mile or more. Stepping aside, he could see the bright light of the sky. "Where does this lead?" He yelled.

"That's the number four smokestack. It's just a shell, purely to add balance to her design," Andrews explained.

Morgan nodded, eyeing the smokestack carefully. This was where the man he chased the night before had climbed down.

Moving through a bulkhead that led to a second engine room, once again Andrews shouted, "This is the reciprocating engine room."

"It's as noisy as the first one," Hunter shouted back. "More."

"Now we know where that constant hum and vibration comes from," Morgan hollered.

"Exactly," Andrews shouted. "The only time you need to worry is when you don't feel the vibration from below."

The engine rooms were filled with men of the black gang, engineers and stokers covered with soot and dust. Their ears were stuffed with cotton, and sweat poured off of them, cutting streams of dripping white flesh from backs that were otherwise black. The temperature must have been unbearable for a man confined to the bowels of the ship. Morgan could see why these men received extra wages for this type of duty.

Most men of breeding would have felt uncomfortable around men who earned their living with bleeding knuckles and groans, but Morgan felt strangely drawn to them. Their lives were the substance of what made civilization work, and if he was to work on a newspaper, he would have to understand them and their pain. The thought of writing about pointless garden parties disgusted him.

Kelly stopped beside two massive pieces of machinery. "These are the pumps, I take it," he shouted.

"That they are."

"But we're in the stern of the ship."

"Not exactly." Andrews was shouting over the engines. "But I should doubt if we'll ever have a chance to use them."

"Not unless you're torpedoed amidships, you won't."

"Come right this way. Follow me, and I'll show you why those pumps are here for ballast."

Kelly pulled Morgan aside. "Those pumps where they are, are practically useless," he said. "It may fit into the design to have them there, but if this ship of his actually hits something, he'll want to have them as far forward as possible." He smiled. "Of course, I build wooden boats."

The four of them moved through the bulkhead door and began a long walk down the keel of the ship. They soon were walking through the noisy boiler room, which was filled with the sound of men shoveling coal into the blazing and towering boilers. Men stepped aside as they passed, and Morgan could see the look of envy written all over their faces. Feeling the intense heat, he could see why.

The noise of the engines and the sound of the intense flame behind them, they began to talk normally. "This is the forward hold area, and there are the watertight compartments—eight of them on starboard and eight of them on port." Andrews pointed out the switches that led to the gears. "They are controlled by an electromagnetic impulse. When the order is given on the bridge, the gates drop, sealing off any flow of water into the hull of the vessel. So you can see, we are our own lifeboat."

Kelly craned his neck toward the top of the doors. "How high do they go up?"

"To E deck." Andrews ran his hand over the surface of the open compartment door. "Even if the hull is breached at the juncture of two of these, we will sustain minimal listing. I believe we could sustain damage along the waterline to up to four of the compartments and notice very little change. Your glasses might slide a might on a wet table, but nothing to notice."

"Impressive." Hunter leaned against the door, testing the strength of the steel.

Andrews beamed. "We like to think so."

Kelly studied the doors. "I think I'll stay with my wooden boats. These steel contraptions go to the bottom rather rapidly."

"Suit yourself, but I think you'd find it quite a chore crossing the Atlantic in one of your boats."

"But I would get there."

"Let's go up to the bridge," Andrews said. "On the way I can show you the Turkish bath. You've already seen the swimming pool. They are the only ones of their kind afloat."

They wandered through the opulent Turkish bath area. Tiled white-and-blue walls gleamed in the light of small lamps beside padded and intricately embroidered massage couches. Pillars rose to the ceiling, giving the place a Moorish appearance like the home of a sultan. A masseuse was giving a gentleman in a towel a rubdown.

"I say, old man," Hunter said to Morgan, "This looks like jolly well spent time. I think we should come down and try our hand at it. What do you think?"

"It looks interesting." Morgan felt somewhat self-conscious having Kelly with them and making plans that only the first-class passengers could enjoy.

"By all means, gentlemen," Andrews joined in. "I think you will find it quite relaxing. Our masseuse here is one of the best. He'll be very gentle with you, though, if you like."

"I'd like that very much," Hunter said. "And Lord knows you could use the relaxing yourself, Morgan."

Within minutes, they arrived on the bridge. The helmsman held the wheel and First Officer Murdoch stood at the telegraph alongside Captain Smith. "Good afternoon, gentlemen," Andrews said. "I'm conducting a little tour with a member of the press."

Smith brushed aside his white beard. "Please, be our guests."

"Captain! Captain!"

The men snapped their heads around at the sound of the alarm, and they could hear fast-running footsteps climbing the stairs. Moments later, Boxhall burst through the doorway, gasping for breath. "Something awful has happened, Captain, something dreadful."

Smith steadied the man with both hands on his shoulders. "Calm down, my boy, and speak slowly."

Boxhall gulped, rocking his head back and forth. "A man has been killed, Captain. There's blood everywhere."

"Where? How?"

"In one of the first-class cabins, sir. The doctor says he's been stabbed, murdered."

Smith's eyes widened slightly and then narrowed as he took control. "Boxhall, come show me the cabin. Murdoch, you have the bridge," Smith boomed as he made his way out the door.

The bridge was silent. Hunter, never one to miss out on excitement, looked at Morgan. "Well, come on, old man. Let's go with the captain." He edged to the door, Morgan on his heels.

Just as they got to the door, Morgan remembered Andrews and Kelly. He turned to make his apologies but could see they were right behind him. The excitement seemed to be too much for any man's curiosity.

He turned to race after Hunter, who was shouting from the nearby stairwell. "Morgan, hurry up or we'll lose them."

THURDAY,
APRIL 11, 1912,
3:45 P.M.

CHAPTER 13

The group arrived at the cabin on B deck in time to see the ship's doctor pulling a sheet over the body of the man on the cabin floor. At first glance Morgan could see the entire room was in shambles. Trunks and chests had been pushed over on their sides, and their contents lay scattered over the carpet in a blanket of wreckage. A man might easily mistake the appearance of the room as something that was the product of a fight, but that was not the case. The murderer had been looking for something. The table in front of the sofa was relatively undisturbed, and several ashtrays, filled to the brim with cigarette ashes, were sitting on the tables, their contents in place.

The doctor got to his feet and turned to face Smith and the small crowd at his heels. "Stab wounds, I'd say, Captain. The man was definitely murdered. The body is still warm, too. It couldn't have happened long ago."

"Was anyone seen about the hallway?" Smith asked.

"Only a steward passing through with a tray."

"Do we know the identity of the man?"

"That's the puzzling thing about it. The cabin was assigned to an American passenger." The doctor took out a list of the first-class passengers. "A Mr. George Sinclair." Patting his pockets, the doctor pulled out a leather passport case. "This is the passport we found on the man, however."

Smith took the case and opened it up. "It's a Serb passport," Smith said. He looked it over, trying to form the words. "It belongs to a Leview Molcan."

Hunter nudged Morgan.

"Excuse me, Captain. May we see the body? I have reason to believe it might be the man I saw on the day we sailed, a man who took someone's ticket."

Smith waved at the doctor to get him to uncover the body.

Bending down, the doctor took the corner of the sheet and pulled it back.

Morgan leaned forward to get a better look. He saw at once that it was the same man with the dark complexion and thin mustache whom he'd confronted in the alley.

The man's dark complexion was made even dingier by a thin veneer of beard. His hair was a wild black, with curls that stood out in bold ringlets. At first glance, his face was almost aristocratic, with high cheekbones and a proud nose. The shabby little mustache and the lack of a clean shave removed that impression quickly. The man's suit, a blue-gray microscopic pinstripe, looked old-fashioned but expensive, like something that would have cost a lot of money twenty years ago. It was worn in places and had a button missing from the bottom of the vest. Morgan studied the shoes. They appeared to be Italian, hand sewn and badly polished. In fact, what polish there was on the man's shoes was smeared and stood out in clumps of black wax in the crease between the sole and the leather upper.

Morgan looked the features of the man over very carefully. There seemed to be no other wounds, and Morgan would have expected to find something, even if it was a bruise. Perhaps it wasn't the man he had dropped the pry bar on.

"Is that the wog you were chasing?" Kelly asked.

Morgan nodded. "But I don't think it was the man from last night."

"You were chasing this man?" Smith asked. "Why?"

"Yes, sir. He stole a ticket. I thought I spotted him on the day we sailed, but I couldn't be sure. We lost him in the second-class area of the ship."

Smith raised himself upright and clasped his hands behind his back. "And why weren't we informed of this?"

Hunter edged himself forward. "I'm sorry, Captain, the mistake was a matter of my advice. Morgan here wasn't sure it was the man, and we saw no reason to alarm or disturb the first-class passengers."

"I gave a full report to Scotland Yard before we sailed," Morgan said. "I should have thought they would have sent you a wire."

Smith turned to Boxhall. "Make a note of this, Boxhall. Send a wire at once to the authorities in London, informing them of this matter."

"Will we have to turn around, Captain?" Boxhall asked.

Smith stroked his beard. "No. Dr. McCoy, I want you to take this man to the morgue. Boxhall, you make certain the companionway is cleared of all passengers. I want no one to see this man taken away. There is no need for panic here."

"Captain, this is serious," Boxhall said. "There is a murderer aboard this ship."

"And do you think that by turning about and disembarking the passengers we'll be able to find him? No, I think not. We will lose two days at least and keep over two thousand passengers boxed up while the police interrogate the innocent along with the guilty. That would be quite an embarrassment to White Star Line."

"But isn't this dangerous, sir?"

"I want you to double the watch. Stop and question anyone of a suspicious nature. Make sure no one is seen wandering about that doesn't belong to their assigned areas of quarters."

"Yes, sir."

Smith turned around to the small group. "Have we all seen enough here?"

Morgan and Hunter nodded.

"Fine. Then, Boxhall, have this cabin sealed. I want no one entering it until we reach New York and the American police have had a chance to see what we have seen."

The small group followed the captain back on deck. One of the seamen had been holding the captain's dog. He handed over the leash on the large hound and Smith bent down to pet the animal.

Hunter pulled Morgan aside as they followed. "Should we have told the captain about the documents?"

"Those papers were to be seen by no one. I think we should find and question this fellow, Major Butt. If we can identify him, then he is the rightful owner, and the whole thing is out of our hair. He can be the one to tell what he knows to the authorities in the United States, and we can stand for questioning as well."

"Surely whoever killed that man was looking for what we now have."

"No doubt."

"Then he will still be looking for them."

"I shouldn't doubt that, either."

"You know this places us in grave jeopardy, old man."

"We do have one advantage now."

"What, pray tell, would that be?"

"The only man who knew we had the documents is now dead."

"A small comfort."

Minutes later they followed Captain Smith back onto the bridge. The idea of a tour at this point seemed spent, and they followed along like a group of whipped dogs. Morgan watched the captain. The man seemed lost in thought. Not turning the ship around was a serious matter, and Smith had made the decision. It was an option that would be open to grave question and consequences. Morgan could see that Smith knew it.

Morgan watched as Smith shuffled through a gathering of dispatches laid on the chart table. He put his hands on a wire and read it, then crumpled it in his hands.

"Tell Phillips to come here at once," Smith barked at Boxhall.

Moments later, the young Marconi operator stepped onto the bridge behind Boxhall.

Smith shoved the paper at the young man. "What is the meaning of this? Why was this wire from Scotland Yard not shown to me immediately?"

Phillips took the paper and looked it over. "I gave this to a steward to give to you yesterday, sir."

Morgan watched as the captain's eyes blazed. "From now on, Mr. Phillips, official wires are to be given only to the ship's officers or to myself. Is that understood?"

"Yes, sir, I understand."

"This delayed communication may have cost a man his life." Smith's voice rose. "I want to see all communication that is not of a personal nature as soon as it comes over the wire. Have I made myself clear?"

Morgan could see the young man's knees shake. Rarely had Smith given in to a show of temper and all could see that this was a grave matter in his mind.

"Yes, sir. I'll make sure everything that isn't personal comes directly to you."

"And whom did you give this to?"

"One of the stewards, sir. He said he'd been sent to retrieve any message from the English authorities as soon as it came in, so I held it for him."

"Boxhall, you are to question all of our stewards. Find out who took it upon himself to deliver this."

"Yes, sir."

3:55 P.M.

Gloria Thompson had arranged a meeting in the ship's gymnasium with Margaret. She was seated on one of the ship's stationary bicycles, pumping away with the small wheel churning underneath her skirt, when Margaret walked in. "Isn't this the most wonderful thing?" Gloria gushed.

Margaret stepped around the padded mechanical camel and drew close to the whirring bicycle.

"And this place is so masculine, too," Gloria added.

"Yes, it is." Margaret turned her head and surveyed the room. Rowing machines with polished oars stood in the middle of the room, and along the wall hung dumbbells and handles attached to weighted pulleys.

A large map was framed in the middle of the far wall, and careful notation was made of each day's progress with the exact mileage of each day's journey recorded beneath a stick pin that marked the ship's position. "The men seem to have thought of everything."

"Don't they pride themselves in doing that?" Gloria chuckled.

"Yes, I just overheard several men discussing the ship. It seems the *Titanic* marks the final triumph of man's ingenuity over nature."

"And what they conquer, they seem to want to do in style. My own husband was in the oil business. I think he believed that man's needs were all solved by the abundance of petroleum."

Margaret smiled. "Why do men take so much upon themselves?"

"To a man who is good with a hammer, every problem appears to be a nail."

Margaret stepped over to the map. "I understand there is a great deal of wagering going on about the distance we put in each day."

"Their attempt at omniscience," Gloria laughed.

She stepped down from the bike and, picking up a small towel she had draped across the handlebars, patted her face. Looking out the window, she spotted the small group of men following the captain. "Isn't that your Mr. Fairfield?"

Margaret turned her head and watched the men pass by. "Yes, it is."

"I do hope I didn't embarrass you by allowing you to dance with him."

Margaret watched him disappear from the view of the last window. "No, it had to happen sometime. Perhaps it was better sooner than later."

"He did seem quite shaken when you finished your dance."

"I'm afraid I hurt his feelings."

"He does seem the sensitive sort."

"He is."

"I prefer that in a man. It makes them more thoughtful, more romantic."

"Morgan is quite the romantic. Unfortunately, he is romantic about his idea of who he is to become."

"It has been my experience that a man who doesn't know who he is, is a man who won't know how he is to treat you. Confidence in a man is so important."

"Why must they always have to prove themselves?"

"Young men need to find themselves. Better they do that while they are young than drag a family into uncertainty."

"The man I am to marry, Peter, understands perfectly well who he is. I like that."

Gloria laid the towel down. "You like that, but do you love him?"

"He is handsome and polite and has the good breeding to care about my future and my feelings."

Gloria walked over to one of the padded leather benches and, spreading out her shirt, turned and sat down. She fingered her topmost button and pulled on it to allow some air down the front of her blouse. "Do you love him?" She repeated the question.

Margaret paced the floor a few steps and then turned back to face Gloria. "I'm not quite certain what the word means any more."

"And were you certain of the word when you and Morgan were sweethearts?"

Margaret blushed. "A girl of ten is always convinced about love."

"And what about a young woman of twenty?"

"I was wrong."

"You were wrong?"

"I was wrong about him, and I was wrong about how I felt about him."

"But you still loved him."

"Yes, I suppose I did."

Gloria reached up and pulled out the large stickpin that held her hat on her head. Taking off the wide-brimmed straw hat, she gently fanned herself with it. "Have you ever watched a farmer?" she asked.

"Yes."

"Well, I was born on a farm in Oklahoma. I didn't always have my husband's money, you know. When a farmer begins cultivating a field, he plows straight and deep furrows in the earth. Then he plants the seeds and dreams of what the crop will look like when it comes to harvest. He expects it, and he waits for it. The love of a young girl is like that. All of your ideas of romance and love are cut deeply into your heart. You put the seed into the ground with every word spoken and every glance exchanged. It's extremely difficult to plant corn and harvest wheat."

"Are you saying that I still love Morgan Fairfield?"

Gloria waved her hat in front of her face.

"If anything, I'm angry with him."

"Another strong, powerful emotion," Gloria observed.

"He chose to leave me while he pursued this dream of his, this illusion of being independent from his family's wealth, this desire to be a writer."

"To become his own man, you mean."

"Yes."

"And all the while you just wanted him to be your man, not his man."

"Is that so wrong?"

"When I fell in love with my John, I was twelve and he was sixteen. I had never seen a more glorious sight in all of my life than him in his torn jeans and bare feet. I would have been perfectly content to be a farmer's wife, if I could just have been his. I was seventeen when we married and was certain that I was the happiest creature that God ever created. But then he found that detestable magazine. He came across it at the barbershop, and it told about the boom in oil. For months it was all he could talk about. He had to go. He had to try his hand at drilling the ground for that black goo."

She leaned forward, making every attempt to look Margaret in the eye. "I begged and pleaded for him to stay. He told me over and over how it was for me he wanted to do this thing, but I knew all along it was for him. Finally, I just had to let him go.

"I stayed and I waited, day after day, week after week, and month after month. Finally when he came home, he had that black stuff all over him. The only thing I could recognize were those sky-blue eyes of his and a smile that was wider than the sunrise on an Oklahoma morning. My John died much too soon, but if I hadn't let him go, he'd have died of a broken heart."

"And you're saying I should just have waited for Morgan?"

"The boy you loved will make a wonderful man. When you plant something and take all the time to cultivate it, it makes little sense to abandon it to the crows just before the harvest, now does it?"

"No, I suppose not. And what about Peter? Peter is so kind to me and has been so very patient."

"Margaret, my dear, that is your decision. All I can say is that with a lifetime of cultivating corn, it's not easy to switch to wheat. It's not easy for you, and it's not fair to the wheat."

4:20 P.M.

Boxhall organized a hastily called meeting of the first-class stewards. Like a convention of penguins, they gathered in the purser's office, milling about and looking most impatient.

The office of purser Herbert McElroy had tiles decorated with blue flowers and green leaves. His desk was polished and gleamed. Nothing was out of place, and several clipboards were piled together in the middle, each containing names and a list of the contents placed by each name in the purser's safe. McElroy was a sturdily built man and had the appearance of a boxer. The double row of brass buttons on his coat only accentuated his full barrel-like chest. His full cheeks bulged out from the sides of his clean-shaven face, and his brown eyes peered out from under his polished cap.

"See here, Boxhall, it's getting on to be the time for us to help prepare the passengers for dinner." The steward who spoke was a portly man with a double chin that quivered when he so much as mumbled. His name was Blanchard, and he held his gold watch open. Noticing the time, he snapped it shut.

"They bloody well need time to prepare, too," a second man spoke up.

"There has been an incident aboard ship."

"An incident?" The portly steward squinted his eyes at the notion. Boxhall could see the man was irritated but not so much as he couldn't have a modicum of curiosity.

"Yes, an incident, yes, and cabin B-24 has been sealed for the remainder of the voyage. No one is to go into that cabin until we dock in New York, and that includes any of you. We want everything to remain exactly as it is."

Fitzgerald blinked his eyes and seemed to step to the rear of the group.

"Dinkins, that is your area. Have you seen any suspicious persons prowling about today?"

"No, sir, I haven't, no one who didn't belong." Dinkins was a proper gentleman's gentleman. He stood ramrod straight and was as thin as a flagstaff. His black hair was pulled neatly over the side of his head and shone with the grease it took to keep every hair glued in position. His high, starched collar stood tall along the side of his neck, biting into the base of his chin.

Blanchard cleared his throat, which was the man's annoying habit when he wanted to speak, as if by making any sort of noise he could produce the necessary quiet that would allow him to take the center of attention. "What sort of incident?" he asked.

"I will come to that directly," Boxhall said.

Boxhall clasped his hands behind his back, rocking back and forth on the balls of his feet. "So, none of you has seen anything strange nor detected anything out of place since our sailing?"

The men looked puzzled. They stared at each other as if they were each expecting some great revelation about something unknown. Blanchard cleared his throat again. "I have had a steward's jacket stolen." He dropped his sizable chin to the topknot on his collar. "At least, I presume it's been stolen."

"When did you notice it missing?"

"I came aboard at Southampton with three, and now I only have two."

"Can you place the time it came up missing?"

"I'm not sure of that. I laid out the jacket I was wearing yesterday on my chair in my room, and this morning when I opened my locker, it was gone."

"This is serious," Boxhall said. "You will have to watch for a man wearing a jacket, then, who is not one of our number. You all know who you are in first class. Did any of you receive a wireless to be delivered to Captain Smith last night?"

Once again the men all looked at each other.

"Might the person in the stolen jacket have taken it?" Fitzgerald suggested eagerly.

A *little too eager*, thought Boxhall, raising an eyebrow to the man. The man's milky-white complexion seemed to indicate ice in his blood.

He seemed suddenly eager to express a suggestion, and Boxhall took note of it. "That might be an explanation," the officer replied. Boxhall paused, letting silence sit in the air.

"But this was an important communiqué from Scotland Yard. It just appeared on the chart table on the bridge this afternoon."

Boxhall's sarcastic emphasis on *appeared* was not lost on any of the stewards. They shuffled nervously.

Blanchard cleared his throat once again. His jaw shook like a plate full of jelly as he spoke. "You haven't told us about the incident, Mr. Boxhall. I suggest you do so, sir."

"A man was murdered in cabin B-24, a cabin assigned to an American, a Mr. George Sinclair."

Like a chorus of bees, the hums from the men's throats rose in unison. Boxhall could tell that the news came as quite a shock. He watched their faces to make sure the surprise was genuine. Even Fitzgerald's milky-white complexion went pale. "It is vital that you say nothing about this to anyone, neither to the passengers nor to the crew. Am I understood? We don't want to cause a panic. We want everything to appear as normal as possible."

Boxhall watched as McElroy scanned the clipboard for the contents of anything that might be registered to that room. "Do you see anything on your list for that cabin, Herbert?"

"Only something very odd. I was given instruction before we sailed to secure a place in the safe for that cabin, but nothing was deposited."

"Yes, that is odd."

"Perhaps he decided to keep whatever it was he wanted to deposit with him. If it was something that was valuable, that might explain it."

"Most thieves have no need to commit murder," Boxhall offered.

"Unless they were discovered in the act," Fitzgerald said.

"Well, that will be all, gentlemen. You all know what you are to do and, more important, what you are not to say. I won't have any rumors flying about." He paused to look the group over. "I would like to speak to Misters Dinkins, Blanchard, and Fitzgerald in private, however."

CHAPTER 14

The sky was a rosy red, like the belly of a giant robin settling down on the largest blue egg ever hatched, the North Atlantic. Morgan stood at the rail with Hunter where the two of them silently contemplated the death of their pursuer. Uneasiness tumbled through Morgan's belly. The man who knew they had the documents was now dead, but the way in which he was dispatched made Morgan aware of the serious nature of what they knew and what they had.

"It is a rather stirring thing to behold, isn't it?" Hunter asked.

"What is that?"

"The sea, old man, the sea."

Morgan was startled by the question. He'd been able to think of nothing but the murder. Hunter, on the other hand, had allowed the view to take possession of his thinking. Morgan lifted his eyes to the setting sun, seemingly seeing it for the first time. He pulled the collar up on his overcoat. There was no wind to speak of, but the speed of the ship caused the cold air to curl around his neck and whisk its way down the back of his shirt. "Yes, I suppose it is."

"It makes a man think about the bigness of the whole thing, eh, what?"

"Yes, it does."

"There is an eternal nature to it that seems to dwarf our smallness."

The idea of Hunter even thinking about time seemed queer to Morgan. Hunter Kennedy and all of his ways screamed out for here and now, never about eternity. "I didn't know you thought about such things."

Hunter chuckled. "Why, old man, I grew up having eternity preached at me continuously. I remember as a child trying to imagine forever. My older brother Jeremy, a constant source of dubious information that stretched from the far reaches of space to the facts of life, challenged me to contemplate the fact that eternity never begins and never ends. Of course, he did this as a constant reminder that his head and his mind were larger than my own."

Hunter spun around. Placing his elbows on the rail, he leaned back. There seemed to be a sense of the daredevil about him. Leaning back over the railing, he appeared to take delight in the look of panic on Morgan's face.

"I tried to think about it," Hunter went on. "At first I was puzzled, and then I was frightened. There was something about this notion that carried with it a warning, a large NO TRESPASSING sign. It was almost like a cliff in my thinking, something that would carry me down into an abyss, sliding down and causing me to fall and fall."

"What makes you think about this now? That man dead in his cabin?"

"Yes. That and the ocean. It seems eternal, as if it never ends." Hunter turned around and once again looked down at the water. "I wonder if I fell overboard how long would it take me to hit the bottom, or perhaps there is no bottom."

"There is a bottom, somewhere."

"Yes, but if one doesn't see it, how does one know for certain?"

"Some things are better to be believed than experienced."

"Ah, but you see, old man, that is one of the great differences between you and me. I want to see things for myself. I have to test life and all that it offers."

"It offers a lot of pain to the unwary."

"And a great deal of joy, I should think."

"God knows all about eternity and tells us in the Bible."

"Ah, God." Hunter turned around with a smile on his face. It was as if he knew a secret he was determined never to tell without a great deal of coaxing. "I can recall my earliest thoughts about God. The mystery and greatness of God used to frighten me. What did He look like, this vast being who never began and never will end? The only picture that came to my mind was that of a huge Mrs. Collins, my first Sunday school teacher. The woman was knowledgeable, benevolent, knew the answers to every question, and kept a ready supply of sweet shortbread for good little boys."

"You didn't think of your father?"

"Only in my worst nightmares did I contemplate God in the image of my father. The ruthless righteousness of that picture was almost too cruel to dwell on. How could there be a God? Where did He come from? How did He get there? How could He be so very powerful? Did He really care about little old Hunter Kennedy like Mrs. Collins said He did?"

"When I think about God," Morgan said, "I think about Jesus. If God isn't like Jesus, then He isn't as good as He could be."

Hunter smiled. "Methinks theology doesn't suit you, old man."

"I suppose it's the personal nature of God that I warm to. I want Him touchable and knowable. Scraping the sky with unanswerable questions seldom appealed to me."

"It appeals to me quite a bit."

"But the central question, I think, is what is your opinion of Jesus? I think your Mrs. Collins would have said that."

"She said just that, and many times."

"And what was your response?"

"I embraced it when I was quite young, hugging it to my breast like a suckling child. Then, little by little, I simply walked away from it."

"You may have walked away from God, but I don't think He ever walked away from you."

Hunter brushed his red mustache aside and breathed a hissing breath from his clenched white teeth. "There is no escape from it. Believe me, I've tried."

He pulled out his gold watch from his coat pocket and pried it open. "It's almost time, old man, and I shall need your help."

"My help for what?"

"Your help in overhearing a conversation."

"A conversation?"

"Yes. I passed a note to Ismay asking him to meet me in the smoking lounge at a quarter of six. I have a screen set up and want you to sit behind it and appear to read a newspaper. With luck, he won't even see you."

Once again, Morgan pulled his collar up. "I can't eavesdrop on you."

"And why not, pray tell?"

"It wouldn't be right."

"And I suppose it's right to allow the man to get away with running my sister down and getting away scot-free."

"No, of course that's not right."

"Well, I may call upon you to testify in court."

Morgan bowed his head. He wanted to help and knew he should, but becoming a sneak had never appealed to him. He always liked to face things head-on, never behind someone's back. "First you ask me to watch you cheat at cards, and now you want me to listen to you drag a confession out of a man. Where will you stop?"

"Morgan, old man, you've seen life from its glossy surface. It's time you contemplated the bottom of the barrel."

The two of them left the ship's rail and walked into the first-class lounge. The polished wood was dotted with brightly burning electric fixtures shaped like small flames that flickered from the sides of the walls. Tables with marble tops were scattered about the room; overstuffed sofas and chairs were upholstered in a pattern of embroidered pitchers and urns on a cream-colored background. They looked comfortable enough for a man to sink into and fall asleep, and Morgan hoped he would do just that.

Hunter chose a place in an alcove that had back-to-back love seats. He reached over, took a screen, and positioned it between the two love seats. Pulling out a comfortable chair, he positioned it alongside the love seat that faced the door. He picked up a newspaper and handed it to Morgan. "Here you are, old man. You just sit behind the screen there and take notes if you can. You will make a wonderful witness with all that righteous indignation of yours."

Morgan took his seat behind the screen, and Hunter plopped down directly behind him. Looking over at the chair, he decided on a better position. He got up and moved it to a spot directly in front of him. That would make Morgan harder to spot and Ismay easier to hear. Retaking his seat, he sighed. "There you are, old man, can you hear me?"

Morgan spoke from behind the screen. "I can hear you perfectly well."

"Splendid."

It wasn't more than a few minutes before Ismay came through the door. The man's dark eyes flashed around the room, and he brushed his handlebar mustache aside. Spotting Hunter, he walked over in his direction.

Hunter got to his feet. "Good to see you, Ismay." He motioned to the chair. "Please be seated. I won't keep you long."

"I hope not," Ismay growled.

"Tell me, do you have a sister, Ismay?"

"What is this? I'm too busy for games. Get to your point—if there is one." Ismay snarled, putting his elbows on his knees and leaning intimidatingly toward Hunter.

Hunter was seemingly relaxed, one arm draped across the back of the love seat. He crossed his legs as he answered. "I just wanted to get your advice. I thought with all your experience and worldliness, you might be able to help me decide the suitable course of action to take against a man who ran down a young girl with his motor car and didn't even stop to help her."

Ismay's mouth fell open a bit. "What makes you think I can help you with legal matters?" he asked nervously, leaning back in the overstuffed chair.

"Well, Bruce, I know you've had experience with just such an incident. Think back to April the twentieth of last year. You surely remember."

Hunter seemed to coil with every word, like a snake preparing for a well-executed strike. He no longer lounged; he was riveted on Ismay.

Hunter shifted forward on the love seat cushions so his knees were almost touching Ismay's. "You should, because that was the night you ran my sister down," Hunter hissed.

"I did no such thing."

"You most certainly did, and I have a witness that is prepared to say so in a court of law." Reaching into his coat pocket, Hunter pulled out a piece of paper. "I have a sworn deposition here with me."

Ismay held out his hand. "May I see that?"

Hunter laughed. "Mercy, no, indeed. You can see it in court along with the English-speaking world. That street may have been dark, but a young woman saw you, and she took down the description of your motor-car along with your license. It may interest you to know that my sister was still alive when this young woman approached her. She may have even lived had you taken her to hospital instead of simply driving off."

Ismay looked shaken. His hands began to quiver. "I thought she was dead."

"Oh, I see. That makes leaving her okay, then. You didn't look closely, did you?"

"She didn't move. I didn't see her. I tried to stop; really I did."

Hunter refolded the paper and stuffed it back into his inside coat pocket. "But you didn't stop for long, now did you?"

Ismay's face looked ashen. He swallowed hard. "What do you want of me? Money?"

Hunter laughed and slapped his knee. "I fear the authorities will want to see you behind bars, a situation I believe I'd find most promising."

"I can pay you."

"I'm certain you can."

"What do you want? Name it."

Hunter smirked and stroked his mustache. "I am traveling first class on this floating palace of yours."

"We can compliment your ticket."

"Mmm, an interesting first step."

"I'll see the purser this evening, and we'll have your fare returned to you."

"And you think a simple boat ride will be enough to secure my silence?"

"I can write you a bank draft when we get to New York."

"Let me think on the matter."

"Yes, please think it over." Ismay pulled on his collar. "That night was a horrible tragedy." He shook his head. "I regret it so very much. Nothing I do can ever bring your sister back. I know that. Of course, it may prove to be an opportunity for you. I must have that paper, however, and your oath that the matter will go no further."

"The young woman who saw you said you did appear to stagger when you got out of the car. What may have been a tragic evening was evidently begun with great celebration."

"I was at a party at my club."

"Perhaps we may find someone who could testify as to your sobriety on the night in question."

"Please, sir, as God is my witness, I had no intention of doing any harm to your sister."

"And if God had been your only witness I'm quite certain the deed would have stayed with God alone." Hunter's green eyes were hard, unreadable.

Ismay got to his feet shakily. "I can only offer to attempt to put things right with you. I will see to the return of your passage and will await your decision on the matter of compensation."

Hunter watched as Ismay beat a hasty retreat across the room and out the door. He got to his feet and stepped around the screen. "Did you get all of that, old man? And what did you think? The fellow appeared to be quite shaken. Strange isn't it how a man's conscience can be hardened with simply God as a witness."

Morgan got to his feet and laid down the paper. "I heard everything." Morgan was filled with a sense of disgust at what he had heard, and just the notion of being made a part of it made his skin crawl. He flicked lint off his collar as if the very motion might somehow make him clean. "Yes, he admitted the deed all right, but I heard something else as well."

"What, pray tell."

"I heard you attempting blackmail."

"Blackmail! Why, dear boy."

"You just like doing things like that to me, don't you?"

"Like what?"

"Dragging me into your vices, taunting me?"

"It's part of the world you need to witness, old man."

Morgan shook his head. "I think that my being a Christian is too much of a temptation for you. You think that by showing me the worst of what you're capable of you're shoving your father's nose into your crimes."

"I'm sorry if I offended you."

"Well, you did. You did something else, too."

"What?"

"You made yourself a very dangerous and powerful enemy."

5:15 P.M.

Margaret's mother April had been changing her clothes for hours. Her bed was littered with layers of colored chiffon and silk of every color and description. Her mood was subject to frequent change and, with it, her attire. Choosing the only dress left hanging, she laid it down and donned her dressing gown. She sat down in front of the vanity mirror and picked up her jar of face powder, pausing to take a last look at her reflection before the application. The powder would make little difference, she decided, since she was wearing the gold dressing gown. She had settled on wearing her pink chiffon dress to dinner. The dress showed enough of her femininity to compliment her but not enough to show a misguided attempt to look young. "Wear the green dress, my dear," she called out. "It is so very attractive."

Margaret stepped out of the bathroom. She twisted her hands behind her back in an attempt to hook that part of her dress behind her shoulder blades. It made her realize why the backless dresses were becoming so popular. Not only were they eye-catching, but they saved the wearer the ritual of throwing her arm out of joint while attempting to put it on. She had already chosen the green dress, and she was glad she had. Arguing with her mother on the impressions her clothes made had always seemed like a waste of time to Margaret. Her mother seemed overly preoccupied with appearance. If someone couldn't tell what kind of person you were by mere conversation, then they weren't worth knowing at all.

"Can you help me with these hooks, Mother?"

"Of course. Come over here and stand still."

Margaret walked over to the dressing table and turned around for her mother.

"I do hope Morgan Fairfield doesn't embarrass us again this evening," April said while she worked at hooking the dress. "By continuing to stare at you, he practically undressed you with his eyes last night."

"Morgan was doing no such thing, Mother. It's just that he hasn't seen me in such a long time, and he was in no position to talk, sitting at the far end of the table."

"You mean sitting with Peter between the two of you."

"I'm certain he'll be quite over it tonight, Mother. I shouldn't worry about it if I were you."

"I am worried." April fastened the last hook and spun Margaret around to look her in the eye. "I'm worried about you, child, about how you will respond to him. You were always so fiddle-headed when it came to Morgan Fairfield."

"That was when I was a child, Mother. I'm a woman now."

April struck her face with the powder, sending a flesh-colored cloud of it up in front of the mirror. Margaret jumped back to escape the flying powder. "Mother, have you lost your mind?"

"Children find it so very hard to part with their little puppy-love infatuations," April went on, oblivious to Margaret's close call with the flying powder. "There is an innocence to it that shows little common sense."

"You needn't worry, Mother. It's all over between Morgan and me."

"Peter is a perfect gentleman, and he will make a wonderful provider. You see to it that you don't ruin your one chance at true happiness."

Margaret picked up an eyebrow pencil. Leaning into the mirror, she began to supply more definition to her blonde eyebrows. "Do you really think that's true, Mother? Do you honestly think this is my one and only chance at true happiness?"

"I most certainly do. Any young girl in England would die to be a part of the Wilksbury family."

"I'm certain their parents would stop at nothing to make it come true."

"Quite so." April shook the powder puff at Margaret, her finger protruding out from it, sending Margaret once again to her heels. "And your parents will stop at nothing to make you happy."

The knock at the door caused both women to freeze. Margaret moved over to the door and listened for the second round of knocks. "Who is it?"

"It's me, my darling, Peter."

Margaret looked back at her mother, while April got to her feet and pulled the dressing gown tighter around her. Margaret opened the door and stepped aside. "Come in."

Peter stepped inside the cabin. Seeing April in her dressing gown, he blushed and smiled in an attempt to make everything appear normal. "Good evening, Mrs. Hastings."

The smell of the room roused his senses. Face powder and perfume were enough to assault the nostrils of any man, especially at their source. Margaret's favorite scent, that of fresh blooming gardenias, was something he could pick up on the breeze. He liked it very much, not only because of its beauty but because it reminded him of her.

April walked toward him, her hand outstretched. "Please, Peter, dear, call me Mother."

"Yes, ma'am, er…Mother." He took her hand and, lifting it, brushed his chin on her knuckles, giving off the slight sound of a polite kiss.

April looked back at Margaret. "Now, I want you two to go ahead without me. I won't be long."

"We couldn't do that Mrs.…Mother. I'm more than happy to wait up on deck until you've finished dressing."

"Nonsense." Putting her hand on Margaret's back, April pushed her to the door. "Young lovers need time to themselves. Soon you two will be a couple, and you have to discover who you are together first."

Margaret picked up her small purse, and Peter opened the door and stepped aside for her to pass. "We will see you at the table soon?" he asked.

April waved her hand at him. "Yes, yes, very soon. Now run along."

With that, Peter stepped into the hallway with Margaret and closed the door.

Peter smiled at Margaret. "You are most fortunate to have such a caring mother."

"Sometimes she cares just a little too much." Margaret gave Peter her hand as they walked up the stairs to the deck.

"All mothers do that."

"Mothers with daughters tend to try to live out their own dreams through them I fear. All the things they never did, they want their daughters to do. Sometimes I'm not certain if I'm living my own life or my mother's fantasy life of the past, undoing all her old regrets."

"Fathers are like that with their sons as well."

"Really?"

"I think it's worse. I mean, you carry the family name and shield, so to speak. There is no room for your own mistakes because you have to undo your father's first. Sometimes I think it's necessary for a man to first of all complete his father's life before he can start his own."

"Does that mean you have to follow along in your father's footsteps?"

Peter stepped aside and pushed the door open that led to the deck. "Somewhat, but not necessarily in the same way."

Margaret stepped out. The evening had a distinct chill to it, and the first stars were low on the horizon.

"Men must do what their fathers couldn't do," Peter went on. "A father who was never home often produces a son who must be home at every turn. Fathers who become lost in their work can very well have sons who play with life. It all balances out in the end. What we can never achieve in our own lifetime, perfect balance, we try to do with resulting generations. Sons find themselves completing the circle of their fathers' lives, before beginning their own."

"And what circle are you completing, Peter, and how long must I wait before you start your own?"

Peter smiled. "My father was the brash captain of industry, and I suppose that leaves me the task of being the dependable, sensitive man."

Margaret curled her arm around his. They stepped over to the rail to watch the rise of the moon. She patted his hand. "Good, I'm glad. I think I prefer your role in life to being married to that of your father's."

He looked down at her and smiled. "Believe me, you are getting the better of the bargain."

"And what about a man who never knew his father?"

Peter stared at her. "You mean a man like Morgan?"

Margaret was embarrassed. She had meant Morgan but didn't want to connect his name to their conversation in any way. Peter wasn't like most men, however. He didn't seem to fear or be intimidated by a woman with a mind.

"Yes, I suppose," she said sheepishly.

"I think men like Morgan have to work very hard at finding out who they are. They have little in the way of a circle to complete and must chart their own course."

Margaret looked off at the water. Peter was describing Morgan to a T. She knew her face was flushed, and if she wasn't careful, he would ask why. "Peter," she stammered, "I should go back and see that mother gets dressed. Could I meet you in an hour?"

Peter backed away slightly. "Of course, my dear." He studied her face.

"I'd just feel better if I knew she was all right."

THURSDAY,
APRIL 11, 1912,
5:40 P.M.

CHAPTER 15

The library of the *Titanic* was systemized with carved and heavily waxed wooden shelves with brass minirails to hold the array of books in place. The polished pigeonholes held a vast assortment of reading material from classics to popular novels. There were shelves of poetry and still others that contained a medley of reference works. The colorful spines of the covers were flanked by rich oil paintings that caught the soft glow of overhead lights. Comfortable chairs and couches were scattered throughout the large room, and alongside them were tables with ball-shaped claws and Tiffany lamps.

Peter walked into the library, and what he saw surprised him. In the corner standing behind a waist-high desk was Hunter Kennedy. The sight of the man in the library made Peter's mouth drop open. He would never have guessed it. He marched over to where Hunter was standing. The man was turning the pages of a newspaper.

"Looking for reviews?" Peter asked.

Hunter looked up. "Mercy, no. This is a Queenstown paper, and yesterday's to boot. The performances in London won't play in Queenstown for another five years, if that. They couldn't be any more backward when it comes to the theater."

Peter smiled and looked around the room. "I just didn't expect to find you in the library."

"Just because I'm Irish doesn't mean I can't read."

"I don't doubt that in the least. I expected you in the smoking room, playing cards."

Hunter grinned. "I see that my reputation precedes me."

"That it does, but from what I hear, you have very little experience with losing."

Hunter laughed. "I do like to keep that to a minimum."

"I should think so."

Peter stepped around the desk, peering over Hunter's shoulder. "And what news have we from the Emerald Isle?"

Hunter turned back to the front page and held it out for Peter to see. "More of the same, Irishmen shooting and blowing each other up."

"Bloody business that."

"Six hundred years of bloody business."

"When will it ever end?"

"I'm afraid not until you English stay in England."

"It's not as simple as all that, is it?" Peter usually kept his political opinions to himself, but there wasn't an Englishman alive who didn't have strong feelings about the Irish question.

"Nothing ever is."

"Is there any hope?" Peter asked.

Hunter turned several pages until he found the article he'd been reading. "There seems to be some hope on the horizon, at least in certain minds."

He pointed to the article. It was headlined "The Promise of War." "There appears to be a rather distant hope that England will soon find herself in a war with the Germanic powers on the continent. The bloke here goes on to explain that if that be the case, they will have their hands so full of English blood that they'll have to leave Ireland to the Irish."

"That sounds rather grim."

"Such is the thinking of Irish patriots. The misfortunes of their ene-mies are what they live for," said Hunter, his Irish accent becoming more pronounced as he warmed to the subject.

Peter mulled the matter over. "My father deals in manufacturing," Peter said. "I'm certain he'd look on the possibility of war with a rather smug, financial point of view."

Hunter slapped him on the back. "There, you see, your family sleeps in the same bed as the Irish Republican Army."

"What a hideous thought."

"War and politics, mixed with money, make strange bedfellows."

Peter looked him in the eye. "Strange, indeed. And what side do you stand on in all of this?"

"I stand on the side of Hunter Kennedy. I've been learning to do that since I was twelve."

"You have no allegiance?"

"None whatsoever."

Hunter folded the paper. "And what brings you to the library? I should think you'd be strolling with the lovely Margaret on your arm."

Peter looked up at the clock on the wall. "She's helping her mother dress for dinner."

"Ah, the womenfolk and their attire. One would think they were preparing for war."

"I suppose they are, and armed to the teeth with the most formidable of weapons, themselves."

Hunter laughed. "Yes, and if you'll pardon me for saying so, your Margaret absolutely bristles with armament."

Peter blushed slightly. "I take that as a compliment."

"Of course. It must have given you quite a start to find Morgan aboard ship, though."

Peter thought the matter over. He knew Hunter and Morgan were friends but saw little need to conceal his feelings. "I like him. Actually, I'm glad he's here."

"Really?"

"Yes, he and Margaret were quite close. I don't think beginning a marriage with a ghost is a good thing to do." Peter held out his hand and opened it. "I never clutch on to things or people, especially people.

When Margaret and I are married, I want it to be because she's made the decision and refuses to look back, ever."

"And what if she decides that Morgan is the one she really loves?"

The idea was a strange one when exposed to words, but Peter had been giving it some thought. "Then I prefer she does that sooner, rather than later. We are going to America to have a bridal shower with American relatives. Returning gifts can be such a messy business."

Peter smiled. He knew Hunter was hoping for a more heated reaction. The Irish actor relished nothing more than stirring people up—something he seemed quite a master at. Peter's logic and gallantry disappointed Hunter. Only, Peter knew that his real feelings were far from gallant. The prospect of Margaret actually breaking their engagement brought him great discomfort, but he could see that Hunter was surprised that the thought had actually crossed his mind.

Hunter placed the paper back in the rack. He chuckled slightly. "You English are given to your proprieties, aren't you? Sometimes I think you'd prefer death by hanging than embarrassment."

"We do work hard at being gentlemen."

"You see, that's where we Irish have you at a disadvantage. We start on the low rung on the ladder and, having come from there, never fear the fall. We may never be humble, but we've had so much practice at being humiliated that it no longer matters."

Peter smiled. He liked this man. "I can see why Morgan likes you. You have candor."

Hunter bowed. "Why, thank you. Yes, our Mr. Fairfield may be American by birth, but he's English by training. Sometimes I think he's so caught up with being perfect that he refuses to be human. He so desperately wants to be the self-made man without help from anyone."

"That's commendable."

"No, that's English. The view from the bottom of the ladder accepts help from any and all directions."

Peter smiled. "Then you can count on me. Should you need help, you have only to ask."

Peter turned to move toward the door, and Hunter followed along with him.

"Perhaps I can be of help to you," Hunter said.

"How is that?"

Hunter smiled. "I think my friend Morgan intends to steal back your Margaret's heart."

Peter stopped in his tracks. He wasn't sure if what Hunter was saying was the truth or just Hunter's way of stirring him up. "That's interesting."

"Interesting, is it?"

"You'd have to know Margaret. No one steals anything from her. She's her own woman through and through." He shook his head. "Believe me, I've tried to convince her of many things and seldom succeeded. The woman won't be bridled or crimped in any way." He leaned in Hunter's direction and lowered his voice. "You should talk with her sometime on the issue of women's suffrage. You'd come out with your head swimming. Believe me, if the women ever get the vote, she may be the first woman prime minister."

Hunter laughed. "Then maybe she'll be the one to free Ireland."

"I shouldn't doubt it. If there's a foreign idea to be found, it will be in the head of Margaret Hastings. Between the two of us, I'm the one who has to curb his tongue. She's a headstrong romantic."

"Will marriage change her?"

"Only an act of God can do that. So, if Morgan has her heart, it's given freely. No one can steal it, and no one can keep it."

5:55 P.M.

Delaney walked out on the forecastle deck. The evening was turning cold, and he pulled up the collar on his overcoat. Looking up, he could see the men on the bridge. They stood behind the massive windows and, for all the world, appeared to be in total control. He knew full well, though, that being in control of a vessel like the *Titanic* was a precarious thing at best.

His eye caught the white tublike structure of the crow's nest high above him. A man in a heavy seaman's pea coat swung his leg over the side and inched down the ladder. Delaney watched him take step after step. In a short time, the man dropped to the deck. Delaney stepped over to him.

"That looks like bitter cold work," he said.

"It is, sir, that it is." The man slapped his arms together to try to keep warm. Delaney looked the man over. He appeared to be twenty at best, thin as a rail and with a white, smooth face that looked like cut glass.

Delaney looked back up at the perch. "You men must have sharp eyes."

"Dees eyes o' mine are the best."

"How do you stand it up there?"

"There's usually two of us up there, and we try to talk a mite. It helps to pass the time." He tucked his hands under his armpits and squeezed down on them to try to put some warmth in his hands.

"I'll be bettin' you could stand a wee bit of the nip."

The man laughed. "That we could, sir, that we could." He beat his arms. "Fact is, sir, when I gets to my cabin, I'm gonna have me some."

"That's a man." Delaney extended his hand. "I'm Donald Delaney, and who might you be?"

"The name is Reginald. Reginald Lee." Looking suspiciously at Delaney's hand, he shook it firmly. Not many first-class passengers were chatty with the regular seamen. Officers in their precious white uniforms were the types they normally socialized with.

"And who's the other gentleman up there?"

"Fleet, sir, Fred Fleet," he said, still wondering about the man.

"And does he take the spirits as well?"

"Any sailor worth his salt has a nip now and then. Fact is, most have it all the time. It does help to pass the time."

"You have some on you now? I could use a smidgen."

"Oh, no, sir. I'm on duty."

"You can't tell me that up there in the cold you haven't been tempted."

"Been tempted a plenty, especially when that cold wind cuts to yer bone."

"And maybe if you had some with you, the temptation might be too much for any man to bear."

Delaney watched the man. He blinked his eyes, and Delaney could see that he was thinking it over.

"'Most ever' temptation is too much for a man to bear sometimes."

"I thought so," Delaney laughed. "Listen, I have some smooth Irish whiskey in my cabin. I might be persuaded to bring you boys a flask of it some cold night."

Lee swung his head around. It was as if they were discussing some state secret and he didn't want to be overheard. "You'd do that, sir? You're a first-class passenger, ain't you?"

"That I am, but I love the common seaman. The officers are a bit hoity-toity for my blood."

Lee gave out a grin. It spread over his face. "Mine too, sir, the truth be known."

Delaney slapped him on the back. "Good. Then we see eye to eye."

"Yes, sir, we do."

"Then in spite of what them officers say, I'll bring you boys some of the good stuff. Nobody's up there to see you, and it might make your eyes a bit sharper if you weren't cold on the inside as well as the outside."

Lee nodded. "Yes, sir, I can see your point."

6:05 P.M.

O'Conner finished the last of the corned beef and laid his fork down. Steerage passengers ate long before it was fashionable for first-class passengers to dine, but dinner for the third class wasn't an event, it was a meal. In first class, only the children ate between 5:00 and 6:00. He kept to himself and for good reason. He wanted no one to recognize him. The idea of becoming close to someone whom he was going to be responsible for killing was something he didn't want to have to carry around inside him. There were too many poor Irish here, too many people like him. He watched them. When he saw them talking and laughing, it was like watching himself, his brothers and sisters, and his own mother and father.

Many languages were being spoken at his table. O'Conner thought he recognized Swedish, and he was sure he could hear German and Italian. The place was a floating menagerie of European immigrants. But there seemed to be little in the way of a language barrier. The common folk all had so much to share in the way of life that they laughed just as easily with someone they could barely understand. He sat back and watched them, sipping his cup of tea.

Several places down from him, he caught the eye of a young woman. Her red hair fell down the sides of her face. She had a cute small nose and eyes of blue that twinkled with mischief when they caught sight of his. He stared back down into his cup of tea. This was the last thing he needed. There must be no attachment of the heart. A man had to do his duty without looking back.

Occasionally, he would glance back at her, and when he caught her smile, he hurriedly looked back down at his tea. The look of the woman sent a shock of loneliness down into his belly. It was seldom the act of killing that bothered him about his work. More often than not, it was the times in between, the times when he could speak to no one, get close to no one. The lonely hours of waiting to be useful were times he was getting to hate.

He knew his square jaw and dark brooding eyes made him, at least according to a lass from his carefree younger days, ruggedly handsome. It was hard to resist the attentions of a woman who was openly and obviously assessing him. Most of the women he saw were those who could comfortably remain strangers. They were ladies of the night, and the streets of Dublin, Belfast, and Queenstown were full of them. Hard times made a woman turn to anything that would fill her plate and put a roof over her head. This woman was different though. She was the kind a man would be content to spend his life with as a friend and the mother of his children. The thought of a wife and children sent pangs of regret deep inside him. It was one of the many things he had to put aside if he was going to be useful to Ireland.

Of course, if Delaney had his way with this ship, he knew this might be his last mission. Everyone was going to die, or as many of the English as possible. Maybe getting close to this woman might not be such a bad idea after all. If he was going to perish with the ship, there would be no need to spend his last few days in pain. The thought gave him some comfort. He lifted his eyes, and this time when the woman looked at him, he returned her smile.

"Here, here, we haven't seen you before." The man slapped him good-naturedly on the back.

O'Conner looked up. The speaker was a young man with hair as black as a raven's wing. He wore a tweed vest over a white shirt with no collar, and a cap pulled low over his forehead. "The name's Killebrew." The man shot out his hand.

"O'Conner's the name." He shook the man's hand.

"You got on at Queenstown, didn't you?"

"Yes."

"I thought I recognized you. I didn't have a chance to speak then, but I'm happy to meet up with you now." Leaning over O'Conner's shoulder, Killebrew lowered his voice and looked across and down the table to the young woman who had been exchanging glances with him. "I see you've caught the fair eye of the lovely lady."

"I hadn't really noticed."

Killebrew laughed. "Oh, you noticed all right. How could a man not notice such a thing?" He lowered his voice to barely over a whisper. "She's prime, too, that one. I'd go ahead with it, if I were you."

O'Conner got to his feet. "Sorry, I got business to attend to."

He got out of his chair and squeezed past the lines of people who were still eating. He did manage to cast a casual glance at the young woman as he went by. There was a look of surprise on her face, mixed with disappointment.

He hurried out the door of the great room and to the aft well deck. A number of people were standing at the rail, smoking and talking. O'Conner nodded to them as he passed. He hurried down the stairs to the Scotland-row hallway and along the row of empty cabins. Occasionally he would see a door opened and people who had already eaten gathered inside. It was easy to find the doors open in the steerage areas. Third-class passengers were a sociable lot.

He passed a number of stairs that were chained. Small signs hung from the chains that read SECOND CLASS ONLY. O'Conner hurried past them. To walk from the great room that the steerage passengers used for dining and congregating to the living quarters for single men meant walking from one end of the ship to the other. Few men made the trip, unless they were bound to do some drinking or wanted to sleep. O'Conner counted on that. He could go back and plant the bomb he had carried aboard without any prying eyes. The other men would still be aft and socializing.

He wound his way into the companionway and down to the room he was sharing with five others. The room was empty. He took out his key and popped open the lock hanging on his locker.

He wouldn't need the steward's jacket for this, but he did want his work pants and the heavy, black wool sweater. Quickly, he changed pants and pulled the sweater over his head. There would have to be some climbing, and the color of the sweater wouldn't show much in the way of dirt and soot.

Reaching into the upper shelf of the locker, he pulled out the knife. It wouldn't hurt to be careful. He just might need this. He slipped the knife into his belt and pulled the sweater over it. Grabbing the bag with the explosives, he tucked it under his arm.

He closed and locked the locker, then went back out into the companionway and down the hall to the steel spiral stairs that led below to the boiler rooms. Winding his way down the stairs, he could hear the sounds of the boilers hissing in the distance and the shovels scraping a constant grating noise. Walking along the catwalk that led from the ship's hold to the boilers, he came to the first set of watertight compartment doors. It would make no difference where he placed the charge, just so it was at the juncture of two of the compartments.

He bent down and looked into the darkness. Reaching into the bag, he took out an electric torch and turned it on. He flashed it up into the compartment. He could see a space there where men worked, but it was seldom used. If he could secure the charge and leave it covered, then he could come back and light the fuse when the time was right.

"Hey, O'Conner."

The sound of his name brought his head back out the watertight door. It was Killebrew. The man had followed him.

"What the blazes are ye doin' down here? If ya have something to drink put away, ya'd be better off with the thing in yer locker."

O'Conner dropped the satchel to his side, his hand opening and clenching.

"You do, don't you? You sly old son. I was just comin' to tell you that bonny girl wants to meet you on the deck back there. She's gonna be a waitin', old son, and I think you'd find a fine thing there."

He eyed the bag that O'Conner had at his side. "First though, we better take a look at what ya got."

Without warning Killebrew snatched the bag from O'Conner's hand. He laughed, holding it back. "Let's us have a sniff of this here mix."

O'Conner reached out to try to take it back, but that caused Killebrew to jerk it away. "Doesn't pay to be selfish," he said. "I share the women, and it's only right you should share the whiskey."

Killebrew turned around and opened the bag. O'Conner lifted his sweater and drew the knife.

"Now, let's just see what ya got here."

Stepping into him, O'Conner put a choke hold on the man and, reaching around, plunged the knife. He held Killebrew up as the man silently squirmed with muffled gasps. Killebrew's arms dropped, and the bag slipped from his hand. In a matter of moments, O'Conner could feel the life passing out of the man and the seeping wetness of blood as it spread across the man's chest.

Calmly, he took out the knife, wiped it over Killebrew's shirt, and stuck it back in his belt. Still holding on to the limp body, he reached down and picked up the bag containing the charge. He slung the straps around his arm and lifted the man with both arms. He proceeded to turn and drag him down the corridor. He would have to find a place for the body, a place that no one would look. O'Conner was used to taking care of the unexpected. It was his job. To a man loyal to the Irish cause, Killebrew's death was a cost of business, and he was numb to anything deeper than that.

Minutes later, he came to the door that led to the hold. He braced the man and shoved the bolt aside. Pushing open the heavy door, he made his way onto the landing. He could see the trail of blood left on the companionway. He'd have to take care of that later. Swinging the body behind him, he carefully went down the stairs. Killebrew's shoes banged on the metal stairs as he dragged him to the bottom. The noise echoed through the large steel compartment.

There it is, the perfect spot. A shiny red car stood at the center of the large room. O'Conner dragged the body toward it. He laid it down and opened the door. *Here you are,* he thought. *You'll get to ride to the bottom in style.* He grinned at his own joke, but his cold, pitch-black eyes were mirthless.

THURSDAY,
APRIL 11, 1912,
7:10 P.M.

CHAPTER 16

Hunter bubbled with enthusiasm as he knocked on Morgan's door. He had on his best dinner jacket with the mother-of-pearl cuff links. When Morgan opened the door, he burst inside, beaming. "You'll never guess who I've been with, old man," Hunter strutted, his thumbs hooked under his black lapels.

Expressionless, Morgan walked back to the dressing table and, looking in the mirror, worked at tying his tie.

"Aren't you the least bit curious?" asked Hunter, crestfallen.

Morgan cocked his head in Hunter's direction. "I'm sure you'll tell me."

Hunter crossed his arms. "Well, maybe I shouldn't." He looked every bit like a petulant child.

"You don't expect me to beg you, do you?" Morgan was fed up with the actor's nonstop theatrics. But, then, seeing Hunter so forlorn almost made him feel sorry for him.

"Well, you should, old man. I've been with your rival."

"My rival?"

"Yes, and I gave the man fair warning of your intentions with the fair young Margaret."

"You did what?" Morgan gasped.

"I told him you intended to steal her back."

"That's crazy. I plan no such thing. She's done with me."

Hunter walked over to the foot of Morgan's high bed and leaned back against it. "I wouldn't be so sure of that, old man. It seems our Mr. Wilksbury is a might worried it might be otherwise."

Now Hunter had Morgan's complete attention. He could tell by the look in his eyes, a kind of burrowing look a rabbit might get from a hungry fox. "I can see the idea intrigues you."

"It does no such thing." Morgan turned back to the mirror and looped the ends of his tie together.

Hunter could tell that in spite of Morgan's protests there was a curiosity about his conversation with Peter. He decided to change the subject to let the matter simmer in Morgan's mind.

"I have a ticket to the Turkish bath for you tomorrow, old man." Pulling the ticket from his pocket, Hunter laid it on Morgan's bed. "It's for 2:00 P.M.. I thought I might go for a swim while you steamed the pain out of that conscience of yours."

"My conscience is clear, unlike yours."

"Clear about Margaret?"

"Why wouldn't it be?"

"Because you seem to have left an indelible impression on the young lady that she finds hard to shake. I don't think this Margaret of yours has settled the matter of her heart. If she had, I wouldn't have got all the talk from Peter I did." He paused, watching Morgan work with his neckwear. "I like the man."

"He is a gentleman. The perfect choice for Margaret."

"Precisely—choice. It is after all, up to her to choose."

"She made her choice when she told him she'd marry him."

"Well, that was when you'd disappeared from her, going off to find yourself. You're here now, and so is she."

"That changes nothing."

"It changes everything. Women are like predators, they need to circle a victim before they pounce."

"Why must you stir things up? What's done is done."

"Well, it's obviously not done in your heart."

Morgan let the strings of his tie drop in exasperation. Placing his hands on the side of the table, he leaned into the mirror. "Hunter, old man," Morgan said, shaking his head. "Why must you do these things? Is it just me you delight in torturing? I know you enjoy toying with people, baiting and befuddling them, but I'm supposed to be your friend. Let me tend to the matters of my own heart."

"That's just it, Morgan. You won't." Hunter's eyes were momentarily soft and pensive.

"I won't what?"

"Tend to your own heart. You English, uh pardon me, you who were raised English, rather, tend to bury and deny all the feelings we Irish live for—love, passion, even sorrow and despair. You, my friend, need to examine that heart of yours. You can't leave it in England and run to New York."

Morgan threaded his gold cuff links into position, happily busying himself so he didn't appear as stunned as he was by Hunter's insight. "You have enough to worry about yourself," he replied.

"And I intend to deal with my heartstrings tonight."

Morgan swung around. "What do you mean?"

Hunter pulled out his silver cigarette case. "Wait till you see the look on Kitty's face when she sees this tonight." He turned it over in his hand. "She will positively flip."

Morgan finally wrestled some semblance of a neat bow under his chin. "And why should she do that?"

Hunter grinned, the sly smile of a cat crossing his lips. "It was a gift from her, a special gift with her name and sentiment on the inside. I think I'll offer old Guggenheim a smoke."

"You wouldn't."

"Oh, wouldn't I? Can you really think of anything I wouldn't do when it comes to taking my revenge?"

"That's despicable."

"I just want to see the look on her face and watch her squirm a mite. Plus, if I can irritate Guggenheim further, he might be itching for another card game. Men who have a lot to prove tend to overplay their hands. I like that in a rich man."

"So you just want to gouge the man for more money?"

"Of course. He must know that Kitty will cost him plenty before I'm through with him." He took a cigarette out of the case and placed it in his mouth. Snapping the case shut, he extracted a match from his pocket and flicked his thumbnail over the tip of it. The match burst into flame. "I want Kitty to pay a price as well." He held the match to the end of the cigarette and puffed it to life.

"That kind of thing is what I was talking to you about. How can you ask for or expect forgiveness when you're so unwilling to give it to others?"

"I can forgive her."

"Oh, really? When?"

"When I see her suffer a fraction of the hurt she put me through. I loved her."

"That attitude has nothing to do with forgiveness. You want your pound of flesh. That's not love."

"And what if I do?"

Morgan shrugged on his dinner jacket and pulled his cuffs to a point slightly below the sleeves. "I think you've grown up hearing about God's forgiveness all your life but seeing little of it. You might understand the concept, but I rather doubt that you know the meaning of the word."

Hunter slipped the cigarette case back into his coat pocket. "Perhaps you're right."

"Of course, I am."

"It's just a difficult thing to let go of. When a man has been wronged as often as I have, it makes him go to great lengths to set things right."

"That is something that belongs to God alone, not to you, not to me."

7:25 P.M.

Benjamin Guggenheim's stateroom was one of the large, ornate cabins that featured a private promenade. Kitty sat at her dressing table, expertly pushing her hair into loops and swirls that would frame her small face. Her hair was thick and jet black. She had worn dresses that showed it at its best, along with her attractive figure. Scarlet and forest-green satin gowns were her favorites since they contrasted with her hair so well. She especially liked dresses that showed off her shapely figure.

"Benjamin, please close that door."

Guggenheim was strolling on the private promenade, smoking a cigar. At the sound of Kitty's voice, he dropped the lit cigar into the ocean and stepped back through the billowing curtains. "Are you cold, my dear?"

Kitty put her hands over her bare shoulders that her emerald-green dress exposed. "Yes, it's freezing."

Turning back to the door, Guggenheim closed the doors to the promenade and secured the brass handle. "I'll ask the steward to see to the heat in this room."

"Please do, darling. When we come back after dinner, I'll put on my white nightgown. You'll like that," she shivered, "but it will need to be warmer."

Guggenheim clasped his hands behind his back and stepped toward her. The very idea of Kitty in one of her negligees was enough to make his blood boil. He traced her soft, perfect shoulders gently with his fingertips. "That sounds wonderful, my dear."

Shivering, she placed a hand on one of his. "I do hope you will stay with me after dinner."

"I won't be long."

"You won't gamble with those men, will you?" she pouted playfully.

"I won't be long."

She turned around on her chair and looked him in the eye. "Please, must we sit at that table again? I simply detest that man."

"You mean young Mr. Kennedy?"

"Yes, he is so very loathsome, and I hate the very idea of you losing money to a gloating Irish drunkard."

Guggenheim lifted his chin. He never enjoyed being reminded of his losses, especially by someone he liked to continue to impress. "Young Kennedy may have won the first round, but I make my way in the world by always winning the last." He patted her shoulders. "This will be a long trip."

She swung back around to face the mirror. "And I'd like to have a pleasant dinner conversation. Please, Benjamin, can we move?" She batted her eyes pleadingly in the mirror.

He ran the edge of his fingers over the back of her long shapely neck. "My dear, I always make it a point of keeping my enemies close to me. I want to know what they are thinking at all times. It's only my friends that I can afford to be apart from."

"Dash it all. I hate the idea of dinner with that man."

"Young Mr. Fairfield will be between you. He seems like a nice enough chap."

"Just the look in his eyes," Kitty was still going on about Hunter, "is enough to make any woman's skin crawl. The man undresses you with them. I can feel him looking right past my dress."

"My dear, you are so lovely, it would be a natural thing for any man."

"Any man but that one. There is nothing natural about that man."

"Just trust me, my dear. I'll see to your Hunter Kennedy."

Kitty looked into the mirror and ran her hands over her bare neck. "What am I to wear tonight?"

"I asked Hans to bring up the emerald necklace and diamond tiara from the purser's safe. They ought to do your dress justice." He smiled and, bending over, kissed her neck.

"Mmm," she purred. "You are a darling."

"It is my great pleasure to please you."

She looked at him in the mirror. The man's large, full chest filled out his starched white shirt, and the smell of bay rum and talcum powder made him masculine, even in his best evening tuxedo. "And when we come back to the room, it will be my pleasure to please you, Benjamin."

The knock at the door snapped Guggenheim's head around. "Come in," he said.

Hans nodded as he carried in a felt-covered box. He stepped over to Guggenheim and, taking a key from his pocket, handed it over to the man.

As Guggenheim unlocked the box, Kitty looked in the mirror and saw a large bandage on the side of the valet's head. He also sported a fresh injury that ran from his temple to a point high on his left cheekbone.

"Mercy," Kitty said, "What happened to you?"

"He took an unfortunate fall last night," Guggenheim answered for the valet.

"I've never known you to be clumsy," Kitty exclaimed.

"No, madam."

"Even the best of men have their mishaps once in a while," Guggenheim went on. "And these decks can be quite slippery at night."

"Please be careful, Hans."

The massive man raised his shoulders and stuck out his chest. He, too, was in evening clothes. Even though he wouldn't be eating with them, he always liked to be available when called upon, and that also meant he had to be appropriately dressed. "Yes, madam."

Guggenheim opened the box and lifted the emerald necklace. The jewels glimmered in the soft light of the room as he dangled them over Kitty's head. Laying the largest of the stones to a place just above her ample cleavage, he leaned down and fastened the gold-and-diamond chain. "There you are, my dear, only added beauty to what you naturally possess."

Reaching back into the box, he lifted the diamond tiara from its place. It sparkled, glimmering like hundreds of tiny stars in the heavens. He placed it gently on her head. "You deserve a crown my darling, but until then, this will have to do."

9:10 P.M.

When Hunter and Morgan walked into the dining room, all of the other guests had been seated. Hunter with his dawdling and puttering had seen to that. Morgan hated arriving anywhere late. "It's inconsiderate," he'd told Hunter in an attempt to hurry him along. They both walked across the room to their seats at the full dining table.

"Here old man, you take my seat." Hunter motioned to the chair beside Delaney while the old Irishman beamed. "I'll just sit here beside Miss Webb."

Morgan glared at him. The man was impossible and seemed bent on chaos at all cost. "I think you should take your own seat."

"Nonsense, my boy," Delaney said. "You sit here by me, and we'll have ourselves a grand old time. I won't even show you my parlor tricks."

"You see," Hunter said, "It's all settled." He quickly took his place before Morgan could offer any more protests.

The dinner of rack of lamb and baron of beef went extremely well. Morgan even enjoyed the conversation he had with Delaney. He kept the matters to the art of writing without delving into the darker areas of Irish politics.

Conversation at the table was lively. At times it was almost comical. Some members of the group were trying very hard to engage people in talk, while a few did their dead-level best to all but ignore others, even people seated at their elbow.

The long table had two people seated on the ends and three on each side. Across from Morgan and Hunter, forming the other brace of two, were Margaret and Peter. They exchanged words with Gloria Thompson, who was seated to Margaret's right. Of course, Colonel Gracie, at Gloria's right elbow, never could seem to get enough of her attention. Delaney was to the right of Gracie and occasionally he would pay attention to Gracie's description of military tactics. Of course, when he wanted to avoid conversation with the man, all he had to do was turn away. Everyone knew he was deaf as a stone. Morgan sat on the end, next to Delaney and Hunter was at his right, doing his best to drive Kitty crazy. Kitty would lean over and try to make talk with April, making sure she did her best to keep her back to Hunter. Guggenheim sat between the two women, watching the conversation the way one would watch lawn tennis.

Hunter would make his attempts at getting Kitty into conversation. He leaned forward and smiled. She jerked her head away, her nose in the air, as if assaulted by some putrid odor. And, of course, the more he tried, the more irritated Morgan became. Several times Hunter caught sight of Delaney watching him and Morgan and their silent exchanges. Hunter could see that the man was amused by it.

Delaney leaned over and lowered his voice. "Are you two boys having trouble?"

Hunter overheard him. "No trouble," he said. "Morgan here just has a great deal of difficulty with how I collect my debts."

Delaney smirked. "Young men always have their spats, though mostly about the female of the species. There's a poem from my native land, what you would call a limerick. It goes something like this: There once were two cats of Kilkenny, each thought there was one cat too many, so they scratched and they bit, in a quarrelsome fit, till instead of two cats there weren't any."

Hunter hooted at the line while Morgan smiled.

Delaney patted Morgan's hand. "So, you see my boy, very little that doesn't involve liberty is worth fighting about, least of all a woman."

"What about two women?" Hunter asked, a sneer on his lips.

"Two women now, is it? Well, that might be a horse of a different color."

"We'll be fine," Morgan said. "Things always seem to look better in the morning."

Hunter could see that Morgan was on edge. When he decided to sit next to Kitty that had put Morgan on the constant alert for the fireworks to follow. He decided it was time to resolve the issue. It wouldn't make Morgan any more comfortable, but at least he could get it out of the way so the man could enjoy his desert.

Hunter was frustrated in his attempt to get Kitty to pay him attention, but he had a plan. He pulled the cigarette case from his pocket and set it on the table next to Kitty's elbow.

Morgan's eyes widened.

Hunter looked across Kitty to Guggenheim. He opened up the case, revealing the sentiment written on the inside of the lid and held it out. "I say, old man, would you care for a smoke before dessert?"

Morgan looked on as Kitty's eyes widened. The band stuck up a lively tune.

"No, thank you," Guggenheim replied, eyeing the case. Hunter knew what was written couldn't be seen from where the man sat, but it amused him to see Kitty squirm.

"That's a very attractive cigarette case," Guggenheim said.

"Oh? You like it? A dear friend, the love of my life, gave this to me. It's a tragic tale of true love betrayed. Let me read the inscription to you."

Kitty dropped her teacup. She grabbed Hunter's hand. "Please, Mr. Kennedy, I should very much like to dance."

The notion caught Hunter completely off guard. He cleared his throat and smiled. "I'd love to, if there are no objections from Mr. Guggenheim."

Guggenheim stirred his tea. "No, please, be my guest."

With that, Hunter sprang from his chair and, taking Kitty's chair, pulled it out for her.

Morgan was distracted by Hunter's latest charade. Delaney reached into his pocket, took out a small bottle, and opened it. He palmed the small brown bottle in his hand and, reaching over his own teacup, allowed several small drops to fall into the tea. Picking up his spoon, he stirred it.

Hunter took Kitty's gloved hand, while seemingly every eye at the table was glued to them, and escorted her onto the dance floor. They began their dance.

"Just what do you think you are doing?" she asked.

"Doing? I was just offering the gentleman a smoke."

"Are you bent on ruining me?"

They spun around the dance floor. "Why should anything I do ruin you? Are you so ashamed of your past that you won't let it into the light?"

"There are some things that I'd just as soon forget."

"Like me, for instance?"

"Yes you, precisely you."

"How very unaccommodating, Kitty, and you of all women should know how to accommodate men."

"What does that mean?"

"You know exactly what it means. You're nothing more than a tart, an expensive one, no doubt, but nothing more than a gentleman's diversion for the evening."

"And you are a sniveling boy with a broken heart."

"We'll just see who does the sniveling before the night is through."

"You wouldn't! Not even you could stoop to do something so low."

"I'm afraid, my dear, that is exactly where you left me. You dropped me like so much used rubbish. How can you expect me to behave any different from that?"

Kitty stiffened in Hunter's arms.

"Perhaps I can make it up to you. I have thought of you so much, you know."

Hunter pushed her back slightly. The woman was truly beautiful, even with the forced smile on her face. "Make it up to me? How?"

"I have my ways." Her smile grew wider. "Besides, in spite of you being so wicked to your loving Kitty, I'd enjoy catching up on our friends. Benjamin isn't keen on the theater set you know."

"Yes, you do have your ways. Hmm, might be interesting at that." He looked down the front of her dress; the emeralds and diamonds sparkled under the crystal chandlers. "All right, then, I'll tell you what we'll do. I have a ticket for Morgan to be in the Turkish bath tomorrow at 2:00. I can meet you in the swimming pool then. It might be fun to see you in your bathing suit." He smiled a wicked smile at her. "Perhaps after we talk at the pool, you might agree to join me in my room."

"All right, then, I'll meet you at 2:00."

When the two of them finished their dance, Hunter returned Kitty to the table and pulled her chair out for her.

Guggenheim smiled.

"Did you two have a nice time?" Morgan asked.

"Yes, we did." Hunter could see that Morgan noticed the change in him. He was more relaxed. There was a sense of victory in what had happened. It was plain to see that Kitty wouldn't treat him like an unworthy servant any longer. He'd made certain of that.

"I'd like to show you my cigarette case, Kennedy," Guggenheim said.

He reached into his pocket and produced a gold case. Guggenheim handed it to Hunter.

Hunter held it. It was heavy, obviously solid gold. "Magnificent," he said. "Where did you get it?"

"From the lady to your right, of course, the love of *my* life."

Hunter read the inscription out loud. TO THE LOVE OF MY LIFE. It was signed KITTY. He smiled and passed it to Morgan to read.

"Very nice sentiment," Hunter said. Taking the case from Morgan, he handed it back to Guggenheim.

Morgan reached for his teacup at the same time Delaney reached for his water glass, accidentally spilling Morgan's tea. "I'm sorry, that was clumsy of me." He picked up his napkin and began to dab at the stain on the tablecloth. "Here, you take mine. I haven't touched it."

"Thank you," Morgan said. He lifted the cup to his lips. Delaney watched him closely. He set it back down. "A very nice sentiment," Morgan said to Kitty.

"Thank you." She nervously dabbed her mouth with a lace handkerchief.

Hunter could see that the relaxing of hostilities had put Morgan at ease. For the first time, Morgan looked at Margaret, at the far end of the table.

Margaret had been glancing in Morgan's direction all during the meal, and while Hunter had caught her looks, Morgan had seemed too preoccupied with saving Hunter to even notice. It amused Hunter. The man had a mother-hen nature about him. He would make a good reporter. A man that absorbed with caring for the welfare of a wayward friend would no doubt work passionately in his concern for society at large.

Hunter nudged Morgan's elbow. He opened his silver-and-gold cigarette case and quietly pushed it in front of him.

Morgan picked it up and read the words TO THE LOVE OF MY LIFE. It was also signed KITTY.

Hunter watched as Morgan tried very hard to appear at ease when he read the words, but it was difficult for the man. His hands gripped the silver case hard, and he rolled his eyes. Had Hunter chosen to, right then he could have dealt a major death blow to the very posh situation Kitty Webb found herself in, and he knew it. It was quite a temptation. But he'd promised to meet her, and he was going to do just that.

Guggenheim asked Kitty to dance.

Kitty sprang to her feet, and the two of them left the table. Morgan and Hunter watched.

"I'd say our Kitty there does have nine lives," Morgan quipped.

Hunter tipped his head in Morgan's direction, surprised. "Well put, old man. Well put, indeed."

Morgan once again picked up Delaney's cup and held it to his lips. "Mmm," he said. "This tea seems a little tepid."

"Go ahead and drink it, my boy," Delaney said. "We'll get you another."

Morgan put the cup to his lips and drank it down. He set the cup down. "That seems a little bitter."

THURSDAY,
APRIL 11, 1912,
10:30 P.M.

CHAPTER 17

Morgan made his way back to his cabin alone. He suddenly felt very sleepy. He was also tired, tired of trying to constantly pull Hunter's fat out of the fire. If the man was going to make an idiot out of himself, he'd have to do it with no help to the contrary. Morgan had always been the perfect choice in school as a hall monitor. He could be expected to keep the other boys from taking two or three of the stairs at a time. The administration expected as much from him, and he never disappointed them.

Responsibility had been a blessing and a curse. It kept his grades near perfect, and it kept him from taking great risks. He hated that about himself. Leaving the safety of his uncle and aunt and risking their displeasure by going to America had been the one chance he had taken in proving his mettle. Keeping his distance from Margaret in the last year had also seemed like the responsible thing to do. For Morgan, it seemed that everything he had tried to exercise control over his life or others had come back to bite him in the seat of the pants. When was he going to learn? People don't need to be controlled; they need to be loved.

He moved down the stairs and for the first time noticed his knees begin to wobble. It frightened him. He grabbed on to the handrail. His eyes drooped. Could he be that tired? Perhaps all the anxiety he had felt for the last two days was finally catching up to him. First the man stabbed in the alley, then saying good-bye. Of course, he couldn't forget seeing Margaret and Peter, and then there was the matter of the man chasing him and trying to kill him. That would be too much for any man to bear up under for long. On top of that, there was his desire to see Hunter free himself from this need for revenge.

He didn't see Fitzgerald watching him from the end of the corridor. Fumbling with the knob on the door, he soon felt the man's hand on his shoulder.

"Are you all right, sir? Would you like me to help you into bed?"

Morgan looked up at him. "I don't know what's the matter. I haven't been drinking."

"Of course, you haven't, sir." The steward opened the door for him. "Here, let me help you."

Taking Morgan's arm, Fitzgerald led him to the bed and helped him sit down. He gently removed the dinner jacket and, lifting Morgan's legs, laid him on the bed. "There you are, sir. I'll make you more comfortable, and then you can sleep."

Fitzgerald untied Morgan's shoes and loosened his tie. Reaching under his chin, he undid the top button. "Is that better, sir?"

Morgan's eyes were glassy. The room seemed to whirl around him, dropping him down, down, down into a deep hole. In a matter of moments, he was unconscious.

Fitzgerald pushed slightly at Morgan's chest, but there was no movement. Stepping over to the low-burning lamp, he turned it up, brightly illuminating that section of the room. He quickly moved from lamp to lamp, turning them up slightly so he could see to find what he had been sent to retrieve.

A screen had been placed in the corner of the cabin to conceal Morgan's trunk. Fitzgerald stepped behind it and opened the trunk. Carefully, he ran his hands through the contents of the man's clothing. If the satchel was in the room like Delaney suggested it might be, then he was going to find it.

He was loyal to the Irish cause. He always had been. Seldom had he questioned his orders, and he'd always been careful before to make sure that what he did was out of sight. To be seen was to limit his usefulness in the future, and he never wanted to do that. Before, he had always been used to carry messages across the Atlantic and occasionally payments for weapons delivered from America. This was different, though. Everything Delaney had asked him to do so far involved greater risks than he'd ever taken before. Stealing the steward's jacket and delaying a message to the captain was one thing, but now there was the matter of murder. The authorities would pursue that. It wouldn't be quite so easy. And if he were found in a passenger's room without reason, he could be dismissed on the spot.

The noise at the door brought him to a sudden halt. Someone was there. He heard a knock. He froze. He dropped to his knees behind the screen.

The door opened slowly. "Morgan." It was Hunter's voice. "I need to talk to you about something."

Fitzgerald's stomach turned over. Why had he hidden? It would have been easy enough to explain his presence. After all, Mr. Fairfield had been drinking. That had been obvious, or so it seemed to him. The man needed help with getting into bed. Why he had attempted to hide bewildered him. Panic had set in. Delaney would never forgive that. It might compromise everything.

Hunter stood over Morgan. "Morgan, old man, are you asleep?"

Morgan was silent.

Hunter shook him. "Morgan, wake up."

There was no movement from Morgan.

Now Fitzgerald was worried. What if Delaney had put too much of the knockout drops in the man's tea? He had assured him that what he had planned to give the man was not nearly enough to cause great damage, but what if he'd been wrong? The dose was just supposed to put Fairfield to sleep so Fitzgerald could search the room and find the satchel, but few things were an exact science. Fairfield was one of his passengers, too. He was certain to be a suspect in any foul play.

Hunter pulled Morgan up from the bed by his shirt. "Morgan, Morgan! What's wrong with you?"

For the first time, there was a groan from Morgan. It was slight and barely audible, but it was a sound.

Hunter slapped him. "Wake up. Wake up."

A louder cry now.

Hunter continued to shake him.

"Mmm...oh, stop." The sound of the man was distant and groggy, but it was a sound.

Hunter shook him once again. "I won't stop until you wake up."

He pulled Morgan's feet from the bed and onto the floor. Putting Morgan's arm over his shoulder, Hunter picked the man up and got him to his feet. "Here, old chap, we'd better go for a walk."

He began to walk the floor of the cabin while Morgan mumbled words that were barely discernible. Morgan dragged his feet and then began to take a few steps. Hunter kept up the pace clear across the cabin floor, stopping to swing Morgan around and move back toward the door.

"You've been drugged old man," Hunter said.

"Delaney's tea," Morgan moaned. "It t-t-tasted odd."

"That's right, he gave you his tea. Do you think it was intended for him?"

Morgan groaned. He shook his head.

Hunter stopped at the pitcher of water on the nightstand. He picked it up and splashed some into Morgan's face.

The jolt shocked Morgan's eyes open. "The satchel," Morgan said.

Fitzgerald leaned forward. He didn't want to miss a word.

"I'll take care of that. I'll take it to my cabin tonight and put it in the purser's safe tomorrow. Don't you worry about it."

"Get it." Morgan pointed to the lower drawer of the bureau. He stuck his feet in his shoes.

Hunter continued to drag Morgan back over to the far side of the room. Stooping down, with Morgan's weight still on him, he opened the drawer. Lifting the satchel, he looped the leather strap over his shoulder and stood Morgan up. "There, I've got it."

Morgan murmured, groggily.

"We'd better get you out on the deck. The cold will help you."

Morgan nodded.

Slowly, Hunter marched Morgan toward the ajar door. He pushed it open with his foot and moved out into the corridor. Turning toward the stairs that led to the deck, Hunter dragged Morgan one step at a time. Up they went. Hunter reached down and helped Morgan negotiate the stairs, grabbing his trousers with one hand and pulling his leg up to the next step. One by one, they climbed the stairs. Finally, they climbed out onto the cold deck and into the night air.

"Here we are, old man. You and I are going to take a bracing walk around this ship. By the time we get back, you may have icicles forming on your nose, but you'll be awake. Then we'll take you in and get some hot coffee in you, not at all like the tea, mind you."

The deck was somewhat slippery, which made them quite a pair to watch. To any casual observer, they seemed to be two men returning from a night of getting very drunk. They slid, with Hunter continuing to brace Morgan and fight the surface of the wood at the same time.

"You've been quite the pip, old man," Hunter said. "You've stuck by me thick and thin, mostly thin."

Morgan tried to focus his eyes on Hunter while he spoke.

"And I've been a bloody fool. I know that now."

"I th-th-thought you'd be gamblin'," Morgan slurred.

"And I would have been if I hadn't wanted to tell you what a blithering idiot I was. This dream of mine, this dream of watching all my enemies fall at my feet and beg for forgiveness is nothing more than a hollow illusion from a hollow man. There's no end in trying to settle scores. I'll never settle the score with my father, and I have no intention of repeating the mistakes that I learned as a child."

Morgan blinked his eyes, still trying to take in what Hunter was trying to say.

"Of course, I hadn't intended on blurting all of that out. Then I saw you in danger. Some friend I would have been not to tell you."

"Why are you saying this?"

"When I talked with Kitty tonight, I saw the hatred and fear in her eyes. This was a woman I loved, or thought I did. Now, I actually feel sorry for her. With nothing to barter but her body, she must be lonely. I understand that feeling because I'm lonely, too. I've managed to ostracize every person who's ever got close to me. The only way I've thought to overcome it is to beat them, not care for them. I think she still cares for me. I want to be able to look myself in the mirror and like what I see, not just on the surface but under it as well."

Morgan nodded.

"And of course I thought of you. You seem perfectly willing to sacrifice your own happiness for a sense of right and wrong. You could sit back and enjoy the fruits of your family's wealth, but no, you want to make something of yourself. You are a bewilderment."

Morgan stumbled, but Hunter grabbed him and straightened him up. "Chances are you won't remember a word I've said in the morning." Hunter laughed. "Perhaps that's a good thing." He grinned. "I'll deny it all."

Morgan shook his head. He was working to try to stay awake. "I'll remember."

"Dash it all," Hunter replied. "Now it will be you that is blackmailing me."

Rounding a walkway on the deck, they ran right into Margaret and Peter coming out of the dining room.

"Here, here," Peter exclaimed, "What seems to be the trouble?"

Hunter swung Morgan around. The man hung on Hunter's shoulder like a rag doll. "Morgan's been drugged. Somebody slipped the old boy a some knockout drops. He's trying to fall asleep, but I won't let him."

Margaret bent over and took Morgan's face in her hands. His eyes were closed. "Morgan, Morgan," she said, "Wake up." She stroked his hair back gently.

Hunter shrugged his shoulders, trying to straighten Morgan up. He carefully got the man's feet under him. "Would one of you be so kind as to fetch the ship's doctor? Morgan here is going to need some attention, and I fear for the rest of the night."

9:45 A.M., APRIL 12

The infirmary of the *Titanic* was a modern one, complete with surgical amphitheater. Morgan opened his eyes to the sound of whispers on the far side of his room. The room was stark white. Bottles of medicine, sitting on brass-barred shelves, filtered the sunlight. Bells seemed to peal in his head, and each beat of his heart slammed his temples. He turned his head on the pillow to see who was doing the subdued talking.

Hunter caught his eye. He was standing and talking to a man in a white smock. "Sleep well, old man?" Hunter shrieked.

The sound of Hunter's voice drove a wedge down the middle of Morgan's head. He grimaced.

"I brought you some fresh clothes, old man." Hunter motioned to a set of tweed togs that hung over a chair. A white shirt and a green tweed jacket, along with a matching pair of knickers that buttoned around the calves. He had also laid a pair of cream-colored knee socks beside some brown shoes.

"Not that," Morgan said, "I hate that outfit."

"You'll be needing to get up and move around some," the man in the white smock said. "Your head must be pounding, and the fresh air will do you some good."

"You listen to Dr. McCoy," Hunter said. "Fresh air and getting back into the process of living will do you a world of good."

Morgan moaned and turned over, putting his back to the two of them.

"Now see here, old man," Hunter reached out and shook him, "we'll be wanting to find out who did this to you and have them punished."

"More revenge, I take it," Morgan mumbled.

"Blimey, you do remember what I said."

Morgan turned back over. "I most certainly do."

"Then if you're going to make me suffer for it and punish me to boot by making me sit on that icy deck with you, you're going to have to get dressed. Besides, Dr. McCoy here needs this bed of yours for truly sick people."

The idea of taking up space jolted Morgan's eyes open. It was just like him to respond to duty, and Hunter knew it. "All right, all right." Morgan swung his feet over the side of the bed. "It's just like you to appeal to my sense of fair play, isn't it? You never let a man rest in peace."

"That's an epitaph dear boy, not a way to live life. Besides, your snoring was scaring the sick people."

"Somehow I think that following you about will be the best way to an early epitaph."

"Early, perhaps, but exciting, nonetheless."

Morgan held his hands to the sides of his head. "Right now, I could use a little less excitement."

"Oh, I wouldn't be so sure about that."

Morgan looked at him, puzzled.

"You should have seen the way Margaret held your head in her hands last night. From what I saw, I'd say you were in for a great deal more excitement."

Morgan put his hands down and smiled. "You think so?"

"I'm sure of it."

"Leave it to you to be certain of a woman's heart."

"It's something you should think about."

"Oh, I have. You may have been a fool to pursue your revenge, but I was a fool to avoid my feelings."

"Now I have a pot of hot tea here and some scones and jam," Hunter said. "It's fresh. It has nothing to do with that cup you had in your hands last night."

"Can you be certain it was the tea?" the doctor asked.

"No, I suppose we can't be certain," Hunter replied.

10:30 A.M.

Peter and Margaret sat with their morning tea in the Palm Court of the Verandah Café watching the two Hoffman children. Margaret enjoyed watching the children. There was a playful innocence about them that she enjoyed. They hadn't a care in the world, no decisions to make and very little in the way of choices. Their father would see to their needs. There was a comfort in that Margaret envied.

The furniture was wicker with heavy green leather cushions. Ivy grew up the trellis-covered walls. High arched windows, combined with the wicker, gave the place the feel of a well-manicured English garden. One could feel as if he were at a garden party without going out into the cold.

The children were lost in bouncing their ball for quite some time while their doting father sat glued to them. The man's eyes were riveted to their every move. He stirred his tea and laughed when they went scrambling for the ball. Soon they had discovered a new pastime. The floor of the café was a checkerboard, laid out in black-and-cream squares. They hopped the squares in hopscotch fashion, taking care not to land on the borders between the two colors.

"Your mother is not enjoying the voyage, I take it," Peter said.

"No, I'm afraid she is not. She is in the writing room, penning some letters to be mailed in New York. Perhaps that will keep her mind off the open ocean. I think she has been somewhat panicky ever since we lost sight of the Irish coastline."

Margaret smiled and sipped her tea. "She does well at night, though, perhaps because she cannot see."

"Oh, what you can't see can't hurt you."

"Yes, exactly."

"I suppose there are times when we see things that we'd rather not see. We can either choose to turn away and not look or we can face them."

Margaret stirred her tea. She could tell that Peter was building up to something, something that involved her and Morgan. For over a year, she had tried to push Morgan Fairfield out of her mind, going to great lengths to do so. It was a difficult thing to do, however. The times of play as a child had a way of weaving their way into a person's heart. There was something about innocent love that left one feeling pure, undefiled, and especially attached to the object of that love. Morgan and her feelings for him had taught her the meaning of the word, and just sitting here and watching the Hoffman children reminded her of those times.

"Perhaps Mother is right. Some things are better to ignore."

Peter held the cup to his lips and looked at her over the rim. "I think you are facing something, Margaret, that you had better not ignore."

"Do we have to talk about that?"

Both Margaret and Peter knew the subject. They had known it ever since they had run into Morgan aboard ship. Had Margaret been certain of her feelings, it would have been something she would have gladly faced, but the indecision that seemed to grow in her by the moment caused her to shy away from it. She did care for Peter, she just wondered if it was love.

"I think we should. In a matter of days, both you and I will be standing in front of relatives and smiling. I should think we'd both want to know if we have something to smile about."

"Oh, dash it all, Peter. Why must you men always be so serious? If you and Morgan insist on pinning me to the wall, I think I'll throw you both over the side and take up with Morgan's friend, Hunter."

Peter gulped at his tea, almost spilling it. Picking up his napkin, he wiped his mustache.

"There are times when women feel like nothing but cows to be owned and herded about. We're fought over, swapped, bartered, and then finally branded. You'd think we were mindless creatures fit for nothing more than a pen."

Margaret knew that when she was in a tight spot, her best defense was to always take the offensive. Men seldom knew what to do with an articulate woman.

"Love means that you care for someone, Margaret."

She glared at him. "Sometimes I think that word *care* carries a different meaning for some than others."

"What do you mean?"

"You care for a garden. You care for a dog. You care for sheep. You care for a house. You supervise it, cultivate it, make it productive, shear it, paint it, and finally bury it. What you don't do is treat it as an equal and give it the ballot."

"I consider you my equal in every way, Margaret."

"Oh, is that so?"

"Certainly. I assume you knew that when I asked you for your hand in marriage."

"And why did you ever do such a thing?"

"Because it was something I assumed you wanted."

"Because I was of the marriageable age? A reasonable conclusion I suppose. After all, what is a woman in her twenties to do with her time? She can't have a meaningful job that requires her brain. She can't think serious thoughts, now can she? She has nothing more to do than sit about and collect dishes, now does she?"

Peter set down his cup. "Perhaps that was Morgan's thinking when he decided to pursue his career. I think he assumed you would be following your own heart while he followed his and that you wouldn't be waiting for him, wringing your hands. If you wanted the man, you should have pursued him like a bloodhound." He paused and smiled. "After all, if you are an equal, why shouldn't you bear an equal responsibility for love?"

Margaret could tell that she had aroused Peter and maybe put a little anger into the man. That was good. She liked to see passion in a man. What she couldn't stand was a man who was willing to sit by and watch things happen to him and merely wait for the outcome. She knew Peter was right about Morgan, though. He had treated her like an equal. She looked Peter in the eye. "Maybe you're right."

"Of course, I am."

"Well, let me ask you one thing, Peter. Do you love me? Really love me?"

"Of course, I do. What a silly question."

"I know you care for me." She searched his eyes with hers. "You've already said that. But I wonder if that is really love or is that something you expect to grow into with time."

"All couples grow into love, Margaret. They begin with mutual respect and care, and over time it blossoms."

"Perhaps that is our problem. You see, I care for you, too, Peter, and I respect you as a man. I suppose the both of us are waiting for love to grow."

"And how will you know when it happens? When you feel about me the way you feel about Morgan?"

FRIDAY,

APRIL 12, 1912,

11:00 A.M.

CHAPTER 18

The purser's office was abnormally calm with the two men at the counter scribbling notes. They made careful notation about all baggage stored aboard. "See here," the first man said, drawing the attention of the man seated to his left, "Here's one that doesn't believe in traveling light, not at all."

The second man leaned over to take a better look. His eyes flared. "Mrs. Charlotte Cardeza of Philadelphia and her son Thomas. They're in B-51, one of the promenade suites." The list underneath their names was long. The man traced the items with his finger and read aloud. "Fourteen trunks, four suitcases, three crates, and a medicine chest." He gulped and continued reading, "Seventy dresses, ten fur coats, thirty-eight feather boas, twenty-two hatpins, and ninety-one pairs of gloves. Mercy sakes alive, has the woman anything left at home?"

"Oh, I'm quite certain she has." The first clerk pursed his lips. "This is just her seasonal traveling ensemble. Bare bones, eh, what?"

"In a pig's eye. Women!"

"Well, it's not just women. Look at this." He pointed to another page with the name Billy Carter written at the top. Running his finger down the list, he highlighted a number of items. "Sixty shirts, fifteen pairs of shoes, two sets of tails, twenty-four polo sticks...and a new Renault automobile."

"I'd love to have a look at that."

"Why don't we then? It'd be a lark. He has it stored in the forward hold." Looking down at the page, his eyes widened. "It says the car is red."

The young men, both in their twenties, were like a pair of puppies at play. The notion of automobiles was one that held great excitement for them. Speed in any form was a great rush.

"As if we have so many automobiles aboard that we will lose track of this one."

"And I'll bet it's a pretty one, too."

"I'll bet it is. Why don't we go down and take ourselves a look?"

"Yes, let's. We'll have McElroy watch the desk."

"All right, you get your cap and I'll tell McElroy."

Minutes later the two men were heading down the lift to E deck. When the machine hit the bottom, the first clerk cranked open the handle and they stepped outside onto the platform. Taking the stairs from there, they were soon on the catwalk that led past the sweltering boilers. Making their way past the men groaning behind their shovels, they tramped onto the landing that carried them past the doors to the watertight compartments and toward the forward hold.

Both of them carried clipboards so they would look serious and official. If anyone should stop and ask them what they were doing, they knew they had a ready explanation. It was the duty of the purser's office to see to all passengers' possessions and the cargo the ship was carrying. The only thing was that this trip was more of a lark for them, the chance to see how the upper crust of society really lived and what they drove about the streets in. They might even have a chance to sit in the leather seats.

Their heavy polished shoes clicked and echoed through the narrow companionway. The floor underneath them was a bright, shiny metal surface with bumps in the metal to give those carrying cargo below an added measure of traction. The first clerk, Smithers, noticed a stain on the metal and called Hankin's attention to it. "I say, what is this?"

"It looks to be paint, red paint."

"Someone spilled it and didn't do a very good job of cleaning it up."

"I should say not."

"Make a note of this," Smithers said, "We'll put it on report."

Hankin scrawled a notation on his clipboard, and the two men continued to the door that led to the forward cargo area. They slipped the heavy metal hasp off the door and, stepping onto the landing, stood and looked over the cargo area.

"There it is," Hankin yelled. His voice seemed to boom through the huge cargo area. He pointed. "Over there."

They stutter-stepped down the stairs. Hankin jumped the last two and landed with a bounce on the heavy metal floor. Smithers followed. Weaving their way around the boxes and crates that were piled on the floor, they soon came to the bright scarlet automobile.

Hankin's eyes bulged. There, in the driver's seat was a man slumped over the wheel. "What do you make of that?" he asked.

"I don't know. Maybe he's asleep."

"Or drunk."

"Well, let's find out," Smithers said, pushing down on the polished silver handle.

Hankin reached in and, grabbing the man's coat lapel, gave him a shake. "Here, here, you can't be sleeping in this place."

The man fell out the open door, his eyes wide, staring into the ceiling of the large cargo room.

"Crikey! He's dead!" Both men leaped back, pinning themselves against a huge crate. Neither had ever seen a dead body before, let alone one sticky with blood. Smithers recovered first and took full advantage by announcing, "I'll get the captain!"

He fell three more times over trunks and barrels on his mad dash to the companionway. Hankin, ashen faced, grabbed his clipboard gingerly with two fingers from where it had fallen in the panic. It had fallen on the dead man's shoulder.

Suddenly the hold was deathly quiet, and Hankin realized he was alone with a corpse. He decided a post near the door would be more prudent. But as he backed away, his eyes never left the body.

It was close to twenty minutes later when Smithers led Captain Smith, First Officer Murdoch, Dr. McCoy, and Fourth Officer Boxhall to the area. Hankin had left the scene untouched. He was also shocked to see that Ismay, the director of White Star Line, had accompanied the group of officers. Hankin stepped back and allowed the doctor to take a closer look.

McCoy lifted the man's arm and pressed on his flesh, starting with the fingers and working his way up the arm. "The man's been dead for some time, Captain. I'd say for eight to ten hours. I won't be able to give you a better guess until I have him in the morgue."

Hankin grimaced at the doctor's touching the corpse. He unconsciously wiped his hands on his pants legs.

"That place must be filling up," Boxhall quipped.

The remark brought every eye in Boxhall's direction. He could see at once that there was no humor to be found on this subject, none at all.

"Search him for identification," Smith said.

Ismay leaned over to get a better look at the man.

Murdoch stooped down and patted the man's pockets. Hearing a rustle in the man's inner jacket pocket, he reached in and pulled out a ticket. He opened and read it. "It's a steerage ticket," Murdoch said. "The man's name is Henry Killebrew. He came aboard at Queenstown."

"That may help you with the time of death," Smith offered.

"Yes, it does."

"Does this mean we turn around, Captain?" Boxhall asked.

"Certainly not," Ismay blurted out. "If anything it should mean that we do all that we can to pick up speed."

Smith pulled himself erect. Laying his hands on the lapels of his coat, he lifted his chin. "We will do nothing to place this vessel in any danger."

"Of course." Ismay seemed embarrassed. "You are the captain. But any thoughts about turning this ship around must be put aside. The authorities in New York are just as capable of dealing with this matter as the police in Queenstown are. The only difference is that by turning around we are going to call a great deal of attention to the matter, unnecessary attention. The publicity would be disastrous. I won't have people thinking this ship is a death ship."

"This is murder," Murdoch said.

Ismay stuck his finger in his watch pocket, which gave him the look of nonchalant authority. With his other hand, he brushed his mustache aside. "The man is steerage class and Irish. They kill each other all of the time."

"They kill the English, too," Boxhall said.

Ismay shot him a quick glance.

"The man found murdered yesterday was a first-class passenger and a Serb," Murdoch volunteered.

"He was only found in a first-class cabin," Boxhall said.

Smith cleared his throat, bringing the conversation to a halt. "Doctor, you will take the man to the morgue and have a report for me in the morning. Boxhall, I want you to make inquiries in the steerage area. Find out whatever you can about who this man knows and who saw him last." Smith looked each person in the eye with a careful look of authority. "Gentlemen, it appears we have a murderer loose aboard the *Titanic*."

1:00 P.M.

Morgan and Hunter had changed into athletic clothes and were both in the gymnasium doing their best to dispel the tension of the previous night. Morgan's head was clearer now, and he cranked back on the rowing machine with ever increasing zeal.

"This is going to put you back in the pink, old man."

Morgan puffed as he pulled hard on the polished wooden oars. He watched as Hunter bumped along on the mechanical camel. "Do you really call that exercise?" Morgan teased.

Hunter grinned as he bounced up and down. He jammed his feet down on the pedals, sending the leather camel's back rising into the air. "Actually, no, I call it amusement. I positively can't ever imagine myself riding a real camel. I understand they smell to the high heavens."

Morgan pushed back with his legs on the rowing machine and leaned back. "I have a feeling they'd be equally offended at the way I'm smelling just about now."

"Don't get yourself too far spent. I still have that ticket for you."

"What ticket?"

"The Turkish bath, old man, the Turkish bath. It will sweat all of that poison right out of your body."

"Sounds awful. Maybe I should live with the poison."

"And you will need to have a massage as well. That ought to do the trick."

Morgan hauled the oars back, straining to increase his speed. "It ought to do the trick, all right. I'll be put into a state of total relaxation, death."

"You're a long way from dying, bucko, believe me, I saw you last night."

"I believe you. Long about this morning, though, I was wishing I had died."

"What! And miss out on my confession of faith?"

"Oh, yes, your confession of faith," Morgan grinned, mockingly.

Hunter crossed his heart as the camel went up and down. "I was true and honest with you, old man. A truer word was never spoken."

"And so you've given up on this quest for revenge?"

"That I have. I'm to meet Kitty when you're taking your steam bath. I'll set things right with her then."

Morgan pulled hard on the oars. "I'm glad to hear that. All this hatred of yours does is hurt you."

"I even spent some time with a Bible in the library this morning."

Morgan looked at him and practically shook his head to clear it. He couldn't believe what he was hearing.

"I think the more words of Jesus I hear, the less I hear of my father."

Margaret and Peter walked by the window of the gym and, seeing the two of them, meandered through the door. "Working hard, are we?" Peter asked.

"I am," Hunter laughed as he bounced. "Morgan over there is relaxing though," he laughed again, only louder, "in his pretend boat."

"The brochure says the gymnasium is designed to give one endless hours of amusement," Peter said. "I see now it's only amusing if one is watching, not indulging."

Morgan groaned as he pulled back on the oars. "We've only been here for a half hour, and already it seems endless to me. Ask me if I'm amused, though."

"Are you amused?" Hunter asked, a smirk on his face.

"I'm about as amused as that camel would be if you were really riding it."

Margaret wound her arm over Peter's elbow. "It does look like quite the he-man enterprise," she said.

"You should join us at the swimming pool," Hunter said. "Morgan here has a Turkish bath scheduled for 2:00, and I have an appointment, but if you'll come down about 2:30, we could all take a nice swim."

"That might be fun." Margaret looked up into Peter's eyes. "Can we do that?"

Peter patted her hand. "Of course we can, my dear." He looked over at Morgan and then Hunter. "The boys here have just issued an invitation."

"That would be jolly," Hunter said. He looked over at Morgan, still rowing and sweating. "Don't you think so, old man?" He slipped off the camel.

Morgan finally released the oars and groaned. He slowly got to his feet. "Yes, that would be nice." He leaned back and, placing his hands on the small of his back, stretched. "Right now I could use a swim, even if it means jumping into the Atlantic itself." He scrambled his black curly hair.

Hunter noticed a look in Morgan's direction from Margaret, a look and a smile.

"Let's hope it doesn't come to that," Hunter said.

Peter laughed, "Yes, let's hope."

"Then it's a date," Hunter said. "You can pull Morgan here out of the steam heat and then join me in the pool."

After Maragret and Peter had left arm in arm, Hunter looked at Morgan and smiled. "Did you notice that?"

"Notice what?"

"How relaxed they both were at the prospect of seeing you again."

Morgan hung his head. "Maybe she's made up her mind, just like I told you she had."

"Oh, I think she's made up her mind all right."

The door opened suddenly, and in strode Donald Delaney. "Just the men I've been looking for."

Delaney advanced on them, his brow wrinkled with concern. "I heard you were ill last night, Morgan. You certainly look fit now," he said.

"Don't let present appearances fool you," replied Morgan. "Who told you I was ill?"

"Actually, the ship's doctor stopped by my cabin to check on my health. Food poisoning, you think? Dr. McCoy wasn't very forthcoming with details," Delaney explained, clenching and unclenching his fists.

"It was poison all right," Hunter piped up, throwing a towel around his neck. "Somebody slipped Morgan here a sleeping potion. We even venture to guess it was in your tea, sir."

"My tea? What? Oh, yes, now I remember. I gave you mine when you spilled yours." Delaney leaned on the mechanical camel.

"I'm shocked gentlemen. I dare say I hardly know what to say, Morgan. I feel responsible."

"Why would someone want to do you any harm?" Morgan asked.

Delaney laughed. "If you knew the list of men who wanted to put a spade over old Donald Delaney's body, you would be truly amazed. I've been told to go to the dickens by the best of them. It's the hazard of being an outspoken Irish writer."

His teeth spread into a wide grin. "Why, when we were boarding this ship at Southampton and you boys were being waved to by the fair young maidens of England, I had a man planting a curse on me from the dock." He snickered. "In fact, a series of curses it was. The most tame one went something like this." He rolled his eyes. "May you be afflicted with an itch with no nails to scratch."

Delaney wrinkled his nose. "Most were much worse, but being as you're such fine young gentlemen, I gave you the one you could tell your mother."

"I'd like to hear the rest," Hunter smirked.

Morgan put his hand on Hunter's arm. "No, that'll be enough, I think." He looked over at Hunter. "We'd better go downstairs if I've got that rubdown and Turkish bath."

"Yes, you're right." Hunter smiled at Delaney. "You just remember all those other curses. They sound like something I would want to use."

"I will, my boy. I will, and I'm so glad you're okay."

Morgan placed his hand on Delaney's arm, "Be careful, sir. And thank you for your concern."

They watched Delaney walk away.

"I thought you had given up cursing," Morgan said.

"But there are so many things that need cursing, like whoever put that poison into your tea last night."

The two men closed the door to the gymnasium and began their walk to the stairs. "What happened to the satchel?" Morgan asked.

"You needn't worry about that. I put it in the purser's safe this morning. It's as secure as it can be."

"I'm glad about that. I don't think I could guarantee my staying awake to watch it another night, not the way I'm feeling."

1:30 P.M.

Boxhall shuffled his way through the third-class area of the ship. The third-class dining area was located amidships on F deck. The dining saloon was actually two rooms divided by a watertight bulkhead. Its walls were enameled white with posters advertising the White Star Line framed and hanging in prominent locations.

The tables were covered with white tablecloths and, as Boxhall walked in, they were already being set for dinner. Knives, forks, spoons and small decanters of vinegar were being laid out. At various intervals along the tables were white enamel water pitchers and bowls filled with fresh fruit. Third class on the *Titanic* was a far better experience than many second-class accommodations on other liners. It was something the White Star directors were extremely proud of. They took every opportunity to show the furnishings in advertisements throughout Ireland and the Scandinavian countries.

The chairs were black with arms that swooped around to provide a place for someone to rest his elbows, and the brown carpet, though rough by first-class standards, was clean and freshly swept. The tables were quite long, seating as many as thirty. But from everything Boxhall knew about these passengers, they preferred the comradeship of numbers rather than intimate settings. There was little in the way of pretense. Boxhall liked talking to these warm and friendly people. *If only one of them misses Henry Killebrew,* he thought.

He stepped through the doors and out to the landing that led to the aft well deck below. Normally this place would be full of people itching to see the ocean or longing for home as they looked off at the horizon. Today, however, with a nip in the air, only a smattering of people milled about. They stood in small groups by the rail. One sight did pick him up. It was Jack Kelly. The boatbuilder was smoking a pipe and watching his two grandchildren play. Like most children, they seemed impervious to the effects of weather.

He bounced down the stairs quickly and caught Kelly's eye. "Good day to you, Kelly."

"And good day to you, sir."

Boxhall waved a hand at the children. "I see someone is enjoying this air."

Kelly leaned back with his elbows on the rail. He puffed a small cloud of aromatic smoke in the air. "Nothing fazes the wee ones. To be a child is a thing of wonder."

"Yes, it is. I have a bit of wonder myself. I'm looking for someone in third class."

"Oh, are you now? And who might that be?"

"Do you know a Henry Killebrew?"

Kelly puffed on his pipe. He drew out the stem and let a small geyser of the white aroma escape his teeth. "Name's not familiar. Did he get on at Southampton?"

"No, I believe he boarded at Queenstown."

"Them are fellers I haven't had much chance to meet. The children and I got on at Southampton. We can ask about, if you like. I'm positive there are some who might know the man. Not many stay to themselves hereabouts."

Boxhall looked at the way the few people on the deck were milling around and talking. "I'm sure of that."

"You wait right here and let me see to one of the ladies keeping an eye on the young ones, and then I can go with you. It might make it easier. There aren't many folk who feel comfortable in talking to a ship's officer."

"Thank you. I sure appreciate your help."

Boxhall watched as Kelly approached two of the older women on deck. They both listened and, looking over at the children, nodded in agreement.

Finishing his conversation with them, he talked to the children and then walked back over to Boxhall. "I like to leave them with older women. The younger women have too much to distract them."

Boxhall noticed several young women giggling coyly and chatting to a few young men who vied for their attention. He smiled. "Yes, I can see your point."

They both walked across the aft deck and, opening the door, stepped into the general room, or great room as it was called. The place looked comfortable with strewn chairs and upholstered benches that had two sides to them. Wooden arms on the benches were spaced at intervals. Tables were scattered and single chairs were filled with men playing cards as they hunkered over the tables.

Kelly moved around the room like a patriarch at a family reunion. He mingled easily with everyone, smiling, nodding, and exchanging greetings. Boxhall was wise enough to stay in the background as Kelly wove his queries into his Irish banter. He didn't have a heart to tell the man that Killebrew was dead. There was no need to cause a panic, and had Kelly known, just a look from the man might have shown something to be wrong.

He stepped up to one card game and got their attention. "Pardon me, boys. The officer here is looking for a Henry Killebrew. Do any of you know the man and, if so, where he may be found?"

"Do ye have money to give him or does he owe somebody?" one of the men chuckled.

"No," Boxhall said, "He owes nothing, and I'm afraid no one owes him, either."

The man laid down his cards. "The way it should be," he said. He pointed across the room. "See the fair lass over there, the one with the two young men hovering about her?"

Boxhall looked and nodded.

"Go ask her. She was asking for him about this time yesterday."

Boxhall touched the tip of his cap. "Thank you."

He and Kelly walked over to the men standing around the chair where the young woman held court. Boxhall looked at the men. "I'm sorry," he said, "but I need a word with the young lady here."

"Awe," one of the men bawled, "you go and get yer own."

A second man mumbled, "Yeah, jest because you're an officer don't give you the right to run off with our women."

Kelly stepped up. "Now, that'll be enough from the likes of you. This is strictly company business. When the good feller here finishes with his questions, then you can go about with all the wooing you got on yer minds."

The small group of men reluctantly shuffled off, but not far.

"Impolite rascals," Kelly said.

Boxhall looked down at the woman. She was attractive and with a smile that flashed when she showed her ample teeth. Her eyes had a certain twinkle to them, and it was plain to see that she enjoyed the attention of men.

He swallowed. One could almost read her mind. It was plain to see that she hoped this conversation wasn't all business. "I need to find out about a man," Boxhall said.

She leaned forward. "Then it be the right place you've come to."

"Do you know a Henry Killebrew?"

She put her hands on her hips. "Where is he? I've been looking for him for a day now. Have ya got him locked up somewheres?"

"When was the last time you saw him?"

"Yesterday, after the noon meal it was."

"And was he with anyone?"

She put her hand under her chin and thought. "Can't rightly say that he was."

Boxhall could see that she was continuing to think.

"He was going to fetch someone, though."

"Who?" Boxhall asked.

Extending her finger, she pointed across the room. "There, that well-built bloke over there. The one with the tam on his head."

FRIDAY,
APRIL 12, 1912,
1:50 P.M.

CHAPTER 19

Morgan and Hunter laughed about the mechanical camel and the sight of Hunter as an Arabian cowboy all the way down the lift. When they stepped into the Turkish bath, the soft lights and dimly lit tile that glistened on the walls quieted them down. "Amazing, isn't it?" Hunter said. "Like something out of the Arabian nights."

"You're the one with the camel experience," Morgan chuckled. "I think you should go first."

Hunter laughed. "And miss the sight of Kitty in her bathing suit? I should say not. What do you take me for, a complete imbecile?"

"Oh, I forgot. This need to indulge your eyes."

"That seems to be all that I'm allowing myself to indulge in these days, what with you bent on reforming my sinful ways."

The tile on the floor was a sparkling array of alternating blue and white blossoms. A number of feet had left water prints that glimmered in the low light. Arching latticework looped the tops of the walls, and painted tiles of blue and green ferns stood out like an indoor painted garden. Overhead, small amber lanterns with brass trim glistened with a subdued shine.

"What have we here?" Hunter asked, looking at the couches that served as massage pads.

In the middle of the room, a husky man with a mustache and skin the color of paste was getting a vigorous rubdown from a bald-headed masseuse who looked to be the figure of Hercules. The man on the couch turned his head to look at them.

"Come on in, gentlemen. Fritz will be finished with me in a moment."

"Oh, take your time," Hunter said. "My friend here is going to broil in one of the steam rooms, and I am going swimming."

"You are missing something really great," the man said. "This is invigorating."

Morgan stepped over to the man and held out his hand. "Morgan Fairfield's the name."

Propping himself up on the couch, the man reached for Morgan's hand. "Archie Butt, Major Archie Butt, to be exact."

Morgan turned his head to Hunter.

"Are you sure?" Hunter asked.

The man laughed. "I ought to know my own name."

"Yes," Morgan said, "You should at that."

Hunter stepped forward. "I believe we have something that belongs to you, Major Butt."

"Yes," Morgan added, "And you'd do us a great favor if you would take it off of our hands."

The man was puzzled. Morgan could see that. His quick smile suddenly disappeared. "You have something for me?"

"Yes, we do," Hunter shot back.

Morgan looked up at the towering masseuse. "I think we should discuss it with you in private, though."

Butt looked up at Hercules, who was brutally kneading his left shoulder. "Fritz, could you excuse me? I think I've had enough for the day."

The giant nodded. Stooping over, he gathered several plush white towels and slowly made his way to and out the door.

Hunter and Morgan remained silent until they were sure they were alone.

Butt swung his legs around and fished for a pair of slippers with his bare feet. He sat forward on the couch. "All right, gentlemen, you have my complete attention."

Morgan and Hunter both looked around for chairs. Spotting two wicker ones of dubious comfort, they pulled them forward and sat down.

Morgan lowered his voice. "Have you been waiting for a certain delivery?"

"What if I have?" Butt mopped sweat from his bald pate.

"The messenger who was sent to bring you that item was stabbed in London on the day we sailed. I was there when it happened."

"Was his name Sinclair?" Hunter asked.

Butt chose to remain silent. He bounced glances between the two young men.

"George Sinclair?" Morgan added.

"What if it was?" Butt asked, determined not to reveal any information to these two characters. His jaw drooped in absolute seriousness.

"Mr. Sinclair had an attaché case intended for you or the War Department. That attaché case was stolen."

"But Morgan got it back," Hunter added quickly.

"And you have it here on the *Titanic?*" Butt asked, looking from one to the other.

"Yes," Morgan said. "We have it, and it would give us great pleasure if you would take it off of our hands."

"Actually, it's in the purser's safe under my name," Hunter said. "There have been several attempts to steal it."

"I shouldn't wonder," Butt said.

"All we need is the proper identification from you, and we'll be all too glad to put it in your hands."

"How do I know you're telling the truth about Sinclair?" Butt asked. "You might be giving me a phony package."

Morgan reached into the pocket of the coat draped over his shoulders. He pulled out the picture of Sinclair and Lilly and handed it over to Butt. "Is this the man?"

Butt took the picture and looked it over carefully. "Yes," he said, "That's George Sinclair, much younger, of course." He looked Morgan in the eye. "And you say he was stabbed?"

Morgan continued to hold out his hand. "I would like the picture back," he said. Morgan could see the look of curiosity in the man's eyes. "It's special to me."

"A souvenir?"

"No, I know the woman in the photograph."

"Uncanny." Butt handed back the picture.

"Yes, it is strange, almost as if God intended for me to come across the incident when I did." He gulped. He knew full well that nothing ever happened apart from God's providence, but such a concept was so hard to explain.

Morgan stuck the photograph back into his coat pocket. "Sinclair was stabbed. He was still alive when they took him to the hospital, but from what I was told, his chances didn't look too promising."

"I'm sorry to hear that. He was an honorable man."

"He did make me promise to get his satchel to you on the *Titanic* and, failing that, to the War Department."

"A man tried to kill us for that thing," Hunter said.

"Yes," Morgan added, "And he himself was murdered on the ship yesterday."

"Murdered? Here on the *Titanic*?"

"Yes," Morgan said. "I assume the doctor has the body."

"And whoever it was that killed the man is still after that case," Hunter added. "He doesn't seem to want to quit."

"I'd be very careful if I were you," Morgan said.

Butt got to his feet, pulled his robe tightly around him, and tied the sash. "I'll go to my room and change. Then I will get my identification for you to see, and you can take me to the satchel. Believe me, gentlemen, if what I think is in that case is actually there, you may have been instrumental in saving a great many lives, that and preserving the presidency."

Butt turned and hurriedly left the room.

Hunter whistled. "Aren't you glad we came down here?"

"That I am. I'll be so glad to finally be freed of that thing."

"All right, old man, we've little time to lose. Tonight will be cause for great celebration." Hunter lifted his arms and swung them around the room. "We can finally enjoy all of this without the cloak-and-dagger."

Morgan nodded.

"All right, I'll put you in that steam bath of yours and be off to meet with a lovely woman whose life I have made miserable."

They both walked through one of the arched doors, and Hunter pointed to a room with a heavy wooden door. Reaching for a red wheel on the wall, he turned it halfway. "That ought to do it, old man. You'll be steamed and pressed in no time and sweat what's left of that poison out of your system."

"It's not too hot, is it?"

"Not too hot, but hot enough." Hunter pointed to the dial encased in glass beside the wheel. It was slightly past the green area marked WARM, and barely into the yellow section marked HOT.

"You should give it about twenty minutes and then come out. I ought to be finished with Kitty by then, but if you should come to the pool and see us there, walk the other way." Hunter smiled.

"Do you have that cigarette case with you?" Morgan asked.

Hunter patted his jacket pocket. Of course I do, old man. I have everything. Do you have your cabin key?"

"Yes," Morgan said. "In my vest pocket."

"Fine, I'll keep my things with me beside the pool, and you'd better take yours into the steam room with you." Hunter looked around the empty Turkish bath area. "Things don't seem too secure at the moment."

Morgan changed into his bathing suit, picked up several thick terry cloth towels, and stepped into the hissing steam room. A brass tube ran along the four sides of the ceiling with steam pouring from its holes. Clouds descended like waterfalls from four sides of the small room and onto the tile floor. From the floor, Morgan could see that there was a second pipe running around the perimeter of the room. Geysers of steam were rising up, to meet the falling steam in midair. Morgan felt like a tropical orchid.

The white tile of the floor was slippery, and a runner made from rubber was the only thing that made it possible to negotiate the room without total collapse. He inched his way, barefoot, to the wooden platform that lay at the far end of the room. Spreading one of the towels over the bench, he lay down.

Morgan closed his eyes and breathed deeply, a sense of relief spreading over him. If this man Butt was in fact the one they were looking for, then life might return to normal. Of course, with Margaret aboard ship, he doubted that anything could ever be normal again.

As a man graduating from Oxford, it was expected that he take his place in society, and of course that meant in his uncle's financial world. That had been counted on. There was little room for what he wanted to do with his life, only what was expected of him. He could vividly remember the evening in Margaret's home when, in casual conversation at dinner, he expressed his desire to write. The look of Margaret's father, not at him, but at her mother, was enough to tell him all about their displeasure at the notion of having a writer as a son-in-law. It was one thing for him to be subjected to rejection, but there was no reason Margaret should have to endure that.

That was the night he had resolved to accept the job with the *Herald* and leave England when he had settled things with Uncle John and Aunt Dottie. He had reasoned that if he could prove himself in the publishing world, even with some small measure of success, the Hastingses might look upon him with favor. Even more important, he might look upon himself with favor.

He had done his best to avoid Margaret, thinking it the honorable thing to do to have something to offer her before he could presume to press their relationship further. He knew now that had been a mistake. He realized that his silence had communicated the wrong thing. She had seen his actions as nothing more than abandonment.

Morgan closed his eyes. The sound of the steam grew louder.

He thought, perhaps, that he'd spent far too much time with the happy endings of books. Life was just not that way. A man couldn't go off on his quest for the Holy Grail and return years later to find the chaste princess still waiting to be his bride. No love was strong enough to endure neglect.

Sweat began to pour off him in beaded rivulets. It trickled down his body forming a small pool on his belly. *This is hot,* he thought.

He opened his eyes and looked at the steam falling from the ceiling pipes. What had been a gentle waterfall of steam was now erupting into an open nozzle of pure heat. *Maybe this is good for me. Maybe it will drive all the poison out.*

He closed his eyes, taking in deep breaths. The sulfuric smell of the steam heat roared into his nostrils and down his lungs. He coughed. His skin was prickly *now*, the heat and the sulfur driving their way into his pores.

He wondered if there was any way he could undo the damage done to his friendship with Margaret. *It's too late now*, he thought. *A man can never be friends with someone else's wife*. The thought of that grieved him. Margaret had been more than a romantic interest to him, much more. She had been his best friend long before he realized he was in love with her. With other boys his age, there had always been the sense of competition, but never with Margaret. He loved her mind and applauded her politics whenever he got the chance. Rather than giving her less power in life, it had always been Morgan's desire to give her more.

Margaret, in turn, enjoyed his way with words on paper. She admired his sense of honor and even shared his spiritual values. She had never seen his Bible reading or even his prayers as something that was unmanly. On the contrary, it had only developed her trust of him and increased her admiration. She attended his track meets and watched him fence in competition, but it was his love for poetry and his deep devotion to God that she had always admired the most.

His eyes opened wide. The sound of the steam pouring into the room had grown to a gush of absolute volcanic proportions. It was hot, hotter than he could ever remember experiencing before. He would need a drink of water and fast. He thought about the red wheel Hunter had turned before he came in. Hunter turned it halfway. Perhaps it needed to be turned down some.

Throwing off his towel, he swung his leg off the bench and onto the floor. The steam was roaring, turning the entire room into a picture of what the inside of Vesuvius must have looked like to the people of Pompeii. Morgan could barely see his hand in front of his face.

The door had a small, thick, round window in it. Morgan wiped it with the back of his hand. He couldn't clear it. He pushed at the door. Something was wrong, very wrong. It was stuck. With both hands around the knob, he pushed harder. The thing didn't budge.

Balling his fists, he pounded at the door, again and again. The sound of his blows echoed down the narrow hall. Morgan held his ear to the door. There was nothing, not a sound.

He leaned back. With a vicious lunge, he sent his shoulder up against the heavy door. It held fast. "Mustn't panic," he muttered. He knew he couldn't lose control and start gulping the searing, wet air into his lungs.

Morgan could feel the heat rising. His head began to spin. Again, he pounded on the door. His blows were weaker this time. He could feel his legs turning wobbly, the strength draining out of him.

Once again, he sent his shoulder crashing into the door. Again and again, he reared back and continued to ram the door, blow after blow, until he became weaker and weaker with the effort.

He turned around. He tried to think if he'd seen a valve on the inside. Reaching up, he waved in the direction of what he thought was the corner of the room. There was nothing, only intense heat. He reached over and tried the other corner. Again, he felt nothing. His heart began to pound, harder and harder. He had to get out of there, and he had to get out now.

Slowly, he moved back to the door. It seemed futile to continue to fight. There seemed to be nothing left for him to do but die.

He hugged the warm wood of the door, pressing his face into the glass window out of pure exhaustion. He began a series of slaps on the surface of the door, beating a slow but steady cadence on the hard wood. It was now hard to stand. His heart was racing, beating rhythmic flutters against the ribs in his chest. He could feel his legs weakening. Then he saw a face in the window. Margaret. Maybe he was dreaming.

He could hear her muffled cries, "Morgan, Morgan, are you all right?"

His pounding on the door intensified, now with new hope. He could feel some pressure being applied on the other side. Leaning back, he sent a weak but solid blow to the door with his now bruised shoulder. Still, no give.

Then he remembered the platform, the wooden bench at the end of the room. He groped his way back to the other side of the room, feeling with his hands out as his knees and legs craved to buckle underneath him. He continued to move slowly, inching forward until he felt the bench rap against his shins. Bending down, he picked it up. It might be his only chance.

Clutching the bench to his chest, he wobbled his way through the searing heat to the door. He put the bench down and wiped the glass. Margaret's face was still there. *Is it a dream?* he wondered.

He held his face to the glass. Summoning up energy, he yelled. "Step back!"

Stooping over, he picked up the bench. Holding it over his head and thrusting with every last bit of strength he had, he sent it crashing into the small glass window. The glass shattered with a sound of pebbles rolling down a metal chute and leaving Morgan's frail body hugging the foot of the door.

Moments later, the door sprung open. Peter lifted him under his arms and dragged his limp body into the hallway.

"Morgan! Morgan! are you all right?"

Morgan coughed.

Suddenly a cascade of cool water dashed over the front of his face and head.

Margaret put the pitcher down and knelt by his side. She lifted his head and held it in her hands. "Go get the attendant!" she screamed.

Margaret stroked his head in her lap.

He felt faint and more than a little nauseated. Any other time he might have reveled in Margaret's caress and attention. All he could think of now was scrambling to sit upright so he wouldn't get sick on her lap. Unfortunately, when his head got as high as Margaret's shoulder he got dizzy and slumped back into her arms.

Peter burst in with the masseuse. Morgan blinked open his eyes and stared at the wheel beside the door to his steam room. The thing was turned all the way over to the right, and the dial was in the top of the red zone marked DANGER.

The men lifted him into one of the padded wicker chairs nearby. Margaret took a towel, dipped it into cold water in a bowl, and began to sponge him off. "Are you all right?" she asked.

"Better," he gasped.

Minutes later, Peter returned from the area of the steam room with the attendant at his side. He held up two broken stubs from something that looked like a walking stick. "These were wedged into your door and broken off."

"What? Who would do that?" he muttered drunkenly.

Peter studied the sticks, then looked over in Morgan's direction. Frowning, he replied, "Someone who seems to have it in for you."

"Should we get the doctor?" Margaret suggested.

"Yes!"

"No!" Morgan interrupted. "I'll be fine. Just a glass of water if you don't mind. I don't want the doctor to think I'm a child or, worse yet, cursed."

"Oh, Morgan, be reasonable," Margaret cooed.

"I'm fine," he insisted, gulping the glass of water Peter offered.

As his color returned to normal, Margaret backed away to Peter's side.

They took a few minutes to relax, Morgan downing glasses of water, each one seeming like it was either his first or would be his last.

"Where is Hunter?" Margaret asked.

"He's in the swimming pool," Morgan said. "We should ask him if he's seen anything."

Morgan bundled the dripping wet towels and dropped the lot of them into the towel bag, picking up a fresh one. They moved out from the arched doorway and down the narrow hall. Peter pushed open the door to the saltwater swimming pool, and they stepped inside. The light was brilliant in comparison to the dimly lit Turkish bath.

Hunter was floating in the middle of the pool.

"All right, you rascal," Morgan called out. "Enough is enough." He expected his jolly friend to spring up from his facedown position.

The three of them fanned out around the pool. Morgan called out again. "The joke is over sport, come out."

"He's not moving," Peter said with alarm.

Morgan dropped his towel and dove into the water. Reaching Hunter's side, he turned him over. His red hair lay in wild fingers across his brow. Morgan was shocked at his blue lips.

Morgan gasped, "Help him! We've, we've got to help him," as he pushed Hunter near Peter's outstretched arms at the side of the pool.

Peter grabbed Hunter's arm and hauled him onto the tile as Morgan hoisted himself out of the water.

"Quick," said Morgan, "We've got to clear his lungs! Turn him over!"

Peter leaned down and put his ear to Hunter's chest. Lifting his head, he looked Morgan in the eye. "He's dead, I'm afraid."

"No, you're wrong!" Morgan pushed Peter aside.

Peter grabbed Morgan's arm. "Yes, he is, I'm afraid."

Morgan heard a wail and vaguely wondered where it came from. Then he realized. It was him.

FRIDAY,
APRIL 12, 1912,
2:15 P.M.

CHAPTER 20

Boxhall wove his way through the chairs and up to the man Bonnie had pointed out. The man sat alone, leafing through an old paper. From the way he was turning the pages of the paper, it appeared to Boxhall that he wasn't reading it at all. He was just using it to try to stay out of sight.

"Excuse me sir. I'd like to ask you a few questions if I might."

The man put down the paper. "Who? Me?"

"Yes, sir, if you don't mind."

The man stuck out his thumb and rapped it on his chest, almost in a boast. "I paid for my passage."

"I'm certain you did, sir."

"I'm on my way to America, same as the rest." He nodded to the room full of people as if to make his point.

"Of course you are, sir."

"Then why the blazes are you pesterin' me?"

"The man just needs some answers," Kelly said.

Boxhall smiled at Kelly. He knew the man was trying to be helpful. "Might I have your name?"

"O'Conner, Howie O'Conner."

"May I see your passport, sir?" Boxhall held out his hand.

"What ya want that for? You ain't no customs officer."

"I need to establish your identification."

O'Conner fished in his coat pocket, finally producing the passport. He handed it to Boxhall.

"You got on in Queenstown, didn't you?" Kelly asked, looking over the passport.

"Sure I did." He waved his hand toward the crowded room. "I got on there, same as most of the people in here." He leaned over in Boxhall's direction. "I ain't seen you askin' them no questions."

Boxhall handed back the passport. "We will, sir."

"Do you remember a Henry Killebrew?" Boxhall queried.

"Nah," the man shook his head, "Should I?"

Boxhall looked back in the direction of the young woman. "According to that young lady over there, you may have been the last person to see him."

"Maybe he fell overboard," O'Conner snickered.

"No, sir, he didn't."

"Them decks can be mighty slippery. I'd think you'd want to watch 'em more careful like. A man starts to drinking and first thing you know, he puts his foot down where it don't belong none."

O'Conner was smarter than that, and Boxhall knew it. Sometimes the Irish were so used to being treated like ignoramuses that they fell into the act just to please the English. "I can assure you, he didn't fall overboard."

"Well, I don't know nothin' about no Henry Killebrew, never met the man, wouldn't know him if he walked up and kicked me in the shins."

"I'm afraid there's not much chance of that."

Kelly shot Boxhall a look and studied him. Apparently there was more to this story than he'd been told.

"Well, I don't know him. He ain't no relative or friend of mine."

"The young woman says he followed you out of the dining room yesterday after lunch."

O'Conner grinned. "There ain't a single man in this room that don't know that lass. She's liable to tell you anything. She's had so many men in that face of hers that I rather doubt she could tell one from the other."

"She knew your face right away," Kelly said.

The remark brought a glare from O'Conner.

"Where did you go after lunch yesterday?" Boxhall asked.

"Where I always go. I went to take a nap, but I weren't follered by nobody." O'Conner swung his head around. "You know this seagoing trip can make a man plenty sleepy, especially after a meal."

"It makes a lot of folks sick," Kelly responded.

"Well, not me." He patted his stomach. "I'm strong as a horse."

Boxhall stroked his chin. There was something about the man that he didn't like. He seemed too coy and a little defensive.

2:40 P.M.

It took a short time for the group of officers to gather at the pool. Smith made sure that one of the yeomen secured the area from casual onlookers. Smith paced back and forth as Dr. McCoy carefully examined the body. He passed Murdoch, practically barking out the words, "We should have turned back for Queenstown."

" A simple drowning, sir," Murdoch replied.

Morgan sat on the side of the pool. His legs were crossed, and for a while his head was buried in his hands. He hadn't known Hunter Kennedy for very long, and any outsider looking in would have found them quite improbable as friends go. Morgan's friends from the past would have found them an impossible match. Hunter was everything Morgan found boorish and reproachable. Still, Morgan loved the man. He had a zest for living that had an unexplained appeal to it.

McCoy lifted his head. "This is no drowning," he snapped.

Every head came up, including Morgan's. Ismay stepped over to the doctor along with Morgan. "Are you quite certain of that doctor?" Ismay asked. Ismay was dressed in a proper dark three-piece suit. It matched his black, waxed mustache perfectly. To Morgan the man was the consumate industrialist. There didn't seem to be an ounce of care outside the ledgers that he maintained a responsibility for.

McCoy turned Hunter's head to the side. "Do you see this?"

The men bent down to get a better look. Behind Hunter's left ear was an open wound. The hair was wet and matted, but beneath it was a red open gash.

"I'd say a blow to the head," McCoy offered.

"Or an accident," countered Ismay confidently. "He may have been careless, slipped, hit his head as he fell."

The men stood up. "Should I prepare a course change?" Murdoch asked. Murdoch was the ideal build for a blue suit with officer stripes. His erect figure and broad shoulders, which he always carried squared away, struck a pose of authority. Morgan could see him as the perfect man to do the perfect thing, so long as it pleased his superiors.

"Where is Boxhall?" Smith barked.

"I believe he's in the steerage area, carrying on some investigating," Murdoch replied.

Smith grunted. "On our *last* murder."

Morgan could see that Smith's mind was whirling. It was bad enough to be saddled with the responsibility of the greatest liner in the world without having the task added to with a series of unsolved crimes.

Murdoch nodded.

"There have been others?" Morgan asked.

The men were silent. Each looked at the other for some signal on how to respond, but none gave one.

"Surely we're as close to New York as we are to Queenstown?" Ismay pleaded. Morgan could tell the man was feeling panicky. He could just imagine Ismay melting on the spot at the notion of limping back to Queenstown with his tail between his legs. Ismay pointed down at Hunter's body. "How do we know he didn't just slip and hit his head?"

"Does the White Star Line want to accept that responsibility?" Murdoch asked. It was a casual question, but by the look on Murdoch's face, it was one he wished he hadn't said as soon as the words were spoken.

The notion caught Ismay by surprise, but Morgan could see that it registered. He frowned, and his eyes squinted at Murdoch. There was a hardness to the look, like a hammer bearing down on an anvil.

"I'm not about to accept any responsibility whatsoever. I merely suggest this man slipping and falling as a possibility. I see no need to read any great conspiracy into this."

"What about it, doctor?" Smith asked. "Is that a possibility?"

McCoy looked up. "I wouldn't rule anything out. He may have even drowned, but he sustained this wound first."

"Who would want to kill this man?" Ismay asked.

Morgan shot him a hard look. He knew full well that perhaps the one with the greatest motive for seeing Hunter Kennedy dead was Bruce Ismay himself. Ismay caught the look from Morgan, and perhaps his own conscience caused him to drop his gaze to the floor.

"That is for a police investigation to decide," Smith shot back.

"Of course," Ismay replied. He looked up. "We can't be having a cops-and-robbers game on this ship. It would create too many questions and too much in the way of bad, very bad, publicity."

"I'm not certain we can protect our passengers if there is a homicidal maniac aboard," Murdoch said.

Morgan got to his feet and wrapped the towel tightly around him. "You didn't answer my question. Have there been other murders?"

Smith looked at him and stepped in Morgan's direction. "You are fully aware of the man we found in the first-class cabin area yesterday." He shook his head. "I'm sorry I wasn't thinking well enough to keep you out of it. You shouldn't have seen that."

"Besides that, are there more?"

Ismay, Murdoch, and McCoy froze. Anything more that was to be said, had to come from the mouth of Captain E. J. Smith, and they all knew it.

"Yes," Smith said, "We had a third-class passenger's body discovered in the hold earlier today. There is no reason to see these as connected, however."

"Would you like me to lay out a change of course, Captain?" Murdoch repeated the question.

Ismay burst into hysterics. "Now see here." He flung his arms up. "If you were to turn this vessel about, we would be held up in Queenstown for days. The *Titanic* would be a marked ship in the newspapers and, more important, in people's minds. How many passengers do you think we'd have for the voyage once we got under way again? This thing would be a ghost ship, and we'd have to return passage to everyone. White Star Line might never recover." Ismay glared at Murdoch. "And that would put you out of a job."

Ismay gazed over the pool area. It was something he was understandably proud of. It was one of a kind. "I dare say, we might never get passengers aboard this vessel ever again. The name *Titanic* would be spoken of by every soul fearful of a sea voyage."

He paused and placed his hands on the lapels of his coat, striking a pose that spoke of authority. "No, you men may sail this ship the way you like. You are the ship's officers. But this is a White Star decision, and I simply won't allow it."

Morgan could tell that Ismay's diatribe had caught both Smith and Murdoch off guard. It was like the ground itself had been swept out from under them. Smith blinked, his cold, blue eyes opening and closing like the lamps on an opera house.

"You are willing to accept this responsibility?" Smith asked.

"I most certainly am," Ismay growled.

White Star Line had started with Ismay's father, and Morgan could almost see the man trying to explain his actions to the dead. To have the entire line go down on his watch was a thought almost too horrible to consider.

"These things are best investigated right away," Murdoch offered.

Morgan stepped forward. "I'd like to volunteer for that role," he said. "I am a reporter."

"Nonsense," Smith blustered.

Morgan knew that at first thought such a suggestion would seem ludicrous. And to make matters worse, he was standing before the man in nothing more than a bathing suit and a towel, not exactly the most imposing of dress.

"I'm afraid this may go deeper than you suspect, Captain," Morgan said. "It may involve a matter of American interest and national defense." In spite of the White Star Line being British, it was in fact owned by his great-uncle J. P. Morgan. The old man had been allowed to purchase it on the condition that it would be available for troop transport should war come to Great Britain. In every other way, however, it was Yankee through and through. It had even been flying the American flag since leaving Queenstown.

"What do you mean?" Ismay asked.

"The man found in the first-class area was a man who had been following me since Southampton. I had something belonging to the American War Department. He evidently wanted it."

"And what was that?" Smith asked.

"I'm afraid I am not at liberty to say." Defiance was something Morgan had had very little practice with. He had summoned every ounce of bravado at his possession to even say what he had said. Hunter's death had done that to him. If his dying was in any way connected with the other murders, Morgan wanted to know about it.

"The man already knows about the first murder," Murdoch said.

Morgan could see that Smith was thinking the matter over.

"I can be very discreet, sir. You wouldn't even know there was an investigation taking place."

He paused before dropping the final bombshell. It was something he had never done before, not in all of his years. However, if he was to play his trump card, now would be the time. "I should mention, sir, that my great-uncle is J. Pierpont Morgan. He will want a full report from me in any event, and I should want to tell him that I've had your complete cooperation." Morgan turned his head to Ismay and Murdoch. "In fact, the cooperation of the entire ship's company."

Morgan could see that his family ties were begining to click in the men's heads. Surely they knew it. They had no doubt been informed about the matter. The idea of having to remind them made him slightly queasy, but if his connections were ever going to be good for anything in this life, he wanted them to be good for this.

"And you say you are a reporter?" Ismay asked. The idea of Morgan's relations with the man who held Ismay's fate in his hands was beginning to have its effect, and Morgan could see it by the change in the man's disposition.

"Yes, I work for the New York *Herald*." Morgan knew that although everything he said was technically true, he hadn't spent his first day in their offices and had never so much as collected a paycheck. Hunter would have loved the deception.

"Perhaps this young man should work on an investigation," Ismay said. "Your own officers have their hands full, and I'm certain he can be of assistance. A reporter's mind is trained for such things."

Morgan could tell that although the captain had said nothing, there was great doubt in his mind. Being his last voyage, by all reports, he had far less to lose by not collaborating than Ismay. He raised his eyebrows. "This must be kept absolutely confidential. If any of the passengers are questioned, one of my officers must do the questioning."

"Perhaps Boxhall," Murdoch interjected. "He's already doing just that."

"Yes, Mr. Boxhall," Smith replied.

"I do need the freedom to interview all of the crew," Morgan said.

"And you shall have it," Ismay burst in. He slipped his arm around Morgan and pulled him closer. "You shall have anything you need, my boy."

Morgan knew full well that Ismay's newfound joy was just another nail in the coffin to the idea of returning to Ireland. The man looked at Smith and smiled. "That ought to satisfy you, Captain. We have our own man on the case. He and Boxhall can have a preliminary report ready for the police in New York."

"And what of your friends over there?" Smith asked the question, motioning over to the far side of the pool where Peter was still comforting Margaret.

"I'll talk to them," Morgan said. "You may be assured of their discretion."

"Fine," Smith replied, "I'll leave it to you then, young man. Dr. McCoy, you can have your men transport the body on a stretcher. I'll have the companionways cleared all the way to the infirmary."

McCoy nodded. They watched as Smith walked off, followed by Ismay and Murdoch.

When the men had cleared the pool area, Morgan turned to Dr. McCoy. "There is something I'd like to ask you," he said. "Perhaps it has nothing to do with this."

"What is it?"

"Did you ever talk to a Donald Delaney about what happened to me last night?"

McCoy put his hand to his chin, thinking the matter over. "I'm sorry," he said, "I can't recall speaking to a Delaney."

4:00 P.M.

The breeze on deck was turning brisk, although Morgan, Margaret, and Peter knew it was no doubt only the movement of the ship and not a breeze at all. The sky had seemed so cold and empty, a blue with no life to it. They had spent the last hour discussing the events of the day and Hunter's death. Margaret, however, wasn't convinced the matter was murder.

"Why should someone want to kill Hunter?" she asked. "He is . . . he was so charming."

"Frankly, Margaret, I only knew Hunter for a little over two days, but the list of people who wanted him dead was growing longer by the day," Morgan replied.

Peter fished in his pocket and pulled out the two stubs of walking stick he had found wedged in the door of Morgan's steam room. "I would say these ought to settle that question," he said. "Whoever killed Hunter wanted to make it a package arrangement." He looked at Morgan. "Whoever it was wanted you out of the way so he could have his way with Hunter."

"And what makes you think it was a he?" Margaret said. "Don't you think women are equally capable of murder?"

"Rather implausible, I should think," Peter replied.

"Maybe not," Morgan said. He thought the matter over. There was at least one woman who preferred Hunter in a lifeless condition, and it happened to be the person he was supposed to meet in the pool. He knew he would have to question Kitty Webb first thing. "And did you ask the attendant if he saw anyone in the pool or Turkish bath area?" he asked Peter.

"The man said that a father and two small children had been playing in the pool after lunch. After that, he went to take a late lunch himself."

The three of them had been strolling the deck. They had stopped to watch the Hoffman children play shuffleboard with their father. "You don't think...?" Margaret began to ask.

"I think we should ask," Morgan answered.

"We know them," Peter said.

They continued their walk over to where the children were playing. "Good afternoon," Peter said. "Lovely day isn't it?"

Peter and Margaret had dealings with the man, and Morgan was content in allowing them to ask the questions. Anything coming from him might seem odd.

"Yes, it is," Hoffman smiled. "A bit chilly, though."

"The children don't seem to mind," Margaret said.

Hoffman brushed his mustache with the back of his hand. "No, children are always the first to know the weather and the last to care."

"Have you taken them to the gymnasium?" Margaret asked.

"Not yet. We were going to do that tomorrow."

"What about the swimming pool?"

"Or the Turkish bath?" Peter added.

"We were there today, after lunch."

"Was it crowded?" Peter ventured.

Hoffman shrugged. "Just a couple of people. The place was pretty empty." He smiled. "I think people are prone to nap after lunch."

"And don't the children take naps?" Margaret asked. Morgan could tell that the man with the children, without a mother in sight, bothered Margaret. For all her bluster about the equality of women and their need to be in the workplace, there was still this notion of children having a mother and Morgan knew it. He rather liked that about her. It spoke of femininity.

"Oh, yes. We've just been having such a grand time, though, that I let them go until they are ready to drop. They sleep well at night then."

"Whom did you see?" Peter asked. "Anyone we might know?"

Morgan could tell the question bothered Hoffman. Peter was trying to be subtle, but his usual candor made this uncomfortable and stilted. Peter had asked the question with a smile on his lips, but his silence after asking it indicated that it was an important question.

"Why do you ask?" Hoffman queried, suspiciously.

"Oh, no reason," Margaret replied. "We were just interested in seeing if this couple we knew were hitting it off. You know how romantic we women are."

Now they were in for it, and Morgan knew it. To have Peter ask a question and Margaret give an explanation indicated some deeper interest and perhaps a collaboration among the three of them. Morgan could tell that Hoffman sensed it, too. A coolness came over him. It was like he was being backed into a corner.

"I saw a very attractive young woman and an older man."

There were no names attached to Hoffman's answer even though Morgan suspected the man might have known them. He wanted to ask if the two people were together but didn't dare.

"Were they together?" Margaret asked.

Morgan's heart melted.

"See here," Hoffman answered, "Why am I being asked all these questions?"

Margaret smiled sweetly. "Forgive me. I suppose I'm just an inquisitive woman, a romantic at heart. You know how we are. We always want to know about the comings and goings of young love."

Margaret never ceased to amaze Morgan. She knew how to use her feminine wiles when it best suited her.

"Women are curious," Hoffman declared. "Too curious, at times."

FRIDAY,
APRIL 12, 1912,
4:45 P.M.

CHAPTER 21

The three of them stood on deck and watched Hoffman hurry his children away. It was plain to see they had learned little from the man, except that he might be able to identify the killer. Of course, getting him into a position to do so without telling him why would be a matter of tricky maneuvering. They would have to know much more before they could attempt to do that.

Peter turned toward them, leaning against the rail. "Now, let's see. How should we proceed?"

"We will have to involve Boxhall," Morgan said, "especially if it means interviewing any of the ship's company."

Peter nodded.

Morgan gave directions. "I think you should question Fitzgerald, Peter. He may have seen something. Then you should get to know Delaney. In fact, we should question almost everyone who sits at our table."

"Please," Margaret said, "not that Colonel Gracie. I don't think I could stand that. Someone would have to come and rescue me from the longest and most boring history lesson imaginable."

Morgan and Peter both laughed.

"No, I think you should find a way to discover Kitty Webb's whereabouts at 2:00 this afternoon."

Margaret looked at Peter and then at Morgan. "Maybe that would best be done by one of you men. She seems to prefer the company of the masculine set."

"You seem to have a knack for this, Maggie." Morgan called her by the name he used to use for her as a boy. It sent a shock to her face and then a smile. "I saw how you handled Hoffman. We were in a tricky spot until you talked about romance."

"Yes," Peter agreed, "very cagey indeed."

"I still couldn't get out of him what I wanted."

"That will come in time," Morgan said. "In any event, she knows Hunter and I were friends and she has no reason to talk to Peter here."

"Except that he's a man," Margaret added.

Peter brushed his black mustache aside.

"I have it." Margaret's eyes lit up. "She spends time every day in the hair salon, primping herself for her evening appearance. What if I go down and make an appointment for the same time with my mother. She would have no reason to suspect us, and there's something about hot irons in a woman's hair that seems to loosen her tongue."

"Capital idea," Peter said.

"I'll talk to Guggenheim's valet."

"A scary fellow, that one," Peter added.

"Yes, and you should have seen the way he looked at Hunter when he had to pay him some of Guggenheim's money the man had lost gambling. I don't think it was a simple matter of paying a debt."

Morgan looked up and saw Archie Butt heading in their direction. He waved Butt toward the group.

"Good afternoon," Butt said.

"Major, I'd like you to meet two very good friends of mine, Miss Margaret Hastings and her fiancé, Peter Wilksbury." There had been a stab of pain as Morgan introduced Peter as Margaret's intended. He thought he caught Margaret's eye to boot and knew she was trying to read his mind.

"Archibald Butt," the man said, extending his hand to Peter. "And where is your friend Mr. Kennedy?"

The group looked at each other, indecision written all over their faces. Morgan knew, however, that if anyone should know what had happened, it ought to be the major.

"I'm afraid Hunter is dead," Morgan said.

The look of surprise on Butt's face was immediate. "How did it happen? You don't suppose…?"

"I'll tell you later, and as to the reason, that's what we'd all like to know."

"I trust it has nothing to do with our business," Butt said.

"I hope not," Morgan replied. "The matter we need to look into is a matter that was my own doing, and if Hunter's death had anything to do with that, I would find it hard to sleep."

"You can't blame yourself, dear boy." Butt put a hand on Morgan's arm. "The fault belongs to the perpetrator alone." Butt stuck his hand into his coat pocket and pulled out a leather-wrapped passport. "You asked to see my identification." He pulled out another equally official document. "This is my White House pass. I am President Taft's military adviser."

Morgan looked them over. "Impressive," he said, handing them back.

"There is work to be done even there," Butt responded.

"Well, I suppose we should go down to the purser's office and see to that item in question."

Morgan could see Margaret and Peter exchanging glances. He had said nothing about the satchel to them. He had no desire to involve them needlessly or put them at risk. It seemed that everyone except Morgan who had come into contact with that satchel and its dangerous contents had met an untimely end.

Morgan bowed slightly to Margaret. "We will see you both at dinner, I suppose."

"Yes," Peter said, "at dinner."

Both Morgan and Butt made their way inside and up the grand staircase. They moved out the side door and onto the deck from there. Soon they were at the door that led to the purser's office, directly behind the bridge. It was a safe place for valuables to be kept as a lot of traffic passed there and many of the people were the ship's crew and officers. People could easily have access to jewelry and carry their valuables back to the first-class area without any chance of running into passengers from the second- or third-class areas.

They stepped in the door. Seated behind the desk was the purser, Herbert McElroy. "Mr. McElroy," Morgan said, "I believe you have something that belongs to me."

"Oh, do I?"

"Yes, my friend Hunter Kennedy put a satchel in your safekeeping last night."

"Then Mr. Kennedy will have to come to claim it."

"That will be impossible. It does belong to me." Morgan looked at Butt. "Actually, to this gentleman now."

McElroy opened a ledger book and ran his finger down a list of names with items that had been checked belonging to each one. He came to Hunter's name and pointed. "Here we have it, a satchel and its contents. It was checked in by your Mr. Kennedy late last night."

"That would be it. May we have it please?"

McElroy lifted his head. "I am afraid that will be impossible."

"Impossible? What do you mean?"

"My orders are strict. No one is to have access to things checked into the purser except the person who checks the item in and others he may designate." He turned the ledger around so that Morgan and Butt could get a good look. "You can see here that there is no one else listed, neither you nor this gentleman."

Morgan took a deep breath.

McElroy closed the book with a bang. "I am afraid there are no exceptions to my orders, not for any reason."

"Mr. Kennedy is dead," Morgan said.

McElroy's eyes bulged out with Morgan's news. Such a thought was shocking. He fumbled with the last page of the entries. "Captain Smith made a deposit in Mr. Kennedy's name this afternoon. It reads, 'personal effects.' I assume he wants it held for the authorities."

"So you see, he can't claim this satchel of mine. He checked it in for me last night because I was in the infirmary. You can corroborate that with Dr. McCoy's records."

McElroy stroked his chin. "And if I look inside this satchel, will I find something in it that can identify you as the rightful owner?"

Morgan and Butt both looked at each other. There was no way anyone could be allowed inside that satchel, and Morgan knew it. Even if the man could look, there was nothing in Morgan's name in the thing, nothing at all.

"I'm afraid not," Morgan said. "You'd just have to take my word as a gentleman."

"I'm afraid, sir, that I cannot do that. You may be a gentleman, but my orders are firm on this matter. If your Mr. Kennedy cannot claim his satchel, it will be turned over to the authorities in New York when we dock. That is all I can do."

Butt put both hands up and motioned to Morgan with an air of acquiescence. Morgan could see that this man was used to bureaucracy. Not only did he have to fight city hall for a living, he was city hall.

"That's all right. Perhaps this is best. If it's as safe in here as Mr. McElroy says it is, then I'm certain the matter can be resolved when we dock."

"It is that," McElroy said. "Until I see Mr. Kennedy walk into my office and have him sign my ledger, that item will not leave my safe."

"Right now, I'd say that was very safe," Butt said.

Morgan nodded.

9:00 P.M.

Dinner was not going to be the same without Hunter, and Morgan knew it. Hunter was a man that irritated so many people who knew him and immensely entertained all the rest. Some people were like that. They couldn't stand neutrality. Love them or hate them as you wished, but ignore them, never. They seemed to cry out for attention wherever they went, leaving a trail of hostility and delight in their wake. Morgan knew he might be able to explain Hunter's absence by a sudden attack of the flu but wondered just how long he'd be able to keep up the deception. Hunter would be sorely missed.

He'd asked Butt to come and take Hunter's place at the table but to make his arrival time late. In spite of the attempt by Ismay to hint that Hunter may have slipped and fallen, Morgan knew better. The man was too spry for a simple fall. Morgan wanted to watch people's reactions at the table very carefully. Only the killer would know that Hunter wasn't sick. Only the killer wouldn't be expecting him.

He took his seat on the end of the table, one seat over from Delaney's place at the end of the long side. The table was already dabbling with their shrimp cocktails, and Gracie was making his first pass with trying to interest Gloria. Guggenheim nodded at him with a smile, and Kitty did the same.

Delaney leaned over toward Morgan. "Where is our Irish friend?" he asked.

"He's not feeling well." Morgan watched the man's eyes. Donald Delaney was already an accomplished liar. Of that Morgan was certain. The man wrote fiction which was often called telling the truth in the form of lies. He also had made it a lifelong habit of fooling the British. One way or another, whether it meant taking their money or taking their lives, Donald Delaney was a very accomplished liar.

"I'm sorry to hear that," Delaney said. "I hope it's nothing serious. We shall miss the old boy."

Morgan's mind raced. From what he'd been able to discover, the IRA would like nothing better than to get their hands on the contents of that satchel. Anything that could involve England in a major European war would be looked upon as good news by the Irish freedom fighters. Had Delaney thought Hunter to be in possession of the satchel? Was he the one who had drugged him in hopes of taking it?

"Just a touch of the flu, I think," Morgan lied. "He might be down for a couple of days, though."

"That's too bad. Maybe I should drop by and try to entertain him."

Surely the murderer won't try to press the issue, Morgan thought. *Then again, Delaney is the crafty sort.* Morgan shook his head. "I wouldn't advise that. The doctor says this thing can be quite contagious, and it seems to affect the oldest people in the worst sort of way. It can be deadly, from what I hear."

Morgan threw the remark in about age more out of spite than anything. Delaney was a man obviously in his late fifties.

"Is that a challenge, or more a way for a young man to gloat to those of us who have lived longer?" Delaney laughed.

"I'm sorry," Morgan lied. "I meant nothing by it."

He picked up a large shrimp, dipped it into the smooth, red cocktail sauce, and bit the end off. To Morgan, shrimp could be largely tasteless. They tended to take on the flavor of whatever they were cooked, broiled, or dipped in. He was glad the sauce had a bit of zip to it. He leaned over to Kitty. "Did you enjoy your swim today?"

The question caught Kitty off guard. "I didn't go for a swim today," she replied.

Guggenheim was being kept busy with April, Margaret's mother, who was seated to his left, or Morgan never would have asked the question.

"Oh, I'm sorry. I thought you were going to meet with Hunter."

"I guess I lost track of the time."

Morgan speared another shrimp. "That can happen."

"I hope he's not too upset," Kitty said.

"Oh, no, I don't think he's upset at all."

"That's good." Kitty stirred her dinner salad, "He used to be a good friend of mine."

"So I understand," Morgan smiled.

9:10 P.M.

The common room in steerage was echoing with the sound of music. A fiddle player drew his bow across a rather shabby but sweet-sounding violin. His gray beard was nothing more than a whisk of hair that came straight down from his chin and curled in gray ringlets over the body of the violin. His eyes sparkled as he pulled back on the bow and then burst out into a bright, cheerful melody.

Kelly watched as people danced in the middle of the room. The tune was a jig, and they clapped their hands and stomped their feet, swinging through a line of partners and smiling. Nights like this were always something to smile about. These people all had the best of their lives ahead of them, and the smile on each face showed it. All, that is, except the man O'Conner. Kelly had been keeping an eye on the man. He wasn't dancing. Instead, he stood to the side nearest the door and just watched other people having fun.

To Kelly that seemed odd indeed. O'Conner was a young man, and young men should be enjoying themselves. The man had even made a point of the fact that the young, attractive woman named Bonnie was of no interest to him. A young single man with no inquisitiveness about the fairer sex or music and without much of a smile that had ever crossed his face, to Kelly's recollection, just made no sense at all. It was like the man was working, and traveling on the *Titanic* wasn't work. It should be play. There was also something sinister about the man, something Kelly didn't like.

Kelly watched as O'Conner sat soulfully on the edge of a table. A group of men were gambling at the other end of the table, and several times they had tried to coax O'Conner into joining them, but each time he had refused. *The man won't gamble, won't dance, won't smile, and won't have anything to do with women,* Kelly thought. *What does he do?*

It was nearing the time when the third-class passengers were expected to be in bed. 10:00 was supposed to be the sleeping time for steerage class. Of course, they could all still hear music coming from the first-class area of the ship long after that. It was something that tended to grate on the minds of those among the list of steerage passengers who were purveyors of a good time, the gamblers and the dancers. Of course, it was explained that with all the women and children and the relatively small space in which they had to live, allowing people to stay up till all hours would be a disturbance. Kelly could tell, though, that the explanation was lost on the "good timers" among them. The place was usually full between 7:00 and 10:00. No one wanted to miss the music while it was allowed. No one, it seemed, but O'Conner.

He watched as O'Conner got up and, with one last look at the room, slipped through the door. Most men who left early did so with a woman on their arm or a cigar clenched between their teeth, but Kelly could see that had not been the case with the strange Irishman. His grandchildren were already tucked into bed, and hopefully they were asleep. Kelly decided he would follow the man.

He walked across the crowded room, circling the dancers to give them a wide berth. If a man on the floor wasn't dancing, he was just as likely to be knocked about. Opening the door, he peered out to the landing and the aft well deck below. He could see O'Conner making his way to the door that led to the series of passages that would take him to the single men's cabins in the bow of the ship.

Kelly waited and stepped back into the great room momentarily. O'Conner had opened the far door and was taking one last look. It was almost as if he wanted to make certain he wasn't being followed.

When Kelly looked back, he could see the man had gone inside and closed the door behind him. Kelly hurried down the steps and made his way quickly across the open deck. Several young lovers stood at the rail looking out into the open sea. It was enough to make any man feel suddenly lonely.

The narrow passage emptied into the dining salon, which was now empty and set for breakfast. Kelly wove his way around the tables and pulled out his pipe and bag of tobacco. The third-class smoking room and bar was on the other side of the dining room. If O'Conner had stopped in there for a drink, he wanted to make sure that the man saw that he wanted a smoke. There was no need to create the notion in the man's mind that he was being watched, especially by Jack Kelly.

The smoking room was spartan by first-class standards, with wooden seats that formed long benches with armrests built into them. They looked like back-to-back park benches in some London square. Around them were scattered a number of chairs, which appeared to be the leavings of what was left from the dining room furniture.

A number of men were seated on the bench, smoking various forms of tobacco products. Kelly preferred a pipe. He found it cheaper than cigars and more satisfying than a cigarette. He also liked the look it gave him. Men tended to listen to a man with a pipe in his mouth. The briar stem carried a hint of wisdom with it, and his was a Petersen, from a well-known Irish pipe maker. His amber root had seen many a night's service out on the sea. It warmed him when little else would.

He stopped past the first set of chairs and surveyed the room. Groups of men were everywhere, but O'Conner was nowhere to be found. That didn't surprise Kelly in the least. The man seemed unsociable. There was no reason to see him smoking and talking with other men.

Pulling the pipe from his mouth, Kelly dropped it back into his pocket and hurried into the bar. The place wasn't full, but there was plenty of drinking going on. The Irish were famous for their fine brewing, and from the looks of the bar, it was being taken advantage of. Irish grown and roasted barley was the key ingredient to their famous Guinness stout. It was a rich, chocolate-looking brew topped with a thick, creamy head. The average Irishman called it "the dark stuff" or used the phrase that brought many a smile, "the blonde in the black skirt."

The smooth-faced bartender was pulling many a pint for the men gathered at the bar, tilting the glass at a precise angle and then patiently topping it off. Kelly looked the place over, figuring that any man at this hour that left the music of the common room would be headed here. He was wrong. O'Conner was not to be found.

There was only one more place, and Kelly headed down the hall that would take him through several common areas with second-class and down through the bowels of the ship to the single men's sleeping area. His mind raced. For any man who knew Jack Kelly, there would be a question. He had grandchildren and had no business in the bow sleeping quarters. His place was in the family sleeping area in the stern.

He hurried. O'Conner had no cause to take his time, and Kelly was determined to see just exactly where the man slept. If he could do that, he might even be able to come back when O'Conner was aft and explore the man's things. There had to be something that would tell him what this silent man was all about.

It was a short time later when he stepped into the companionway that led to the men's rooms. It was empty, with several halls that led to storage areas of the ship. Kelly's heart sank. If the man had already turned in, he might never discover the room he was using. He slowed his pace and walked carefully.

Suddenly one of the doors opened at the far end of the hall. Kelly quickly darted into a hallway and waited. Pushing his head back out, he could see O'Conner with a bag in his hand, closing the door. He slipped back into cover in the hall. Looking around, he could see no escape. If O'Conner came back down the hall and happened to look in his direction, he would be there, all too apparent for the man to see. Kelly's mind raced. He had to find a story to tell the man.

He waited for a short time, but much to his surprise, O'Conner didn't appear. *What happened to the man?* Kelly wondered. Pushing his head back out slowly, he could see the hallway was empty. That puzzled him. There was no place else to go.

He stepped lively down the hall in the direction of O'Conner's door. Then he saw the stairs that led down to the cargo area and the boiler rooms. *Why would he go down there?* Kelly wondered.

Taking the stairs, he curved around the spiral steps to the area on the deck below. Several signs read NO PASSENGERS ALLOWED.

Getting to the bottom, he peeked around the corner. He could see O'Conner in the distance, in the area of the ship to the bow side of the bulkhead that led to the boiler rooms. The man was climbing through a watertight door. Kelly watched.

He swiveled his head around. There was a tool closet at the base of the stairs. Reaching over to it, Kelly opened the door. Axes and wrenches hung in neat order, and a small space at the front held a mop, bucket, and push broom. That would be the place to hide. Kelly left the door open and stuck his head back down the hall to see if O'Conner would emerge.

Moments later, he spotted the man shinning back out of the compartment. He was now empty-handed. Kelly walked lightly over to the closet and, stepping in, closed the door. A short time later he heard the sound of footsteps outside the closet door. The man stopped on the landing, almost as if he was remembering something or, worse still, suspected another presence. Kelly held his breath.

He moved on, and Kelly heard the man's feet on the stairs. Going out onto the catwalk bothered him. What if O'Conner had indeed forgotten something and any minute would be back this way? Still, he couldn't leave now. He had to see what the man had carried up that compartment door.

He opened the closet carefully and moved out onto the catwalk. He reasoned that if O'Conner did appear once again, from where he was he could make a dash for the boiler rooms. He didn't belong there, but at least stokers would be working there.

Walking down the catwalk, he came to the door O'Conner had used. He bent down and looked inside. There was nothing but total blackness. He climbed inside. Inching his way up the side of the hull, he came to some stairs. He climbed up, feeling his way as he went.

Coming to a section of the ship where the two compartments met, he could feel a hatch above him. He ran his hands along the top of the compartment and stopped. His hands touched something, and his imagination ran wild. It had the feel of dynamite, sticks bound together by tape.

It had been bolted and screwed into the steel of the compartment wall and covered by a smooth coat of grease. A man with a light might have missed it, but not one finding his way around by the tips of his fingers.

Kelly wiped his hand on the leg of his pants and slowly began to back down the stairs. Moments later, he was at the bottom. Then he heard something that made him freeze—a man's footsteps.

FRIDAY,
APRIL 12, 1912,
9:30 P.M.

CHAPTER 22

The sight of Archie Butt at the table in Hunter's place created quite a stir. Morgan could see that. He had handled the questions well, but he couldn't tell which was worse, the sight of Hunter's empty seat or another person at the table in his place. He finally concluded that it was best that Butt was there. Decorum prevented people from asking too many questions about Hunter's absence. After all, how polite was it to drone on about a man being gone in front of someone taking his place?

Guggenheim hadn't asked many questions about Hunter's not being with them. Morgan couldn't decide if it was because the man already knew of Hunter's fate or if the man's status in life, and the fact he was used to having all the answers, prevented him from asking such a question.

Delaney kept Butt in good company. He obviously relished the fact that the man was an assistant to the president of the United States. That fact alone made sure that he was filling Butt with great description about the Irish cause and the injustice he could see being dealt by the British government. Morgan watched the passion on Delaney's face.

The band struck up a chord of music, and the director of the band turned around to face the audience. Morgan noticed that Delaney stopped his diatribe the moment the room was at a hush. He thought that was a rather fortunate thing, since by then his voice would have been the only one being heard. With the pause, Butt motioned toward the band area, catching Delaney's attention. The man turned around and stared with the rest of them.

"We have some announcements and introductions to make," the band leader said, raising his voice. "We have some honeymooners with us on this voyage." Wallace Hartley was a bandleader who believed in doing everything in a proper and dignified manner. He even had the selections that the band played numbered so that all he had to do was say the number and every member of the band knew instantly what to play.

Taking out a slip of paper, he proceeded to read the names of the first-class honeymoon passengers. Each stood and bowed, blushing, to the polite applause of everyone in the dining room.

There was a moment of some concern in the introductions, one of those times when no matter what was done, it would be the subject of dinner-table buzz. Hartley read the names off, "Colonel John Jacob Astor and his lovely bride, Madeleine."

From across the room, Morgan could see the Astors slowly get to their feet. He could also clearly hear the buzz of gossip from the next table. One woman remarked, "She will never be accepted in society, I don't care how rich he is." Astor was in his tailcoat, and his wife wore a green-sequined gown that showed off her auburn hair. It was their honeymoon and a long one taken to stop the tongue wagging over this, his second marriage. Madeleine Astor was younger than even John's son Vincent and was beginning to show that she was in a family way.

Delaney leaned over and whispered in Morgan's direction. "The man has no concept of how people really live. I heard he once said, 'A man who has a million dollars is as well off as if he were rich.' Imagine that."

Butt added to the gossip as the Astors took their seats. "He is quite bright however. The man invented a brake for bicycles and a device for flattening road surfaces. Wall Street listens to him as well. There was one occasion where he was missing on his yacht in the Mediterranean for sixteen days, with no word. The money markets fell like a rock."

Hartley wasn't finished, however. "We also have an engagement to announce. The lovely couple is going to America for their bridal shower."

Morgan glanced at Margaret. She seemed uncomfortable, not at all as one would suspect a soon-to-be bride to look. It was April's gaze, however, that lanced him through the heart. The woman was looking smugly at him, not Margaret or Peter. It was almost as if she could see the pain in his heart and was taking her final revenge on him. He turned away.

"I am pleased to announce the engagement of Peter Wilksbury to Miss Margaret Hastings of London," Hartley called out. "Perhaps the lovely couple would like to stand and lead us in this next dance."

Peter seemed supremely proud, but Margaret was still shaky as she got to her feet. Morgan watched her force a smile. Peter led her away from the table as a rancher would display a prize heifer at the local livestock show. Morgan knew that wasn't his attitude at all, but right this moment he wasn't prepared to give anyone the benefit of the question. April had no doubt done this. She sat in her seat with the pompous posture of a peacock.

The next thing Morgan saw was Captain Smith walking toward their table. The man stopped beside April and was evidently asking her to dance. It was a nice touch. Morgan had to admit that.

"They make a lovely couple, don't you think?" Butt asked.

"Which one?" Morgan replied dryly, "Margaret and Peter or the captain and her mother?"

Butt roared at the notion.

Guggenheim got up to dance with Kitty.

The idea of simply sitting there while Margaret danced with Peter made Morgan antsy. It was one thing to be left in the lurch, and quite another to take on the appearance of an uncared-for wallflower. He glanced over at Gloria, who was obviously thinking the same thing. To make matters worse, it seemed that Gracie was doing his best to entice her into a dance.

Morgan quickly got to his feet and excused himself. He knew that would leave Delaney all by himself, but at this point in time, he just didn't care. He stepped around the table and, standing behind Gracie, smiled at Gloria. "Pardon me, Mrs. Thompson, didn't we agree to the first dance?"

"Why yes," she gulped, "We did indeed." Turning back to Gracie, she did her best to put the man off. "I'm sorry, Colonel, but young Mr. Fairfield and I have this dance. You will excuse me."

Morgan stepped around and pulled out her chair. Leading her to the middle of the dance floor, he wrapped his arm around her and led off. Hartley was leading the band in a Strauss waltz, and Morgan and Gloria moved to the music beautifully.

"Thank you, Morgan. You are a most merciful man. You know if I could be assured that the colonel's conversation on the dance floor would be any different from what he subjects us to at dinner, I would gladly oblige him."

"Some men seem to be absorbed in only one thing."

"And just what are you absorbed in tonight?" She batted her eyes and smiled coyly.

"That's hard to say." Morgan moved gracefully with the music. "I have so much to think about."

"Not having your friend at the table must make things quite boring for you. He seems so spirited."

"Yes," was all Morgan could manage.

Gloria looked around to where Peter and Margaret were dancing. "And perhaps you're thinking of Margaret there."

"I was, but I'm trying not to now." He looked at Gloria. "It's very difficult to think about another woman when I'm dancing with one so beautiful."

Gloria laughed. "You do that so well, Morgan. Maybe you should have done more of that when you had the chance."

"Yes, I suppose I should. We tend to learn our lessons all too late in life."

"That is nonsense. You have your whole life ahead of you, and no amount of pressure from Margaret's mother is about to change that. I've talked to Margaret. She's a very bright lady but a bit confused now. I think knowing your heart would change all that."

"I can't do that. She's engaged."

"There's nothing about the sacredness of engagement where I come from."

"It wouldn't be the gentlemanly thing to do."

"And you think Peter is being the gentleman when he's about to marry a woman who loves someone else?"

Morgan's mind raced at the question. There had been so many mixed signals that he was beginning to doubt his own eyes and ears. Gloria was a woman, though, and they all appeared to carry with them this extraordinary sense when it came to love and matters of the heart. She expressed herself, too, in a way that seemed so confident. Of course, it was a confidence that involved him. There was little risk for her. "Do you really think Margaret still loves me?"

"Did she ever love you?"

"Why, yes. She's loved me all of her life, and I've loved her since passing the stage where all females were silly creatures."

"Are you certain she loved you?"

"Yes, as certain as I am about anything that has ever happened to me."

"Then that has never changed. Love is never something that goes in and out of your life on a whim. My minister at home used to say that all love comes from God. If His love never changes and He never decides to not love a person He has once decided to love, then I think it would be safe to assume that real love between people doesn't change, either."

Morgan was confused. Two sets of thoughts roared through his mind. There was what was expected of him by society and what he wanted to do at the moment.

"A woman doesn't grow up loving someone, only to change her mind, not unless, of course, she thought there was no chance that love would ever be returned."

"What am I going to do?"

The music suddenly stopped. Morgan and Gloria stood at attention, almost refusing to return to the table. "I'd say you have to make a decision."

Morgan stared at her. He seemed powerless, or at least he felt that way. Now with the world and those at dinner knowing that Margaret and Peter were engaged, anything he might do would seem totally out of place and even reprehensible.

"You have to decide if you're going to tell Margaret that you love her and want her or if you're going to remain a gentleman."

Morgan saw Boxhall walking in his direction and knew that he'd obviously been informed about his role in the investigation. He only hoped the man would be discreet enough not to say anything too specific in front of Gloria. There was no need to worry her.

Boxhall stood at attention in front of them. He was in his best dress uniform with the two rows of polished brass buttons. The band started playing once again.

"I understand we're to be working together," Boxhall said.

Gloria stared at Boxhall, obviously taking the man in. Her smile showed a look of approval.

Morgan motioned his head in Gloria's direction while she was turned away and eyeing Boxhall. "Yes, but I think we should discuss that later. Have you met Mrs. Gloria Thompson?"

"No, I haven't had the pleasure," Boxhall bowed slightly at the waist.

"This is the ship's fourth officer, Joseph Boxhall."

"Charmed, Mr. Boxhall." Gloria took his hand and curtsied.

"I hope you and Mr. Thompson are having a pleasant voyage," Boxhall said.

"Mrs. Thompson is traveling alone," Morgan said.

"Oh, yes, I am. I am a widow you see." She looked back at Morgan and then at Boxhall. "How could a woman have otherwise when surrounded by such fine gentlemen."

Morgan looked at Boxhall. "Why don't you dance with Gloria? I think I'm going to go out on deck for a while to clear my head."

Morgan walked out the doors that led to the open deck. He turned first and saw that Gloria and Boxhall both seemed to be having a good time. From across the room he could also see Margaret. Peter was having a conversation with a small group of people, but Morgan could see that Margaret was staring at him, unable to take her eyes off him. It made him feel uncomfortable.

9:50 P.M.

Kelly crouched beside the plate that formed the door to the watertight compartment. There would be no escape. If O'Conner had indeed come back to check on his work, there was no place to go. There would also be no explaining. Kelly knew he had no reason to be where he was other than the obvious one—that he'd followed O'Conner.

The sound of footsteps grew closer, and then Kelly's eyes brightened. They were coming from the direction of the boiler room. Taking hold of the top of the door, Kelly slid out and onto the catwalk.

"Here, what is this?"

The man was a chief engineer. Kelly could see that from the cap he wore. A sturdily built fellow with a pudgy face and side whiskers of brown hair. His cheeks were like vanilla pudding, with a dotting of blackheads over them that made them look like sprinkles of chocolate. He was more surprised than anything else, but the surprise soon turned to anger.

"What are you doing here? No one is supposed to be in this area. I'll have to put you on report."

Kelly got to his feet and dusted himself off. Once again, he worked at rubbing the grease from his hands. He rubbed them on the legs of his trousers. "There's a bomb aboard."

"Nonsense." The man gave Kelly a shove. "There's just a man who's drunk and not where he belongs."

Kelly stumbled with the shove but steadied himself against the bulkhead. "Listen here, there is a bomb aboard." He pointed to the compartment. "It's right up there next to the aft wall."

"Sure it is." A sickening grin spread over his face, and he sweetened his voice in a mocking sort of way. "And who left this bomb? Was it the fairies?" He moved up close to Kelly. "Why don't you just go to bed and sleep it off, old fellow."

Kelly pointed again. "But I tell you, it's up there. Why don't you have a look for yourself?"

The man snorted in disgust. "See here, I'm a busy man, much too busy to go chasing after the fairy stories of some drunken Irishman."

"But, I'm not drunk." Kelly leaned into the man and exhaled a breath. "I haven't had a drop."

The man stepped back and waved his hand over his face. He was acting as if Kelly were drunk and seemed determined to prove the point. "You old Irish types are all alike. You plow into the sauce and invent silly stories. Only thing is, this time you've picked on the wrong bloke. I ain't about to go rumblin' about in the dark on the word of an old man from steerage. What were you down here looking about for, anyway?"

"I followed the man who planted it."

"A likely story."

"It's no story, I tell you." He pointed back to the compartment. "Just go and have a look for yourself."

"Not bloody likely. I got myself a crew back there." He jerked his thumb over his shoulder to make his point. "And they're hard at work to keep you no-accounts types on a steady course. Do you expect me to leave my work to chase down some story?"

"Look, go and find Officer Boxhall. He can vouch for me. The man who planted that bomb was someone Boxhall was questioning earlier today."

"Oh, sure. Now you'll have me running all over the ship to find an officer. Then what will I say? Excuse me, sir, but there's an Irish passenger who says there's a bomb." He laughed. "What do you take me for?"

The chief pointed back in the direction of the stairs. "You just go back to where you came from and sleep it off. You go on with your story-telling to someone who'll listen to you, and I'll get on about my work."

Kelly looked back at the stairway. For all he knew O'Conner was up there. He might even be in the hallway waiting for him and with all the commotion this chief was making, it was sure to draw attention. There would be some tall explaining to do if the man caught him in that area. He had grandchildren and a berth in the aft family segment of the *Titanic*'s living quarters. He had no business in the forward single men's section of the ship, and O'Conner knew it.

"Look, just call up to the bridge and tell Boxhall that Jack Kelly's down here. I tell you, he'll come a runnin'. He knows who I am."

The chief grabbed Kelly by the shirt. "You just come along with me. If Boxhall won't come and get you, one of the yeomen will."

With that, the man practically dragged Kelly with him into the boiler room. The men there were sweating and shoveling coal into the flames of the forward boilers. When the chief came in with the stranger seemingly on a leash, every eye was fixed on him. The men leaned on their shovels to get a better listen.

The chief held onto Kelly's shirt and motioned with his head to the suddenly still men. "You see what you've done? You're already costing me time. You'd better be right about this, or it'll be my hide and yours as well."

"Oh, I'm right." Kelly peeled the man's hands free from his shirt. "And when you get a hold of Boxhall, you're gonna be a blinkin' hero."

The chief picked up the pipe used to communicate with the bridge and blew into it. Kelly knew that it sent a whistle to the bridge that would cause someone to pick up the other end. "You'll see," Kelly said.

"I bloody well better see."

Moments later, Kelly heard the sound of a hollow voice from the end of the tube. "What do you want?" it asked.

Kelly could see the chief pause for a moment. It was as if he hesitated in telling the whole story. "I got a man down here that wants Boxhall."

There were a few moments of silence and then words from the other end of the tube. "Boxhall's off duty."

"Then send a yeoman down here. I got a passenger who won't go back to where he belongs."

Kelly's heart sank. From the way this man acted, Boxhall had been his only hope. "Now listen to me. There is a bomb in your watertight compartment. For all I know, it may be a timing device. That thing could be ready to blow even while you're taking the time to call me a liar. If you won't go yourself, then have one of your men do the dirty work."

Kelly could see the man was thinking it over. He looked back at one of the stokers who, along with all the rest, was leaning on his shovel. "Finnian," he said, "Pick up that lamp and come with me. We've got a man we need to prove to be a liar."

Kelly breathed a sigh a relief. His fear of a timing device hadn't been just a ploy. The thought had come to him, and it sent shock waves up and down his spine. In a matter of moments, the three of them were standing next to the compartment door. Kelly pointed into the blackness. "It's right up there. Take the stairs up to the hatch, and then feel along the top of the wall. Make sure you go all the way over. You may not be able to see it 'cause it's covered with grease, but it's there all right."

The man moved through the compartment door, and Kelly and the chief stuck their heads in and listened to him climb the stairs.

Moments later they heard the man. "I ain't seein' nuthin' here, chief."

The chief looked at Kelly. "See there, nothing!"

"Run your hand along the top of the wall," Kelly called out, bending down and sticking his head under the door. "It's there, right next to the two compartment walls."

There was a pause before they heard the next sound. "There's somethin' 'ere, chief. I don't know nuttin' 'bout what it is."

"Don't touch it!" Kelly yelled. He backed out and looked at the chief. "Now does that satisfy you? Why don't you just go and find Boxhall?"

Kelly waited with the chief while Finnian went to find Boxhall. The minutes crept by like hours. Just the thought of being so close to a bomb powerful enough to puncture a hole in the *Titanic*'s hull was enough to make even the chief begin to sweat. Kelly took a great deal of pleasure in that.

When Boxhall finally showed up, it seemed like it had been more than an hour since the stoker had been dispatched. Boxhall walked forward from the direction of the boiler room, Finnian trailing along behind him. "Here, what is this?" Then, he spotted Kelly. "What are you doing here?"

"You know this man?" the chief asked.

"Of course I do," Boxhall replied, "And he's a good man."

Kelly smiled at the chief, who was looking rather sheepish.

"What's all this about, Kelly?"

"The man you questioned earlier today, O'Conner, I followed him." He pointed to the compartment. "He planted a bomb in there. I saw it, or rather felt it, for myself. It's up against the top of the stairway, next to the compartment wall."

Boxhall stripped off his jacket and rolled up his sleeves. "I'll have a look. Chief, I'll need a lamp and you to follow me with some tools."

"Me, sir?"

"Ah, the blazes with him," Kelly said. "I'll go with you." Kelly gave a hard look at the chief. "He might get lost in there."

It took them a short time to unbolt the bomb from its anchor. It was secure, safe enough from the normal jarring of the ship. Kelly removed several screws while Boxhall held the lamp. Kelly pulled it off of the wall. They came down the stairs and into the light.

Kelly held the bomb in his hands and turned it over for a closer look. "No timing device here," he said. "He uncurled a rather long length of fuse that had been taped to the side of the device. "I'd say our man planned to come back on cue, unwrap this thing, and light the fuse."

"The captain will have to see this," Boxhall said. "And we have an arrest to make."

FRIDAY,

APRIL 12, 1912,

10:10 P.M.

CHAPTER 23

Morgan stepped out onto the deck and pulled his coat collar up around his neck. The tiny slip of a moon cast an eerie glow on the water, almost as if they were on a large pond and not the ocean. The vast darkness of water seemed almost placid. The night was cloudless, and Morgan could almost swear that he could see every star that God had ever created. They stood glowing in the night, calling out to him with tiny voices of shining beauty.

He walked over to the rail and, placing his hands on the slick and glistening wood, watched the water as it passed by. The light from the stars and the moon was dim but managed to kiss the top of the swell the ship made as it sliced its way through the sea. The lights from the *Titanic* herself, however, cast the most powerful glow on the water. The hum of the engines beneath his feet made Morgan see the vessel as a living thing, almost as if she had eyes that could peer through the gloom.

He looked along the railing at the glow of the floating city. It was a blaze of light. It was easy to see why Andrews had such affection for her. She was a product of his mind, something come to life from pencil and paper and now a living, moving thing through the timeless ocean. Almost an act of defiance against nature itself, the *Titanic* was created to carry the best of this new century through a troubled water and into the place of dreams, the place where each member of the crew and every passenger longed to be. The black form of the giant of the sea was cutting through everything that mankind had feared in the past, the limits of his thinking and the barrier to a new world.

Morgan could feel the solid steel under him. Rigid and proud, the *Titanic* was the mark of all they could ever hope to do. If modern man ever had a boast to make, ever had a fist to raise to the sky in proud acclaim, it was the *Titanic*. Morgan could see that in the spit and polish of her officers and hear it in every proud boast of a first-class passenger who could afford her price. The old fears of man were making way for the glittering, proud, bold noise of the *Titanic*.

Morgan had always viewed the sea as a dark, powerful, and mortal enemy. It had taken his parents and his childhood, at least the normal childhood every other boy he had ever known had experienced. His childhood had been Lilly, and she had been in every way like a mother, a mother with no husband to point to as to what a man should be like. That had been the place of books in his life. In the poetry of Tennyson and the words of Sir Walter Scott, he had found the meaning of manhood: duty, honor, sacrifice, and giving one's self for the benefit of others.

Life itself had seldom been like the life of his mind, however. His Uncle John was a steady enough man, but cold and given to the accumulation of wealth. There was no self-sacrifice. His teachers in school had gone about their duties but without the panache and dash that Morgan imagined to be the product of true manhood. It had been his fencing instructor, a German, Wolfgang Erhart, who had earned his respect. Wolfgang had been a graduate of the school in Heidelberg. Like most other graduates of that school, he had the dueling scar on his cheek to prove it. Most of the other boys thought him pompous and overbearing, but Morgan just saw him as manly and undefiled.

The man handled the saber like it was a part of his arm, a practiced extension of his very quick mind. Morgan had been a very good student, not only watching the man's moves but listening to the reasoning of the brain that produced them.

It was only of late that the Bible had attracted his attention. What had been only stories before came alive for him in a school chapel. A missionary from India, James Cook, had talked to the young men of Oxford and challenged their faith. It was as if the man was speaking only to Morgan. He alone could hear the words, even though they boomed across the entire assembly. He had challenged the young men to follow Christ into the crucible of life, to be different, to surrender one's own self. Morgan had got to his feet with a number of the other young students when the challenge was issued. The act of standing before his classmates, perhaps even in spite of them, had burned the missionary's words deep into his heart.

For Morgan, all of life and its smallness seemed pale when compared to that moment. It was then that he had decided to make a difference with the talent he had been given with the written word. If he could sway the hearts and minds of people with what was expected of them as ladies and gentlemen of culture, if he could help in bending their wills in some small way to the will of the Almighty, then his life could truly count.

And now, here he was in pursuit of fulfilling his feelings. *Perhaps this is a test?* he wondered. Compared to the scope of doing what was right, how important were his feelings for Margaret anyway? And what was right? This was a question that always seemed to plague him. Was it right to let Margaret marry a man she could never love in the way that she loved him and spend the rest of his own life thinking about her, where she was, what she was doing? Or was it right to defy convention and tell a woman promised to another man that he loved her?

Morgan began to wander the decks. He missed Hunter. It was almost as if by not going to his cabin and trying to sleep, he could prevent the sound of silence. The man had never seemed to leave him alone. He was constantly knocking on his door with his latest scheme to pass the time, however shocking or improper. But that was the way of the man, defying convention and racing toward the edge of life. It was the thing that made him so irritatingly lovable.

The chill of the night air knifed through Morgan's jacket. Even though the air itself was a dead calm, the *Titanic's* movement through it was enough to send most people running for cover. Morgan could feel the vibration of the engine, never changing, always the constant hum.

He stepped into the salon that opened into the grand staircase. Several couples were making the parade up the stairs, while others waited for the lift. Somehow, coming down the stairs was an event, a place to be seen. Walking up it, however, might have been thought of as sheer work.

He looked up to see that there were at least two couples who stood by the upstairs balcony edge. Perhaps that explained the people climbing the stairs. Someone was there who could still watch. All was not lost.

Turning to a set of smaller stairs behind the sweeping staircase, Morgan made his way down into the reception room. The place was well lit with blazing chandeliers and deeply upholstered red and yellow furniture. The best feature of the moment, however, was the fact that it was empty.

He dropped into a large upholstered chair and stared at the wall. He was feeling lonely, as difficult as that was to admit. The man had that way about him. Of course, the announcement about Margaret's engagement only seemed to make him lonelier still. It had been published in the papers in London and no doubt declared at a party or two. But he hadn't been there. He'd never had to deal with it.

Reaching into his pocket, he pulled out the picture of Lilly he'd found. Somehow, as lonely as he felt, the sight of Lilly was a comfort to him. Her face smiling in the picture seemed to say, "I love you."

He had, since finding the picture, discovered the man's name to be George Sinclair. Lilly looked perfectly happy and in love as she stood beside him. *Could there be contentment in love alone?* he wondered.

Looking up, he saw Margaret coming down the stairs. She was the last person he thought would be prowling about. "What are you doing down here?" he asked.

"I was looking for you."

Morgan got up and stepped away from the chair.

Margaret came closer, suddenly noticing the picture. "And who is this?" She took the picture from his hand and held it closer. "She is lovely."

"That is the woman I told you about. You remember Lilly, my governess as a child."

She smiled at him. "That's sweet. She's beautiful. I don't think I remember her like this." She handed the picture back to him. "There aren't many men who carry pictures of their nursemaids around with them. She must have been very special to you."

"She was, very special. Of course, as you know, I had no mother. Lilly was the only real mother I ever knew."

He looked once again at the picture and dropped it back into his pocket. "I don't normally carry her picture, but I just came across it under the most unusual of circumstances. It was in a gentleman's bag that was entrusted to me, a man I've never met before."

"That is intriguing."

"Yes, isn't it?"

"Well, women aren't always exactly what you may think they are."

"I just never imagined that Lilly had a life of her own apart from me."

"That seems to be a rather masculine trait."

She looked at him. It was a look of sympathy, and it made Morgan feel somewhat ashamed. She must have known how much the announcement at the table had hurt him and had come to find him to offer some consolation. Pity was something he didn't need. He walked toward the window that looked out on the water. He spoke into the window, but loud enough for Margaret to hear. "You told me there was no hope. I should have listened."

She put her hand on his arm. "That was cruel of me, and I'm sorry. I had been hurt, and perhaps the idea of seeing a little pain in you for a change was too great of a temptation."

"It was painful."

"And I could see that. I should have known that if you didn't care, you wouldn't have had any cause for distress. I think I just believed that your need for a career and to prove yourself was deeper than any feelings you had for me."

"Margaret." Morgan sighed and turned around to face her. "I have seen so many friends of my aunt whose husbands are making money but are essentially unhappy men. They've never…never…never…"

"Never what, Morgan?" Margaret asked nervously. Morgan's eyes were on Margaret, but she could tell he was looking inward, struggling to give voice and reality to something deep in his soul.

"They've never tested themselves, never risked failure. They live inside of four walls, with an occasional stroll in the park. That is a life not worth living, and their wives suffer for it. No man who is unhappy can make the woman he loves happy."

Margaret looked deeply into his eyes. It wasn't a look that was an attempt to study him or even to try to find out what he was thinking. It was a look of understanding and one of adoration. "Why didn't you tell me how you felt? I would have understood."

"I suppose I just didn't feel that it was fair. I couldn't come to you with some promise based on a job I hadn't even started. I had nothing to offer you."

"Nothing but your love."

He bowed his head. "I just didn't think that was enough, not when other men could offer you so much more."

"No man can offer a woman more than his love."

Morgan slipped his arm around Margaret's waist and pulled her closer. The silence between them was deafening. Both of them stood seemingly teetering on the edge of a cliff. There would be no turning back.

"And I do love you, Margaret. God help me, I do. I've always loved you."

Margaret raised herself on her toes and kissed Morgan's lips. He gripped her tighter, and they held each other close.

Releasing him from the kiss, she looked sheepish. "Now, what will we do?"

"I have no idea. I like Peter."

"And that announcement tonight—mother will absolutely die."

"Margaret, I think you should think this matter over very carefully. You and I are making quite a decision, and I still haven't even started my first day of work."

"There you are with this job thing again."

"How can I help it? I have nothing to offer you, and Peter has so much."

"I thought you were offering me your love." With that, Margaret wheeled around and paraded toward the stairs.

Morgan started to follow her but decided not to. Maybe it was best. Margaret could think and so could he, if he could actually sleep.

11:30 P.M.

T urn them cocks." Chief Engineer Nordstrom was quickly losing patience. They'd had the fire burning in coal bunker number 6 since before they'd left the docks at Southampton, and all the dousing and mucking hadn't helped. The men were growing weary with it, and so was he.

"The cocks?" The man shouted back the question, almost as if he hadn't heard.

"Yeah, turn them cocks. We're gonna rake this stuff all out and put this thing out if it's the last thing I do. The old man wants to make full steam. That Ismay has some kinda speed trial in mind for this old girl, and we gotta get ready fer it."

The old stoker shook his head and mumbled a series of curses. It was bad enough dealing with a fire without the added pressure of having the director of the line breathing down your neck.

He began turning the wheel that would release the seawater into the boiler room. The large spigot began its deluge with a trickle, and then as the stoker turned the wheel, the trickle soon became a raging torrent of ice-cold seawater. The water poured over the floor in sheets of freezing brine.

Nordstrom signaled to the six men standing at the far side of the large room. Each of them was watching the water, and even though they all knew what would be next, he could tell they were dreading it. "Come on, me boys. Let's get to doing it."

The water was shallow, barely up to their ankles as they waded toward the smoking coal bin. Each man came forward like lambs to the slaughter. They were used to the conditions in the boiler room. Steam and the intense heat of the boilers coated them in sooty sweat. This would be different, though. They'd be standing in freezing water, raking hot flaming coals into it, and perhaps on top of their feet to boot.

"Is that enough?" The old stoker called out.

"No, let 'er go," Nordstrom shouted. Nordstrom had been working on putting the fire out or waiting for it to burn itself out for almost a week now. It was frustrating. On top of his other duties was the headache required to keep the steam up with two of the boilers down. Of course that was because of the fire in bunker number 6. It had reached an explosive point tonight when the chief of engineering said the captain had lost his patience. Now Nordstrom was determined to see it extinguished. The crew of men watched the veins on his head bulge when he screamed, "I want this thing out!"

The stoker turned the wheel one more slow half turn to the left. Water poured into the fast-rising pool on the floor. It rose ankle deep.

Nordstrom pointed to one of the engineers at the far end of the room. The man was standing on the bulkhead, watching the water rise. "Go get the pumps. When we have this thing out, we'll have to start pumping out the water."

"Might be tricky to get the pumps working up here."

"Just do it," Nordstrom shouted. "I don't care."

Several men moved back to get the pumps ready to put into place. It would be quite a task to join the hoses that would bring the pumps into operation to coal bunker number 6 and the forward boiler rooms.

Even then, they could only be expected to pump out two to three inches a minute. *Those main pumps are just too far astern, everybody knows that,* Nordstrom thought.

He motioned the three remaining members of the crew into action, pointing to the smoking door of the coal bin. "OK, open 'er up and start raking."

One of the men reached out with the blade of his shovel and threw the latch back from the bunker. Edging the tip of the blade into the door, he pried it open. With a swift jerk, he yanked back on the second door.

Smoke began to pour out the open doors of coal bunker number 6. The fresh flood of air seemed only to make the fire burn hotter. The men turned their neckerchiefs around, covering their noses and mouths. They began to cough and retch as they picked up the long rakers and began to pull on the burning coal.

The fiery rocks hit the water with a sizzle, sending more steam into the air, mixed with acrid smoke. Nordstrom bobbed and wove against the smoke to try to catch a glimpse of just how far the fire reached. The lumps of coal glowed deep in the coal bin. Much of it was resting on the hull itself.

Nordstrom cursed. It couldn't be worse. The whole bunker would have to be dumped into the freezing water on the floor. Only then would the fire be out. He looked at the stoker on the wheel. "Open 'er up more," he yelled.

The man gave the wheel another half turn.

The men continued to rake the flaming mixture into the water. They moved forward, shoving the long-handled rakers deeper into the burning coals.

The water now rose to the height of the men's calves. It was a bone-chilling cold that sent shivers up their spines. But even as they worked, the sweat poured off their backs in rivers of salty rivulets, cutting streams of white into their black, soot-caked backs.

Nordstrom pointed at the hot spots. "Over there, get that over there!"

The men grudgingly complied, shooting out the muckers into the heat of the fire. Slowly, they pulled the burning rocks into the water. The flaming rocks sizzled and barked as they hit the soggy floor.

"More," Nordstrom yelled.

They bent their backs, dragging still more into the water.

Nordstrom watched as the men with the hoses from the pump arrived at the door. The water was spilling over to the next room. He knew they'd had enough. Turning back to the stoker on the wheel, he yelled. "OK, shut it down."

The old man began to spin the wheel to the right. In a matter of moments, he had the seawater turned off.

Turning back to the men at the pumps he yelled out. "You three, spell these men."

There was to be a shift change. He knew men could stand only so much. They'd have to keep it up until all of the coal was in the water. It wouldn't just be the burning coal either. There might just be a spark of a hot spot he hadn't seen. No, it would have to be all of the coal in bunker number 6. They'd take care of the mess later. The bunker was on starboard. He knew full well that the men had been using coal all along starboard. If the *Titanic* was stationary, they might even detect a list on the bridge, but since it was moving, there would be no chance of that, not until they'd had the time to make up for it. *Besides*, he thought, *if they have any complaints, they have only themselves up there to blame.*

SATURDAY,

APRIL 13, 1912,

10:45 A.M.

CHAPTER 24

Morgan ate an unusually late breakfast at the Palm Court of the Verandah Café. He eagerly dug into a mixture of bacon, mushrooms, and tomatoes and tried to adjust himself to a cup of coffee. It would be a different thing for him. His preferences had been trained in a typically English fashion, and the taste of coffee was somewhat bitter on his tongue. He had heard about the drink's wonderful properties in waking and keeping a man up, however, and felt it would be worth the price of a little bitterness. He hadn't been able to sleep much during the night. Several times he'd got up to check his watch, just to see how long he would have to endure the darkness. Of course, he'd mercifully fallen asleep close to dawn, but out in the North Atlantic, dawn came quite early.

He looked up in time to see Peter Wilksbury walking past the outside trellis window. If he'd had a paper, he would have gladly held it up to take refuge behind it. Guilt still raged inside of him for kissing Margaret last night. He felt like a cad.

"Oh, there you are," Peter said, spotting him. "I've been looking for you."

Morgan motioned to him. "Come on over and have a seat."

Peter had a lot of bounce in his step. Obviously, Margaret had said nothing. Just the thought of having to guess if Peter knew about what had happened sent torrents of guilt tumbling through Morgan's soul. *Should I tell the man?* Morgan wondered.

Peter had on just the type of outfit that Morgan hated: a green-tweed jacket with matching knickers and knee-high brown stockings. His cream-colored shirt and green bow tie showed him to be the perfect country gentleman. Peter pulled up a chair in front of him and, sitting down, signaled for the waiter. "You seem to be taking breakfast quite late."

"I had a hard time sleeping." Morgan searched Peter's eyes. Did he know about Margaret?

"That must be hard, with Hunter's death." Peter looked up at the waiter. "I'd like tea and some fruit." The man nodded and waddled off. Peter leaned forward. "I have good news. Do you shoot?"

"Do I shoot?"

"Do you do any trapshooting?"

"I'm afraid I don't have a great deal of experience in that," Morgan said.

Peter patted Morgan's arm. "That's right, I'd forgotten, you're a city boy. My father has his country estate and I grew up shooting birds on the fly. Well, I have us lined up to do some trapshooting off the poop deck at noon. Guggenheim will be there shooting, and I thought we might use that as an opportunity to question him."

Morgan was amazed. Peter seemed to have no idea that anything was amiss with Margaret. There wasn't the least bit of a hint in the way he looked or the way he spoke. Morgan would have felt better if there had been. As it was, he felt like a grown man taking candy from an unsuspecting child.

"Doesn't that sound like a grand idea?" Peter went on.

"Yes, splendid," he said absently.

The tea and fruit arrived and Peter picked up the silver serving pot and poured a cup of what smelled like Earl Grey tea into the blue and white cup marked "*Titanic*." Morgan noticed Peter's thumb covering the word etched in gold on the cup. *Titan...Titanic*, Morgan mused. His study of Greek mythology tickled his mind. *Titans, the product of the union of heaven and earth, a lawless bunch,* he remembered. *And cast down by a higher power,* he thought. *The old girl seems to want her name branded on everything in sight. She was like a proud but possessive woman, always reminding you that her favors were only on loan.*

"Morgan, Morgan my boy. I say, if we can get his mind on something else, maybe he might let something slip," Peter said. "And good shooting requires great concentration."

"If that's the case, I doubt I shall be able to hit the deck itself," Morgan quipped.

"You'll do fine. Just keep the lead in the air."

"I suppose I should congratulate you." Morgan broached the subject of Peter's engagement. The subject continued to nibble away at his insides, and he knew if he didn't at least bring it up and give Peter a chance to talk about it, it would continue to haunt him.

"Congratulate me for what?"

"Your engagement." Morgan took a slug of the bitter coffee. It seemed to fit the occasion. "That announcement last night made quite the splash."

"Oh, that," Peter laughed. "Something Margaret's mother put together. I shouldn't worry about that if I were you. We both know that Margaret loves you."

The words sent a spray of coffee from Morgan's lips. He quickly covered his mouth with the napkin. "What? What are you saying?"

Peter smiled. "Look, I know when I've been whipped. I can do almost anything but change a woman's heart. No man can do that, not even you."

"But she's promised to you."

"Yes, and it's a promise I shall not hold her to. I'd be a cad to do a thing like that." Peter sipped his tea. "I know there will be some embarrassment to the thing and we'll have to contact those people invited to the wedding shower, but that's easily enough done. I shouldn't worry about it if I were you."

"You seem quite calm about something so devastating."

Peter sat forward, the smile disappearing from his face. "Resigned, perhaps, but calm, never. I knew about her affection for you when I first asked for her hand. Frankly, I was shocked when she accepted. I think she did that to simply tell you something in the papers that she didn't seem able to say in person. I think I've lived with your ghost for months now, and I'm glad it's out in the open."

He picked up his tea. "There are times when a woman changes her mind at the drop of a hat and other times when she can't change her mind if her life depended on it."

"Perhaps you're mistaken. It could be that Margaret simply needs to get me finally out of her system."

Peter laughed. "I think she needs to get you finally to the altar."

Morgan could hardly believe the switch. Here Peter was trying to do his best to gracefully give Margaret away and Morgan was himself suggesting that she belonged to him and even encouraging the man not to lose hope. It was the sort of dutiful, gentlemanly thing that both men had been trained to do from birth and the kind of behavior that drove Margaret absolutely mad.

"I wouldn't lose hope, if I were you," Morgan said. "A marriage takes two people and only heaven knows where my mind will be by the time this trip ends. Besides, I know she cares deeply about you and respects you."

"Ah, there's the rub. It would seem that the both of us care about one another, but *care* can only go so far. Her thinking about you goes much deeper than that, as deep as love."

"You and I both know that love blossoms in time. It needs time, time undisturbed by me."

"And what man wants to see his bride walking down the aisle and know that she'd prefer to see another man waiting in front of it? Not many, old boy. When would such a thing happen, when she has a child and can transfer feelings of love to a little one instead of you? I think that would be a miserable experience."

Morgan watched Peter's expression. There was a sadness in the man's eyes, one that anyone would pity.

"I won't do that to myself," Peter went on, "and I can't do it to someone like Margaret, someone I really care for."

Morgan spotted Boxhall as the man made his way through the dining area. "There you both are," Boxhall said. "I have some good news for you."

Morgan motioned toward a vacant chair, and Boxhall laid his cap on the table and took a seat.

"We have our murderer," Boxhall said.

"Who?" Morgan asked.

"The man is a steerage passenger who got on at Queenstown." Boxhall picked up a spoon and began nervously to bounce it up and down between his thumb and index finger. "He has ties to the Irish revolution and was planting a bomb aboard the ship." He put down the spoon. "It was a merciful thing for all of us that he was followed."

"I'd say it was," Peter added.

"How did a steerage passenger get into the first-class area?" Morgan asked.

"He had a steward's jacket in his locker. That would have given him access to the entire ship."

"How did he get that?" Peter asked.

"That's something we're not completely certain of, just yet."

"And what reason would he have to kill the man in the first-class cabin and then murder Hunter?" Morgan asked.

Boxhall seemed uncomfortable with the question. He raked his teeth slightly over his upper lip in a nervous fashion. "We know he was looking for something in the cabin, something he didn't find. Perhaps, he was just a thief. We do know that he killed a steerage passenger and planted an explosive device."

"But that still doesn't explain how he came to have the jacket," Morgan said. "Nor does it explain Hunter's death."

"I'm afraid we may have to suppose that the death of your friend was accidental. Perhaps he slipped and hit his head."

"And what of the jacket?" Peter asked.

"The man obviously has an accomplice on the ship," Morgan added.

"Nor does it explain how Morgan came to be shut up in the steam room with the steam on high and the door jammed."

Morgan could see that the word of his own attempted murder was news to Boxhall. The man blinked and once again picked up the spoon.

"We didn't say anything about that," Morgan said. "Frankly, it seemed rather inconsequential after we found Hunter."

"I'll have to look into that," Boxhall said.

"Yes, we have what looks like pieces from a cane that were jammed into the door of Morgan's steam room," Peter offered. "There was nothing to rob and no connections to Irish independence whatsoever."

"All right, all right," Boxhall laid down the spoon, "The three of us will explore the matter." He leaned toward the two men. "But let's keep this to ourselves. In all my years at sea, I've never seen or so much as heard of multiple murders aboard ship. There is petty thievery of course, but nothing like this. Everyone on the bridge is quite shaken. Ismay and the captain seem delighted to have this thing solved, and I think it's best not to disturb that notion."

Boxhall got to his feet, followed by Morgan and Peter. He turned to leave but then almost in an afterthought looked back at Morgan. "I say, old man, that was bloody good, your introducing me to Gloria last night. She is a magnificent woman."

"Yes, she is," Morgan said. He stood still while Boxhall left the café and Peter looked at him rather oddly.

"What's wrong?" Peter asked.

"He called me 'old man.'"

"Yes, a rather common term among the English, I should think."

Morgan could feel his eyes moistening. "That was Hunter's way of addressing me. I guess I'd forgotten how very much I miss him."

Peter put his arm around Morgan's shoulder. "I rather imagine that you would. The two of you seemed to be becoming such fast friends."

Morgan nodded.

A short while later the two of them made their way to the stairway on C deck that led down to the aft well deck. They would have to pass through the well deck area in order to get to the poop deck at the very rear of the ship. A chain blocked the stairs. A sign hung from it that read FIRST-CLASS PASSENGERS ONLY. Beside it stood a seaman carrying out his seemingly important role in keeping the layers of English society completely separate.

Peter smiled at the man. "We're going to do some trapshooting."

The seaman unhooked the chain and stepped back.

There wasn't a man alive who didn't realize the great distance between the upper levels of British society and the working poor. It was a fact, a daily fact of life. The thing about the *Titanic* was the relatively close space that confined them together. Even though the *Titanic* was the largest ship afloat, in London a man had to take a taxi from Soho to Whitechapel to be able to see the sooty nature of the English poor. Here, one had only to step to the B deck balcony, off the Palm Court, to see it. Many couples did, too. Even as Morgan walked down the stairs he could see several finely dressed couples standing at the railing above and pointing below, like visitors to a human zoo.

The thought annoyed him. Even worse, he and Peter would be on the stern of the ship firing shotguns at clay pigeons, well within earshot of the third-class passengers around them. Somehow, he had never been able to recover from the idea of being a part of the upper class.

There was so much reality that he felt he was missing out on with his full stomach and soft bed, so much pain and so much hardship. The challenge to follow Christ that he'd heard at Oxford from James Cook was surely something that couldn't be enjoyed from the ease of the first-class section on the *Titanic*.

The two of them walked through the steerage passengers on the aft well deck to the stairs that led up to the poop deck area. A number of eyes studied them, these two finely dressed men, Peter in his knickers and bow tie and Morgan in his blue blazer and Oxford rep colors. At the top of the stairs, they had to parade in front of another group of steerage passengers. These people were seated along rows of shellacked benches that faced the open ocean. The benches provided a rather relaxed view of the sea, even though from time to time a man might be showered with soot from the smokestacks, if the wind was blowing the wrong way.

The docking bridge stood on a white platform that separated the seating for the steerage passengers from the very stern of the ship. The docking bridge stood high above the deck area with stairs on either side; it had white handrails that ran around a teak deck. It was complete with its own telegraph column to the bridge and engine room along with a separate steering helm that was used in the process of easing the *Titanic* into port. It covered the width of the stern area, and Morgan and Peter walked under it, giving it a close inspection.

Guggenheim and his valet stood with Boxhall and a seaman at the end of the poop deck. The seaman was making adjustments to a contraption Morgan could only guess was used to throw the clay targets off the fantail. Guggenheim was impeccably dressed in a black coat and white pants with a pearl-gray vest and open white shirt. Around his neck was a flaming-red silk ascot. He held a double-barreled shotgun, open and draped over his elbow.

His valet was even more impressive in a cutaway day coat with gray trousers. The man's shiny black shoes were covered with gray spats. His stature filled the day coat, and his chest stood out like a barrel full of hard nails. But what caught Morgan's eye right off was the sight of the bandage on his forehead.

"Good afternoon gentlemen," Guggenheim said. "I'm pleased you could make it."

Peter's eyes danced at the sight of the velvet-lined cases that lay on the deck. The shotguns had checkered grips that shone in the sun. "The pleasure is all ours," Peter replied.

Guggenheim looked at Morgan. "I am sorry to hear that your friend is not feeling well."

Boxhall shot Morgan a quick glance.

"Thank you," Morgan said. "I'll pass on your regards." It was very difficult for Morgan to talk about Hunter as if he were still alive, especially to a man who may well have been responsible for his death.

"You both know my valet, Hans?"

Peter nodded at the man.

"I've seen him," Morgan said. He looked at the man. "I see you've had an accident."

Guggenheim chuckled. "It seems Hans here is too tall for certain sections of the ship. He will have to be more careful." Guggenheim looked at Morgan and Peter. "So, you two gentlemen are sportsmen?"

"I shoot quite a lot on my father's estate," Peter said.

"I'm afraid shotguns are not my weapon of choice," Morgan added. "Actually, I prefer the foil."

Guggenheim's eyes widened. "Did you hear that Hans?"

"Yes, sir, I did."

"Hans is actually quite good with a sword. He was trained in Germany."

"My fencing instructor was German."

"And who would that be?" Hans asked.

"Wolfgang Erhart. I studied under him for six years."

"I know of zis man," Hans said. "You have learned well."

"I hope so."

"Perhaps you and Hans here can favor us with an exhibit this afternoon. We have the squash court reserved for 3:00."

Morgan looked at Hans. The man was trying very hard to suppress a smile, but it was plain to see that he was hoping Morgan would say yes. It was also easy to see that he was supremely confident. "I think I'd enjoy that," Morgan responded.

"Splendid. Then it's a match. We have a collection of foils, épées, and sabers. I'm certain Hans would give you your choice of weapons."

Morgan smiled. "Oh, no, I'd let your man choose."

Guggenheim laughed. "You don't want to do that. Hans much prefers the saber. It's the most brutal of the weapons. A man could get scarred, at the very least."

"Then your valet will have another to match the one he already appears to be carrying," Morgan said.

That brought laughter from both Guggenheim and Hans. Peter tried to smile, but the seriousness of the event made him stop short.

"Are you taking advantage of everything the _Titanic_ has to offer?" Morgan asked.

"I'd say I am." Guggenheim hefted the shotgun. "There aren't many given to shooting, however."

"I was looking for you yesterday afternoon," Morgan lied. He was thinking he was becoming more like Hunter all the time. "Where were you?"

"At what time?"

"Around 2:00."

Guggenheim placed his hand on his chin, studying the question. "Ah, yes, I was gambling in the smoking room."

"With whom?" Morgan asked. He could tell Guggenheim was growing impatient with the questioning.

"What does it matter with whom?"

"I just wondered if you had a chance to recover what you lost to that same group you were with the other night."

It was obvious the reminder wasn't appreciated.

"I believe Baxter was there."

"Too bad Hunter couldn't have been there with you."

Guggenheim's eyes flashed. "Yes, that is too bad. All right, gentlemen," he said, "Let's begin. Choose your weapons."

Peter immediately picked up the shotgun he'd already been eyeing. Morgan bent down and selected the smaller of the two that remained. There was no sense in making a complete fool of himself by taking one he couldn't even aim quickly.

The view from the fantail of the ship was impressive. The *Titanic's* massive triple screws churned up the water, leaving a wake that seemed to go on for miles. It was impossible for something that large to pass through even the deepest water without leaving its mark, and however temporary that mark might be, the *Titanic* was doing her best to make her presence known.

Morgan couldn't resist turning around and looking at the impressive length of the great ship. It was over 882 feet and 9 inches long, more than twice the length of a soccer field, and her black hull seemed to go on and on when viewed from here.

"Quite extraordinary, isn't she?" Boxhall asked. "She's 104 feet from the keel to the bridge with a gross tonage of 46,328. Her 29 boilers and engines produce over 46,000 horse power and she has a maximum speed of between 24 and 25 knots. A grand lady she is."

"Yes it, uh, she is," replied Morgan, amazed at the ease with which the officer rattled off numbers as if they were familiar as his birthday. "Why are ships seemingly always called after the female of the species?"

Boxhall smiled. "I suppose it's because men sail on them, and we do develop a love for the ships we sign onto."

"And do you love the *Titanic?*"

"Passionately!" Boxhall replied.

"Here, here," Guggenheim said, "Plenty of time for that. Let's begin our shooting, eh, what?"

The men moved into position and Boxhall gave the signal for the seaman to release the first target. The chunking sound of the machine sent a clay target spinning off into the blue. Guggenheim threw his gun to his shoulder, eyed down the barrel, and squeezed the trigger. The clay target shattered in midair.

"Fine shot," Peter exclaimed. He held his gun to his chest. "Pull," he shouted.

The second clay bird went spinning off. Peter rested the large shotgun on his shoulder and trained his eye on the small bead in front. The explosion was followed by the far off puff of the disintegrated target.

Boxhall applauded.

Morgan sheepishly stepped forward. He turned to Guggenheim. "You asked earlier about Hunter. I should think that after the way he treated you in that card game, he'd be the last man whose welfare you'd care about."

Guggenheim's eyes sharpened. "I always care about the men who embarrass me. It's my friends I largely ignore." Turning to the seaman, he gave the order, "Pull."

The man snapped off the target. Morgan placed the gun to his shoulder and followed to clay bird into the air. He squeezed the trigger. The gun rocked in his hands from the explosion, jarring his shoulder. Morgan watched as the target continued on its downward course into the ocean.

"You must lead it," Guggenheim said. "Always be there before your opponent."

"Who are we talking about?" Morgan asked, "The bird or Hunter?"

SATURDAY,

APRIL 13, 1912,

2:00 P.M.

CHAPTER 25

Margaret and April had been looking forward to their trip to the styling salon. Margaret wore a tan-colored skirt and jacket, a lace blouse that had ruffles down the front, and a wide-brimmed brown hat. April had gone all out. Her salmon-colored dress was nearly to her ankles, and she wore white shoes with pearl buttons. Her hat, dyed to match her dress perfectly, swooped low over the side of her head. Pearl-white and salmon ostrich feathers hugged the wide brim, fluttering softly. Both women had spent almost an hour in preparing for their appearance with Jean, who was the French hairdresser recommended by one of the stewards.

Margaret had at first resisted her mother's notion of spending so much time to get ready to go and have their hair done, but April was adamant. The best of society's women would be having their looks put into place. It wouldn't do to turn up in a shabby appearance. Besides, if one didn't have the hairdresser's respect, he wouldn't do his best work. There were times when Margaret knew better than to argue such logic with her mother, and this was one of them. Margaret had made certain that Kitty was having her usual work done at the same time.

The salon smelled strongly of ammonia, and floating through the air was a hint of what one might sniff coming from the bottom of a seldom-used fireplace—burning hair, masked by an overbearing aroma of French perfume. It was like a cloud of chemicals resting on a field of blossoming flowers. One didn't quite know whether to gag or breathe deeply.

Jean greeted them as they stepped into the salon. "Bonjour, Madame and Mademoiselle. If you would please step over this way." He wore a white shirt with puff sleeves that were held in place by garters; his trousers were a matching white. Tied around his waist was a flowing red sash that dangled down to a point just below his knees.

We're getting our hair done by Sinbad the sailor, Margaret thought. But April didn't seem to notice, or if she did, she pretended the man was perfect in every respect.

Margaret spotted Kitty right away. Her hair was already wet and wrapped in a towel, awaiting the next stage of preparation. She sat in a chair, showing some interest in one of the many magazines that featured the apparel of Paris for the upcoming spring. "Good afternoon," Margaret said.

Kitty dipped the magazine slightly and peered over the top. She nodded. "Afternoon."

Margaret sat down beside her. "I'm so very glad to find you here. I've wanted to be able to talk to you, and our table doesn't allow a great deal of conversation unless you happen to be seated next to the person with whom you wish to talk."

"Yes, I know." Kitty nodded at April. "I have spoken to your mother, though. A charming woman."

Margaret looked over at April and smiled. "Yes, she is. I'm a very lucky girl."

"I should say you are, and preparing for a wedding too, I see."

Margaret knew enough about Kitty's situation to know that the subject of weddings was no doubt a painful one. A woman who was planning one always seemed to talk of little else. She decided to put the woman at ease, and perhaps cause her to want to talk. "That remains to be seen," she replied.

She could see that her response caught Kitty off guard. The woman put down her magazine and leaned in her direction. "You sound like you have some doubts."

Margaret looked over to make sure that April was occupied. "Honestly speaking, yes, I do." She looked Kitty in the eye. "I'm not quite certain I want to settle into a life of one man with a house and children just yet. There's more of the world to see and more people to meet."

"More men?" Kitty asked the question with a knowing smile on her lips. It was as if she'd discovered a dark secret in a young lady who wasn't supposed to have any.

"More of everything." Margaret knew she would have to do her best to keep Kitty's interest up if she was going to get her to talk at all and what better way to do it than make her believe that she was in on the ground floor of a potential scandal. Few women could resist such a thing.

"I must say, I'm surprised."

Jean stepped over to them, a sickly smile underneath his pencil-thin mustache. How the man managed to work under these conditions continually was a mystery to Margaret. He lifted his finger and wagged it in the air. "Now, now, you must not get too distracted. In a few moments more, you will be all mine."

Kitty waved the man off, obviously very interested in hearing more of Margaret's story. It was one thing to be interrupted and another to be stopped in the middle of juicy gossip.

"You must have known more men than Benjamin Guggenheim." Margaret made the statement, even though for most women it would have been considered an insult. She'd already laid the groundwork with her own scandal. It was only right that Kitty play along, or so she hoped.

Kitty smiled slyly. "Yes, you could say I have."

"Men are such amazingly simple creatures when you come right down to it," Margaret went on. "When a girl knows what to do, they can be so very predictable."

Kitty laughed. "Oh, yes, they can, very predictable."

"I seem to have run into a tight spot here on ship," Margaret said. "Perhaps you can give me some advice."

Now Margaret could see that Kitty was interested. A tight spot for Margaret would be a nice piece of gossip. In a way, Margaret hated telling her anything about her personal life, but if she was going to get the woman to talk, she might have to.

"I can't imagine what a girl of your family could possibly run into here that would give her any difficulty."

"You see," Margaret started, "Even though I am engaged to be married, there's another man aboard ship who loves me."

"Oh, really!" Kitty's eyes brightened. "Do I know him?"

"Yes, I think you do." Margaret knew she would simply dangle Morgan's identity in front of Kitty for a while. It might keep her talking. "He's someone I had a relationship with in the past, and now here he is. Has anything like that ever happened to you?"

The question was a bold one, and Margaret knew it, but she thought she had the hook just about set.

"Yes, it has." Kitty gulped. "Can you keep a secret?"

"Why, yes," Margaret said, "I've told you mine."

"Well, you haven't told me everything."

"Oh, I will. You can rely on that."

"Well, then, it has happened to me, and on this very trip."

"Really? How are you dealing with it?"

"The young man was someone I knew in show business." Kitty shook her head frivolously and giggled. "Someone I neither expected or wanted to see ever again." She leaned forward. "You know the past can come back to haunt you, and you must prevent it. Men like to think they are the only love you've ever known."

"Your Mr. Guggenheim might frown on a man from your past."

"Yes, I'm afraid so. It seems to be all right for men to be experienced but not for the women they love."

"They can be so very possessive. You'd think they want jewelry no one else has ever worn."

Kitty laughed. "No, they seem to take some pride in that. That piece I wore last night was once owned by one of the crown princes of Europe. Benjamin takes pride in announcing that. They want desks owned by famous people and houses lived in by royalty; it's only their women they want to have never even been seen by another. It seems the feminine gender is their prize possession."

"Possession?" Margaret asked.

"Yes. Sometimes a woman can feel like an accoutrement to a man's attire. Benjamin takes almost as much trouble in my apparel for the evening as I do."

"Is that so?"

"Most certainly."

Margaret looked around the salon. "And do you come here every afternoon?" she asked.

"Why, yes, I do."

"Were you here yesterday afternoon?"

Kitty's eyes probed Margaret. It was easy to see that in spite of the personal questions, it was this one question that seemed to make her the most uncomfortable. She squirmed in her chair. "Yes, I was here."

"Do you come here at the same time every day?"

Kitty looked over to Jean and raised her voice. "I was here yesterday afternoon, wasn't I, Jean?"

The man turned from April and smiled, then advanced, shaking his finger. "Yes you were, but you were late you bad, bad girl." He laughed and went back to his work on April.

"There," Kitty said, "I can't seem to stay away from the beauty salon. A girl has to stay in tip-top form you know."

"As to this other man," Margaret went on. "Do you think that his exposing the nature of his past relationship with you would have made Mr. Guggenheim angry?"

"Of course, it would have."

"Then what am I to do?" Margaret asked innocently.

"Speak to the man. If he's a gentleman, he will understand."

"And was your past lover a gentleman?"

"Unfortunately not."

"What am I to do if he doesn't listen to reason?"

Kitty leaned closer. "Obviously your fiancé is a man of means. If it's worth it to you, you can try bribery."

"And what if that doesn't work? You must know how irrational men in love are."

"Then, my dear, you must prepare for the worst." Kitty's head sank.

"And what did you have to do?"

Kitty's eyes narrowed. "I don't think I will have to worry." A broad smile spread over her face. "I think my own problem is solved."

3:00 P.M.

The squash courts were near the waterline and, with no natural lighting to speak of, had a number of bright, overhead lights that were kept protected from errant squash balls by brass wire cages. It smelled of sweat but had the appearance of a freshly scrubbed operating room with its white walls and parquet floor. The floor's glow of newness made one almost hesitate to step on it.

Morgan had changed into something more comfortable and athletic. He had on a pair of his khaki slacks and a white shirt, open at the collar and of a generous fit. He chose his new oxfords to wear. They were tan with bottoms that were spongy and could be relied on to maintain a steady footing.

"I say, old boy, do you think he'll show?" Peter asked.

"I'm sure he will. He didn't flinch even when I told him who my fencing instructor was and how long I'd studied under him. In fact, he seemed rather anxious."

"Do you think Guggenheim will come along?" Boxhall asked. The officer had been released from some of his regular duties in order to assist Morgan in investigating the murders aboard the *Titanic*. It had taken quite a bit of persuasion to convince the captain to continue what he saw as a charade. But at Ismay's insistence, he had done so. Ismay, it seemed, was still a mite gun-shy about what Morgan might report to his famous great-uncle.

"He'll be here," Morgan replied.

"I don't see how he could miss it," Peter added. "The man is his employee. He'll want to see what he's made of."

"I'm certain he already knows that," Morgan said. "That man is sly enough to find only the best when it comes to a personal servant, a man of grace who can defend himself and his boss."

"Do you mean a bodyguard?" Peter asked.

"I'd say so."

"And a rather intimidating one to boot," Boxhall added.

Morgan shook his head, deep in thought. "That man is dangerous."

"He's a big one," Peter observed.

"Oh, I don't mean Hans. I mean Guggenheim."

"How so?" Boxhall asked.

"He strikes me as something akin to a South American boa constrictor, so subtle in his movements that you almost think he's a part of the jungle. He moves ever so slightly that it's easy to take your eyes off him, but you dare not. He's steady, his eyes and senses trained on you alone. And when he strikes, it's swift and sure, taking you in his arms and choking the life out of you." Morgan was growing more and more animated in his description. "He strikes me rather like what I hear of his business ventures. He swallows you whole, without a trace left."

"Sounds bloody ruthless," Peter said.

"My uncle's bank has had some dealings with him, and they view every transaction from a safe distance." Morgan shook his head. "You know, I warned Hunter about that man. I told him he was making a dangerous enemy."

"You think Guggenheim killed your friend?" Boxhall asked.

"I'm not sure. Frankly, I'd find that hard to believe unless he had some compelling reason we're not aware of. Such a thing is much too risky for a man of Benjamin Guggenheim's stature."

They watched as Guggenheim and Hans stepped though the far door. Hans was carrying over his shoulder a collection of cases, which undoubtedly contained the swords, along with a large bag.

"Of course, he may have had someone close to him who did it," Morgan added, "someone who just got a little too carried away."

"You mean someone like Hans over there?" Peter asked.

The men looked over at the formidable-looking man as he put the swords on the floor. He was well decked out for a fight, with red pantaloons that were tied around soft leather calf-length boots. The boots looked almost like slippers on the bottoms but Morgan recognized them as foot apparel often worn during dueling. His cream-colored shirt was open, with a lacing of brown string that reached from the bottom of his massive chest to the top.

"Yes, someone just like him," Morgan replied. "We'll see how he handles his anger this afternoon."

"Good afternoon once again, gentlemen," Guggenheim said.

"I see your man is ready," Peter leered.

"Oh," Guggenheim looked around at Hans, who was bending over at the waist and turning circles to limber up, "I think he's ready all right." He looked at Morgan with a smirk. "We'll see how your schoolboy chum has learned his lessons."

Morgan took the insult good-naturedly. Bravado was something he was used to handling when it came to swordplay.

Hans walked over with the equipment he'd been carrying in his bag. He handed Morgan a thinly padded vest with a red heart painted on the chest. "There you are," he said. "You'll be safe."

"Do you practice here every day?" Morgan asked.

"Yes, every afternoon."

"So, I take it you had the court yesterday afternoon."

"Yes," Hans glared at him. "I had it from 2:00 to 4:00."

"And you practiced by yourself."

"I have not found anyone who shares this passion of mine," he smiled, "until now."

Morgan strapped the vest into place. Safety was a relative thing when it came to fencing. A well-placed thrust could easily penetrate the lightly padded vests that men often referred to as *paper shields.*

Hans pulled out two leather gloves and pulled them over his large hands, fixing them into position by alternatively mashing his fingers in between the fingers of the other hand.

Morgan took out a small pair of leather gloves that he carried for the weather. They would have to do.

"And now the mask," Hans said. He tossed Morgan a small semimask made from wire mesh. Men seldom went for a man's eyes, but in the heat of battle, one could never tell. Hans pouted in Morgan's direction, sticking out his lower lip with an air of contempt. Picking up a foil, he tossed it at Morgan.

Morgan caught it and inspected it. The blade gleamed like new money, and the handle seemed to be balanced. The basket hilt was carefully wrapped with brown leather. Morgan tested the hard rubber ball that had been secured at the tip. His was firm. He could only hope Hans's was as well. "I thought we were using sabers," Morgan said.

Hans motioned nonchalantly with his free hand. "We begin with these. If I see you can use them, we may go to the saber."

The man seemed determined to be condescending. Morgan noticed he was sporting a fresh bandage on his head. "I wouldn't want you exerting yourself until you've fully recovered."

"Oh, zis thing." Hans touched the bandage. "Iz nothing. I took a fall."

Morgan shot Guggenheim a glance, then refocused on Hans. "I thought you banged your head on something low."

"It matters not." Hans waved him off.

"Perhaps something fell on you."

Hans glared at him. Morgan knew he'd hit a nerve. No doubt it had been Hans who had dropped the heavy object on him and Hunter on the night they docked in Cherbourg. Maybe Guggenheim didn't take lightly to losing, or perhaps it had been the valet's idea entirely. In any event, he'd got what he deserved, and Morgan wanted to make him pay even more. The man may have even carried the need for revenge into the Turkish bath and swimming pool.

Peter stepped over to Morgan. "Are you sure about this, old boy?" He looked over at Hans, who had stepped aside and was conferring with Guggenheim. "This doesn't appear to be a game to that man."

"It's not."

"Well then, what is it?"

"It's the way a man proves his mettle, sheer combat."

Peter put his hand on Morgan's sword and ran it along the solid steel shaft of the blade. "I really think you should stick to the pen."

Morgan chuckled. "I've no doubt that I'll write about it later. It'll make interesting copy, I should think."

"No doubt," Peter agreed.

"All right," Guggenheim announced, "it's time you two gentlemen have at it."

Boxhall pointed to the viewing loft above them. The row of seats stretched atop the wall at the back of the two squash courts. "I think we should all wait up there. We'll get a better view."

Guggenheim nodded.

"I'm not certain I want to see this at all," Peter added.

When the small group had taken their seats in the observation loft, Hans turned and raised his sword for approval. Morgan got the picture of a gladiator turning to face the emperor for the last time. Swiveling around, the man positioned himself. "En garde," he said.

Morgan touched his sword to Hans's foil. They began to maneuver, circling each other like dogs in an alleyway, lightly flicking their blades and ringing out ticking noises that sounded like a telegraph with the steel blades.

Hans began a series of thrusts, sending his forward foot advancing and dancing with jabs and slashes.

Morgan twisted his body and parried with his blade, repelling each and every thrust the man sent his way.

Hans smiled and stopped momentarily. "Very good," he said. "You must have attended your classes."

"That I did." Morgan launched a surprising slash that pushed Hans back on his heels. Morgan continued the attack, which Hans repelled, raising his foil to fend off the blows and then dancing to one side.

"You do have nice form," Hans said. "Your way with a sword is not at all like you shoot." He paused and smiled. "But now, the way of children is over. We fight."

With that, Hans began his own series of slashes, sending each one overhead to Morgan's face and shoulders. He handled the foil as a cruel man might whip a horse that refused to move, each blow coming down harder and still harder. Morgan could see that the man's style was far more suited for the saber, that of a cavalryman on horseback murdering an enemy.

Each and every blow sent Morgan's hand flying up to stop the crashing oncoming blow with the hard edge of the blade.

"I'm afraid the foil doesn't suit you, sir," Morgan said.

"Is that so?"

Morgan could see the man's face flush with anger. He was used to intimidating an opponent, and it was plain to see that Morgan had no intention of backing down.

Hans once again started with yet another series of slashes. Side to side, from his right shoulder, down to Morgan's right leg, and then from his left shoulder to Morgan's left. He was slashing large Xs in the air, each designed to make contact and perhaps even cripple Morgan.

The lightly padded body armor they both wore wasn't designed to take serious blows of the nature Hans was trying to deliver and both of them knew it. Broken bones, or worse, could result from the type of com-bat being dished out.

Morgan danced out of the way of the blows, spinning like a ballerina on the stage and glancing off each of the man's blows with a flick of the foil. Then he rushed him, locking hilts with the man.

Hans grinned. He was strong and he knew it. There would be no pushing him over. The two men got very close, in a deathlike grip.

"You should have come and faced us like a man that night at Cher-bourg," Morgan said. "Instead, you ran away."

Morgan watched the man's eyes bulge, his mouth widen and his teeth begin to grind. "I don't know what you're talking about." Hans spoke the words almost syllable by syllable, slowly and deliberately.

"Oh, I think you do."

With that, Morgan gave him a shove and once again danced away from a downward blow Hans sent in his direction. The near edge of the man's sword grazed Morgan's left hand, starting a trickle of blood.

Hans grinned and started a sideward windmill slash. Morgan ducked as the blade went sizzling overhead, and with an upward thrust, sent the tip of his foil into the German's chest. The ball struck the painted heart and seemed to startle or take the man by surprise.

"Touché," Morgan announced.

Hans dropped his sword to his side.

There was polite applause from the gallery and enthusiastic clapping from Peter.

Morgan held his sword. "I want you to know, you won't find me with my back turned to you in the swimming pool."

"And what is that supposed to mean?"

"Don't you know?"

"All I know is that the next time I face you, it will be with a saber."

SATURDAY,

APRIL 13, 1912,

4:05 P.M.

CHAPTER 26

W e'll be getting close to that time," Phillips said.

Jack Phillips was a twenty-four-year-old wireless operator, living out the adventure of his life. The Marconi equipment aboard the *Titanic* was the finest piece of wireless communication available. During daylight hours, a message could be sent for over four hundred miles and at nightfall the range escalated to over twelve hundred miles. Phillips and his assistant, twenty-two-year-old Harold Bride, found those numbers hard to fathom. The other number they didn't believe was the cost to send a wire. A three-dollar fee was charged for every ten-word message, and fifty cents a word was charged after that. The passengers of the *Titanic* could afford it, though, and as far as Jack was concerned, what could be afforded could and should be charged.

"I guess we'll get plenty busy when the sun sets," Bride replied. "You ought to go and get yourself some food. After all, the ship's paying for that."

Both Phillips and Bride were technically employees of the Marconi wireless company, even though the roster of the *Titanic*'s crew listed them both as junior officers. The fact remained that all they got from White Star Line was room and board. Marconi paid their salaries. While they usually got very little sleep, they were both determined that what wasn't collected in the form of *room* would be made up for in the way of *board*.

"Yes, and when they all get to dinner, I swear, all they must do is sit around and talk about who they haven't wired just yet. They must have nothing better to talk about."

"It's a good thing for us," Bride said. He held his hands up and wiggled his fingers. "Sometimes I think these fingers are solid gold."

Phillips laughed. "You'd better hope they're flesh and blood. I wouldn't let some lead-fingered kid work this key, and I won't let one with gold fingers do it either."

In most places, Jack Phillips couldn't have passed for more than nineteen or twenty at best. His pug nose and twinkling eyes had a boyish charm to them. Harold Bride looked to be all of twelve, with hollow cheeks and large doleful eyes that gave him the appearance of a choirboy. Neither of them had ever shaved.

Phillips shuffled through a number of the incoming telegrams. It was easy to let the things pile up in the heat of battle, and the battle heated up at night. The airwaves buzzed all the way across the Atlantic when the sun went down, and it was all either of them could do to take a message and stack up the undelivered ones. It might take them all of the next day to deliver the messages.

"Here, what have we here?" Phillips held up a wire and showed it to Bride.

"That's a wire from the Cunarder *Caronia*. It came in last night along with tons of hope-you're-having-a-wonderful-time messages."

Phillips read the message:

Captain, *Titanic*—

Westbound steamers report bergs, growlers and field ice in 42 degrees North from 49 degrees to 51 degrees West, April 12.

Compliments, Barr.

"I figure Barr must be the captain of the *Caronia*," Bride said.

"Why haven't you taken this to the bridge?" Phillips asked.

"That position is still a good ways off. I got bogged down with paying customers, I suppose."

"OK, don't worry about it, old man. I'll take it up on my way to dinner." Phillips stuck the wire into his pocket.

He sat down on Bride's bunk. Lifting up the younger man's pillow, Phillips's eyes brightened. "I say, what have we here?"

"Hey!" Bride, sprang from his chair and tore the magazine from Phillips's hands. "That's mine." He held it away from Phillips's prying eyes.

"What is it?" Phillips danced around Bride as the man kept the magazine behind him.

"I'll let you see it when you've finished eating and I can go. It's kind of a fashion magazine, from Paris, France."

"Ooh-la-la," Phillips said.

"That ought to make you eat in a hurry."

Phillips squashed his hat on and opened the door. "Oh, it will, old man, it will. You just see that you don't wear out the pages while I'm gone."

"Oh, I won't do that. It'll be in absolutely pristine shape by the time you get back. You just save me some of that custard, you hear?"

The cold breeze of the evening air was starting to make its presence known in the small little radio room. Phillips threw Bride his jacket and laughed. "Here's something to keep you warm if those pictures don't do the job."

With that, he closed the door and headed straight for the dining room.

4:15 P.M.

Morgan took the time to change in his cabin. He put his blazer over the white shirt, but he left the oxfords on. The deck was slippery, and the soles seemed to have a remarkable ability at gripping the wood. He'd been quite happy with the way they had performed on the squash court.

When he took the stairs, there was a remarkable spring in his steps. Combat seemed to agree with him, although most casual observers to his life would have never guessed it. He'd always taken to the sword. Perhaps it was the fact that it reminded him of all the books he'd read as a child. The idea of being a modern Lancelot appealed to him.

Peter and Boxhall were still on deck. They stood at the rail and, when they caught sight of him, began to chuckle.

"There he is," Peter said, "the most heroic Morgan Fairfield."

"Well, how does it feel to defeat the Hun?" Boxhall asked, in obvious reference to the German race. "I fear we shall all have to be doing just that before long."

"Don't make too much of it. The foil is a subtle weapon. He was being kind to me. He's far more suited to the saber."

"That may be," Peter said, "but you made him look foolish, and in front of Guggenheim."

"That's a dangerous thing to do," Boxhall added.

"I've already crossed swords with the kaiser today. I doubt I'll do it again."

"Why don't we go up on the bridge," Boxhall said. "I don't think you had much of a chance to see it, and Ismay may just be there."

"Lead on, Macduff," Morgan said.

The men started their brisk walk along the rail. One could seldom walk a great distance on the *Titanic* without being impressed by its enormous size. It was like a small city with all of its glamour and none of its squalor. There was no litter to be seen, and the crew made constant attempts at keeping the ship in polished form. For many, it was the power of the thing that seemed so awesome. As the hum of the engines rose from the steel below, a passenger could feel confident.

The papers had declared her to be the final word in oceangoing travel for all time. Morgan knew that newspapers were given to superlatives, especially the English press, about something they viewed as their own. They hated being reminded that the ship was financed and the White Star Line owned by an American conglomerate. Of course, as J. P. Morgan's great nephew, that fact wasn't lost on Morgan.

The name *Morgan* carried a certain amount magic to it, along with its share of ridicule, inspired by envy, no doubt. Morgan certainly had no great affection for the rich, but his great-uncle's wealth had come to him as a result of energy combined with an enormous amount of shrewdness. For most people, however, it was the vulgarity of his wealth that caused the negative reaction.

"Morgan." The sound of his name brought him to a halt. Stepping out of the doors that led to the first-class lounge was Molly Brown, the woman he'd seen gambling with Hunter during the Cherbourg stop. She had a well-dressed couple with her.

Morgan looked ahead at Peter and Boxhall. "You go ahead. I'll join you in a bit."

"I sure am glad to see you," Molly said. "I've been looking for that friend of yours, that Irish rogue who took me for over a thousand dollars." She chuckled. "He was worth it, though. The boy was great fun. I thought that easterner would split a gut when your friend kept calling him *Goggenhem*."

"He called Benjamin Guggenheim that?" the woman who was at Molly's elbow inquired.

"You bet he did, and several times, too, even after the fella warned him."

Molly looked at the woman. "Oh, I should introduce you." She smiled. "Fact is, you've got a lot in common. Morgan, meet Mr. and Mrs. Morgan."

Morgan recognized the woman at once. He'd seen her in the society pages almost on a constant basis, and her name wasn't Morgan at all. She was Lady Lucy Duff Gorgon, the international fashion designer. Her clothes looked it, too. She wore a mink draped over an ankle-length, green silk dress with long sleeves and matching jacket. Her hat had a small brim that wound all the way around with fur instead of feathers hanging from it. He could only guess that the man next to her in the black suit was her husband, Cosmo.

"Pleased to meet you," Morgan said.

"Jolly good to meet you," The man said, shaking Morgan's hand.

"And who are your parents, young man?" the woman asked.

Morgan was used to that. In society, if a man wasn't over the age of thirty, or even if he was and was still not recognized by sight, a man's pedigree was his most important asset. "My parents are both dead now. They died when I was a child. They were the Fairfields of Newport."

"Pity," the man said.

"But of course," the woman exclaimed, "I knew your mother, a wonderful woman."

"Yes, she was."

It puzzled Morgan slightly that the two of them would be traveling on the *Titanic* under assumed names. Certainly, the passengers in first class would be the picture of high fashion. Some would no doubt know her by sight. If he hadn't seen her picture so often or hadn't seen her at his aunt's home at parties, he wouldn't know her. But as it was, here he was, a man, and he knew her. He could only guess their decision to use the name of Morgan was to be a slap in the face to his great-uncle. They no doubt had heard he'd be onboard ship, and he would have if a sudden illness hadn't prevented it. The name choice was no doubt a matter of their personal entertainment at what they thought would be his uncle's expense.

"Where's that scalawag friend of yours, Morgan?" Molly asked. "I miss him. It's not easy being a woman and traveling on the most romantic ship afloat, you know." She shook her head. "I see couples hand in hand everywhere, and at night I can hear them creeping through the halls and knocking on doors. A lady like me needs a few laughs, and that friend of yours was good for that."

"I'm afraid he's not feeling too well," Morgan lied.

"Oh, I get it." Molly's eyes twinkled. "Been drinking, has he? Well, you just tell him that when he sobers up I intend to get my money back, all of it and some of his."

"I certainly will."

"And you tell him to watch out for that Guggenheim feller. The man had blood in his eyes. And he'd better not run into that valet of his on this deck in the dark, either. It's a long swim to New York."

"I'll tell him just that." He bowed slightly to the woman calling herself Morgan. "Pleased to meet you, Mrs. Morgan, and you, sir."

"Our pleasure, chap," the man replied.

Morgan hustled to try to catch up to Peter and Boxhall before they left the bridge. The last thing he needed was another reminder of someone who wanted Hunter dead. The list was long. At least he could scratch Molly Brown from it.

The sight of another passing steamer caught everyone's eye. The vessel was in the semidarkness. Its lights were on, and from where Morgan stood, he could see it was flashing Morse code signals to the *Titanic*. It was some comfort to know they weren't quite alone on this endless ocean.

It was a matter of minutes before Morgan ran up the stairs leading to the bridge. Boxhall was pointing out the telegraph column that was used to send messages to the engine room.

"I say, Morgan, come over here and look at this." Peter seemed excited to see him. "This thing can deliver messages almost instantly."

Morgan took note of Captain Smith standing with his hound beside him. The man was special, like a rock, and even if he'd been in another line of work, E. J. Smith would have still been a captain. Some men were just born to a position, and no amount of career shuffling could ever change it. He would have had another title—dean, president, professor—but he would have been a captain all the same.

Morgan thought that was true about his being a writer, too. It wasn't that he loved words, it was that he loved the feelings produced by words. He was also a student of people and would often be caught watching total strangers, trying to imagine what their life was like. He'd embarrassed his Aunt Dottie on numerous occasions by not only staring but by taking notes. People didn't just become something. They were born something and found out about it in time.

"What was our distance yesterday, Boxhall?" The captain asked.

"From noon yesterday till noon today, she covered 519 miles, sir."

Smith nodded and stepped toward the window. His hound dutifully followed. Even though there was nothing to see from the animal's perspective, he knew his place, and that was by Smith's side.

Boxhall dipped his head in Morgan's direction and spoke in a low tone. "I'd say we'll do better today."

Morgan watched as a seaman came through the door. The man was scrawny with a heavy, black wool sweater that mushroomed to a point just below his chin. He came to a stop next to the captain's elbow and held out a message. Smith's eyes were transfixed on the open water ahead. It always amazed Morgan how a man could look at the same ocean he'd seen for years and always look for something different, something out of place. He had to have his mind on something.

Smith took the message and turned back to Boxhall, "Have we received any reports of ice?"

"No, sir, not yet."

In an aside to Morgan, Boxhall lowered his voice and added, "But I suspect we will."

Smith opened the message, lifting on the flap of the envelope and tugging the thing so as not to tear it. Morgan saw the faintest hint of a smile cross the man's lips. He handed the paper back to the messenger and announced, "They have the fire out in coal bunker number 6."

Boxhall was far enough away so that his asides couldn't be heard. "Bloody good, that."

"Why is that?" Morgan asked.

"Yes, why?" Peter joined in the whispers.

"I'm no metallurgist, but I don't much care for having a blazing fire on the hull while we're making our way through arctic waters. It might weaken the thing."

"You mean we could have a tear?" Peter asked.

"I doubt that," Boxhall said, "Not without running into something."

"Well, that's a relief," Peter sighed. "I wouldn't say that water out there was something I'd care to take a swim in."

Boxhall's face turned sober. "I shouldn't think so. With the temperature of that sea, I don't think a man could last much over twenty minutes. Of course the *Titanic* was never built to launch swimmers." He chuckled. "It was built to be unsinkable and I for one would like to keep it that way."

The captain turned around and recognized Morgan. Reaching into his coat pocket, he pulled out a manila envelope. "I have something for you to see young man. It was turned in by one of our crew early this morning. They found it near the swimming pool."

Morgan took the envelope and opened it.

"Honest man, I should say," Smith added.

Morgan slid the item into the palm of his hand while Peter and Boxhall looked on. It was a diamond earring. It sparkled in Morgan's hand as he turned it over. The thing was a solitaire diamond in the shape of an oval, obviously quite valuable. He thought he had seen it before. He just couldn't quite place it.

"Most likely, it was lost by a passenger who will no doubt report it missing," Smith said. "I thought that since it was found in the place where the incident took place that you'd want to see it."

"Most thoughtful of you, Captain." Morgan dropped the diamond back into the envelope and handed it to Smith.

"I don't think Guggenheim's valet would be wearing that," Peter snickered.

"It may not even be connected to the murder," Morgan replied. "That swimming pool is very busy in the late afternoon and morning." In spite of his words to the contrary, he couldn't shake the feeling that he'd seen that piece of jewelry before. He'd like to know to whom it belonged.

"We might know its significance if no one reports it missing," Boxhall said. "Something that valuable is bound to be missed."

"That does puzzle me," Peter said. "I can't understand why there weren't more people there when Hunter died."

"Perhaps someone shooed them away," Boxhall said.

"It's simpler than that," Morgan said. "If you go down there early tomorrow afternoon, I doubt you'd find anyone. Everyone knows you shouldn't swim less than two hours after lunch. That's the conventional wisdom, and this ship is filled with people who constantly stake their lives on conventional wisdom."

"Not Hunter," Peter added.

"Exactly. That's the last thing Hunter was."

Boxhall rocked back and forth on his heels. "I wouldn't say that time was all that good for Kennedy. Perhaps the traditional thinking is right."

Morgan stared at the man. The irony of the thing wasn't lost on any of them.

A few minutes later, Bruce Ismay stepped onto the bridge. He seemed relieved to see Morgan. "There you are, my boy. Have you heard the news? Our murders are solved."

"All but one."

Ismay wrinkled his brow. "Which one?"

"Hunter Kennedy. He was killed when Boxhall was interviewing the man who attempted to sabotage the ship. It couldn't have been him."

Ismay brushed aside his mustache and stuck his hands in his pockets. "Well, I for one think your friend's death was an accident. He just slipped and hit his head."

"I have reason to believe that it didn't happen that way."

"Suit yourself, but I think we've found the only murderer we're going to find."

Morgan stepped closer to the man, not wanting to be overheard by others standing on the bridge. He spoke in a low tone. "Pardon me for asking, but it's just part of my job you understand."

"Asking what?"

"Can you tell me where you were yesterday afternoon between 1:00 and 3:00?"

Ismay blinked, removing his hands from his pockets. "You mean I'm a suspect?"

"It's just routine. I'm asking this question of everyone. You may have seen something or someone out of the ordinary."

Morgan watched as Ismay raked his hand over his face. He could tell the man was worried, perhaps worried that Morgan might actually know the reason he was happy to see Hunter dead, whether he had performed the deed or not.

"I was in my suite, napping."

5:30 PM

Margaret and April came out of the salon with more than new coiffures; they emerged with a sense of power. The brisk breeze bothered April, and she kept patting her hair. Margaret, however, loved it. She stepped out onto the deck and, facing the bow of the ship, lifted her chin. The cold breeze made her feel alive.

She spotted a mother and a young boy along the rail. What caught her attention, though, wasn't so much the look of the two of them as what the boy had in his hand. He was walking along the rail with the stub of a cane, raking it on the surface of the metal railing and making as much noise as he could.

"Margaret," April tried to get her attention, "We need to go inside. It's cold out here."

"In a minute, Mother." Margaret stepped forward to meet the woman. "Good evening. It's a mite chilly out here tonight, isn't it?"

"Yes." The blonde woman was wearing a baby-blue dress that showed off a sparkling white blouse. Her hat was pulled low. She looked back at the boy. "Wesley seems impervious to the cold. He can't seem to get enough of seeing the ocean."

"A typical boy, I suppose."

"I'm not a boy." The youngster raised himself to full height. He wore brown knickers and a wool jacket with a cap pulled down over his blond page-boy hair.

"He's ten years old. We're meeting his father in New York." She laughed. "I'm sorry we didn't introduce ourselves. "I'm Susan Holmes, and this is my son, Wesley."

"Pleased to meet you." Looking back at April, Margaret waved her hand to signal her out of the doorway. "I am Margaret Hastings, and this is my mother, April."

"Oh, yes, we saw you last night. Congratulations."

"Thank you," April said. She slipped her arm around Margaret, pulling her tight.

"We're very proud of Peter, aren't we dear?"

Margaret smiled. "Yes, Mother." She looked at the boy. "I was just wondering about that cane your son has. I have a friend who lost his. May I see it for a moment?"

"Of course. Here, let me have it, Wesley." The mother reached out and pulled it from the boy's hand. "It just fell from the sky."

"Margaret, do we have to do this?" April asked. "We really must get ready for dinner."

"Fell from the sky?" Margaret asked.

Susan handed the cane to Margaret. "We were on the deck below yesterday afternoon, the one with the glass that sticks out over the water. Someone must have dropped it from the deck above. It's broken, and perhaps they were just throwing it away."

"Yes, maybe so." Margaret turned it over in her hands. The cane was almost half-length. It had been broken and from the looks of it, it could have been the dark cane from which they had found pieces stuck in the steam room door. The large handle was silver with several dark spots on it, and carved at the top was the single initial, B.

Margaret shuddered at the thought that she might have the weapon that killed Hunter in her hands.

"Could this be your friend's cane?" Susan asked.

"Yes, I'm afraid it very well could be. Can you tell me what time it was dropped into your hands?" Margaret smiled at the boy.

"I think it was about 3:00, or perhaps a little bit before that. Was that when your friend lost it?"

Margaret nodded. "Yes, I think it was."

Susan pressed the cane into Margaret's hands. "Then you take it to him. Perhaps it can be repaired. It's a beautiful handle, and if nothing else that can be salvaged."

"I'll show it to him. If it's not his, I'll return it to you."

SATURDAY,

APRIL 13, 1912,

7:30 P.M.

CHAPTER 27

The gathering in the first-class lounge was a hastily called one. Boxhall began by relaying the information about the bomber found aboard the ship. That was shocking enough. The fact that Margaret had sent word about an important new piece of evidence had the group anxious, though, as she passed it around. "I think the fact that it was thrown overboard and the time are meaningful," Margaret said. She studied the cane and passed it on.

Boxhall examined it. "Whoever dropped it must not have been aware of the glass on the promenade deck. That deck is so low in the water, relatively speaking." He moved his hands to a side-by-side position, angling them toward the group in a forty-five-degree position. "The glass is tilted out to allow the air in and still keep any high seas off the deck. It lets people see without getting wet."

"And that's the only deck with such glass?" Margaret asked.

"Yes, the only one."

"Bloody good, that," Peter added, "otherwise they'd have known better and given it a fling."

"Yes," Boxhall replied, "They no doubt didn't even hazard to look down, just dropped it over the side and mistook the sound of the cane hitting the glass for the sound of the hull."

"They probably don't even know it's still aboard," Margaret added.

Morgan took the cane from Boxhall, pulled the two broken pieces from his pocket, and matched them. They fit perfectly. He ran his hands up the silver handle and held the stain up close. It did appear to be blood. It made him angry. This was a cold-blooded, calculated act. Someone tried to get him out of the way and then killed Hunter with the thing.

"That appears to be blood," Boxhall said.

"Yes," Morgan agreed.

"And that B inscribed at the top could only mean Benjamin Guggenheim," Peter offered.

Morgan handed the cane over to Peter. "Or Bruce Ismay."

Peter's eyes widened. "I hadn't thought of that."

Morgan could see that Boxhall was uncomfortable with the notion of the manager of the White Star Line being a murderer.

Peter clinched his fist and gritted his teeth. "He could be the bloody Prince of Wales for all I care. Odd thing though," Peter went on, "Why only the one initial? I'd think a man would want both. And if only one, why the first letter of the man's first name?"

Peter was beginning to grow on Morgan. The man still knew what was the proper thing to do and what wasn't, like any English gentleman should. It was plain to see, however, that he was loosening up. "It doesn't prove a thing," Morgan said. "The thing might be stolen, or we just might be looking for someone we don't know at all, say a John Brown."

"It does give us a big hint," Margaret said.

"You did well." Peter patted her hand.

Morgan broke into a half smile. "Maybe the B stands for Boxhall?"

The group stifled a chuckle.

"Of course, if it had been our officer friend here, he would have known to throw it farther from that place on the ship."

Boxhall wasn't amused. "I should think Ismay would have known that, too."

Morgan nodded. "You're right, he would have." Morgan mulled the idea over. Ismay had to have known about the deck below him. He could have panicked and not thought much about it, but that was doubtful. No, this was a cold, calculating murder. If Ismay had done it, he would have planned the disposal of the cane better.

"So then we're all settled," Peter said. "Benjamin Guggenheim is our murderer."

"Not so fast," Morgan said. "I don't think he would stoop to something like that. He may be vindictive and he may have wanted to see Hunter under the heel of his boot, but kill him? I don't think so."

The group spent some time circulating the substance of their own interviews and observations from those they considered suspects. One by one they circled the group with their thoughts. Morgan told them about his suspicions that Hans, Guggenheim's valet, had already attempted to harm them.

"Look," Morgan said, "even though my initial reaction to Peter's assertion about Guggenheim is somewhat negative, it's obvious there was a first attempt on our lives and Hans had to be responsible for it. I doubt seriously if the man ever takes a sneeze without Guggenheim's approval."

When it got to the subject of Ismay, however, Morgan was reluctant to tell all that he knew. He even felt somewhat ashamed for being involved with what little he had been. Not that he wanted to provide any cover for Ismay, but he hated the thought of being used for blackmail.

"And you say Bruce Ismay had a compelling reason?" Peter asked.

"Yes, I'd say so, something that might prove ruinous."

"And yet you can't tell us what it is?" Margaret asked.

"No, I'm afraid I can't. The matter is a confidential one, and frankly I'm embarrassed I heard it at all."

"But you did," Peter nodded.

Morgan hung his head. "Yes, and from what I heard it sounded like blackmail to me. I know Hunter would deny that if he were here, but I can only tell you what I heard. I can assume that if I thought it was blackmail, given that I'm not involved in any way, Ismay most certainly did."

"Then I'd place my money on him," Margaret said. "Men of importance can become quite desperate when they see their world crumbling down around them. They could panic and do something just like this."

"Don't forget Boxhall's observation," Morgan said. "He picked a spot and dropped the cane in the only place on the ship where it wouldn't hit the water."

"Everyone can forget in a moment of panic," Margaret reasoned.

"But this wasn't a panicked act," Morgan said. "It was cold and calculating."

"Well, my pick is Guggenheim," Peter said. "Even if the valet did the deed, Guggenheim's the man responsible. He missed you the first time, but he didn't miss Hunter on the second."

"You're forgetting where Hunter was hit with this thing." Morgan bounced the cane in his hand.

"What difference does that make?" Peter asked.

"He was hit behind the left ear." Morgan said. "Now would you really turn your back on Guggenheim's valet?"

"Not on your life," Peter responded.

Morgan pounded the palm of his hand lightly with the handle of the cane. "Something else just occurred to me."

"What's that?" Boxhall asked.

He was growing more curious by the minute. Morgan could tell that Boxhall had been resistant to a passenger having anything to do with the investigation, although the man had been nice about it. Now, however, with the observations Morgan was making, he could see a newfound respect growing in the officer.

"Given the position of the wound and the fact that we all agree that Hunter had to have his back to the murderer, I think we can agree on two things: one, Hunter trusted this person or took them lightly, and two, the person was left-handed. That rules out Hans. I spent my afternoon crossing swords with the man. He is definitely not left-handed."

Margaret scooted forward on the sofa. "You haven't told us what you think, Morgan. Who do you think killed Hunter?"

"I'm not certain just this minute. If I had to venture a guess, though, I'd say it was Kitty Webb."

"Preposterous," Peter exclaimed. "Women don't do things like that."

"Listen, I'm open to persuasion. She's already doing something most women wouldn't think about doing," Morgan said. "I think she was feeling desperate, and besides, Hunter did have a scheduled meeting with her at the time of his death." Morgan allowed his words to soak in and then added, "And she did have access to anything Guggenheim possessed. That cane was well within her reach, if it is his."

"I'm afraid I just can't see a woman clubbing a man over the head," Peter said. "Poison would be the most likely method for a female to murder." He thought it over and looked at Morgan. "And she would have had to have the boldness to come into the steam room and the strength it took to jam that cane in your door and then break it off." He shook his head. "Not likely. Women don't even think about how those types of things operate. The idea of jamming your door never would have occurred to her."

Morgan could see that Margaret didn't at all like the idea of women being made out to be incompetent and lumped into the same ball. "So, you think women are incapable?"

"Er, why no. I didn't say that."

"You certainly implied it."

"I think Peter has some valid points," Morgan said. "This doesn't seem like a typical thing for a woman. Hunter may have taken her lightly enough to turn his back on her, but would she have known how hard to hit him? Bruising him would just infuriate the man. And she would have to jam that cane in the door very hard and then break it off with her bare hands."

"I see your point," Margaret said.

Morgan watched Peter. Margaret had swooped down on him and agreed with Morgan on essentially the same point. It was something Morgan could see was painful to Peter. He almost felt sorry for him.

Boxhall nodded and smiled. One could tell he was glad he hadn't made the same observations as Peter. "I'm not sure we know everything there is to know about the events here," he said. "And I don't think we know all the players. We do have a terrorist that we captured last night, and while he couldn't have done it, he might have an accomplice. Don't forget, Hunter was carrying this mysterious bag of yours, the one that's now in the purser's safe."

"What makes you so certain the man didn't do it?" Peter asked.

"Because I was interviewing him at the time. My notes have the time clearly marked."

Morgan observed two men enter the lounge area. They were both carrying canes. He watched them closely and then pointed them out. "There goes our foolproof evidence."

They turned to watch the two men. They were depositing their canes into a large brass umbrella stand just inside the door.

A short time later, Fitzgerald came walking into the lounge, He was carrying a silver tray high above his head. He spotted Boxhall and the group and walked in their direction. "I was sent to find you, Mr. Boxhall."

"Yes, what is it?"

"This tray is the dinner for the man being held prisoner. You do have the key to the storeroom where he is being kept, don't you sir?"

"Yes, I do."

"You are to let me in and stand by while I see that he is fed. The captain doesn't want him left alone with any of the eating utensils. When he finishes his dinner, I'm to take everything with me."

"You want me to stand out in the cold while you feed that man?"

"If you please, sir. Of course, you are more than welcome to join us."

"Ugh," Boxhall exclaimed, getting to his feet. "Well, it seems that duty calls." He bowed slightly. Reaching into his pocket, he pulled out the key. "I seem to have the key."

Thomas Andrews, the architect, was someone who left no stone unturned. With his ready notebook, he seemed to constantly prowl the *Titanic*, looking for anything out of place. Often, it wasn't something out of place, it was something that needed improvement. He wasn't haughty enough to think that a ship he'd designed would be perfect in every detail on the first try. Besides, he loved the *Titanic*. The ship was like a woman, someone he was in love with and wanted to look her best. He had already noted that the coat hooks in the first-class staterooms would require three screws instead of two.

He was in the suit he was going to wear to dinner, but he had loosened his tie and contented himself in his work. When the captain told him about the prisoner being kept in storeroom B, he knew at once that this was a detail he hadn't counted on. There had never been a time when any of the builders had imagined a brig on a luxury liner like the *Titanic*. Nor did he think such a thing should be constructed. Nevertheless, plans ought to be made. Plans always ought to be made for something one never intended to happen.

Smith had been right to put the man in the storeroom behind the bridge. It faced out on the open catwalk just behind the radio room. There were two such rooms that could be kept secure by lock and key, and he was in the first of those rooms, trying to measure and decide which one would be better suited for a thing of this nature.

Storeroom A was where the weapons were deposited, another precaution few saw any need for. It was required, however. Many things seemed to be required that no one dreamed would ever be used. Some were proudly bragged about, like the watertight doors, and people had laughed about the *Titanic* having any lifeboats whatsoever.

Andrews carefully looked over the bomb on the table. The eight wrapped sticks of dynamite would no doubt have created quite a hole in the hull. From what he'd been told, the device had been positioned at the junction of two of the compartments. The explosion may have buckled a third or perhaps even a fourth. According to Andrews's calculations, that wouldn't have been enough to sink the *Titanic*. Five, perhaps, certainly six, but not four. The ship would have been greatly damaged and limped into New York a day or so behind schedule, but it wouldn't have floundered. He tested the locks on the door to the cabinet that held the revolvers and ammunition. They were secure. Boxhall was the man who held the keys. That gave Andrews some comfort. If terrorists were aboard ship, these guns might be needed.

He measured the room. The one the prisoner was being kept in was identical in its dimensions. He'd be able to tell a great deal about any modifications that might be needed by sizing up storage room A. His eye was immediately drawn to the vent between the two rooms. He measured it. The thing was twelve inches by sixteen inches. Andrews backed away and looked at it. It would be too small for a man to squeeze out of. Still, he would make modifications to it. He scribbled a notation in his notebook. When they docked, he'd see that bars were placed over the vent.

He heard the prisoner cough. The man could be heard very well from where Andrews stood. It was a second sound that snapped his head around, however, the sound of Boxhall's voice outside the door.

T his is the place," Boxhall said. "I'll go in with you. The man might be dangerous."

Fitzgerald nodded and stepped back to allow Boxhall to unlock the door. This hadn't been his assignment at all. Delaney had told him about the man and had given him specific instructions. Delaney had made a special point of the fact that this man wouldn't be allowed to fall into the hands of the authorities in New York. Delaney wanted Fitzgerald to relay his assurances about that and to let him know he hadn't been forgotten. It had taken some trickery to get the assignment, an arrangement Fitzgerald hoped Boxhall wouldn't check on. The man was suspicious enough of him already.

Boxhall turned the key and opened the door. "All right," he said, motioning to O'Conner. "You just move back into your corner."

O'Conner shuffled back into the corner of the room.

Fitzgerald could see that there had been a cot placed in the room, along with a chair and table. The captain had even seen to it that a lamp and a Bible were present. Evidently, the captain had some repenting in mind for O'Conner. The man took a seat in the chair, sliding the leg irons under it. Fitzgerald had no idea where they'd managed to dig those things up. He set the tray on the table.

"All right," Boxhall said, "here's your dinner. Now eat up."

"I ain't hungry."

"You'd better eat."

O'Conner eyed the tray. "I'm not about to be eatin' with no Englishman standing over me like I was some kind of prized lapdog." He looked up at Boxhall. "Especially you."

Fitzgerald knew that Boxhall had taken charge of the man's capture and it hadn't gone easy, either. Both he and Delaney were hoping Fitzgerald would be able to get a few minutes alone with O'Conner. The man had to know their plans, and Fitzgerald was curious about what O'Conner was responsible for.

"I have no liking to making friends with someone who practices sabotage," Boxhall said. "Our instructions are to watch you eat and take back all the utensils and the tray, immediately."

"Well, he can stay." O'Conner looked at Fitzgerald and pointed. "But I won't have no English officer looking over me eating."

Fitzgerald shrugged and smiled sheepishly. This was working out just as he planned. O'Conner was a quick one. Fitzgerald knew O'Conner was somewhat the performer. He was giving Boxhall the tough, dumb mick act, and it was a routine the officer was buying.

Boxhall took out his watch and popped open the lid. "All right. I'll go up to the bridge, but I'll be back in twenty minutes. You watch him, Fitzgerald. That man could put a knife to your throat, even if it is a butter knife. When you're done, count all silverware and napkins. Is that understood?"

"Yes, sir. I understand."

"Now, I will lock the door behind me so you'll have no way out until I come back in twenty minutes."

"I'll watch him."

"See that you do." Boxhall pointed over to O'Conner. "You behave yourself. Don't add a murder to your crimes, or we'll see you hang."

"You'll see me hang anyway." O'Conner looked over at Fitzgerald and then back at Boxhall, giving off a sly smile. It creased his lips slowly. "You can only hang a man once." He chuckled, his eyelids drooping low in a sinister manner.

Boxhall cleared his throat. He opened and stepped through the door. Both O'Conner and Fitzgerald listened to him turn the key and then heard the sound of his footsteps on the catwalk.

Fitzgerald backed up against the door and smiled. "That was a nice touch, that line about hanging more than once."

"I think it took the old boy by surprise."

O'Conner scooted his chair forward and pulled the silver top off the tray. "Chicken! What, no beefsteak?" O'Conner stirred the peas into the mashed potatoes. "I would think the only prisoner aboard would get the best." He laughed.

"You did try to sink the ship."

"And I would have, too, if it hadn't been for that Irish traitor."

"Speaking of that, did you have anything to do with the murder of that other Irishman, the actor?"

"Murder? You've had another murder?" O'Conner seemed genuinely surprised, and that puzzled Fitzgerald. Of course, he really didn't know the man. Maybe he was just being coy.

"Yes, yesterday afternoon."

O'Conner cut into his chicken. "You mean the one who saw the two of us in the first-class companionway, the man you're a steward for?"

"Yes," Fitzgerald hung his head, "bad timing that?"

"You picked the worst time to ask to see the bomb."

"Yes, I suppose I did. I was just curious."

"Yeah, I remember the man, red hair."

"That's the one."

"Well, I don't know what you're talking about." He crammed another piece of chicken into his mouth. "I found the cabin number in my pocket," he chewed his way through the words, "just like the big fella said it would be."

"That was me. I'm the one who left your jacket. I didn't think you'd kill him though."

"There was no other way." O'Conner shrugged. "The man was in the room. You think he was going to stand by while I searched it?"

"What about the steerage-class passenger, the one found in the automobile?"

O'Conner cut his chicken with the knife and stuffed yet another large piece into his mouth. "I'm hungry, and that officer's coming back in twenty minutes."

"What about it?" Fitzgerald asked again.

"Yeah, bloody well right I did." He ground the food in the back of his mouth, mumbling his words. "He followed me. Found out about the bomb." He scooped mashed potatoes onto his fork and shoveled them into his mouth. "Did you tell the big cheese about the redhead seeing us?"

"Of course I did. I tell him everything."

"Then maybe he did the poor bloke in himself, did his own dirty work for a change." Sliding the peas onto his knife, O'Conner stuck them into his mouth. "Speaking of him, how's he plannin' on getting me outa here?"

Fitzgerald gestured with his hand, as if to ward off a nonexistent fly. "Don't worry about it. He's got a plan. I'm to bring you a file to work on those irons, and before we dock I'll work out a way to get the key from Boxhall."

"Good, you do that. Then I'll figure out a way to get the old man who put me in here."

The sound of footsteps on the catwalk brought both men to silence. O'Conner stuffed a large portion of the rest of the food into his mouth while the key was being turned. Boxhall opened the door and stepped inside.

"OK, pick up the tray." Boxhall was all business. "I've got work to do besides being nursemaid to a criminal."

Fitzgerald stepped over to the table and covered the remainder of O'Conner's dinner.

"Let me see the knife, fork, spoon, and napkin," Boxhall barked. "Then you get back to work."

Fitzgerald held them up. Putting them back on the tray, he turned around and made his way out the door.

"Next time you'll have to eat faster," Boxhall said. "We've no time for chitchat."

"Well, I'll just be sure and do that. With you rabid English types, a man never knows what his last meal will be."

Boxhall turned, stepped out, and closed the door. Fitzgerald had already gone down the stairs and was headed back to the galley. Placing the key in the lock, he turned it.

Quietly, the door to storeroom A opened. Andrews stepped outside and held his hand up to his mouth to silence Boxhall. He turned and locked the door behind him. He motioned to Boxhall to join him on the other side of the catwalk.

When the two men stepped over to the port side of the bridge, Andrews leaned into Boxhall's face. "I have some news for you. Something you need to hear."

SATURDAY,
APRIL 13, 1912,
8:30 P.M.

CHAPTER 28

A tiny hint of the moon cast a cold, light-blue glare off the flat, calm sea. It was a sight seldom seen on an Atlantic crossing, the kind of sea and sky that might lull a sailor to sleep with its calm boredom. The sky was a blaze of stars that caused the men on the bridge to watch the sky more and the water less.

Second Officer Lightoller was in charge of the bridge, and Boxhall worked on the charts, trying to make certain his settings were correct. "Have you ever seen flatter, calmer sea?" Lightoller asked.

"No, I haven't, not for some time."

"It's been a mild winter for the North Atlantic."

"Yes, and that worries me." Boxhall looked up from the charts. "The mildness will have the ice flowing farther south, along the current. It'll be there in larger pieces, too."

Lightoller nodded. "We'll have to keep a sharp eye."

The dim light on the bridge cast ominous shadows over the dials of the ship's compass, and the blackness of the sea met the night sky with hardly a change in color. It was like being trapped inside a large ball of black glass, with stars sprinkled on the ceiling.

"Have we any reports of ice?" Lightoller asked.

"I picked up a report at Southampton and another at Queenstown," Boxhall said. "The latest word when we left Queenstown was that over twenty steamers had reported seeing ice. Some have been forced to stop. I take it there were some rather immense icebergs."

"I doubt if we'll stop."

Boxhall nodded, reluctantly. "The French liner *Niagara* sustained minor damage."

"Really?"

"Yes, I'm afraid so."

"Where was that?" Lightoller asked, stepping over to the charts.

Boxhall put his finger on the charts and with a red pencil drew a series of lines. "The reports I get indicate a rather large ice field stretching from here, 46 degrees North, to 41 degrees North and spanning from 46 degrees West to 50 degrees West."

"That puts our course right in the middle of it."

"That it does." Boxhall dropped a ruler on the chart and extended the *Titanic*'s course with a blue pencil. "I figure we'll cross it at 42 degrees North, 47 degrees West." He pointed with his finger to a spot near the *Titanic*'s proposed route. "The *Niagara* hit the berg right about here."

"Blimey!"

"We ought to do plenty of bobbing and weaving tomorrow night," Boxhall said.

"Just as long as we do it at the right time."

Both men laughed. It was a kind of nervous laughter. The *Titanic*, after all, was unsinkable.

"Let's just hope we don't break any china," Boxhall said.

The men both looked up in time to see Captain Smith step onto the bridge. The man was wearing his dress whites, obviously on his way to dinner. His faithful Afghan was following dutifully by his side. "Everything under control?" he asked.

"Yes, sir," Lightoller said, stepping over to the large window. "The sea is a flat calm. I'd say we have the perfect weather for a crossing."

"Any reports of ice?"

"None other than our Queenstown reports," Lightoller replied.

Smith nodded.

"I did get a very disturbing report from Andrews earlier this evening," Boxhall said.

"What was that?"

"He was working in the storeroom next to the prisoner and overheard a conversation the man had with one of our stewards."

Smith fastened his eyes on Boxhall. The matter obviously had his full attention.

"One of our stewards?"

"Yes, sir, I'm afraid so. His name is John Fitzgerald. It would seem the man is in collusion with our prisoner. I suspected him of stealing a steward jacket earlier in the voyage. The jacket enabled this O'Conner fellow to pass among the first-class passengers and cabins undetected. I think Fitzgerald was also the man who intercepted and delayed the message sent to you from Scotland Yard, the one identifying the room number of the passenger who was killed. The man had stolen the ticket."

"Arrest him."

"I don't think that would be wise, sir."

"Why not, pray tell?"

"There appears to be another man aboard who is party to the plot. In fact, this man may be the mastermind of the entire scheme."

Lightoller stepped over, and Smith drew closer. The entire situation had sent a sense of panic into the officers on the *Titanic*. A wartime environment on a luxury liner was a circumstance few of them had been used to dealing with. "Go on," Smith said.

"The identity of the man is unknown to us at this time, I'm afraid. But if he has another bomb with him and we arrest Fitzgerald, we might never know until it's too late."

"What do you intend to do?" Lightoller asked.

"I plan on having Fitzgerald continue to deliver the man's meals. We'll have someone stationed in storeroom A when the meals are taken in. Perhaps the man will slip and give us the confederate's name. In the meantime, I'm having the steward watched like a hawk."

"Be careful of that," Smith said. "We wouldn't want him to grow suspicious."

"I will. I'm having this Morgan Fairfield and a few of his friends alerted to follow his movements and, of course, telling the two of you."

Smith shook his head. "That's not wise."

Boxhall hated the idea that the captain didn't approve of his plan. The impression that anything he might do could reflect in a way that seemed unwise sent a chill down him. "Why is that, sir?"

"Fairfield is a passenger, a young passenger. I know who his famous relative is, but still, I don't like the idea that we're placing such a grave responsibility on someone who is supposed to be our guest."

"I've listened to the man discuss the case. Frankly, I was surprised. He seems wise beyond his years and appears to have a good head for this thing. I don't think you have anything to worry about, sir."

"You had better hope that you don't," Smith shot back.

Lightoller smiled.

"If there is another bomb aboard, you are the one I am holding responsible for its discovery, not some passenger. I will enter this in the log and it will be your name that's written there, not the name of Morgan Fairfield. Do I make myself clear?"

"Yes, sir, perfectly clear."

9:00 P.M.

Morgan made his way along the deck toward the first-class dining room. The night air was chilly, but it stimulated him. He still found it hard to have Hunter gone. The man was always pounding on his door at dinnertime, eager for the next round of verbal fisticuffs at the table. At the time, it had been something that Morgan dreaded, but now he missed it. For whatever his misplaced reasons were, Hunter was the spoon that stirred the fizz.

When Peter stepped out onto the deck, Morgan was actually glad to see him. Maybe it was because he missed Hunter, or perhaps he was developing a genuine fondness for Peter after all. "Good to see you," Morgan smiled.

Peter turned the collar up on his coat. Morgan had been standing on deck and perhaps was used to the night chill, but for Peter the sudden exposure was a shock. He stamped his feet. "I do hope the ladies are not long in coming."

"Oh, they'll be along directly. You know how women are."

"I'm beginning to find out."

"Well, the food will be hot and you'll be getting lots of congratulations tonight."

"Morgan, you and I both know the woman loves you."

"Peter, she's your fiancée. I can't stand the idea of taking another man's betrothed."

"I'm afraid you'll have to get used to the idea. Facts are facts, and a woman's mind is too difficult to change. Don't you give me all that talk about being the proper gentleman. If we did things your way, you'd be the perfect lonely gentleman and I'd be the gentleman married to a woman who loves someone else. Now wouldn't that be a fine kettle of fish, two perfect gentlemen, two perfectly miserable gentlemen."

"She said yes to you once. She can say yes again."

"She can, but she won't, not now."

Morgan laughed. "Well, aren't we a fine pair? You won't take her and I won't let you give her up."

The humor and irony of the situation caught both men completely off guard. They began to laugh, Morgan's hand on Peter's shoulder and Peter's hand on his. It wasn't until Morgan looked up and noticed the two women standing in the shadows that he stopped laughing.

Peter continued his laughter until he noticed that Morgan had frozen in his tracks. He stopped his bold laughter and wiped his eyes, then slowly turned around.

"Good evening, gentlemen." April Hastings's voice was not hard to miss. It was cold and deliberate.

"How long have you two ladies been standing there?" Peter asked.

"Long enough," Margaret replied.

Peter dipped his head in Morgan's direction. He spoke in a low tone. "Oh."

The women stepped forward, out of the shadows. There was a look of extreme anger all over Margaret's face.

"Look, we're sorry if—" Peter didn't get the chance to finish his sentence.

"Sorry about what? You were just deciding who was going to get to care for me. So far as the both of you are concerned, I'm nothing more than a piece of unwanted property, an old horse whose upkeep has suddenly become more than you expected to pay."

"That's not it at all, Margaret," Morgan said.

"Oh, it isn't? You're too much of a gentleman, and Peter here doesn't think he can ever win my total affection. He seems to want to predict my every thought from here until the day I die. And if he can't be assured of that, he doesn't want to bother. You're both so possessive, possessive and pretentious."

"But Margaret, we're both—"

Margaret cut Peter off, once again. "Both what? Looking after my own welfare? Did someone give you the duty of being my father and assign me the role of a six-year-old? Well, I already have a father. And in case you haven't noticed, I'm a full-grown woman."

Both Morgan and Peter shook. They felt like dogs with a pail of cold water thrown on them, too shocked to move or even howl.

Margaret quickly removed the opera-length glove from her left hand.

"What are you doing?" April asked.

"Please, Mother, this is my decision, not yours and certainly not either of these gentlemen's." Grabbing the ring on her finger, she slowly twisted it off. She stepped toward Peter and slammed it into his hand. "Here, this is yours. Take it."

"Y-y-you don't have to do this," Peter stammered.

"I most certainly do. If I can't be trusted with my own heart, how can you trust me in a church to mean what I say when I say *I do?*"

She glared at Morgan. "And you."

Morgan almost jumped back at the words.

"You don't even care enough about me to ask me. You take all of our years together and everything we've meant to one another, our entire friendship, and presume to hand me over on the basis of your pitiful honor. Well, I hope you and that honor of yours will be happy together." She lifted her head. "Come, Mother, we're late for dinner."

With that, she steamed off toward the doors that led to the dining salon.

April drew closer to Morgan. "Young man, this is all your fault. I hope you're happy now." She left, following Margaret.

The two men were still shaking. Morgan had never felt worse or more embarrassed.

Peter hung his head and shook it. "It seems we've made a terrible mistake." He looked off in the direction the women had taken. "Perhaps it would have been best if we'd drawn swords and fought for her." He smiled. "No, you would have had the sword, and I would have used my shotgun. That way they could have at least had the satisfaction of grieving over our bloody corpses."

Morgan laughed, even though it didn't seem funny in the least. It was a time, though, when nothing could be said that would ease the pain, and he knew it. First Hunter and now this. He felt empty inside.

"I'd better go inside to dinner," Peter said. "There's nothing I look forward to more than an hour of cold conversation and hot baron of beef."

Morgan nodded. He could tell Peter was in just as much pain as he was. He was simply handling it better. Right now, the last thing Morgan wanted to do was look up and see Margaret's face, even if she was at the end of the table. "Yes, you'd better go. Maybe you can talk some sense into her."

"I doubt it."

Morgan turned and wandered down the rail, making his way to the forward well deck of the ship where the breeze was stiffer. But the cold night air could never match the chill Morgan carried about inside. His eyes were drawn momentarily to the sight of the man climbing the crow's nest. There at the base of it stood another man, a man Morgan thought he recognized. Even at a distance, Donald Delaney's beard was hard to miss.

"Morgan, old boy, wait up."

Boxhall was headed in his direction from the bow of the ship. From the looks of the man, Morgan could see that something was worrying him. Boxhall's tie was askew, which was rare, and he was almost panting for breath.

"I'm glad I caught you before you went in."

"Well, I am, too. It's pretty late, though. What seems to be wrong?"

"I'm afraid the list of suspects in your friend's murder grows longer."

"How is that?" Morgan had a mixture of dread and elation at the thought. On the one hand, the timing meant he'd have to double his efforts. New York was only a little over three days away. On the other, he'd almost excluded, for one reason or another, anyone who might have had reason to see Hunter dead.

"That Irish terrorist we have locked up. Andrews heard him in a conversation with that steward of yours, Fitzgerald."

"Fitzgerald?"

"Yes, I'm afraid so. It seems the two of them are working together, and there's a third party connected with the both of them, most likely a first-class passenger."

"Someone connected with the Irish rebellion?"

"It would appear so."

Morgan's mind raced. It was hard to think of someone connected to the Irish cause other than Delaney. It was a thought he didn't want to consider, however. The man seemed so pleasant. Of course, Morgan's association with the rest of the passengers had been limited. For all he knew, there might be scores of zealots aboard. But then there was Hunter. How many of them knew him, and why would they want him killed?

"I don't understand. Why Hunter?" Morgan asked. "He wasn't connected to the government."

"Evidently Hunter happened across those two when our prisoner was showing Fitzgerald his bomb. Hunter may have never seen what they thought he saw, but Fitzgerald passed the word on to the third member of their party."

Morgan shook his head. "Hunter saw nothing. I'm certain of that. The man couldn't keep a secret if his life depended on it. If he had seen something, I'd have been the first person he told about it."

"Precisely! And remember, whoever killed Hunter tried to kill you as well."

The idea was a sound one. His being trapped in the steam room was just too close to the time and place of Hunter's death not to be related.

"You could still be in danger," Boxhall said.

"I doubt that. I mean, they've already discovered the bomb. What they might think Hunter saw would be of no consequence now."

"I wouldn't be so sure of that. And if anything does happen to you," Boxhall took Morgan's elbow and led him over to the rail, "I'll have only myself to blame."

"How so?"

"They may think the matter of the bomb has ceased to be a danger to them, but Hunter saw the both of them, and we have only one of the two locked up."

"And you think Fitzgerald will try to do me in to protect his identity?"

"That's just what I fear, and I had the captain refrain from locking the man up. Now, seeing you, I wonder about the wisdom of that. I thought that perhaps we could see who Fitzgerald talks to and spends time with, anything suspicious about the man. Also, the third party might have a second bomb, and it would help if we had some idea of who it might be."

"What do you want me to do?"

Boxhall dug his grip into Morgan's sleeve. "Listen, old boy, I want you and your friends to keep an eye on Fitzgerald. Do nothing. Just report anyone he talks to directly to me, understand?"

"Yes." Morgan nodded. He smiled. "That will be an odd situation. I'll be watching him, and he'll be watching me."

"Yes, I suppose it will at that." Boxhall paused, thinking the matter over. "Listen, I didn't think about the danger I might be putting you in when the captain suggested arresting Fitzgerald. If you want, I'll go arrest him now."

"No." Morgan shook his head. "The entire ship's in danger. I couldn't think of having you do a thing like that just to make things better for me. I'll be careful. I'll watch myself."

Boxhall put his arm around Morgan's shoulder. "You do that. I'm afraid you've become more than just a paying passenger to me."

Morgan smiled. He'd been feeling so very much alone. He couldn't tell, though, if the sudden rush he was feeling was from his constant need for noble self-sacrifice, from the notion of putting himself in jeopardy, or from the genuine expression of concern from Boxhall. "I appreciate that. I'm not sure of how much help you can count on from my friends, however. Some of us seem to have had a falling out."

"I'm sorry to hear that. I hope it's not serious."

"I'm afraid it's worse than serious, but I'll try to deal with it."

"Good man. Now, everything I have is on the line here. The old man would just as soon keep you out of this, your being a passenger and all, so I'm taking a great risk by even telling you what I have."

"I understand. I won't let you down."

Morgan walked to port of the well deck and climbed the stairs. Delaney should be at dinner and so should he. He'd be talking to the man soon enough. Right now, he just wanted to be alone with his thoughts.

Up ahead, standing by the rail, Morgan caught sight of a man in a black suit and black hat. He was smoking a pipe. The aroma of the tobacco was carried on the breeze, and the night air was livened with a scent of tobacco mixed with cognac. It wasn't until the man turned around that Hunter spotted his white clerical collar. The graying beard that covered his face was neatly trimmed, giving his face a manly, chiseled look. "Good evening, sir," Morgan said.

"Yes, it is. A fine evening, too." The man looked out on the water. "God has done a great and wonderful thing, wouldn't you say?"

"And what would that be?"

"Why, He's created this mighty ocean." The man stuck out his hand. "I'm Reverend James Rosscup."

"Morgan Fairfield's the name." Morgan shook his hand.

"You look somewhat troubled, Mr. Fairfield." Rosscup pulled the pipe from his mouth, blowing a steady stream of smoke into the night air. "Is there anything I can do to help?"

"Thank you for asking." If the truth were known, the idea of anyone trying to help Morgan out of a mood was as foreign to him as the backside of the moon. Throughout his life, he had always been the one to try to help others buck up. Now the shoe was on the other foot, and it seemed odd. Only Hunter had knifed past his defenses and taken the time to know him.

"I lost a very good friend recently." Morgan shook his head. "I seem to find myself losing more and more of my friends." Morgan's mind couldn't leave the thought of Margaret. It had been his decision to run off to America and seek a future of his own choosing. He felt like he had indeed lost Margaret. He was just now beginning to see how painful that was. She'd been his best friend for so long, even if she was female. That in itself had been a strange thing. It was peculiar for a man to feel that close to a woman.

"It does leave a hole when that happens, doesn't it?"

"Yes, a monstrous hole." Morgan leaned against the rail, parking his foot on top of the bottom rung.

"I find that holes need to be filled. I do it in my yard and my life as well."

"I am going to find a new job."

"That may help for a short time."

"A short time?" Morgan was curious. He looked away from the water and directly at Rosscup.

"All of those things are of a temporary nature. Sometimes God allows things and people to be taken from us in order to create holes. They've been there all along, of course, it's just that we're often so busy, or have done such a seemingly good job with filling the holes with something temporary, that we've never seen them before."

"I've always enjoyed time to myself. I'm a writer, and when I can spend part of my life with my own thoughts, I feel in touch with my feelings. I can also think thoughts that deserve to be written down."

"Then you should treasure the holes."

The idea of treasuring pain was a new one. If that were the case, right now his treasury seemed to be full. "Normally one might think so, but it always helps to have someone to go to, someone who can hear."

Rosscup moved closer and put his arm around Morgan. "Perhaps that's a role our Lord wants to play in your life, only before you've always been too busy or perhaps never recognized the need. In Isaiah 6, one of my favorite passages, the prophet tells about his response to losing a friend. He writes: 'In the year that king Uzziah died I saw also the Lord sitting up on a throne, high and lifted up, and his train filled the temple.'"

Rosscup tapped out the dottle from his pipe on the rail. The bowl of the pipe was hot to the touch, and he jerked his hand away from it. Then he let it lay in his hands. On an evening as cold as this was, something warm was welcome. There was a sweet but firm innocence to the man. "The choice is yours, young man. When everything that stands in God's place is taken from you, those things that you depended on, you can either get bitter, fill the hole with something temporary, or see God. There are no other alternatives."

"Do you think God can use those times to show you how important someone was to you, someone you took for granted?"

Rosscup slipped the hot pipe into his pocket. He nodded. "Yes, I think so. The overlooked person in your life has much to teach you. Perhaps a time like the one you're going through can open your ears to him."

"*Her*, reverend, *her*." He stuck his hand out and once again shook Rosscup's, only this time more vigorously.

SUNDAY,
APRIL 14, 1912,
9:00 A.M.

CHAPTER 29

Jack Phillips stepped contritely onto the bridge, the wire in his hand. There was nothing he hated more than the feeling of being a failure, and he carried the two-day-old ice warning, knowing he had been. He knew very little about navigating a ship, but enough to know that what changes might have been made in the ship's course two days earlier to avoid the ice field would be next to impossible now.

There had always been an uneasy alliance between the Marconi company and White Star Line. Marconi wanted to keep the lucrative wireless trade as the sole property of the company. Therefore, Marconi made the agreement with the liners that included thirty words a day of free communication that was not billed to White Star. The shipping firm was proud to advertise the fact that the latest in wireless equipment was aboard, one of the marvels of modern technology. It made the passengers feel safe and gave them something to entertain themselves with. The passengers' friends would be so impressed upon receiving a wire sent by someone at sea. It was a novelty that almost all of the first-class passengers were taking advantage of, some many times a day, and all at exorbitant rates.

Phillips was well aware that most of the ship's officers didn't view the wireless with any degree of seriousness. They saw it as a toy for the rich, a sort of grown-up attempt at talking to playmates. The thrill of chattering to a chum by using a string and attaching two cans to it was very much like the looks he saw on people's faces when they passed him the script of a wire. He hoped the captain would look on the wire that way, at least one more time.

Captain Smith was in his dress blue uniform. His coat hung down to a spot midway between his waist and knees. It was a style that was a bit old-fashioned, but what else could be expected of a seaman's uniform? It was his best daytime outfit, however. He was scheduled to conduct Sunday services in the first-class dining salon at 10:30.

Phillips approached the man cautiously. "Captain, I have a wire for you, an ice warning." He handed the telegram over and stepped back.

As Smith read it, he tried to explain. "I'm afraid we've been very busy, and this was mislaid by mistake."

Smith looked up at him while he read the wire. He handed it over to Murdoch. "It's from Captain Barr on the *Caronia*. Read it and then post it for the officers on the bridge." Casting a glance over at Phillips, he made sure the timing on the message was clear. Even though the words were directed to Murdoch, their intent wasn't lost on Phillips. "It's two days old."

The look Smith gave Phillips was bone chilling. "I want these ice reports brought to me at once."

"Yes, sir, it won't happen again."

"See that it doesn't."

Murdoch studied the message carefully. He stepped over to the charts, traced his finger over the map, and gave out the bad news. "The area Barr indicates in his message is north of our present course, Captain. I would assume that with the southerly drift of the current, we'll be right on top of it."

"Keep a sharp lookout," Smith responded.

"Will we be having our customary lifeboat drill today?" Murdoch asked.

"No, we'll belay that. We haven't enough lifeboats for all the passengers and there's no need to alarm them needlessly."

"Aye, aye, Captain."

Smith stepped over to the window and ran his hands over the ledge. "Besides," his voice sounded calm, almost as if to reassure himself, "this vessel is perfectly safe. I shouldn't worry about that if I were you."

Phillips knew that Sunday morning on White Star ships was supposed to include a boat drill where all hands, passengers, and crew were instructed to assemble in life jackets at their boat stations. Having too few boats, however, would only make the passengers nervous. Smith was a man given to following all of the rules, but he also knew the delicate state of mind of the average passenger. Several people who had never sailed before were already in a state of constant tension. A few even refused to sleep at night, and one wouldn't venture out of her cabin.

"Will that be all, sir?" Phillips kicked his heels together to get the captain's attention.

Smith waved him off with the back of his hand. "Yes, that will be all."

Leaving the bridge, he rounded the catwalk and stepped back into the radio room. Bride was tapping out several messages on the wireless.

Collapsing onto the cot, Phillips stripped off his coat and loosened his tie.

Bride swung around, a broad smile on his face. "Here, here, you look like your cat just died."

Phillips shook his head slowly. "No, but I think I almost did. You remember that wire you gave me from the *Caronia*?"

"Sure."

"Well, you were late in giving it to me, and I stuck the thing in my pocket. I just took it to the old man."

Bride blinked, his eyes wide open.

"We need to make sure those things get delivered up to the bridge as soon as they come in."

"That's a hard thing to do at night. I have my desk filled with outgoing wires from 5:00 on. Does the old man know we had a breakdown last night and didn't get this machine up and running until 5:00 A.M.?"

"No, I didn't tell him that."

"Well, we're absolutely swamped." Bride picked up the pile of unsent messages.

"I know, but we have to do it. Those ice reports are important, and, besides, it's turning colder out there."

10:20 A.M.

The dining salon was filling up fast with Sunday worshipers. Morgan could see Margaret and April in the third row, with Peter two rows behind them. Evidently, whatever Peter had tried to communicate with her hadn't worked. Morgan didn't think it would. Margaret had always needed time to mellow.

He spotted the Reverend Rosscup walking through the door. The man's black garb, complete with black vest, made him hard to spot in the darkness, but in the light of day he stood out like a lump of coal in the snow. Morgan scooted to his left in the row of seats, making room for the man. It was something he didn't do lightly, as it put him right next to Colonel Gracie.

"It's good to see you, young man." Rosscup slid in, taking his seat.

"Nice to see you, Reverend." He nodded to his left, acknowledging Gracie.

Rosscup opened his prayer book and began to read, no doubt to prepare himself for the service.

Gracie leaned over to Morgan. "I say, have you had a good morning so far?"

"Just breakfast and my Bible so far this morning," Morgan replied.

"Bully for you," Gracie replied. "I've had quite the time of it myself. You see, I've always prided myself in staying in top condition, something I picked up from my cousin Teddy, Teddy Roosevelt, the former president."

That Gracie should seek to impress him by casually mentioning a prominent name didn't surprise Morgan in the least. First class on the *Titanic* was a place where people worked hard at impressing others with what they knew and, more important, who they knew.

"I've spent most of my time in the library, up till now," Gracie went on. "You know I write about military history, don't you?"

Morgan's heart sank. He hoped and prayed Gracie wouldn't insist on relating the substance of his book.

"Well, I do." He slammed the palm of his hand against his stomach. "So, it would be all too easy to let myself go. Therefore, I had a game of squash with the resident professional aboard, then took a swim in the pool."

"Sounds vigorous," Morgan said.

"Well, I didn't stop there. I went to the gymnasium where I had an appointment with the attendant. The fellow gave me a right good work-out, and then it was back to the pool. Say," Gracie stopped, almost mid-sentence, "I saw the fellow there who's seated next to you at the table so often."

"Who might that be?" Morgan asked.

"The Irishman, Delaney. He wasn't swimming. He told me he was just taking a walk someplace where he didn't have to be outdoors. That's funny, eh, what? I saw him there the other day with that friend of yours, that Kennedy fellow."

Now Morgan's ears did perk up. "When was that?"

"Hmm," Gracie stroked his chin. "Now, when was that? I think that would have been Friday afternoon, sometime after lunch. I remember that because I thought it was foolish of the Irishman to swim so soon after eating. You know what they say."

"Yes, I know what they say."

"Well, the older Irishman wasn't swimming, that was plain to see." He laughed. "That was, unless he planned on getting his suit wet."

Morgan felt like kissing the man. He had placed Delaney where Hunter was killed, and on the very afternoon. After what he'd learned from Boxhall, he had a hunch Delaney just might be the third person involved in the bomb plot. The man had already lost his hearing to a bomb, why not his life? Of course, had the bomb successfully exploded and sunk the *Titanic*, Delaney would no doubt have a place in a lifeboat, being a first-class passenger.

The members of the orchestra took their places. The service promised to be the event of the morning, and the music would help to lift people's spirits. There had been very little outdoor activity, except by the heartiest of souls.

The service started with Captain Smith standing in front and having everyone sing a hymn of the sea. It began with the words "Eternal Father, strong to save" and concluded with a prayer "for those in peril on the sea." Morgan thought the words of the hymn to be especially appropriate, even though they weren't quite comforting. He noticed several women with their handkerchiefs dabbing their eyes. The service was billed as something from the High Church of England, but the White Star Line had its own book of common prayer, and they used that, with Captain Smith leading the reading.

When the service ended, the group began to file out. Morgan noticed Margaret and her mother, April, linger near the front of the room. They undoubtedly wanted to speak to the captain. He followed Rosscup out the door.

The air was brisk, sending most of the group flooding onto the deck quickly indoors. Morgan and Rosscup stepped to the rail, however. The feel of the crowd in the dining salon had made both men just a bit claustrophobic. It felt good to be cold, and for the first time in a long while, Morgan enjoyed the look of the open sea.

Rosscup took out his pipe and the leather pouch containing his tobacco. "Very nice service, don't you think?"

"Yes, sir, it was."

The man crammed a pinch of tobacco into the bowl of the cherry-tinted pipe and tamped it down with his thumb. He looked up at the *Titanic's* superstructure high above. "This is a magnificent ship. It's too bad we expect too much from it."

"How is that?" Morgan asked.

"Our society has a great deal of pride in what we're capable of performing, and I'm afraid this vessel is the embodiment of all of that pride and vanity. The extent of our national haughtiness seems to know no bounds."

Morgan looked up at the gigantic smokestacks, the front three belching streams of black smoke into the cloudless blue sky. It was easy to see why all those who saw her brimmed over with pride. All they knew as a civilization was tied up in the *Titanic:* strong, powerful, clever, exotic, and the cream of English society. Morgan related to the expectations of the ship. He, too, had so much placed on his shoulders, so many things that were expected of him. He, too, was on a maiden voyage to the New World. He, too, was expected to turn a tidy profit, no matter what.

Rosscup took out his matchbook and, turning his back to the wind, struck a match and plunged it into the bowl. He puffed the thing to life. Shaking the match into a sliver of smoke, he flipped it into the sea. "I fear for us at times."

"Why is that?" Morgan asked.

"Earlier today I overheard one of the passengers trying to comfort a distraught woman as to the safety of this vessel. He told her, quite emphatically, 'Not even God could sink this ship.' And while that may have been a comfort to her, it sent chills up my spine. It's a dangerous thing to tempt God."

Rosscup sucked hard on the pipe, and smoke billowed out. It was an aroma Morgan rather enjoyed. "The prophet Daniel recorded the words of King Nebuchadnezzar," Rosscup said. "'*And all the inhabitants of the earth are reputed as nothing: and he doeth according to his will in the army of heaven, and among the inhabitants of the earth: and none can stay his hand, or say unto him, What doest thou?*'"

"A rather sobering verse," Morgan said.

"Yes, quite. Well, I'm off on a walk. I prefer to do my smoking on deck. Somehow the conversation of the smoking lounge leaves me colder than the deck."

Morgan watched the man walk off just as Margaret and April stepped onto the deck. Margaret caught his eye. Morgan walked hurriedly in her direction. "Margaret, may I have a word with you?"

The question brought both women to a halt. "What more could you say than you've already said?" Margaret asked.

"I do have an apology to make, and I pray you'll hear it. I have no expectations, of course. I just need to say it."

"We haven't time for this," April said.

"I also have some news about the other matter, news that I think will interest you." He looked at April and then back at Margaret. "This is something I think only you should hear." Morgan hoped it would peak her curiosity. If he couldn't tempt her into hearing him out, he at least hoped that some news about Hunter's murder would be enough to entice her.

"Well, I never—" April said.

"It's all right, Mother. Morgan wants to share some news about his sick friend, Hunter. As to his apology, humility in a man is such a rare thing. It shouldn't be missed."

"I'll wait for you in the cabin, then. You won't be too long, will you? It is turning quite cold."

Margaret looked at Morgan and then turned to April to reassure her. "No, I don't think this will take very long."

April obviously had a great deal of confidence in her daughter's new-found resolve. She lifted her chin in disdain and hurried off in the direction of the cabins.

"Now, what about the matter of Hunter?" Margaret asked. She obviously wanted to make it clear that she wasn't the least bit interested in anything that had to do with their relationship.

"Boxhall told me that they've discovered a confederate of the man who is locked away for trying to blow up the ship. He thinks Hunter may have seen the two men plotting together."

"That's interesting."

"Yes, it is. It's even more interesting when I tell you who it is. You must promise you won't panic, however."

Margaret narrowed her eyes. The idea of being considered a panicky woman was one that made her angry. Morgan could tell at once he'd used a poor choice of words. "Of course, you won't," he said. "You're not the timid type."

"I most certainly am not."

"The man in collusion with the prisoner is our steward, Fitzgerald."

"You don't mean it."

"I most certainly do. There is also word of a third member of their party, someone higher up. Boxhall would like us to watch Fitzgerald closely in hopes he may lead us to the man."

"I'll do that." She shook her head. "I never liked the man, always too cool and proper."

"I suppose women have a natural sense for these things. Men are instinctively ignorant of feelings."

"Yes, they are, as you should well know."

"Which brings me to the other matter I need to discuss with you."

"Listen, if you're trying to talk me out of breaking off my engagement with Peter, you can forget that. He spent most of last night trying to convince me that you loved me."

"He did?"

"He most certainly did. The two of you men are most disagreeable. Both of you seem bound and determined to shove me off on the other." She planted her fingers on her blouse and nodded her head, "for my own sake of course."

"No, that wasn't what I was going to talk to you about."

"It wasn't?"

"No. I was remembering a time when I was nine and climbed that big oak outside your home. Do you remember that?"

"Of course, I do. I thought you'd never come down."

Morgan smiled. "The truth is, I couldn't come down. I couldn't come down, and I was just too proud to ask for your help."

Margaret's mouth dropped open. "Why are you telling me this?"

"Because in some ways I'm still nine years old. When I get something in my mind and find that I'm stuck, I'm just too proud to admit it. I rebelled at the notion of living a life of ease off the proceeds of my trust fund, and the idea of a position with your father or my uncle made me feel like less of a man. I've always seen myself as the hero who desired hardship, hardship that seemed never to be my lot in life. Being wealthy, warm, and well thought of seemed to be the way of a coward. I'm more afraid of dying warm in bed having never known pain, dirt, duty, and courage."

"Morgan, I know all this about you. I've never known you to be a coward in any way."

"Except one."

Margaret looked him straight in the eye. Even without saying it, Morgan could tell that she knew exactly what he was going to say. It must have been her intuition.

"The only thing I've been cowardly about is my feelings for you. I didn't think you could care enough for me to wait, so I never asked you to. I didn't think I could ever be good enough to provide for you in a way that didn't present an embarrassment. I wasn't certain you could ever be proud of me. I knew what I needed to do, but I was too ashamed and too cowardly to ask you to be a partner to it. I climbed that tree and was stuck, but I couldn't bring myself to ask for your help."

"Morgan, what do you take me for?" Her eyes were soft, almost teary. Morgan could tell she wasn't going to be harsh, even though he felt like he deserved it. "You don't think me some china doll made only to be taken down and dusted do you?"

"No," Morgan said.

"Well, I'm not. Just because I'm a woman doesn't mean I can't be just as heroic as you can be. I'd freeze and starve if it meant doing it with the man I love."

Morgan started to speak, but she stopped him. "Now I know what you're going to say. Of course, my parents will be upset, but I don't care. I don't have to live the rest of my life as daddy's little girl. I'm not, you know. I belong to the man I give my heart to. That's my choice, not my mother's, not my father's, and not Peter Wilksbury's decision."

"What are you saying?"

"I'm telling you that I love you, Morgan Fairfield. You infuriate me, but I love you. That hasn't changed since the time I stood at the base of that tree, the time you seemed so helpless, pretending you just didn't want to come down."

"You knew?"

"Of course I knew. I may have been six, but I wasn't stupid."

"I don't know what to say."

"You don't?" She smiled.

"All I can say is that I love you, Margaret. I love you, and I will always love you."

"There, that wasn't so bad, was it?"

"No."

"Now, what else would you like to say?"

Morgan gulped. He looked around as several people went scurrying by, driven by the cold. "Could you ever consider?" The words seemed to stick in his throat. "I mean, I know this is sudden, and I wouldn't blame you in the least if you said no."

"No to what, Morgan?"

"Would you marry me, Margaret?"

Margaret nodded. "Yes, Morgan Fairfield, I'll marry you."

He grabbed her, pulling her close. "April the fourteenth, this is the luckiest day of my life." Brushing back the blonde curls that fell from her bangs, he kissed her softly.

"Morgan, one thing I would like to know."

"You want to know if I'm still determined to write?"

"No, I want to know how you ever got out of that tree."

SUNDAY,
APRIL 14, 1912,
12:00 P.M.

CHAPTER 30

The food was set out in the Palm Court, and it was a dazzling array of sliced ham and beef, with oysters on ice. The clam chowder was the biggest hit of the day. Just the sight of the steam rolling out of the bowl was enough to warm the heart, with the cold air such as it was.

Morgan kept his eye on Delaney as the man made his way through the line. He fell in behind him and shuffled along in step. His mind raced back to the time that Hunter had talked about the satchel behind Delaney's back. *How much had he really heard?* Morgan wondered.

"Good to see you, Delaney." Morgan spoke to the man in a loud voice, but Delaney didn't turn or seem to notice him.

When they had made their way through the line, Delaney turned and saw Morgan. "There you are." He nodded toward the steaming chowder on his tray. "This looks powerfully good, doesn't it?"

"Yes, it does." Morgan spoke the words slowly, making sure Delaney could read his lips. "Why don't we have a seat over there?"

They both made their way to the table, and Morgan made sure Delaney was settled before he began launching his salvos. "My friend, Hunter, says the Irish are just looking to grab power."

The remark made Delaney mad. Morgan could see it at once.

"And where is he? Still sick?"

"Yes, I'm afraid so."

"Good, then maybe he'll take a turn for the worse. No Irishman that doesn't have the good of Ireland pulsing through his veins is worth his next breath."

"I understand you saw him at the swimming pool on Friday afternoon," Morgan said.

"No, I didn't see him at all on Friday." Delaney cut into his beef. "Who told you that?"

"One of the swimmers who got out of the pool."

"Well, I don't swim, so that couldn't be."

"He must have been mistaken then," Morgan said.

"Either that or he's a liar."

Morgan could see that the remark about Irish independence had set the man on edge. It was something he'd always seemed defensive about. For the next ten minutes, Morgan spent his time trying to recall every argument against Irish independence he'd ever come across. He would launch each challenge at Delaney, working as best he could to provoke the man. With each idea floated, Delaney's responses were heated and growing more and more caustic. Several times Morgan had to smile at passersby, nodding to reassure them the two of them weren't coming to blows.

Finally, he felt he had Delaney right on the edge. It was the place he'd been guiding the man to. He dropped his napkin on the carpet. "I understand the Irish thugs who commit these," he bent down to pick up his napkin, making sure Delaney couldn't see his mouth, "outrages," he continued, "are nothing more than cowards hiding behind the skirts of their women." Grabbing the napkin, he straightened up in his seat.

"Another lie." Delaney growled a set of curses under his breath. "We protect our women from the English. We don't hide behind their skirts."

One of the stewards came quickly over to their table. "Pardon me, gentlemen, but I'm afraid your conversation is unsettling the rest of our guests."

"My apologies," Morgan said. He looked at Delaney and smiled. "I think we've quite finished here." With that, Morgan got to his feet and dropped his napkin on his still half-full plate. He bowed sweetly to Delaney. "I bow to your wisdom, sir. I think you've said quite enough."

1:40 P.M.

B ride and Phillips worked feverishly to try to make up for the lost time the wireless had the night before. It was a grueling job, requiring all their concentration.

"I say, I don't think what they're paying us is quite worth this," Bride said.

"I should say not," Phillips responded. "Four and a half pounds a month doesn't go far, eh, mate?" The company was making far more than both of the men's meager salaries and they both knew it. For the Marconi company, this was going to be a profitable voyage, indeed.

The slight pause at the key was greeted by the clatter of an incoming wire. Bride got out his pad and listening carefully to the headset, jotted down the message.

White Star steamer *Baltic:* Captain Smith, *Titanic.*

> Have had moderate variable winds and clear fine weather since leaving. Greek steamer *Athinai* reports passing icebergs and large quantity of field ice today in latitude 41°51' North, longitude 49°52' West. Last night we spoke [with] German oil tanker *Deutschland*, steaming to Philadelphia, not under control; short of coal; latitude 40°42' North, longitude 55°11'. Wishes to be reported to New York and other steamers.
>
> Wish you and *Titanic* all success.

Bride ripped the message off of his pad and handed it to Phillips. "You'd better get this to the old man right away. It may just help pull your fat out of the fire."

Phillips read it. "You bet. I'll do that."

He slung on his coat and buttoned it up, taking the time to tighten and straighten his tie. Dashing out of the radio room, he was soon on the bridge. Smith was still in his dress blue uniform, his Afghan by his side. He stood beside the charts, looking over Boxhall's shoulder.

"Sir," Phillips said, "We have a wire from the *Baltic*." He handed the communication to Smith. "It's another ice warning, sir. It just came in over the wireless, and I thought you'd want to see it right away."

Smith grunted, taking the paper from Phillips's hand.

Phillips stood, doing his best to maintain a posture that resembled attention. The glare he'd taken from the captain earlier still haunted him, and just then he'd have done anything for a smile or a "well done" from the man.

Smith read it and then stepped closer to the charts for a look at their position. He traced his finger over the line Boxhall had drawn, stopping at the point reported by the *Baltic*.

"Will that be all, sir?" Phillips asked. "Should I send a reply?"

"No," Smith said. "That will be all." He folded and stuffed the message into his coat pocket. "You can go back to your duties now."

Turning on his heels, Phillips left the bridge and soon was back in the radio room. He stripped off his jacket and loosened his tie, watching Bride work. Things were hectic enough without being uncomfortable. He couldn't be on the bridge talking to the captain without doing his best to look spit-and-polish, but he was darned if he was going to work that way.

Bride swung around on his swivel stool, a look of anticipation on his face. It was a blank stare that almost begged for an answer. "Well?" he asked.

"Well, what?"

"What did the captain say."

"The man said nothing. He just took the thing and mumbled." Phillips shuddered. "You know how it is. When you do something right, you get nothing. When you do something wrong, you're drawn and quartered."

He pointed to the wireless. "Here, let me have a turn at it. I have my shirt off."

Bride smiled and got up from the stool. He took out a handkerchief and, with great ceremony, dusted it off. "There you are, sir," he chuckled, "Warm for your bottom and hot for your ears."

No sooner had Phillips taken his seat and clamped the headphones onto his ears, than he began to hear a signal. It was being tapped out to all Atlantic shipping. Phillips picked up his pencil and began to take down the message. It was from the United States Hydrographic Office in Washington, relaying a message from the German liner, *Amerika*. *Amerika* was broadcasting the fact that she had just passed two huge ice-bergs at 41°51' North, longitude 50°8' West.

Bride heard the message. "Another ice report. Are you going to take it to the bridge?"

"I just came from there, and I have my coat off. No, thanks. I'd rather be horsewhipped than made to face that man twice in the same hour." He folded the message and stuck it in his pocket. "Besides, it sounds a lot like the last one. If those old boys can't figure out that we're sailing into a sea of ice, I'm quite certain one more message won't do the trick."

2:15 P.M.

Morgan, Margaret, and Peter were walking the chilly decks, doing their best to place Fitzgerald anywhere near where the satchel had been discussed. "Hunter talked about it behind Delaney's back," Morgan offered. "We know now how useless that was."

"I should say so," Peter exclaimed. Morgan had related his lunch with Delaney to the two of them.

They watched as Bruce Ismay approached. The man, in spite of the chilly weather, refused to wear a hat or overcoat. He was in his blue serge suit, stopping to chat with each passenger who was braving the nippy conditions. Many of the passengers had confined themselves to the promenade deck or were staying indoors and watching the passage from comfort.

He spotted the three of them and, although he seemed nervous to Morgan, his face widened with a smile. "Good afternoon," he said. "We seem to be making good time."

Margaret crossed her arms, wrapping them around her shoulders. "It is terribly cold."

"Yes," Ismay replied, "We're in icy seas, I'm afraid. We've already had several reports of iceberg sightings." He reached into his pocket, pulling out a wire. "The captain passed this on to me."

Morgan took the telegram from the *Baltic* and read it. "Are we going to stop and help this tanker, the *Deutschland?*" he asked. He passed the telegram around the group.

"No, but we will get word to other steamers in the area. I shouldn't worry if I were you. I think we'll arrive in New York on Tuesday night rather than Wednesday morning. We've managed to light two additional boilers."

"So we're going faster?" Margaret asked. "Isn't that somewhat reckless?"

"Somewhat, but I shouldn't worry. We're only doing twenty to twenty-one knots. I think we should surprise the people in New York when we arrive." He ginned at the announcement, obviously taking great pride in the *Titanic's* progress.

"It's so cold for April," Margaret said.

"We are in among the icebergs," Ismay announced rather cavalierly. "The crew is keeping a special watch out for ice, though, and we're heading for the corner."

"The corner?" Peter asked. "What's that?"

"There is a great underwater plateau stretching from the coast of Newfoundland," Ismay said. "It's called the Grand Banks. In order to avoid the ice, ships generally follow a more southerly route until reaching an area that's called 'the corner.' From there we dash almost due west." His eyes brightened, and his smile widened. "That's where we'll open her up and see what this old girl can really do."

"And so we're following this southerly route?" Morgan asked.

Ismay laughed. "Not as far south as Boxhall would have had us go, but far enough to avoid any great danger, I should think."

"And when do we reach this corner?" Peter asked.

Ismay craned his neck, looking back to the bow of the ship. He was thinking the matter over. "Before dinner, I should think, around 5:00."

"A steamer passed us last evening," Morgan said. "It was flashing Morse code signals."

"Yes, that was the *Rappahannock*. She was signaling us that she'd passed through a heavy field of ice." He held his hand up toward the rail. "But as you can see, we've been at full steam all day and haven't seen a thing. I wouldn't worry if I were you. These small steam ships tend to exaggerate. What can you expect of Americans?"

Margaret and Peter both laughed, but Morgan held his peace.

3:30 P.M.

Margaret set off for a walk. She was still trying hard to find the best way to break the news about Morgan's proposal. The fact that she'd told him yes would shock her mother, and Margaret knew it. There had been so much resolve in her attitude when the two of them had last talked, a resolve that talking to Morgan had broken into a thousand pieces.

When she spotted Gloria coming out of the first-class lounge, Margaret's eyes brightened. She'd need all the courage she could summon to talk to her mother, and Gloria would help. "Gloria," she spoke the woman's name loudly, "I'm so very glad to see you."

Margaret's voice spun Gloria around. "There you are," she said. "It's good to see you."

Margaret shivered in the cold air. "Yes, but we haven't picked a very good time for it, have we?"

"No, I suppose we haven't."

The two women locked arms and sauntered off toward the stern of the ship. The wooden deck seemed a bit slippery in the cold air, like ice in the making. "I have something I need to tell you," Margaret said.

"Let me guess. You and Mr. Fairfield."

"Yes, Morgan has asked me to marry him."

"Isn't that a mite inconvenient, having two fiancés?"

"It's a long story. I broke off my engagement to Peter. Frankly, I never wanted to see either of them again."

"Obviously that resolve didn't hold for long where Morgan was concerned." Gloria was smiling, almost snickering.

"No, it didn't. Of course, it leaves me in an awful dilemma."

"What's that? Getting married to the man you love?"

"No, explaining it all to my mother and father."

"I take it they had great expectations where you and Peter were concerned."

"Yes, great expectations."

"I should think you could simply remind your mother of the importance of love when it comes to marriage."

"I don't think that will work. You see, I rather doubt if she's ever loved my father. I think that for both of them marriage is a way of entwining social connections. My marriage to Peter was a way of continuing her own marriage to my father."

"That is too bad."

"Yes, my feelings for Morgan as a child were the first real feelings I'd ever known."

Gloria slipped her arm around Margaret. "I can understand your fears. You must understand something, though, my dear. When a woman begins her life with a man, it is largely built on the love she's known. It would have been so very easy to have your marriage one of duty. That's what you've known. But somewhere in the midst of this colorless, emotionless background of yours, you ran into a boy that you genuinely loved, a boy who is becoming a man. Leave all of that behind you, my dear. Leave it all and cling to this man. He is your future, and your feelings for him are the ones you want to pass on to your own daughters."

Margaret knew the truth of the words even as Gloria spoke them. This woman had become a godsend to her, an older sister she'd never known. "I know you're right. I do love Morgan."

"You are not your mother. I'm only sorry she wasn't a lot like you when she was a girl. You have too much of life ahead of you to call a halt to your feelings."

Gloria bit her bottom lip. Margaret could see that the woman was studying her. "Peter is a fine man. I shouldn't worry about him. Believe me, the worst thing you could do to that man is give yourself to him in a passionless commitment."

"I'm sure you're right. I know I hurt him deeply. He's such a gentleman."

"And the hardship will make him stronger. You can't control his feelings, though, only your own."

4:15 P.M.

The air was turning colder, dropping in a matter of minutes from fifty degrees to forty-five degrees. Just those few degrees of temperature were more than enough to drive the heartiest of souls inside. The aft well deck was almost clear when Boxhall walked through it. He stood at the door to the great room. In the third-class area of the ship, a small make-shift band was already tuning up their instruments, and Jack Kelly was watching his grandchildren dance. They seemed eager to do so, even without music.

He smiled as the children began to dance to the two violins and the mandolin that were chattering out an Irish jig. Seeing Kelly across the room, Boxhall made his way over to the man. "Seems pretty lively already," Boxhall said.

The old Irishman smiled and slapped a knee with his gnarled right hand. "To be sure, my boy, to be sure. Will ya be staying for a dance?"

"No, I'm afraid not. I'm just making my rounds."

"Too bad, you're gonna miss a good time tonight. I can promise you that. We'll be coming into icy waters shortly, I take it," Kelly said.

"Yes, we've already had a few warnings. We ought to be turning the corner close to sunset, though, and later than that if I have my way."

"We should go farther south," Kelly said.

"Yes, I know, and we would be doing that if they'd followed my original course."

Kelly got up and patted the man on the back. "I'm sure you're doing your best up there. I just wish them brash so-and-sos wouldn't put so much store in them newfangled water traps of theirs. Thinkin' like that can only bring a ship to ruin."

"I need to ask you something," Boxhall said. "You seem to have a good eye for people."

"I try."

"The man you led us to the other night, did you ever see anyone talking to him?"

Kelly scratched the side of his head, sending the fine tufts of reddish-gray hair flying over his left ear. "Funny you should be askin' that. The day he got on, I seem to remember him climbing the stairs on the aft well deck and standing up by the chain that separates us from first-class."

"Did you see him talking to anyone?"

"That may have happened. There was someone standing by the chain, I just can't remember who. Mostly, I had my eye on O'Conner. I figured what he was doing was the place for a curious woman. You know how they always want to see to things that don't belong to them, not all mind you, but a few."

"Yes."

"Well, he struck me as somebody trying to find out what the first-class deck looked like, and that was peculiar. I mean, he'd just come down here from the thing when he got on at Queenstown. What more could he see than he'd already seen? And he couldn't have got a better view than we already had from the well deck. But there might have been somebody there he was talking to, come to think of it. Why do you ask?"

"Because the man was not working alone. We do know he was in collaboration with one of the stewards. We know there's a third man involved, too, maybe one of the first-class passengers."

"That figures. That type is somebody I sure wouldn't trust to work alone."

"Well, if you can think of anything, you let me know. We're a mite worried there might be a second bomb."

He started to walk away, but Kelly grabbed his arm. "Look, if you're worried about that, we don't have much time. You'd better do something."

"Do what?"

"Get the man to talk."

"Now how do you expect me to do that?"

"Put the fear of God into him."

"I'm not about to go and bounce him around that storeroom. Somebody might hear."

Kelly's eyes had a twinkle to them. "Oh, you don't have to do that."

Now Boxhall was interested.

"I'd just wait till it's late tonight. Get some help, and you go and take the man up on deck, near the bow."

"Then what?"

"I'd latch onto his britches and hold him over the side. Threaten to drop him over if he doesn't talk. You can say you'll report him missing and nobody will be the wiser. I should think that'll loosen him up considerably."

"Sounds dangerous."

"Might be, but is it any more dangerous than having a second bomb aboard that you can't locate?"

"I can see your point. I'll think it over."

"You do that. You think it over. Meantime, you keep a watch out for ice."

Boxhall started toward the door. He called back over his shoulder. "We'll keep good watch. Don't worry about that."

SUNDAY,

APRIL 14, 1912,

4:40 P.M.

CHAPTER 31

Boxhall made his way across the well deck, he climbed the stairs swiftly. Rounding the corner that led to the first-class decks, he spotted Margaret and Gloria. The sight of Gloria perked him up a bit, and he smiled. "Good evening, ladies. A bit nippy out here for you, isn't it?"

Gloria smiled. Boxhall could tell she enjoyed seeing him. He only hoped she enjoyed it half as much as he liked the sight of her. "Yes, a fine evening," Gloria said.

"Do you think we'll have a lot of stars tonight?" Margaret asked.

"I should think we would." He lifted his head up. The sun was getting low on the horizon, but there wasn't a cloud. "It ought to be quite the sight. I'd expect to see a number of shooting stars." He smiled. "You ladies can wish to your hearts' content."

"And will you do your best to make our wishes come true?" Gloria asked.

There was something about the woman that made Boxhall know that she said much more than the words alone might indicate. Some women had a knack for such a thing, and he could see that Gloria Thompson was one of them. "I'll do my best."

The sound of scampering children brought their heads around. It was the two small Hoffman children, with their father playfully giving chase.

"I've never seen a father who doted on his children more," Gloria said.

"Perhaps so," Margaret said, "But the man seems odd to me. He seems to avoid all mention of his wife."

Gloria stepped in front of the path of the children and spread her arms in a playful manner. They screamed, delighted that someone else was joining in the game of chase. With their father in hot pursuit, they darted behind two of the deck chairs.

"There, now I got you," Hoffman shouted. He grabbed them, and they clung to him like mussels on a pier.

Margaret, Boxhall, and Gloria stepped closer to the man and the two laughing children. "You seem to be having fun," Gloria said.

The man stared into the faces of the two children. "Oh, we are. We're having the time of our lives." Putting the two children down, he ran his hands over their faces. "All right you two, run into the lounge and hide. I'll see if I can find you."

The children both ran off, laughing.

"You certainly seem to be the devoted father," Gloria said.

"Thank you. I try to be."

"I notice you're alone. Are you a widower, sir?"

The man's face turned sour. "I am alone."

Gloria could see the question made him ill at ease. "I asked because I'm a widow. I had no children, though."

"Excuse me," he said. "I have to go tend to the children." With that he hurried off in the path the two children had taken.

"That's odd," Gloria said.

"Yes, it is," Margaret agreed.

Boxhall was dumbfounded. He'd seen nothing unusual about the exchange. "Why would you say that?"

"I would think if the man was indeed a widower that he'd have told us so," Gloria responded. "Especially after I gave him the opportunity. If his wife was waiting for him in New York, wouldn't you think he'd have said so?"

"Of course he would have," Margaret concurred.

"You women are quite the detectives. I should think a man wouldn't have a secret to his name around the two of you."

6:00 P.M.

Second Officer Lightoller stepped onto the bridge. Lightoller's four-hour watch would last until 10:00 P.M., and he was determined to get a good night's sleep when it was over. Lightoller had been with the White Star Line for twelve years, since January 1900. That had been a glorious day, the start of a new century and the start of a new career all at once. He had left the seventeen-thousand-ton *Oceanic* to join the forty-six-thousand-ton *Titanic*.

His original position had been that of first officer, the position he held on the smaller liner. Captain Smith had brought on an old ship-mate, Henry Wilde, as chief officer, which knocked William Murdoch into the position as first officer. Naturally, Lightoller had to move down the ladder to second officer, a position he'd been told would only be temporary, but it was disappointing, nonetheless.

Lightoller had led a rugged life. He'd been shipwrecked on a deserted island, prospected for gold in the frozen Yukon, and worked for a time as a cowboy in Canada. These adventures provided him with not only a far greater range of experience than the average ship's officer but the fodder for many a nighttime story as well. Now, he was a career seaman who fully expected to be commanding his own ship some day. He read men well and expected them to adhere to the strict letter of the law and was thought to be short with a man who used poor judgment. These qualities, and the vast amount of experience he had as a man, made him a good friend and a bear of a man to serve under.

"It's time for dinner." He announced it to First Officer Murdoch, knowing the man would want to eat.

Murdoch buttoned up his coat and put on his hat. "You might want to know that we reached the corner at 5:00 P.M., but the captain had us continue almost sixteen miles farther south before we made our turn. I suppose he was somewhat concerned about ice."

"Rightly so," Lightoller replied.

Lightoller recalled the ice warning sent earlier in the day. Smith had shown him the message from the *Caronia*. "Mr. Moody, can you calculate the time in which we will reach 42 North to 49 to 51 degrees West?"

Sixth Officer James Moody was a young man, only in his mid-twenties. He was tall, clean shaven, and when given the chance could be quite levelheaded. Lightoller saw a knowing look come over the man's face. He knew exactly what he was looking for.

He stepped over to the charts and surveyed them closely. "I'd say we ought to be there around 11:00, sir."

The timing didn't sit well with Lightoller. He'd hoped to be asleep by then. Of course, with the promise of a vast ice field they'd have to traverse, he doubted he be able to sleep a wink. He would try, however. He knew he shouldn't be so nervous. Spending most of his life in solitary pursuits had often made it difficult to rely on the judgment of others. It was a habit he'd have to break.

"Close the blinds." He gave the order to the yeoman. The man stepped behind the bridge area and closed the blinds on the aft window of the wheelhouse. This shut out the lights of the *Titanic* that would otherwise stream through the window. Now the only light in the room was the dull, radiant glow that came from the compass, and that of the small lamp hanging over the charts that were spread over the courseboard.

Seaman Samuel Hemming stepped onto the bridge and gave a small salute. "The ship's navigational lights have been lit, sir."

Lightoller stepped over to the large window in the front of the bridge and stared into the growing darkness. "Hemming, I want you to go forward. See that the fore scuttle hatch is closed." He was staring down and looking at the light coming from the hatch. "We are in the vicinity of ice, and there is a glow coming from that thing. I want everything totally dark before the bridge, nothing that might interfere with our ability to see an obstacle in our path."

He watched as Boxhall took a star sighting. The man was responsible for navigation, and Lightoller saw no reason to criticize his work. So far, every thing had been accurate as far as Boxhall's work was concerned. Lightoller was certain the man would go far; he just didn't want him to go farther and faster than he did.

The one thing about Boxhall that might hurt him, as far as Lightoller was concerned, was the fact that he tended to want to get the right things done without necessarily caring that it got done the right way. Of course, the right way was always the British way, and as far as the *Titanic* was concerned, it was the White Star Line's policy.

Boxhall had wanted to take the ship even farther to the south before turning the corner. Lightoller smiled as he watched the man take the star sighting. At least, if he was going to err, Lightoller was glad he was doing it in the area of greater caution. If Ismay hadn't been aboard, he was almost certain they would have followed Boxhall's original course. *Too bad*, he thought. *I'd have gotten more sleep tonight.*

Lightoller had been impressed with the way Boxhall had taken to the security matters aboard ship. The man was the cautious type, but Lightoller was sure he could get a bit wild, too, if he had to. Boxhall was a big man, and the night O'Conner had been captured he had seemed more than willing to beat a confession out of the man. Lightoller knew Boxhall was more than a little concerned about the possibility of another bomb, perhaps more concerned about that than he was in keeping regulations. He was busying himself now with pinpointing the location of the ship on the map and matching it up with the ice reports they'd received. He'd have to bear watching, though, at least until Lightoller retired for the night.

6:30 P.M.

D elaney paced nervously back and forth in his cabin. Things were getting a bit touchy, especially after O'Conner had been captured. The *Titanic* was the pride and joy of more than the English maritime industry; she was the embodiment of all they prided themselves in as a nation, especially in the way of luxury and ingenuity. A catastrophe involving the *Titanic* would produce world news and perhaps even bring the haughty English to their knees. It was the only thing he could think about.

The knock at the door sent him scurrying across the room. He unlocked it and yanked the thing open. It was Fitzgerald. Delaney hauled him into the room and, stepping into the hall, looked both ways. The companionway was empty. Fitzgerald had taken some precaution. Delaney stepped back and closed the door behind Fitzgerald, locking it once again.

"How did this happen?" He stepped in Fitzgerald's direction, almost spitting out the words. "I just don't understand."

"I don't know for sure." The man was backing up, almost instinctively. "I suppose there was a man in steerage who became suspicious. The man followed him."

Fitzgerald looked at him with a quizzical look. "How did you hear my knock?"

Most of the time, Delaney knew he should have been more cautious about his ability to hear. On this day, however, he didn't want the man banging away at his door. Fitzgerald was enough of a deadhead to let anything slip and just at the wrong time, too.

"I had my hand on the door," Delaney lied. "I felt the knock. Lucky thing for you. I don't want anything that might attract attention, least of all you banging on my cabin door."

Fitzgerald gulped nervously.

Delaney shook his head. "So he was followed, was he?" He made sure he kept his eyes focused on Fitzgerald's lips. The man might be too inquisitive for his own good. "Nosy people, always poking about where they don't belong."

"The man is an Irishman."

"An Irishman?" The very idea of being betrayed by an Irishman was almost too much to bear. It stuck in his throat.

"Yes." Fitzgerald took a few more steps back, almost as if he wanted to prevent any blows. "He followed him right to the spot where he planted the bomb."

Delaney moved toward him. "Where's he being kept?"

"He's being kept in a storage room behind the wheelhouse. I've spoken to him. I didn't know what to say, so I told him you had a plan."

"Good thinking," Delaney breathed a sigh. The last thing he wanted was for O'Conner to go shooting off his mouth. "We don't want the man to panic and talk."

"That's what I thought. I told him we'd get him a file. They've got some old leg irons on him."

Delaney paced around the room like an overgrown cat in a very small cage. "Well, we've got to get O'Conner out of there. Who has the key to the place?"

"The fourth officer, a man named Boxhall. I shouldn't try to get the key from him though, if I were you. The man is quite the imposing figure and would promise to be quite rough and ready."

Delaney walked over to the window and opened the curtain. The sky was dark now, with nothing but the passing sea. "Is there any other place where a key is kept?"

"Yes, there is. In the purser's office they have a lockbox. All the keys to the ship are kept there."

"Is the box secure?"

"I'm not certain of that. It may be locked, but then again it may simply be shut."

Delaney took a seat on the sofa and buried his head in his hands. He began to rub his bearded face. It was his way of forcing a thought when his mind seemed blank. Suddenly, he jerked his head up. "All right, you go and find out. I don't care what you do. Make some sort of pretense. If that box is locked, find out where they keep the key. If it's unlocked, you come right back and get me. Do I make myself understood?"

"Yes, sir, I understand."

Delaney got up and walked him to the door. "Make certain you are not followed. I want every contact that you and I have to be able to pass close scrutiny. They may be watching us at this very moment."

Fitzgerald nodded his head. Opening the door, he peered outside.

"That's it," Delaney whispered as he pushed him out into the companionway. He closed the door and stood for a moment with his back to it.

The next twenty minutes seemed to drag by like hours. Delaney paced the room, back and forth. Nothing seemed to be going right. O'Conner had planted the bomb but hadn't been careful enough to watch his backside. He still didn't trust Fitzgerald. The man was in the right position to be of service to the cause. He'd managed to work his way up to being a first class steward, but that didn't make him a brave man, or even a smart man, for that matter. He'd carried payments for guns and a few dispatches, but this kind of work required more than that. Fitzgerald was curious when he didn't need to be, and the man Hunter had seen them. Now, this Morgan Fairfield was asking questions, asking questions and testing his patience. Why? What could he suspect?

Outside the door, Delaney heard Fitzgerald's voice. The man was exchanging pleasantries with two women.

The door opened, and Fitzgerald poked his head in. He caught Delaney's stare. "I'm sorry, but you said you didn't want any knocking."

Delaney waved him in. "Come in and shut the door. Are you sure you weren't followed?"

"Yes, I'm certain of that. I saw Miss Hastings in the hall with her mother, but I waited until they passed before I came in."

"Well, what did you find out?"

"The box with the keys hanging in it is unlocked. It's on the bulkhead wall right beside the purser's desk."

"And who's on the desk now?"

"Just McElroy. I think the other two men who work there are in the ship's mess hall."

"Good, then we haven't a moment to lose. You will come with me, and I'll have McElroy gather a few of my things from the safe. When I have him out of sight, you can get the key to the storeroom."

Delaney grabbed Fitzgerald's sleeve and twisted it. "Now listen carefully. Take the key to the man and tell him to hide it. He is not to use it under any circumstance until we near New York harbor. Then he is to go to the purser's office and get that satchel, by force if necessary."

"By force?"

"Yes, we must have those papers. Make it clear to him that they in no way are to reach America."

He moved to the doorway and then stopped in his tracks. "I'll go first, and you should come a few minutes later. I don't want anyone to see us together, ever again. Is that clear?" He knew that perhaps he was overdoing it with the man trying to make sure he got the drift of everything he said, but it was better to offend him than to make a mistake.

Fitzgerald nodded. "Yes, I understand."

"Fine, then I'll go. Give me five minutes, and I'll meet you at McElroy's desk."

Delaney climbed the stairs and stepped out onto the deck. He could tell at once that the night air was turning chilly. The sun going down always seemed to have that effect, but this night was far worse than most. He grabbed the cold rail but quickly pulled his hand away.

He saw Ismay walking the deck in the opposite direction and smiled. "Evening to you, Ismay."

"Yes, good evening." Ismay seemed to bounce, doing his dead level best not to appear cold.

"Turning a bit chilly, isn't it?"

"Yes it is. It was thirty-nine degrees the last time I looked."

Delaney slapped his arms underneath his armpits. He shivered. "Then it'll be freezing before we know it."

"I expect so." In spite of the temperature, Ismay never lost the smile he gave out to paying passengers. The man was doing his best to keep a stiff upper lip, no matter what. "These are icy waters."

"Well, let us hope your men are taking every precaution."

"Oh, that they are." Ismay craned his neck around and looked up at the crow's nest. "We have men with sharp eyes up there and more in the wheelhouse. I don't expect we'll have anything sneaking up on us tonight."

"I should hope not."

He left Ismay to survey the nearly empty deck. Most people with sense had gone indoors. It took him some time to reach the base of the wheelhouse, the place where the stairs led down to the purser's office. Now he slowed down. There was no reason to get there with a great deal of time to spare.

The door to the purser's office was a wide one, separated into two parts. The top half was open, and the bottom half had a ledge that served as a counter. Delaney could see McElroy seated behind his desk. He had a white crockery cup in both hands with the White Star insignia emblazoned on it. He seemed to be cradling the thing, more for warmth than anything. "Good evening," Delaney said.

McElroy put down the cup. "Good evening, sir."

"Delaney, Donald Delaney."

"Of course, Mr. Delaney." McElroy got up from his ladder-back swivel chair and rounded the desk. "And what brings you to see us this evening?"

Delaney smiled. "I seem to have got myself into a bit of a pinch."

"Is that right?"

"Cards, you know. A man has to pass the time some way."

McElroy nodded. "I understand, sir. Perfectly."

"I'm afraid I haven't been too lucky, and for an Irishman to admit that is quite a cause for embarrassment."

McElroy smiled.

"But my luck is bound to change, and I have a feeling it will tonight. My blood boils in the cold weather, and that's a good sign." His grin was almost unbearable.

Glancing back down the companionway, he could see Fitzgerald coming his way.

"Well, how can I help you sir?"

"I have some extra cash money in that safe of yours." He scanned the wall. There it was, a large metal box hanging on the bulkhead wall. It was flat and took up about four feet by four feet. He was sure that's where the keys were stored. "I was wondering if I could draw some of it out. It takes money to make money, you know."

"Yes, sir, that's what I hear. How much do you require?"

"I think I should go with you. I'm not sure how much I might need, but when I see what I have left, that will tell the tale for me."

McElroy reached down and undid the latch on the inside of the door. He swung it open. "Of course, sir. We'll go back there together."

"Brilliant. I might get lost."

McElroy fished in his coat pocket, pulling out a brass ring filled with keys. He spun them around his finger. "Well, I have the keys. I'll have to let you into the area myself and then make certain everything is secure when you're finished."

"Splendid." He made his way through the door. "I must say, you people make certain that you have everything in its place."

"That we do. We have everything on the ship that's of value under lock and key."

Delaney smiled and followed McElroy down the stacks and into the area where the safe was located.

SUNDAY,
APRIL 14, 1912,
7:30 P.M.

CHAPTER 32

J unior wireless operator Harold Bride took the opportunity to keep the accounts current. The alternator tended to run hot on the apparatus, and they had given it very little rest. He had shut the motor down, giving it and him a much needed breather. So many messages had been sent that the silence of the machine came as a welcome relief. He laced his fingers together and stretched them.

Reaching over to the wall, he clamped the switch back into position, sending an electrical charge through the wires and surging through the apparatus. When it came back on, he listened to the sudden clatter and dropped his pencil. A ship that was obviously close by was sending the message. The signal was strong. Picking up the headphones, he clamped them over his ears and reached for the pencil once again. The message was being repeated, and he copied it furiously.

"Ice report from the *Californian*. Latitude 42°3' North, longitude 49°9' West. Three large bergs five miles to southward of us."

Bride quickly tapped out a message, acknowledging the warning. Sparks jumped from the machine as the key was pressed.

Ripping off the headphones, he shrugged his jacket on and headed out the door. He continued buttoning the thing as he stepped onto the bridge. Spotting Second Officer Lightoller, he held out the message. "Sir, a message from the steamer *Californian*, an ice warning."

Lightoller took the message and read it.

"She sounded close by, and I thought I ought to bring it to the bridge right away."

"Good thinking," Lightoller said. "Mr. Moody, would you relay this message to the captain? He's at the à la carte restaurant on B deck."

"Yes, sir."

Lightoller handed the wire to Moody and, stepping over to the charts, turned on the small light. He traced his finger down to the reported position. "She is close," he said. He looked up at Moody, who was putting his cap into place. "Also, speak to the ship's carpenter. I noticed the air temperature was 39 degrees. Tell him to take care that we don't have the fresh water freeze aboard."

"Aye, aye, sir."

"Will that be all?" Bride asked.

"Yes, for now. Keep a close watch on the ice reports, though, Bride. We're in icy waters, and I want to know all reports at once. Is that understood?"

"Yes, sir." Bride pivoted on his heels and left the bridge.

7:40 P.M.

Morgan and Peter were working hard at taking their walk before dinner. They both shivered in their suit jackets, and only Peter was wearing an overcoat. The cold air sliced away at their faces. Peter edged closer to the rail. "I say, old boy, I don't think I've ever seen the sea looking more calm. It's like one great big pond out there, except there are no swans."

Morgan stepped out, braving the wind created by the movement of the great ship. He placed his hands on the rails and looked into the starry night. "Yes, I should think if there were swans out there, they'd have to be in their overcoats."

Peter pulled the collar of his coat up around his neck. His face was a parchment white against the cold. "It may, indeed, be cold out here, but not nearly so cold as my seat at the dinnertable."

"I wouldn't worry about that, if I were you. If anything, Margaret will be much more uncomfortable than you will be."

"Oh, fine, two fidgety people sitting next to Margaret's mother. How will I ever keep my food down? Are you sure you wouldn't like to swap places for the evening? I should think it would be the least you could do."

Morgan laughed. "And, of course, no one will notice that. It would never come up, would it?"

"I suppose you're right." Peter shook his head. "There's nothing I like more than being the subject of an entire evening's conversation," he said, with a jaded tone in his voice.

He put his arm around Morgan's shoulder. "You are going to owe me, you know. So much, in fact, that your grandchildren will be paying the debt."

"Yes, I expect that's true."

Both men looked up to see Bruce Ismay heading their way. Like Morgan, he was without an overcoat, but he had his hands in his pockets, doing his best to smile. Morgan was carrying the broken cane in his hand, while Peter had the two broken pieces in his overcoat pocket.

"Going for a stroll?" Ismay asked.

Morgan could see that Ismay had spotted the silver handle of the cane. "Yes," Morgan said. "We both thought it would make the dining room seem even warmer."

"I should say it will," Ismay replied. "What's that in your hand?"

Morgan held it out. "It's what's left of a walking stick. It does have your initial on it, so we thought it might be yours."

Ismay grabbed it, looking it over. "It's not mine, sorry to say." He turned it over, examining the broken end. "I'd say it's the worse for wear." He handed it back to Morgan.

"Yes, I'd say so."

Ismay looked around at the deserted deck. "People have all taken to the lounge, I'm afraid, and on such a beautiful night." He forced a smile. Looking at Peter, he brushed his mustache aside, showing a set of gleaming white teeth. "It's a very romantic night, too. We ought to catch sight of a number of falling stars."

Morgan and Peter exchanged glances. It was apparent Ismay still had the matter of Peter's engagement in mind. It was something both men would have to get used to until they docked in New York, and they both knew it. Until then, there would be many awkward moments.

"I haven't seen many people out," Ismay said, "except for that Irish writer."

"You mean Delaney?" Peter asked.

"Yes, I saw him a short while ago up near the wheelhouse."

"Did you happen to see our steward, Fitzgerald?" Morgan inquired.

"As a matter of fact, I did, shortly after I saw Delaney. I assumed he was on ship's business. Has the man been serving you well?"

"Oh, quite well," Morgan replied.

"Yes," Peter added, "A splendid fellow."

"Good, good, I'm glad to hear that. The White Star Line likes to employ only the best help." His smile disappeared, and he looked from side to side. "You must be somewhat relieved that we've apprehended the man we were all seeking."

"I don't think that answers all of our questions," Morgan replied.

"Why not, pray tell?"

"There's the matter of Mr. Kennedy," Peter offered.

Ismay shook his head. "So, you still don't think that was an accident?"

"No, we don't," Morgan said. "We think someone had a very good reason to want him dead, a very good reason."

"I can't imagine what."

"Oh, you can't?" Morgan asked, "Not even yourself, Mr. Ismay?"

The man practically exploded. "Me?" He waved his hand in an animated fashion. "Mercy sakes, no. Why should I want the man dead?"

Morgan knew the man was quite the accomplished actor. He was doing his very best to maintain a level of innocent purity. "Hunter seemed to think you might have reason to not want him aboard the *Titanic*."

"What did he tell you?"

"Something about a sister of his."

Morgan knew he was taking quite a risk by even intimating he might know about the hit-and-run accident. If Ismay was the killer, there would be plenty of reason now not to stop with Hunter. Still, he couldn't resist. He had to see the man's reaction.

"That's a terrible lie." Ismay's eyes bulged. In spite of the cold, Morgan could see beads of perspiration forming on his forehead. The man's head looked like a boiled egg, freshly removed from the scalding water.

"What is?" Morgan asked.

"That story about the man's sister."

"And which one would that be?"

Morgan knew that in many ways what he was doing to the man was cruel, jabbing the knife in and slowly twisting it. He didn't want to tell him, however, exactly what it was he knew, and he was certainly ashamed of how he came to know it.

"What did he tell you?" Ismay asked.

Morgan tucked his hands under his armpits for warmth. "Actually, he told me very little." Morgan knew that was true. Most of what he'd really learned about the event had been from Ismay's own lips, even if Ismay didn't know it. "He said something about his sister's death."

"Yes, poor man. He was under the illusion that I had something to do with it." Ismay shook his head. "That's false, of course, but you know how people are when something gets stuck in their head."

"Yes, I know."

"Well, I hope you have other suspects, young man, because I'm afraid you have a dead end where I am concerned. The idea of a murder aboard one of my vessels is simply terrifying to me. Even if I had good reason, I'd pick a better place for it. Why would I want the notoriety?"

"Well, you're probably right there," Morgan said, "unless, of course, the notoriety of what he might say would be worse."

"Nothing could be worse, absolutely nothing."

He pulled out his pocket watch and nervously fidgeted with the lid, trying to open it. Finally, he looked at the time. "I should go up to the bridge and check our position. If you will excuse me?"

"Certainly," Morgan said.

"Keep them steering straight and true," Peter said.

They watched him walk off.

"The man is right about one thing," Peter said.

"What is that?"

"Ismay is a corporate creature first and last. I should think if he were going to kill Hunter that he'd pick a better spot, someplace in New York."

Peter pointed to the end of the cane Morgan was carrying. "I'd think he'd also find a better place to get rid of that."

Just as the men started to go into the lounge, they noticed a man in a blue jacket standing in the shadows. "Is he gone?" the man asked.

"Is who gone?" Peter asked.

"Ismay." It was Boxhall.

"How long have you been standing there?" Morgan asked.

"Just a few minutes." He stepped out from the darkness and into the light. "I was waiting to speak to the two of you, but then Ismay walked up. I have a proposition for the two of you."

"A proposition?" Peter asked.

"It's dangerous," Boxhall replied. "Could be very dangerous."

The men drew closer, suddenly interested.

"It might mean finding out the identity of Hunter's murderer."

"We're interested," said Morgan. He looked at Peter.

"Very interested," added Peter.

"This is something I can't involve any of the crew in. It would mean their jobs. It would surely mean mine, if we're caught."

"Mean your job?" Peter asked.

"Yes, it's illegal and highly improper, but it might be our only way to find out. It involves our prisoner. We've had someone listening in each time Fitzgerald has delivered a meal, but so far the man hasn't given out a name. We know the prisoner knows the man though. I just don't think we can afford to wait. Whoever this third party is might have another explosive device with him. For all we know, it might go off tonight."

"What would you like us to do?" Morgan asked.

"Just meet me at the steps to the wheelhouse at 11:30 tonight. You'd better bundle up, too. It promises to be freezing."

"What are we going to do?" Peter asked.

"We're going to put the fear of God into that man. If he won't tell us the other man's identity, let's see what he does when he thinks he's going to die."

"That sounds risky," Morgan said.

"It's plenty risky. You won't be able to ever tell a soul we did this."

"You're not going to kill the man?" Peter asked.

"No, we're not going to kill him, just make him think these are his last few moments on the earth. Let's see how he talks then." Boxhall looked at the two men. They were both young, and neither seemed to be the type to do such a thing. Of course, he wasn't the type either. He just couldn't get the notion out of his mind of a second bomb. If one did go off and people were killed and injured, he'd never be able to live with himself if he thought there had been something he could have done but didn't do. He knew that what he planned went far beyond the boundaries of proper behavior, especially for an officer, but he no longer cared.

"Are you both in with me? I really have no one else."

"Yes," Morgan said, "I am."

"Me, too," said Peter.

"There will be no turning back, you know."

8:45 P.M.

Second Officer Lightoller was looking at the charts when Captain Smith stepped back into the wheelhouse. "And how was the dinner, sir?"

Smith brushed his beard aside. "Excellent, quite a nice affair." Smith stepped over to the large window. "Has there been any change?"

"No, sir." Lightoller stepped over to join the captain. "There's been no change. It's a pity, though, that whatever breeze we had before has disappeared."

Smith stared at Lightoller. He knew the man had been to sea at age thirteen and was a man of great experience. Smith made it a point to know his men, which was why he could have guessed what Lightoller had in mind.

"Even the small surf the breeze might have created," Lightoller went on, "could show us ice quicker."

Smith nodded, "Quite."

Lightoller looked out over the dark water. "We do have good visibility though. I should think that even if one shows us its blue side, we'll still have sufficient time to make course corrections."

Lightoller referred to the practice of sea ice. No matter how massive the berg was, it would often get top heavy as the sea melted away at its bottom and roll over in the water. When that happened, the new surface of the berg would be almost blue—which made seeing it all the more difficult, especially at night.

Smith looked up at the crow's nest. "Who's aloft?" he asked.

"Jewell and Symons, sir. Fleet and Lee come on at 10:00."

"Good. Make sure they keep a good watch up there."

"I don't expect us to enter into the area we've had the ice reports about until 11:00 or 12:00, sir. Shall I wake you?"

"No, only if conditions change. If we should pick up any haze, anything at all, I want you to reduce speed. Is that clear?"

"Yes, sir. I have just over an hour left on my watch. Murdoch will be in charge after that."

"Fine," Smith smiled, "Then you get some sleep."

"I will, sir, and you should, too. Tomorrow will be a big day. I almost hate to see it end."

"Yes, I do, too."

Lightoller watched as Smith stared into the night. There had been great speculation that this would be the man's last voyage. It was a touchy subject, though, and one Lightoller in no way wanted to bring up. There was a sadness written on the man's face, however, almost as if he wasn't looking into the darkness at all. It was as if he was looking back over the years, years spent on the sea.

8:50 P.M.

Abigail held up two dresses, one a white dress with sparkles on it that made it shine and the other a pink satin gown. Abigail was

Madeleine's size, and Madeleine liked the fact that she could see first-hand just what her dresses might look like before she put them on. "What do you think, Johnny?" Madeleine asked.

"I think you'd look lovely in either."

John had just returned from the smoking lounge where he'd had a good game of cards, and Madeleine, as was her custom, had waited for him before choosing her dress. Pleasing him made her feel special, and she wanted to make sure that what she wore did please him.

She watched Abigail's face beam as she held up the white gown, draping it over the top of her maid's uniform. "Do you like that, Abby?"

"Yes, ma'am, ever so much."

"What do you think, Johnny? Should I wear that one?"

Astor laughed. "I can't seem to fight women. If I can't say no to you, what makes you think I can say no to the two of you?"

"Oh, John, you spoil me."

Astor stepped up behind his wife, who was standing in her gown and watching Abigail hold up the dresses. He placed his hand on her shoulders and gently kissed her neck. "My dear, this is nothing like the way I plan on spoiling you."

She placed her hand on his. "You are too sweet to me, darling." She looked back at Abigail. "Let's take the one you like, Abby."

Abigail curtsied and laid the pink one on the bed. "I'll help you, ma'am."

Astor stepped away while Madeleine took off her dressing gown and pushed her arms into the sleeves of the white gown. She stepped into it. "You do like it, don't you, Abby?"

"Yes, ma'am. You look so very beautiful in it."

Madeleine patted her stomach. "I'm afraid I won't be able to wear it for long."

Abigail blushed.

"I'd like you to have it when we get to New York, Abby."

"Oh, ma'am. I couldn't do that."

"Of course, you can. I insist on it."

"You're most kind."

Madeleine looked back at John, who had been listening. "Being kind is what I do best, isn't it Johnny?"

Astor stepped her way and once again placed his hand on her shoulder. "I think you're the kindest, most gentle creature I've ever known. I've been married to the opposite of that, and I must say I much prefer this."

Turning around, Madeleine put her hands up to his face, gazing into his eyes. "My darling, being kind to you is what I live for."

9:35 P.M.

B ride had decided to take a break before the heavy wireless traffic that usually came at the end of the day. It was evident that people made plans for their messages during dinner because shortly after that, both men found themselves busy at the key. They would have to take turns to keep fresh. Phillips tapped away at an already-long list of pending messages. They'd already been able to reach Cape Race, and that would mean even more traffic over the wireless.

He finished his message and suddenly heard an incoming warning:
From Mesaba to Titanic and all eastbound ships,

> Ice report in latitude 42° N to 41°25' N, longitude 49° W to 50°30' W. Saw much heavy pack ice and great number large icebergs. Also field ice. Weather good, clear.

Ripping the message from his pad, he speared it on the spike with incoming messages and mumbled. That made a total of six ice messages they'd received. He couldn't leave his work to deliver it to the wheelhouse. It would just have to wait.

11:00 P.M.

J ack Phillips grew more and more impatient with the late-night messages being sent back and forth from Cape Race. There seemed to be no end in sight. The stack of wires remaining had reached what he saw as a mountain of paper with scrawled words. Sparks from the machine leaped in a blue arch as he tapped out the latest having-a-wonderful-time-wish-you-were-here message.

Suddenly, he winced in pain. A loud signal from the nearby *Californian* was blowing his ears off, it was so close by. "We are stopped and surrounded by ice," it blasted.

Furious, Phillips roared back with an equally loud and hot message. He rapped feverishly with the key. "Shut up, shut up. You're jamming my signal. I'm busy. I'm working Cape Race."

That seemed to be enough. The operator on the *Californian* must have gotten the idea. There was no response. Phillips blew out a breath. Now he could get back to work.

SUNDAY,
APRIL 14, 1912,
11:20 P.M.

CHAPTER 33

Boxhall was standing at the base of the stairs when Morgan and Peter walked up. They were a little early, but it was obvious that Boxhall had been there waiting, perhaps even thinking over what had to be done. Both men were in their overcoats, and it was a good thing. The temperature had dropped. The water itself was thirty-one degrees.

"All right," Morgan said, "We're here. Now, what's this plan of yours?"

Boxhall looked out over the rail. The decks were deserted. Lights were ablaze, and a number of people were still milling about the smoking room and first-class lounge, but at this hour, and given the icy conditions, it was doubtful many would come venturing out onto the deck.

"I want to ask the prisoner a few questions. We've got to find out who this third man is and if he has another bomb."

Morgan and Peter looked at each other. Morgan knew that most likely, whatever it was that Boxhall had in mind was risky at best. The idea frightened him, but it also seemed like the best thing to do if he was going to find Hunter's killer.

Boxhall looked up the stairs. "The man is up in the storeroom. I have the key."

"You're not planning on roughing him up are you?" Peter asked.

"No, I'm planning on the three of us taking him out onto the forward well deck. We'll lift him up and hold him over the side."

Peter gulped.

"That's why I wanted the two of you to help. I don't want the man to fall. I just want him to think that we might very well drop him over the side."

"Isn't this dangerous?" Morgan asked.

"Only if we're caught."

"I don't know," Morgan said. "The man might just slip."

"That's why I need you two. I figure that with the three of us that we can get a good grip on the man. I'd do it alone, but then it might be dangerous."

"We can't have you go at this alone, old man," Peter said. "Can we, Morgan?"

Rarely had Morgan ever been a part of even schoolboy pranks. It just hadn't been his style. He'd always been the model child and the young man who could always be trusted to do the right thing. It was one of the things he knew Hunter played on, his tendency to always think and do the right thing. Had Hunter been in his place and had he been the one floating in the pool, he knew what Hunter would have done, and in a heartbeat. He heard himself saying the words, even though he didn't feel them inside. It was almost as if he were a bystander, listening to someone else. "No, we can't. Let's do it."

"Good," Boxhall said. "Then follow me."

The three men headed single file up the stairs to the area on the deck behind the wheelhouse. Shortly, they were at the darkened door to the storeroom. Boxhall took out his key, inserted it into the door, and turned the lock. The men stepped into the room, leaving the door open. Reaching for the switch, Boxhall turned on the lights.

O'Conner groaned, tossing under his blankets.

Boxhall stepped over to the bed. Reaching down, he threw back the man's covers. "Let's go. This is where you get off."

"What the blazes are you doing?" O'Conner asked.

"You'll see," Boxhall said. "You're going for a little swim." Boxhall pointed at the man's shackled feet. "Grab them," he shouted.

Peter latched onto the man's feet, as he began kicking. Taking out a long piece of cord, Boxhall grabbed the man's wrists and looped it around them. He looped them several times and tied a quick knot.

"Hey, you can't do this."

"Just you watch me." Boxhall took out a handkerchief and crammed it into O'Conner's mouth. "You tried to blow up the ship and kill innocent women and children. You don't deserve to continue this ride."

He pointed to Morgan. "You take his arms, and both of you follow me. I'll go ahead and make sure no one is between us and the deck."

Morgan lifted the struggling man up, and with all the kicking and squirming they could handle, they wrested the man out the door between them.

Boxhall stood by as they stepped onto the catwalk, then closed and locked the door. "All right, follow me."

They moved to the stairway with Boxhall in the lead. It was a slow process with O'Conner squirming and kicking his best with the leg irons on. Morgan felt sorry for Peter. Even though he had to look at the man's frightened and angry face, it was Peter who was taking all the bruises.

Morgan was very thankful when they finally stepped down the last of the stairs and to the well deck. The crow's nest was some fifty feet above them, but both the lookouts would be staring straight ahead. They wouldn't be looking down. At least Morgan hoped they wouldn't be.

"Here, this is it," Boxhall said. "This ought to just about do it. Have you both got a good grip on the man?"

"I have," Peter said. "If I don't hold him tight, he'll kick me to death."

Boxhall leaned over O'Conner and spoke in a low voice. "You'd better relax. You start kicking and squirming, and somebody is going to drop you."

O'Conner's eyes widened. His loose clothing was no match against the cold.

"All right, let's hold him over the side," Boxhall snapped. "We'll point him to the bow, feet first." He placed his hands underneath the man, and the three of them lifted him over the rail.

Morgan watched the water slide by. There were now small chunks of ice that glowed in the *Titanic*'s light. In the distance, he saw another strange sight. It appeared to be the lights of another steamer.

"Now," Boxhall spoke in a slow and deliberate tone, "I'm going to ask you some questions, and if we don't like your answers, we're going to drop you in the Atlantic. There's no reason for us to keep a man aboard who won't cooperate. No one will be the wiser. As far as anyone is concerned, you tried to escape and fell overboard."

O'Conner shook his head, as if silently pleading for mercy. It was a strange transformation. The man had obviously been a hardened criminal. Empty threats would have no doubt gone unheeded. This was different, though. It was a threat that could be seen and felt. The danger was all too obvious. The sight of the water passing below would have been enough to frighten any man. Morgan was concerned himself, and he had both feet on deck.

"Now," Boxhall went on. "I'm going to take that thing out of your mouth so you can answer a few questions. But be careful. If you kick up an uproar, I'll stick it back in and we'll drop you right here. Do you understand?"

O'Conner nodded his head vigorously.

"Fine. That's good."

Boxhall pulled the handkerchief slowly from the man's mouth. When it was out, O'Conner's breath rose in a ghostly steam. He panted.

"Now we know you had a bomb. What we want to know is, is there another bomb?"

"No," O'Conner gasped. "That was it."

Boxhall leaned over, pushing his face up next to O'Conner's. "Are you sure?"

"I had the only one."

"Fine, now one more thing. We know Fitzgerald the steward is working with you. Who's the other man, the first-class passenger?"

O'Conner blinked at the question. Turning in a fellow comrade was obviously something that was repugnant to him. He greeted the question with silence.

"We're going to find out anyway. You don't think Fitzgerald will be quiet when we hold him over the rail, do you?" Boxhall twisted the man's collar. "Of course, that will be tomorrow night, and you'll be at the bottom of the sea." He shook the man by the collar.

There was a pause.

"Hold him out more," Boxhall said. "We don't want to get wet." He looked O'Conner in the eye. "Is one day more of your secret enough to die for?"

O'Conner coughed. "No, I reckon not."

"Then who is it?" Boxhall growled.

"Delaney, Donald Delaney."

Now, Morgan's curiosity was aroused. "Did he have anything to do with Hunter Kennedy's death?"

The men could hear the ringing of the bell high above in the crow's nest. Boxhall looked up. "What the blazes is wrong with them?"

Morgan had a perfect view of the bow. He looked up and could hardly believe his eyes. There in the distance was a gigantic iceberg. It towered some several stories high with a peak that was looming up in the direction of the *Titanic*. The icy monster appeared for all the world to be a floating white Rock of Gibraltar. "That's what's wrong," Morgan shouted. "Iceberg."

The word snapped Boxhall's head around as the bell sounded out a clear second and third ring.

11:39 P.M.

Sixth Officer Moody picked up the phone from the crow's nest. Fleet's message was startling and to the point. "Iceberg right ahead."

"Thank you," replied Moody. He set the phone back in its cradle. Turning to First Officer Murdoch, he relayed the message. "Iceberg right ahead, sir."

Murdoch stepped out onto the wing bridge to get a better look. He could see the features of the icy mass moving toward them. He leaned back through the door and shouted out his orders to the helmsman, "Hard astarboard."

The yeoman swung the wheel to the right. Unlike an automobile, one had to turn the wheel right in order for the ship to come aport.

Almost simultaneously, Murdoch shouted orders to Moody. "All stop. Full speed astern."

Moody swung the handles of the telegraph into position. First, "All stop." The chief below must have heard the bell ring and seen the order. Then, he swung it into position for the second order, "Full astern."

Just as soon as Murdoch gave the orders, he realized it was already too late. There was no way the *Titanic* could be brought to a halt in time. They had spotted the berg at five hundred yards. At her trials, the *Titanic* had taken eight hundred and fifty yards to stop when traveling at twenty knots. Here, evidently in what was the middle of an ice field, she was doing twenty-two and one half knots, a speed that covered thirty-eight feet per second.

He stepped back into the wheelhouse and moved quickly to the red alarm button. It would sound a bell below. He left his finger on the button for a full ten seconds. That would give the men time to clear the way before he threw the switch that operated the vaunted watertight doors. Taking his finger off the button, he threw the switch on the doors.

Stepping back, he watched along with Moody as the berg slid closer. The ice mountain was at least seventy-five to one hundred feet above the surface of the water. Murdoch knew his quick action had prevented a head-on collision, but it remained to be seen how much damage would be done.

A mere forty seconds had passed since Fleet had phoned the warning. The scraping noise on starboard made every man on the bridge aware that it was not nearly enough time. They watched the berg slide by as it continued to chafe the side of the great ship. Large chunks of ice fell on the forward well deck.

"Hard aport," Murdoch yelled. "We have to try to clear the stern." He stepped back onto the starboard wing bridge and watched the iceberg continue to hug the starboard, dropping ice onto the deck as it passed. Soon, it drifted free and disappeared into the darkness behind the stern.

It wasn't more than a minute before Captain Smith had hurried to the bridge. "What have we struck?" he asked Murdoch.

"An iceberg, sir. I pulled hard astarboard and reversed the engines, and I was going to pull hard aport to try to take us around it, but she was too close. I could not do any more."

"Have you closed the watertight doors?"

"They are already closed, sir."

Boxhall seemed quite out of breath when he ran onto the bridge.

"Mr. Boxhall," Smith said, "I want you to go below on starboard and determine the extent of our damage. Report back to me as quickly as possible."

"Aye, aye, sir."

Boxhall ran out the door and back down the stairs to where Peter and Morgan were waiting. They had all three put O'Conner back where he belonged. It seemed ironic. Boxhall could breathe more easily that there was no second bomb, but there was something even worse, an iceberg. "You two had better get to your cabins," he said. "I'm going to assess the damage below."

"Is it serious?" Peter asked.

"We're not certain of that, but I'd wake Margaret and her mother, if I were you."

Peter looked at Morgan. It was obvious that he was wondering if that were his place any longer.

"Yes, I think you should," Morgan said. "Here, you'd better give me the cane first. If I can find Guggenheim in all this mess, I'll ask him if it's his."

Peter pulled the cane from his overcoat pocket and looked at Morgan with a frown. "You don't give up, do you?"

"No, I don't."

In fifteen minutes Boxhall was once again in the wheelhouse making his report. The captain and Ismay had been joined by Thomas Andrews. "There is no sign of damage above F deck," Boxhall said. "The orlop deck is flooded forward of number 4 watertight bulkhead, however." Boxhall knew that was a bad sign. The orlop deck was the lowest one on the ship, and any flooding there was merely a sign of what was to come. "The postal clerks are shifting the mailbags to the office on G deck."

"Do me the favor of determining our exact position," Smith said. The man seemed cool, almost cold. His years at sea had trained him not to overreact or panic. Boxhall liked that about the man.

A few moments later Boxhall put down the instrument and looked up from the charts. "Sir, I put our position at 41°46' North, 50°14' West. Of course, that's a rough estimate, but it's the best I can do at the moment." He scribbled the position down on a piece of paper and handed it over to Smith. The man stuffed it in his pocket.

"Andrews and I will have a look below," Smith said. "In the meantime, you gentlemen will assemble all the officers."

With that, Smith and Andrews both left the bridge and made their way to the radio room. Phillips was continuing to tap out messages to Cape Race. Andrews's mind raced. He didn't know the extent of the damage just yet, but he could imagine the worst. Seeing the situation firsthand would tell him all he needed to know.

"Is there a problem, sir?" Phillips asked. He was unaccustomed to seeing the captain in the confines of the small radio room, and his being without his jacket and tie further embarrassed him.

"We've struck an iceberg." Smith handed over the paper with Boxhall's scrawled position recorded on it. "Send out a CQD with this position on it."

Andrews could see that the words struck Phillips like a hammer. *Come—Quick—Danger.* It was no doubt something the man hoped he'd never have to use.

"Yes, sir. Right away, sir."

Smith and Andrews both left the radio room with the sound of Phillips's spark buzzing in their ears. They quickly made their way below through the series of stairs that would take them into the deepest portion of the ship. Standing on the rail near F deck, they watched as the water poured in. Andrews jotted his notes in a somber but dispassionate manner.

"Sir, I make it a rise in the water level of over fourteen feet in just ten minutes," Andrews said.

Smith said nothing. He continued to stare at the surging water. Seawater, the color of gravestone, poured out of the forward compartments. The smell of the brine, mixed with steam, left a taste of salt on the tip of a man's tongue.

"It appears to me that we have a breach in five of the eight watertight compartments on starboard," Andrews said. "I would say the transverse bulkheads will not serve us well here; they only go up to E deck."

The decks were numbered starting with the boat deck on top and followed by decks A through F. Underneath them was the lower deck and then the orlop deck that Boxhall had said was being flooded. In spite of all the talk about the *Titanic* being its own lifeboat, Andrews knew full well that was not the case. The watertight compartments only surrounded the first third of the ship. After that, the boiler rooms would fill up.

Andrews went on. "Only the first of the compartments extends up to C deck. Had she rammed the berg head on, it would present little for us in the way of danger. Bulkheads two and eleven to fifteen extend to D deck, but three to nine only go up to level E. With this fifth compartment flooding, the water will rise to E deck and spill over into the next, like the filling of a series of ice cube trays."

Andrews made some calculations in his notebook, looking up occasionally to see how fast the water was rising. "Captain, she can float easily with her first two compartments flooded. She can even float with the first four gone. But she cannot, I repeat, cannot stay afloat with five compartments flooded."

Smith looked ashen. He gripped the rail on the landing with both hands. "How long do we have?"

"An hour I'd say, two at the most."

"We'll have to assemble the crew and prepare the lifeboats," Smith said.

Andrews shook his head. "They won't be nearly enough."

12:20 A.M., APRIL 15

The fatigue of the day was finally getting to Phillips when Bride came back. Both young men were giggling over the idea of so large and impregnable a vessel ever sending for help from anyone. "What are you sending?" Bride asked.

"CQD, old boy."

Bride hunched over Phillips' shoulder and loosened his tie. "Well, send out that SOS. It's the new code and it may be our last chance to use it."

Both men laughed and Phillips began sending out the new international distress call, SOS.

"So you say we hit that iceberg?" Bride quizzed him.

"Yes, the captain looked pretty serious about it."

Bride laughed. "The man looks serious about his porridge in the morning. Why don't they just poke a hole in the other side and let the water out."

Both men laughed, and Phillips continued his call for help, this time with the new signal.

"Amazing," Bride giggled, "We have the fanciest ship afloat and we'll probably wind up being towed into New York by some old dilapidated ship."

"We got picked up by the French steamer, *La Provence*," Phillips said.

"Lot a good the frogs will do us. I shouldn't care to depend on them."

Phillips listened. "Cape Race has our message now. They're sending it out to other ships."

"About time."

12:25 A.M.

Fifty-eight miles away, twenty-one-year-old Harold Cottam was coming to the end of a very long stretch of work in the wireless room of the Cunard liner *Carpathia*. He was the lone radio operator aboard ship and had been on duty constantly since 7:00 A.M. the previous day. He stood up and arched his back. The last thing he wanted to hear was another message, and he thought briefly about shutting the blame thing off. He knew he should have closed everything down a half hour before, but he was waiting for the receipt to a message he'd sent to the liner *Parisian*. *When is that thing going to come?* he wondered.

He had been listening to the land station in Cape Cod to pass the time, which evidently had a stack of messages for the *Titanic*. Sitting down once again at his machine, he worked the dials until he thought he had the frequency of the *Titanic*. There seemed to be a rare moment of silence from Phillips, and Cottam began to signal the *Titanic*. "I say, old boy," he tapped out the words, "Cape Cod has oodles of messages for you. Are you still there?"

It felt good to catch the *Titanic* asleep at the switch. He knew that's just where he should be.

Almost before Cottam could finish, Phillips fired off the distress signal, giving the *Titanic*'s position. Even in the cloud that seemed to hang over his mind, the SOS caught his attention. It was a new one, and he knew he needed to pay attention.

He returned the signal, acknowledging it. "Are you sure?" he tapped out. "Should I tell my captain?" Cottam was flustered now. "Do you require assistance?" he asked.

The message back was firm and quick. "Yes. Come quick."

Cottam tore the message off the pad and raced up to the bridge. "It's the *Titanic*. She's struck an iceberg, and she's sinking."

The officers aboard each looked at one another, seemingly in disbelief. "Are you certain it's the *Titanic*?"

"Yes, sir, I am. Where's the captain?"

"He turned in a half hour ago."

Cottam waved the message in the air. "We'd better wake him for this."

MONDAY,
APRIL 15, 1912,
12:35 A.M.

CHAPTER 34

S tewards passed through the steerage-class area, pounding on the
doors. "Everybody up. Put your life jackets on and assemble in the
common room."

Several faces peered out the doors at the men. "What's happening?
What was that noise we heard?"

"Nothing to be alarmed about. The captain's orders are to have you
all gather in the great room. Now, get dressed and get at it."

In a matter of minutes the companionways were filled with people,
some in a state of half dress. They banged into each other in the confusion.

Jack Kelly had heard the alarm and was dressing his two grandchildren. "Let's go. We've got to get ready."

"Why, grandfather? I'm sleepy."

"We're just having a game tonight," he smiled. "First we're going to see who can get dressed the quickest."

"Is something wrong?"

"No, nothing's the matter. We're all playing a game. Now, let's see how fast you children can get into your clothes." Kelly knew enough about the lifeboat capacity to know that if the ship was in fact in real danger, there would barely be enough room for the women and children. The men would stand no chance at all. He also knew something about the layout of the *Titanic* that few others knew. He was grateful now that he'd taken that tour.

When the children were dressed, he pulled on their warmest coats and tied their vests around them. With the children in tow, he stepped out into the hall. People were passing him on their way to the common room, with the stewards herding them along like sheep. He watched them go by and then headed in the opposite direction. Somehow, some way, he had to find Andrews or Boxhall. He knew if the *Titanic* had closed its watertight doors, the chances of staying afloat would be greatly diminished.

He moved the kids in front of him and down the hall, passing several stragglers as they made their way quickly to the rear of the ship. Coming to the elevator he had taken on the tour, he pushed the bell. The doors opened. Stepping inside, he pushed the button that directed the contraption to A deck. From there, they took the stairs to topside.

It was there he found Boxhall. The man was firing off a distress rocket. He lit the fuse, and he and a seaman stepped back as the thing rocketed into the black night. The children watched the explosion as it ripped through the sky above them.

"Boxhall," Kelly called out. "You've got to have them open the watertight doors."

Boxhall stepped back and stared at him. The man was animated and excited. "I've been ordered to fire off our rockets. There's a ship out there."

He pointed out into the distant darkness. Stepping over to the rail, he motioned for Kelly to join him. "There it is, out there." Kelly stepped over to look. Some five to ten miles away, they could both make out the masthead lights of what appeared to be a ship. "It's out there," Boxhall shouted. "They have to see our distress signals."

"Never mind that." Kelly said. "You have to tell the captain to open the watertight doors."

Boxhall pointed to the wing bridge on the wheelhouse starboard. "There he is, you tell him."

Kelly looked up and saw the large white-bearded figure of the man standing in the open of the wing bridge. He knelt down beside the children. "You two stay right here with Mr. Boxhall. You can watch the rockets go off."

He could see they were both apprehensive about being left behind, but he patted both of them and headed up the stairs to the wheelhouse.

At the top of the stairs, near the door, he ran into another officer. "I have to see the captain," Kelly said.

"Who are you?" the man asked.

"I'm Jack Kelly, and I have to talk to him. We can save this ship."

"Go back with the other passengers, Mr. Kelly, and await your turn on the boats."

"And who are you, sir?" Kelly asked.

"I'm the chief officer, Wilde. Everything that can be done is being done. Now, you go back and join the rest of the passengers."

Captain Smith stepped out toward the door and yelled over both Wilde and Kelly to Second Officer Lightoller who was making ready to lower a boat. "Lightoller, load the boats from A deck. It will be easier that way on the women and children."

"Aye, aye, sir," Lightoller yelled back.

"Captain Smith," Kelly yelled, "I must speak with you. This boat doesn't have to sink so fast."

Wilde pushed Kelly back. "Now see here," he said, "you leave this area. You're disturbing our work. If you keep this up, I'll have you arrested."

Kelly ignored him. He yelled all the louder. "Captain, I have something you have to hear."

This infuriated Wilde all the more. He gave Kelly a shove that sent him flying out the door and onto the landing. "I won't warn you again," he growled, stepping forward. "You get back to where you belong."

"But it's important that I speak to him," Kelly said, working to get up from where Wilde had pushed him. "Lives can be saved."

Smith stepped to the doorway. "What seems to be the trouble?"

Wilde pointed to Kelly. "This man is not cooperating."

"Captain Smith, I need to speak to you." He wiped his hands on his pants. "Lives can be saved."

"And who are you, sir?" Smith asked.

Kelly motioned his hands forward in a plaintive plea. "You must remember me. I'm Jack Kelly, the boatbuilder. I was taking that tour with Thomas Andrews when we left Queenstown."

Smith looked confused. "I'm not quite certain I remember you, Mr. Kelly. Believe me, Mr. Wilde is right. We are far too busy here to be disturbed."

Kelly threw up his hands. "But, Captain, I tell you lives can be saved. You need to listen to me for a moment."

Wilde looked back at Smith. "I'll take him below, Captain, and turn him over to one of the yeomen."

"No, I'll hear him out," Smith said. He looked at Kelly, his brow wrinkling. "Make it quick, Mr. Kelly. I don't have a moment to lose."

The moment was cut short by the sound of escaping steam from the boilers. The crew below were blowing them out to avoid water coming into contact with the fire and causing an explosion. The sound was deafening. It was soon joined by the noise of another of Boxhall's rockets.

The three men waited the noise out, each afraid to speak over the sound. When the steam was cut off, Kelly broke into the silence. "Captain, you have to order the watertight doors opened."

Both Wilde and Smith seemed shocked by the suggestion. "And why should I do that?" Smith asked.

"I don't know the size of the split in the hull, but I imagine it's dragging us down by the head. When you closed those doors, you made sure the water would not fill the hull of the boat evenly."

"We can't do that, Mr. Kelly. We'd lose all our boilers and our power, too."

"Captain, when that water drags us down past the anchor chains, we'll open ourselves up to another twelve to fourteen feet of water. Next, you'll have the cargo bay doors and windows underwater, and that will only let in more of the sea. Plus, you have your best pumps near the engine room. You can't even use them effectively as it stands now." He wanted to grab Smith's collar and shake the man into action, but the only man he could reach at the time was Wilde. He dug his claws into

Wilde's overcoat sleeve. "You've got to open those doors, Captain, not close them. It's too late for that, much too late."

"I'm afraid that won't stop what we have on our hands now," Smith said.

"No!" Kelly roared, "But it will slow it down. You'd have more time for rescue. Wouldn't it be better to have a dark ship still afloat at dawn than a set of blazing lights going to the bottom?"

Both Smith and Wilde exchanged glances.

"Do it, Captain," Kelly barked. "Do it now. There's not a moment to lose."

"I'm afraid we'll have to consult with Andrews," Smith said. "He is the builder of this vessel. I'd have to hear it from him personally."

"Then get the man," Kelly roared. "I'll talk to him."

"We have no idea where Andrews is," Wilde said, "but you're welcome to search for him, if you've a mind to."

Kelly made his way back down the steps. He felt defeated and alone with his thoughts. Everything he said had made sense. He could see it in their eyes. Watching the people milling around the deck, searching for a place on too few boats, made his spirits sink even lower. What if he couldn't find Andrews, or, worse yet, what if he found the man and it was too late to stop the increasing flow of water belowdecks? It was frustrating.

He reached Boxhall as the man was lighting another rocket. "Where are the children?" he asked.

Boxhall stood up and watched the rocket blast off from the deck. He followed its trail into the sky, watching it burst overhead. "Your grandchildren?"

"Yes, where are they?"

Boxhall pointed to a boat halfway down the side of the ship. "I put them on boat No. 5. I didn't think you'd mind under the circumstances."

Kelly craned his neck over the rail. He could see the two children in the nearly empty boat. He began to count. "Why are all the crew members on that boat?" he asked.

"I think most of the passengers went down to A deck," Boxhall replied. "We couldn't wait to bring them back up. I looked around and got on as many people as I could, but Murdoch up there is hurrying us along."

Kelly shook his head. "Maybe it's for the best."

12:55 A.M.

Near the first-class port entrance to the main stairway, the band had assembled and began a series of jaunty melodies. A number of the passengers had gathered around them, some clapping their hands to the ragtime music that at any other time would have signaled a time to dance.

A number of the passengers were doing their best to appear calm, with several men assuring their wives. "You'll be fine," one said. "I'll be along directly when they come back for the men."

Peter was going to get Margaret and April, and Morgan was confident Peter would do his best to get the women prepared. Meanwhile Morgan waited impatiently for them on deck, anxiously scanning the crowd. It worried him that they were taking so long. *Where can they be?* he wondered. *Why haven't they come up to the boats?*

He listened as Second Officer Lightoller shouted out the orders. "Women and children only, please. Women and children."

Suddenly stepping out onto the deck was the other party he'd been looking for, Benjamin Guggenheim, with Kitty and Hans. Guggenheim and Hans were dressed in their best evening clothes, tailcoats and starched white shirts. Both men wore silk top hats and white silk scarves around their necks. They looked for all the world like men prepared to spend a night at the opera. Kitty was wearing a scarlet dress with a ruby necklace around her neck and a diamond tiara on her head. She wore opera-length white gloves and a fur. None of the three wore life preservers. Hans was carrying one that was evidently intended for Kitty.

Morgan stepped forward. "I can see you're ready for this," he said.

"But of course, my good man," Guggenheim responded. "We are always prepared."

"I have something here you seem to have lost," Morgan said. Reaching into his overcoat pocket, he pulled out the silver end of the cane. "Does this belong to you?" he asked.

Guggenheim took the cane. "Why, yes, it does. Where did you find it?"

"Someone tried to throw it overboard." He watched Kitty and Hans for their reactions. Both of them looked at the cane and then back at Guggenheim. They seemed more interested in what he would say than they were in the fact that Morgan had what was left of one of his walking sticks.

Guggenheim turned the cane over. "It seems they ruined it in the process."

"No," Morgan said, "I think it was broken before that."

"That's a pity."

Lightoller called out, "Women and children only."

Putting his hand to his hat and politely tipping it in Morgan's direction, Guggenheim smiled. "You'll pardon us, but we have to see the lady to her boat." He looked at Kitty. "Come along, my dear. We must not be late."

Kitty cocked an eyebrow in Morgan's direction. There was a haughty, ladylike expression on her face. "Good-bye, Mr. Fairfield."

Morgan nodded back. He couldn't tell if her expression was a look of relief or one of pity. Her *good-bye* had seemed rather final. It was almost as if she was certain she'd never see him again. *Perhaps she's right,* he thought.

Escorting Kitty to the boat, Guggenheim held her hand as a crew member assisted her. The men operating the davits leaned back on the ropes to prepare to lower the boat. Guggenheim bent down and blew Kitty a farewell kiss. "Tell my wife I went down like a gentleman," he said.

Standing straight up, he looked at Hans. "Shall we retire to the lounge for a brandy, old man?" He smiled tranquilly at Morgan. "You will excuse us. I am glad you found my cane." The man's look was one of complete calm, like he had ice water flowing through his veins. "You are most welcome to what's left of it."

It was several minutes more until he saw Peter with Margaret's mother. Peter had her by the arm, practically dragging her to the boat that was still being held with Kitty and the other women in it. Morgan couldn't believe his eyes. April's hair was disheveled and with her life jacket on, along with her yellow coat, she looked like a cross between a teddy bear and a banana.

Morgan ran to them. "Where is Margaret?"

"She won't come," April screeched, "not without you."

Morgan was dumbfounded. "Where is she?" he asked.

"We left her in the cabin," Peter replied. He pushed April toward the boat. "I was hoping to see you. Perhaps you can talk some sense into her."

"I won't go," April cried out, "not without my daughter."

Morgan took her other arm. "Mrs. Hastings, you must go. Peter and I will go and get Margaret. We'll put her on another boat. Time is precious, though, and tending to you is keeping us from her." He didn't want to make the woman feel any more guilty than she was already feeling, but at this point he didn't much care. There was no way he could leave Peter wrestling with Margaret's mother.

"I can't go without Margaret," April wailed.

"But you must go," Peter said. "The boat is here, and you are here. Morgan's right. When we have you safely off, we can go get Margaret."

The woman dug her heels in, scuffing them on the surface of the deck. She continued to wrestle the two men and then broke into hysterical bawls.

"Please, madam," Lightoller said, "We must send this boat away at once. If you're not in it, it will have to leave without you."

"No! No!" April cried out. "I won't go without Margaret." She began a series of screams, clawing at the rail and refusing to budge her feet.

Peter reached around and gave her a sturdy slap across the face. It silenced her, jerking her head up in shock. "Now, get on this boat at once," Peter barked.

April lifted her feet and sheepishly stepped into the boat. Both Morgan and Peter helped her in to the point where others could take over in the boat. Lightoller gave the signal, and the seamen operating the ropes began to lower it.

Peter blew out a blast of breath. "I can't tell you how often in the past I've wanted to do that. I should be ashamed of myself."

"But you aren't, are you?" asked Morgan

"Not in the least." A smile spread over his face. "I can tell you one thing, though, you won't have to worry about April Hastings ever longing for that son-in-law she never had." He chuckled.

"Let's go get Margaret," Morgan said.

"We may have it worse with her than we did with her mother," Peter responded.

1:10 A.M.

Boat No. 8 had only thirty-eight aboard in a vessel designed to hold sixty-five. Lightoller was still looking for women and children when he spotted the elderly owners of Macy's department store, Isidor and Ida Strauss. He signaled them forward. "Please, madam, we have a place for you, but we must leave right away." He held his hand out for her.

"No," she said. "I will not go without my husband."

"I'm sorry, but I'm afraid the boats are for women and children only," Lightoller said.

"Then I will not go," Mrs. Strauss replied. She placed her hands on her husband's arms and held him tight. "I will not be separated from my husband. As we have lived, so we will die, together."

The crowd around them was composed entirely of men. One of them stepped forward to reason with Lightoller. "There are plenty of seats aboard, surely no one can object to an elderly gentleman accompanying his wife."

Strauss spoke up. There was a nobility about him. "No, I do not wish any distinction in my favor that is not granted to others."

His wife turned to their maid. "Ellen, you must go. You can do us no good now."

"Please, ma'am, don't make me."

"Yes, you must go." She took off her fur coat and placed it on the woman's shoulders. "This is my parting gift for you. Wear it well. It can do me no good here."

The maid began to sob, and Lightoller helped her onto the boat and gave the signal to lower it away.

1:15 A.M.

Jack Kelly pressed through the crowd of first-class passengers on starboard. He was looking for Andrews, hoping to spot the man before he was lowered into a boat. Somehow, he couldn't imagine Andrews ever leaving the ship. It was his baby, the dream of a lifetime. First Officer Murdoch was in charge. The man seemed dignified, and Kelly thought the air of calm he was exhibiting may have prevented some of the passengers from recognizing the danger.

"I won't get into that thing," one woman declared. "Floating in that silly boat out on the ocean. Ridiculous!"

"You need to get in the boat, madam," Murdoch responded.

"Why must I do that? Isn't it safer here on the ship?" She grabbed onto her husband, holding his arm in a death lock. The woman was bundled in furs, with a long dress that reached to her ankles. The mounds of padding from the life jacket gave her shape a whimsical look. Feathers and pearls cascaded over the side of her hat.

"Do as the man says, my dear," her husband responded. He was being as brave as possible with an obviously headstrong woman. "We'll all be along directly." He looked at Murdoch in an obvious cry for help. "Please tell her there is sufficient space for all of the first-class passengers."

Murdoch didn't respond to the plea; he merely swung himself around the woman in an attempt to move her along. "Please, madam," he said, "we need to get this boat away at once."

The woman continued to try to reason with both her husband and Murdoch. "This ship is perfectly safe. It's the *Titanic*. You can't expect me to climb into that little boat and be lowered into that cold, black ocean."

"You must go," Murdoch responded.

"I won't go, not without my husband."

The man gave Murdoch a plaintive look. "Can't I go with my wife? She's very fragile and delicate." He looked around at the crowd of men standing by. "I see no other women nearby; can't I go with her?"

"Yes," Murdoch responded, a sense of exasperation in his voice. "By all means, get on with the woman."

Kelly spotted several of the gamblers he had seen during his tour of the ship. The men were laughing and nudging one another. "I passed that rumor they were taking men on the port side," one of them laughed. "I thought that would clear the way for us."

A second man roared with laughter. "It obviously worked," he said.

Kelly watched as the men climbed into the boat. Evidently, their ruse had worked. It would seem that many of the women had hauled their husbands to port with the hope they would be allowed to go together. There seemed to be no waiting women at the moment.

Kelly tugged on Murdoch's sleeve. "What about the women and children in steerage?" he asked. "They're down there, shut up in the common room."

"I can't be bothered with that just now," Murdoch shouted. "They'll be let out in due course."

Kelly stumbled away from the man. Few officers could think about more than one thing in the midst of a crisis, and obviously Murdoch wasn't one of them.

Turning around, Kelly caught sight of Bruce Ismay. The man was busying himself with giving out orders, obviously unwanted and unheeded. He flitted back and forth like a bee over a field of clover, first moving to the seamen on the davits and then back directing the passengers. "Let's move along ladies," he said. "We need to move quickly. Get these boats down at once," he shouted.

"But it's only half full," the officer standing by the boat shouted.

"These small boats can't hold that number in the air," Ismay howled. He shook his head, determined to make his point. "Lower it half full, and it can pick up people from the gangway."

The officer looked over the side and then screeched at Ismay. "The gangways aren't open!"

"Lower this boat immediately. Don't you know who I am?"

"Look, I don't care who you are." He pushed Ismay back. "Right now, you're just another passenger. Stand aside."

Kelly could see Ismay's embarrassed look. The man wanted to do everything he could. The trouble was, with his direction for the *Titanic* to make all possible speed into an ice field, he'd done enough already.

MONDAY,
APRIL 15, 1912,
1:25 A.M.

CHAPTER 35

Both Morgan and Peter burst into Margaret's cabin, only to find it empty. Even so, they searched every area, hoping they might find her cowering in a corner. Peter was flapping his arms like a bird, beside himself with fear and rage. "She was here. I left her here. I said we were coming back for her."

"Which is probably why she's gone," Morgan said. "We'll have to search the ship," Morgan yelled, raising his voice. "I'll search the lounge, and you can go to the library and dining area."

"You don't think she'd be reading do you?" Peter asked.

"Heaven only knows what that woman will do," Morgan answered. "You know that about her."

Peter shook his head. "If she's anything like her mother, we may need six men to carry her to the boats."

"Let's hope it doesn't come to that."

Both men headed off in their different directions, rushing past crying women and the men who were doing their best to console them. Morgan's mind wandered over his last few days with Margaret. *Where can she be?* he wondered. He moved into the now deserted grand staircase area. Circling around it, he came to the room where he and Maragret had talked, the lounge. There, standing by the mantel, was Margaret and Thomas Andrews.

"Peter and I have been looking everwhere for you," Morgan said.

"I've been right here, talking with Mr. Andrews."

"Well, come on," Morgan tugged on her arm. "We haven't a moment to lose. We have to get you on one of the boats."

"Just what I've been telling her," Andrews offered.

"Well, I'm not going, not if it means leaving you."

Morgan shook his head. "You don't understand. If you don't go, I can't go."

"Fine, then we'll stay together."

"We'll do no such thing." Morgan was getting impatient. He tried pulling gently on her arm. but it was all too apparent that Margaret wasn't moving. She was like a stone statue. "I can swim very well, and I plan to survive this thing," Morgan said. "I love you and have every reason to live. I can't very well plan on swimming if I have you to worry about, now can I? You'll kill us both."

He knew very well that with the temperature of the water a man's chances as a swimmer were practically nonexistent. He was counting on the fact that Margaret wouldn't know that as well.

"It's not fair," Margaret said. "Why are women allowed to go and not men? Must we always be treated like china?"

"Listen, we're not going to make this an issue of suffrage, are we?"

"And why not, pray tell?"

Morgan turned to Andrews, pleading with him for help. "Can't you reason with her?"

"Miss Hastings, in all the time I worked on building this vessel and preparing her for passengers, there was not one single woman I worked with. Had there been, perhaps we'd have sufficient lifeboats. Women tend to look to those matters while men are more concerned with steam and speed. If we look at the issue of fairness, I think it's only right for the women to have the boats."

"You see there," Morgan said, "it is fair. Now, let's go to the deck."

Margaret turned and placed her arms around Morgan. She held him close. "I've known you practically all of my life, and I've loved you for all of that time. I won't leave you now, not when I finally know that you love me. I want to die loving you, not hating you for leaving me all alone."

It was then that their attention was drawn to the doorway across the room. Hoffman stood at the door with his two small children. "Please," he cried out, "can you help me?"

Morgan and Margaret both stepped over in the man's direction. "What seems to be the problem?" Margaret asked.

Hoffman looked down at the two children. They were in plaid coats and hats, their black curls streaming down underneath their caps. "My children won't go with strangers. They are afraid of the boats. Can you help them?"

Margaret stooped down beside the two little boys, their large brown eyes staring into hers. She wrapped her arms around them. "Now, there's nothing to worry about with those boats. They're perfectly safe."

The two youngsters blinked at her, their eyes widening.

"You must go with your father and let him put you on a boat. It will be fun."

The two boys clung to their father's legs, like monkeys on the high branch of a tree.

"They won't go," Hoffman said. "I've taken them up to the boats, and they won't get in. They're afraid of the strangers on the boats."

"Perhaps if Miss Hastings was to accompany them," Morgan said, "then they wouldn't be so afraid."

Margaret looked up, glaring at Morgan. She didn't like his tactic one bit.

"Yes, perhaps that might work," Hoffman said. He stooped down eyeing the children. "What about that children? What if Miss Hastings here were on the boat with you?"

The oldest of the boys nodded.

"You see, Margaret," Morgan said, "You are needed. You won't let your female pride cause these boys to perish, will you?"

Margaret stood up, ramrod straight. Her eyes were riveted on Morgan. "You're awful. Why must you men always win?"

"This isn't a matter of winning and losing, dear, it's survival. I'll do better on my own, and these boys will survive."

She lowered her voice. "You're despicable, Morgan Fairfield."

Within a matter of minutes Morgan and Margaret had taken Hoffman and his children up to port. What appeared to be the last of the boats were being filled. The officer in charge waved them over. "Over here!" he shouted. "Women and children only."

Morgan moved Margaret and the boys over to the side of the small boat. Morgan looked at her. "I think we'll need to get you on first so the children can come in."

"Morgan, you know I don't want to do this."

"You've made that perfectly clear, darling."

She clung to his arms. "I love you, Morgan."

"You don't hate me for making you survive all this?"

"I hate being alone, and without you I feel alone."

Morgan kissed her softly. "You'll get over it, dear. Think of me when you hear the word *love* because I'll always love you." With that he helped her into the boat.

Hoffman picked up the two boys and kissed them. "Now you two be good," he said. "Don't give Miss Hastings any trouble." He held out one child after the other, Margaret taking them and placing them in a seat.

Looking down into the boat, Morgan noticed Mrs. Holmes, the woman whose son had found the cane. Margaret nodded at her. It was then he spotted the boy. The youngster was cowering underneath a seat, obviously hiding from the officer who was loading the boat with women and small children. There was fear in the youngster's eyes and a look of despair from the mother.

The group gathered around the boat were husbands and fathers, all saying their last good-byes to the women they had placed aboard. The officer was seating the last of the women when he noticed the small boy. "Here now," he shouted, "You get out of there. This boat is for women and children only."

Mrs. Holmes looked up at the officer. "He is a boy. He's only ten years old."

"That's a man. Now you get out of that boat."

Morgan watched the young boy begin to cry. "No, please," he wailed, "I don't want to stay. I want to go with Mummy."

Mrs. Holmes got to her feet in the boat. "He is a mere boy. You can't make him stay with the men."

The officer simply ignored her. He shook his head. "He's too old to go with the children. He'll have to stay with the men."

"But we have empty seats here," Margaret cried out. "You can't make him stay while we have empty seats." The Hoffman children clung closer to her. The sound of the argument seemed only to make them more insecure.

Morgan looked the boat over. There were at least five empty seats left, but it was equally obvious that the officer had no intention of bending the rules. The man raised himself to his full height and hardend his jaw.

"I have my orders, women and children only."

"But he's only ten," the boy's mother called out.

"I have specific instructions, children are nine years of age or younger. In my book he's a man."

At that word, the youngster began to cry all the louder.

The officer reached into his pocket and pulled out a revolver. He waved it at the child. "Climb out of there," he shouted. "If you don't climb out of that boat, I'll blow your brains out where you are."

The boy kept crying as he slid out from the seat. His mother grabbed him and hung on.

The officer continued to hold the gun in his right hand, but with the left, he reached down and grabbed the child by the collar. "We don't have time for this," he growled. "We must lower this boat."

He lifted the child up from the boat, by the collar of his coat. All the while, the boy proceeded to holler. It was a mournful, plaintive cry, like a lost soul being sent to certain doom. The officer looked at the seamen manning the davits. He snapped his order to them. "Lower away."

Morgan could tell the man was quite anxious to simply have the boat disappear. There was no waiting for others to arrive and fill the empty seats, women and perhaps youngsters who met his definition of a child. It was as if by sending it over the side, he could put the whole unpleasant business out of his mind.

As the seamen lowered the rope wrapped around the davit, Morgan could hear the cries of the boy's mother. Her screams of anquish pierced the darkness, knifing through the sounds of bedlam with a note of personal anquish. The boy kept up his crying, sinking to his knees beside the pile of rope that was lowering his mother.

Morgan stepped to the rail. He could see Margaret looking up, and their eyes met. The very idea of once again finding her and then losing her seemed unbearable. He did manage a faint wave, one last good-bye. Stepping back from the rail, he knew he had a few things left to do. He had to find Peter and tell him that Margaret was safe, and then there was the matter of Hunter's killer. Any normal person would have concluded that the murderer was destined to perish with the ship, but Morgan wasn't so sure about that.

Moving through the crowd of men, he bumped into Major Butt. The man was wearing his life preserver, an overcoat, and a black bowler. "My stars," Butt said, "You're just the man I was hoping to find." He took Morgan by both shoulders and shook him. "I thought you might be gone by now."

Morgan looked over the side of the ship. "I fear we shall all be gone before long."

"That's why I needed to find you," Butt said. "We have to get that satchel out of the purser's safe and see it safely away before the last of the boats are gone. We can have one of the women take it to the War Department, if need be."

By this point, Morgan was so lifeless inside that the thought that he could be of any use at all seemed to be a shock to him. Still, it seemed like the thing to do. If he could spend his last hour saving lives in the future, then perhaps something might be made worthwhile. "All right," Morgan said, "let's go."

The two men started for the purser's office. A short while later, they found themselves in a surprisingly lonely companionway. What had been a bustling place, with people shoving and others waving their fists, a mere half hour earlier was now nearly deserted. McElroy was standing behind his desk busily stuffing papers into a carrying bag when the two men walked in.

"We've come for a satchel," Morgan said. "The satchel you wouldn't let us have earlier. Now it's doubtful it will ever reach the War Department if we don't see it safely away."

McElroy scratched his head. The man looked haggard and beat, his tie askew and his shirt open. It was obvious that the rush on people's valuables had taken quite a toll on him. The British were used to order, and since midnight, everything and everybody aboard the *Titanic* had been total chaos.

He pointed his finger at the two of them, his memory taking hold. "Oh, yes, I remember you. You want the dead passenger's satchel."

"It's not his satchel," Morgan said. "It belongs to the United States Government."

McElroy waved his hand. "Whatever. I can't say at this point that I really care. I'm gathering papers for the purpose of insurance, and then I'm leaving. It's too late to save the old girl now."

"Then, you won't mind if we have the satchel?"

"No, I couldn't care less at this point. The thing was not insured, and my hands are washed of the whole affair."

Morgan and Butt both looked at each other, the traces of smiles on their faces.

McElroy pointed back at the stacks. "It's in the third row, bottom shelf. Help yourselves."

Both Morgan and Butt rifled through the stacks of abandoned belongings. It took several minutes to find it, but there it was. Morgan recognized it at once. He picked it up and handed it over to Butt. "Here it is, and you're welcome to it."

Butt had a grin pasted across his pudgy face. His eyes sparkled. "Thank you. You can't possibly know what this means."

The two men stepped out into McElroy's office in time to see him leave the room. They watched as he turned and greeted a man in the companionway and then darted to his left in the direction of the deck.

"We'd better get out of here," Morgan said. "We haven't much time."

"After you," Butt said, bowing politely.

Morgan raced out the door in the direction McElroy had taken, barely taking the time to notice the man standing next to the door. When Butt cleared the door, however, Morgan heard the sound of a blow. Turning around, he saw Butt slumping to the floor. The man held an iron bar. He reached down and pulled the satchel from Butt's fingers.

"Hey!" Morgan cried out. "Who are you, and what do you think you're doing?"

The man grinned. "The name's O'Conner, and what I'm doing is for Ireland."

Morgan recognized the name of the man at once. Boxhall had told him that much. He gave chase as the man raced down the companion-way. Rounding the corner, he saw an empty hall and a door. Morgan took it. It opened into the grand stairway, and there racing down the stairs was O'Conner.

Morgan took the stairs two at a time, doing his best to close the distance on the man. The stairs were tilted, and it made running on them difficult. When he reached the sloping bottom of the polished floor, he grabbed for a banister to keep his footing.

Running out the door he thought the man had taken, Morgan found himself in a group of men mingling on the enclosed promenade deck. They were huddled in a group, obviously discussing plans for their last minutes. The sight of Morgan coming through the door obviously took them by surprise. He was a rare sight, a man not looking for a boat. Morgan could see the man with the satchel on the other side of the group. O'Conner brushed them aside and soon exited a door on the other side.

Morgan followed, brushing past the men and opening the door. He took the stairs in front of him, stairs that were set at a deeper pitch slanting downward. The floors all seemed cockeyed. He opened the door at the end of the stairway. All at once he found himself in a room that was a mixture of confusion and familiarity.

The Palm Court slanted in his direction, with carts that he had to push out of the way. Several tables and chairs were overturned, and glasses and dishes were strewn all over the floor. Some of the trellises had fallen to the floor, while others hung with the ivy suspended down over the doorways.

O'Conner stood in the middle of the room. Setting the satchel on the floor, he braced himself and picked up a chair. Morgan approached the man and circled him. The man held the chair up and bluffed a throw. Morgan stopped, and O'Conner heaved it in his direction. Quickly, Morgan ducked as the chair flew past him.

"Get back," O'Conner yelled, pointing at him.

Morgan continued to circle the man. The man was bigger than he was. The only thing Morgan could count on was his quickness and determination. "What makes you think that what you're doing is for Ireland?" Morgan asked. "Don't you know that what you're carrying could prevent a war?"

"An English war with English blood," O'Conner barked. He picked up a second chair and held it up.

"Irish blood will be spilled just as quickly," Morgan shot back. The man was edgy. Morgan could see that. There was a coolness to him, though. Death was the coin of the realm for a man like this. It wasn't a subject found in a book. Morgan knew he had to find the man's weakness.

"Well, tonight it will be mostly the rich English that get their come-uppance."

Morgan lowered his head and charged the man like a bull. If he was going to take this man down, he'd have to do it all at once.

1:50 A.M.

The confusion around the launching of collapsible C was getting impossible to handle. It had taken more than a dozen men to turn the boat into an upright position, and for each one of the eight crew members that participated, it only seemed right that they should be aboard. Time was running out and they knew it.

They moved the upright boat to the edge of the roof of the wheel-house on top of the officer's quarters. The water was rising. It lapped against the edge of the roof. The entire bow area had been covered and from where they stood, they could still see the eerie green lights of the cargo area glowing from under the water.

Bruce Ismay was among the men with the collapsible. He was doing his best at giving directions, a task he warmed to. "Make sure you have the oars secure," he shouted.

Nearby, a large group of men had been prowling the ship in search of a boat. Many of them were steerage-class passengers who came to the deck late with their women and children, only to find that most of the boats were already gone. Now they were turning into a mob. The sight of the collapsible was almost too great a temptation for them. McElroy was in charge of the boat, and he didn't like the looks of this swarm of men one bit. He hurried the members of the crew along as they uncovered the boat.

"There's one, boys," one of the members of the mob shouted, "Let's get it." With that, they began to rush the boat.

When McElroy saw the mob forming, he drew his revolver. As the men rushed, he fired several warning shots into the air. "Here, stop at once," McElroy shouted. He waved the gun in the air as if to make his point. "We'll have no panic here. There is no more room. You go back. Go back to the starboard deck. Not all the boats have left."

The men slowly began to edge back. The deck was slippery and angled down at the bow, toward the surging water. It was plain to see that there was little time left, but the sight of McElroy's pistol promised a surer and even quicker end. The men grudgingly backed up, turned around, and left the roof of the wheelhouse.

Turning back to the group, McElroy gave out his orders. "Slide her down, men. We'll let the water take her when it comes up over the well deck."

Ismay stepped into the boat along with a few others while the rest of the men shoved the boat forward.

1:55 A.M.

In all of the pandemonium and racket, Second Officer Lightoller had forgotten all about the wealthy women in boat No. 4. It was just over half full, and he was still searching for any women and children who might be found.

John Jacob Astor approached him with his wife Madeleine. "Excuse me, sir, my wife here is expecting a child, and she is quite nervous. Might I be allowed to accompany her?"

"No, I'm sorry, sir. The boats are for women and children only."

Madeleine hung onto his arm. "Oh, Johnny, I can't go without you."

Astor patted her hand. "Nonsense, my dear. You take this boat, and I'll follow along with the men later. I'll be all right." He kissed her and helped her to step into the boat. Stepping back, he took a cigarette out of his case and lit it.

Lightoller gave the order to lower the boat, and Madeleine watched as Astor waved good-bye.

MONDAY,
APRIL 15, 1912,
1:55 A.M.

CHAPTER 36

M organ caught the man's midsection with his shoulder, sending both of them catapulting into the sagging trellis. They went sliding back with the angle on the inclining floor. Morgan sprang to his feet and knocked over a table as he scrambled toward the man.

O'Conner met him head-on. Swinging his fist, he sent a hard right to Morgan's jaw, launching Morgan backward and into the overturned chairs and tables.

As Morgan got to his knees, the man picked up the satchel and headed for the door that led to the grand staircase. Morgan stumbled to his feet. He was determined. This man wasn't going to be allowed to get away, not now, not after everything he'd been through to get that satchel and keep it safe. If Hunter hadn't been killed for that thing, the both of them had certainly been stalked.

He limped toward the door, picking up speed as he angled over the tiled floor. There was no way a man could walk upright on the *Titanic* any longer.

He swung the door wide open. Stepping out onto the balcony area, he spotted O'Conner at once. The man was clambering down the first set of white marble steps, hanging onto the satchel with one hand and the oak banister with the other. Given the angle of the ship, it was almost as if he were climbing up the stairs, although the room was designed just the opposite.

Morgan jumped, launching himself into midair. He landed on O'Conner, separating him from the satchel and flattening him on the landing that was in the middle of the stairway. From there a middle staircase separated the stairs, and at the bottom the brass Hermes held a glowing light. The stairs fanned out around Hermes and widened, forming a sweeping series of marble ledges over the polished floor.

Morgan and O'Conner rolled down the lower set of stairs, Morgan hanging onto the man, tumbling over and over until they spilled out onto the slanting tile. It seemed odd to Morgan that they were rolling down the stairs. They seemed almost flat in the way the ship was going down. He felt the floor beneath him give way, like a large bubble that had burst. The *Titanic* had only minutes left, and Morgan knew it.

He got to his feet and hauled O'Conner up by the lapels of his coat. Morgan delivered a blow to the man's jaw, which sent O'Conner stumbling backward.

O'Conner rolled over. Working hard, he got his feet under him. He grinned at Morgan. It was a kind of knowing grin, the kind Morgan might see in a fencing contest when one of the contestants knew he'd taken a man's best and still had more to give. It was a look of yet uncaptured victory. "Is that the best ya got, little schoolboy?"

Morgan motioned the man forward with his hands. "No, I've got more, lots more. Come and get it."

"You're gonna be a dead man when I'm done with you," O'Conner said.

Morgan worked at circling the man. It was hard to maintain footing on the slanting floor, which was almost a forty-five-degree angle. It was like standing on a rooftop. Morgan was counting on his ability to do just that, however. "I have news for you. In a matter of minutes we're both going to be dead men."

"I don't really care. I'm dying for Ireland. You're dying for nothing." With that, O'Conner rushed him, sending his fists flying with a series of roundhouses.

Morgan backed away instantly, and O'Conner fell forward, unable to keep his balance. The man had landed on his hands and knees without delivering a blow. Like a newborn giraffe, he scrambled to his feet awkwardly.

Morgan stepped into him, delivering a punch to the man's stomach. It doubled him over.

O'Conner unleashed a sudden uppercut that caught Morgan by surprise. It rattled his teeth and sent him backward on his heels.

Morgan shook his head and stroked his chin with his hand. This time it was his turn to smile. "Is that the best you can do? I would have expected more from a brawler."

The taunting infuriated O'Conner. It was just what Morgan had been counting on. An angry man might think he could whip the world, but the brain doesn't respond well to irrational emotion. O'Conner went into a fury. He ran at Morgan, and the two men locked arms.

They were like two bulls fighting for a herd of cows, awkwardly stumbling and wrestling on the slanting floor, each afraid to lose his footing and equally afraid not to try.

O'Conner tried to swing and plant a blow on Morgan, but the two of them were too close together. Morgan began to hammer away at the man's midsection. It was the one area he could reach reasonably well and have the effect felt. O'Conner staggered backward.

The room seemed to whirl as the men embraced and grunted for power, turning each other around. Morgan could see the tilting of the overhead light. The gold that was inlaid into the iron spacing between the balusters glinted with the light from above, and several times he could make out the innocent, cherubic look of Hermes as he held up his lamp at the foot of the stairs.

O'Conner was a powerful man. Morgan could tell that. He knew also that his best chance was to keep close to him so the man couldn't get off a full punch. Grabbing him by both lapels, O'Conner held him and pushed him back. The angle of the floor was unstable. The stairs, along with Hermes and his lamp, were behind Morgan.

O'Conner had a longer reach. He held Morgan out, almost suspending him. Launching a punch, he slammed his fist into Morgan's face, whose head jerked back like a punching bag. O'Conner spun him around. Now Morgan was looking at the stairs. Throwing another right, O'Conner connected with Morgan's jaw. The blow was a shock, and once again O'Conner spun him around.

O'Conner reared his right hand back to deliver what he thought would be a final blow. "And now, my schoolboy friend, I plan to leave you right here and let the fish finish you off."

Morgan knew he couldn't just stand there in O'Conner's grasp and let the man deliver another blow. With every ounce of his might, he pulled himself straight down to the floor, slipping out of O'Conner's grasp and collapsing onto the slanted tile.

O'Conner's blow went right over Morgan's head. His force and the power he was trying to exert sent him tumbling over the top of Morgan and directly into the bronze feet of Hermes.

Morgan braced himself on his knees. He felt wobbily and spent. Deliberately placing one foot flat, he slowly cranked himself upright. Turning around, he saw O'Conner at the foot of the statue. The man was not moving. He was lying there, his legs flared out. He looked like a broken doll dropped from the top shelf of a child's closet.

At the top of the landing, Morgan saw the satchel. Slowly he started stepping over the stairs. He could no longer call it a climb, so great was the angle of the ship. They were like bumps in a well-traveled road. Reaching the landing, he picked up the satchel.

"Fairfield!" Morgan heard the familiar voice. It was the voice of Donald Delaney. "I see you have our satchel."

Morgan turned around. "I'm afraid this isn't yours."

"Of course it is." Delaney braced himself against a pillar in the middle of the room. "You have no idea what we've gone through to get that thing."

"Like murder?"

"Of course. The murder of a few spies is nothing compared to the wholesale slaughter of an entire nation."

The rumbling noise belowdecks told Morgan that things were beginning to break loose below. It wouldn't be long now. He could tell that Delaney had heard the noise, too. "Don't try to pretend you didn't hear that," Morgan yelled. "I know you can hear well enough."

"Perhaps so, but it does serve my purposes to be deaf from time to time."

"Like the time that Hunter said we were carrying the satchel and he wanted to get a better look at what was in it?"

"Yes. That was very helpful. I'll admit that." He held out his hand. "Now, give me the bag, boy."

Morgan saw the cane Delaney was carrying. It made him angry. The man had obviously used one before, perhaps on Hunter. Morgan took a few steps down the stairway. He was keeping Delaney on the other side of the middle banister.

"I talked to doctor McCoy. He told me he had said nothing to you about my being drugged. You lied."

"Yes," Delaney smiled, "And a poor lie it was, too. But we had to try to put you to sleep boy. We needed that satchel you're carrying and had no desire for any harm to come to you. After all, you're an American. Our war isn't with you; it's with the bloody British."

"Your war is with everyone who loves decency and honor, it would seem. You tried to blow up this ship."

"Yes, sacrifices have to be made to drive home our cause." Delaney smiled. "But you see, we didn't need to do that." Delaney raised his hand to the overhead chandelier, which was now rocking forward in a slow deliberate motion. "God Himself has intervened. He is on our side."

Delaney glanced down at the cane in his other hand. He raised it slightly. "Don't make me use this. I really don't want to."

"And why wouldn't you? You've had plenty of experience."

"Give it to me, boy. Give it to me now."

"I'll leave it right here." Morgan had reached the statue of Hermes where O'Conner was sprawled over the floor. The cherub held the still brightly lit lamp with his left hand, while his right hand was extended, palm up to the sky. Morgan looped the handle of the bag over the hand of Hermes. "First, you have to tell me something."

Delaney's eyes widened at the sight of the satchel. He lowered the cane. "Of course, what is it?"

"Be honest with me now, no lying. At this point it would serve no purpose. After all, we both know we're going to die. "Did you have anything to do with the death of Hunter Kennedy?"

Delaney shook his head. "Somehow I knew he was dead." He looked up at Morgan, smiling. "You're such a poor liar boy. I knew he wasn't sick like you said he was. No, I had nothing to do with it. Why should I? I liked the boy. Quite a bit, actually."

"Then you didn't hear that he'd seen your bomb?"

"Of course I heard that, but I didn't believe he knew what he saw."

"And why not?"

"The man was an actor. Do you honestly think he'd pass up a moment to be dramatic? I doubt it. If he had a story to tell, everyone would have heard it."

Delaney stepped closer to where Morgan had hung the satchel. The hand of Hermes was tantalizingly close to him now, and Morgan edged closer to it as well.

"Now, will that be all? I've really told you everything I know about your friend's death."

"Of course," Morgan said. He lifted his hand in the direction of the hanging satchel. "Take what's yours."

Delaney reached out, and Morgan cranked back his arm and let fly with a stiff punch to the man's face. The blow sent Delaney reeling along the floor. He slid along the face of the stairs. Morgan stepped over close to him.

"Y-y-you said you'd let me have the satchel," Delaney slurred, rubbing his jaw. The man was still on his back and made no attempt to get up.

"Maybe I learned something from Hunter. I might not be the poor liar you take me for."

The cracking of the paneling on the wall jerked both men's heads around. Moments later, the entire wall collapsed. Tons of water flooded the stairs and the balcony. It was a sight to send any man into an instant panic. Torrents of seawater poured through what had once been solid walls.

The water hit the floor with a shock, sweeping Morgan off his feet. The foam curled and raged over the tiles. Tumbling him over and over, Morgan felt the stairs and the remains of what had once been bookshelves and pillars. The water blinded him, and the sudden shock of the icy sea took the breath right out of him. He could barely see what was next. The doors that led out onto the deck stood right before him, and he was hurtling toward them like a bullet out of a gun.

He slammed into the edge of a door with his right shoulder, only to have the raging water carry him past them and spill him out onto the deck. He fought as he grasped the rail, breathing hard as the sea pressed him to the deck.

The *Titanic* was leaning now, getting ready to take its final plunge. Rolling over, Morgan struggled to get to his feet. There was no way of standing up. The stern rose in front of him and along with it what looked to be hundreds of screaming people.

Morgan could see the look of panic on their faces. Men, women, and children scrambled to get to the highest point of the ship possible. They were trying hard to breathe as long as possible and to fight the inevitable plunge into the bottom of the sea.

He looked up the rail and saw a woman clutching a child. The woman was Irish with wavy red hair. There was a look of panic on her face as she held the crying baby. "You'd better jump," Morgan yelled. "Don't let the ship drag you down with her." Morgan slammed his arm over the rail, grappling to keep his feet under him.

The water surged over the sinking bow of the great ship, sending sheets of icy brine over the forecastle. Morgan leaned over the railing. He had forced Margaret into her life jacket and into a lifeboat, and that gave him some comfort. The boats below were being rowed away, and already he could see that the oarsmen were keeping their distance from the swimmers in the water. The shouts and screams of the men below went unanswered.

He climbed over the rail and watched the approaching flood. The sea was dark and still, and in the distance he could see the stars as they winked at him over the dim ice field. He stepped off, his arms spinning in wide circles.

2:45 A.M.

Morgan stroked with his arms on the surface, hand over hand. He had given up his life preserver and frankly felt glad he had. The chill of the water would kill him long before he had a chance to drown, and in a way he imagined it a pleasant death. His legs and feet already felt numb; soon the rest of him would join them. He kicked them now, more out of memory than feel. Without the cumbersome life preserver on, he could make better distance, although for the life of him he didn't know where to.

For some time he had heard the sound of people in the water. Their screams had been a sharp, almost mournful cry, like some great voice rising in protest to a sudden blow of injustice. Now, however, they were getting more and more quiet. The voices were almost like an enormous field of crickets, chirping away at the darkness, only to die out in the light of dawn. There was a great pity in Morgan's heart. This was now a sea of sorrow. His own death and the sadness of it would be mixed with many hundreds more.

The noise of the *Titanic* when it sank had been the most mournful of all. The sound of the great ship breaking up on the surface had been like the ship was screaming herself.

Morgan let out a silent prayer. *O God, remember me as Your child. There is so much I want to do to serve You. Only You know best. If I can serve You best beside Your throne right now, then I leave it with You.*

As his head bobbed in the water, he could make out what appeared to be a mound of people. At first glance he almost wondered if it weren't some large piece of ice that men had found, something that floated above the surface. Such a thing would be ridiculous of course, but at such a time all hope was a ridiculous thing.

The group clung to the sides of the floating platform, and as Morgan swam closer he could see that it was one of the collapsibles. The thing had evidently been overturned, and the men were all working hard to keep it on the surface, shifting, balancing themselves, and trying to even the load.

Second Officer Lightoller was in charge of the boat. He stood on one end. Spotting Morgan swimming, Lightoller pointed toward him. "There," he yelled, "a swimmer in the water."

Morgan swam closer. It was obvious that the sight of another man to be rescued was not all that glorious. One of the other men on the boat growled. "We ain't go' no more room, Mr. Lightoller. Shove 'em off and let 'em find some other place."

Lightoller ignored the man as Morgan swam closer. "All right, keep your balance. Make some room for the man at the side. He has no life preserver on. Clear a space."

A number of men were still in the water doing their best to hang on. They moved aside, and Morgan soon found one of the edges. Reaching out a cold hand, he grabbed on and began to pant.

One of those on the raft leaned over to Morgan. "I'm Nordstrom, mate, Eric Nordstrom. I'm one of the stokers. You do yer best to hang on here. We got ourselves some blokes up here what are gonna die. When we slips enough of 'em over, we'll drag ye up."

"Perhaps I should just swim on," Morgan said. The cold was unbearable, and Morgan at this point would much rather have drowned than cling to that boat like some icicle dangling in the water.

"Nonsense, mate. Ye jest hang on a bit." Nordstrom looked around. "It can't be much longer fer many of these here gents. If ye still got some life in ya, we'll have ya up in no time."

In a matter of minutes they had lowered two bodies into the water. Morgan felt a strange sensation on his legs. It amazed him that there was anything to feel at all. It wasn't the touch of a leg, however, it was somebody's hand, and whoever it was, was alive. The unseen hand was pulling on his trousers. "There's somebody down here," Morgan cried out. "Somebody under the boat."

"Can you get him?" Lightoller called. He looked around at the men clinging to the top of the boat. "I don't think anyone up here is going back into that water."

"All right," Morgan said. "Hang on. I'll go get him." Before he went under, he turned for a final look at Lightoller. "You just get whoever this is a place up there."

Morgan ducked down under the boat and came up underneath. There clinging to the overturned seats was a man. He'd obviously been trapped under the boat. Morgan couldn't see him in the total darkness. Reaching out his hand, he felt the man's face. "I'll get you up," Morgan said. "Hold on."

The dark figure tried to respond but his words all came out as frozen gibberish.

"Just let go," Morgan said. "Trust me. I'm a strong swimmer, and I'll get you out on top."

Taking him from behind, Morgan put his arm around the man's neck. He took a breath and sank beneath the boat. Moments later, Morgan and the man he was towing came bobbing to the surface. "Here he is," Morgan said. He swam up to the edge of the boat. "Haul him up."

Several men, one of them the stoker from the *Titanic*, Nordstrom, reached down and hauled the man out of the water. Nordstrom leaned back and caught sight of Lightoller. "It's Bride, sir, the radio operator."

Bride's teeth began to chatter.

"We have Phillips over there," Lightoller said. "But I don't think he's going to make it."

"Let's haul this other feller up," Nordstrom said, "The one who went under fer Bride here."

"Yes," Lightoller replied, "by all means."

Morgan felt the men's arms under his own. They began to pull. Soon he was lying on the top of the boat. He was too numb to feel the cold, and the feel of shivering was almost an unconcious act, something he neither tried to do nor felt. He looked at Nordstrom and mouthed, "Thank you."

A short time later, Morgan struggled to his feet. He knew if he were going to survive freezing to death it would mean getting to his feet and moving around as much as was permitted on the small surface. Only those who were lying down, unable to move, were in the process of dying.

Morgan surveyed the faces of those lying still. There was every type and description and then, then his breath almost left his body. It was Peter. The man was lying still, near Lightoller's feet.

Morgan edged his way forward, taking care to turn to the side so he would disturb as few people as possible. In a few moments, he was close to Peter. He stooped down next to him and felt his face. Peter's face was clammy and chalky white.

Morgan leaned down. "Peter." He touched his face once again. "Peter, it's me, Morgan."

Peter's eyes blinked open. "Morgan," the sound came out in a raspy manner. "I thought I'd never see you again."

"Here, Peter, we've got to get you on your feet."

Peter slowly shook his head. "No, I can't. I can't even move."

"Try," Morgan said.

"Just promise me two things," Peter said.

"Of course, anything."

Peter smiled. "Promise me that you'll love Margaret and that you'll name your first son Peter."

MONDAY,

APRIL 15, 1912,

3:30 A.M.

CHAPTER 37

F ourth Officer Boxhall had only one other sailor aboard boat No. 2, and the prospect of staying adrift for days was one he didn't want to think about. The monkeys, which was the name given to the cabin boys, a collection of ten- to twelve-year-old boys in the *Titanic's* employ, had given out baskets of bread to the boats before the boats were lowered away. Of course, those same boys were technically classified as men, so even though they did their duty and handed out blankets and bread, they had to dutifully stand by and watch as half-empty boats were lowered.

That fact alone sickened Boxhall, and he could barely stand to look at the baskets of bread, let alone eat. He looked at the boat, trying hard not to count the empty seats. *Twenty-five people,* he thought. *We could have saved forty more.*

Boat No. 2 had been lowered from port, and First Officer Murdoch had taken men after all the women and children were loaded, at least those who could be found. There hadn't been much time though. Ismay had insisted the boats be lowered only half full, fearing that they wouldn't be able to hold the same number in the air as they were designed to hold on the water. Such thinking amazed Boxhall. If the boats had been tested, then surely they would have known the capacity.

The gangways were supposed to be opened when the boats hit the water. He'd been told they could pick more people up there. But they were closed. No one had bothered to tell the men who were supposed to open them just what their job was. The lack of preparation seemed scary to Boxhall. No one seemed to know what to do, just when it was most important to know exactly what to do.

He did take some comfort in the fact that Gloria Thompson was aboard his boat. At least someone he knew and cared about survived. His mind raced on to the number of others, however. He kept seeing faces and wondering just where those people were. *Too many people and so few boats*, Boxhall contemplated.

"Do you think we'll see a ship soon?" Gloria asked.

"Ma'am," the sailor on the tiller answered, "we may float around out here for days on end."

Gloria looked at Boxhall for some word of encouragement. It was something he didn't feel. His spirits were lower than they had been in years, in spite of the fact that he had so much to be thankful for. "I think that by morning, this ocean will be crawling with ships," Boxhall responded. He wasn't really sure if he believed that. He just knew he needed to say it.

A woman near the middle of the boat pointed to a faraway glow to the southeast. "There's lightning over there," she cried. There came a slight boom, and then the light died away.

The seaman at the tiller disagreed. "It's a shooting star."

"Maybe it was a cannon," Gloria suggested.

Boxhall could tell that she was given to seeing the best in things. No matter what he said, he was determined not to get his hopes up until he saw the hull of another ship.

Fifteen to twenty minutes later, a second distant report boomed out. They could see the faint trace of a rocket. It looped with an arc of light over the night sky. Now, Boxhall was getting excited. He stood up and peered into the darkness. It took another fifteen minutes before an additional rocket was seen. This time Boxhall could make out the faint green glow of a navigation light.

Now everyone aboard boat No. 2 was excited, even the gloomy sailor at the tiller. A number of women began to clap.

It took what seemed like hours for the people to see the hull of the steamer. The ship was slowing down and beginning its search. Boxhall reached into the box of equipment and pulled out the last of the green flares. Snapping off the top, he struck the end of the flare, which erupted with a shower of green phosphorous. Holding it over the side of the boat, he began to wave it overhead in a broad sweeping motion.

A short time later the steamer drew near. Boxhall cupped his hand over his mouth and shouted. "Shut down your engines and take us aboard. I have only one sailor here."

"All right," a voice called back.

"The *Titanic* has gone down with everyone aboard," a woman screamed.

Boxhall barked back at her. "Shut up!"

The woman fell silent.

The *Carpathia* soon pulled up alongside the small boat and dropped a rope ladder.

"All right," Boxhall said, "All of you follow my orders. I'll send you up one at a time, and we'll secure a rope around you during the climb. We don't want any of you falling."

It took the group the better part of a half hour to climb up the side of the *Carpathia*. Members of the *Carpathia*'s crew took each of the passengers and wrapped them in a warm blanket. They then led them off to warm quarters for something they said would be hot and liquid.

"I'm Second Officer Bisset," a man said to Boxhall. "I'm to escort you to the bridge. Captain Rostron is waiting for you there."

"What's he like?" Boxhall asked.

"We call him the electric spark. Captain Arthur Rostron is a man of high energy. On occasion, we see him lift the bill of his cap on the bridge and murmur a silent prayer. I saw that myself tonight after he laid out plans to look for you. The man used everything he could think of to nurse more speed from this girl. He shut down even the hot water aboard ship, putting all the power into the engines." Bisset smiled. "The old man managed to take a vessel whose top speed was fourteen and a half knots, and make her do over seventeen."

Boxhall followed the man obediently to the bridge. When he stepped into the door, he saluted Captain Rostron. "Fourth Officer Boxhall," he said.

"Has your ship gone down?" Rostron asked.

Boxhall knew the answer was obvious, but he also knew it was something that needed to be asked. "She went down about 2:30. We struck the berg at 11:40 and immediately began to determine the extent of the damage. Five to six of the watertight compartments had been compromised. There was no way she could be saved. It went down by the head." Boxhall was continuing his explanation of the disaster, but Rostron interrupted him.

"Were many people aboard when she sank?"

"Hundreds and hundreds!" Boxhall said. "Perhaps a thousand! Perhaps more!" Tears were beginning to form in Boxhall's eyes. He felt responsible. If he were the highest ranking officer left, perhaps he was responsible. To make matters worse, he'd been so consumed with finding a second bomb that he wasn't looking out for an iceberg. Maybe his eyes would have made all the difference. The numbness of guilt swept over him. "My God, sir, they've gone down with her. They couldn't live in this icy cold water."

"Thank you, mister," Rostron responded. "Go below and get some coffee and try to get warm."

5:08 A.M.

When the light of dawn finally appeared, there seemed to be a stunning sight out on the water. A number of the *Titanic*'s survivors stood at the rail and pointed. "Oh, look, look," one woman cried, "Sailboats, sailboats out on the water looking for our dear people. There must be a great rescue underway."

As the light got better, it became obvious that these weren't sailing ships at all, but icebergs. The first rays of the sun glinted off them, turning them to a pink, mauve, blue, and then white.

Boxhall stood next to Gloria on the deck. Both of them were transfixed by the sight of the ice on the placid water. "It's so hard to believe that something so horrible could come from something so beautiful," Gloria said. She sighed. "I find that scene so tranquil and peaceful."

"Things aren't always what they seem, are they?" Boxhall said. "The *Titanic* seemed to be unsinkable, but we know better now."

"Yes, we do," Gloria said. "You know, I'm almost amazed they were so presumptive to name that ship the *Titanic*. The Titans were half humans that longed to be like God." She shook her head. "For that pride they were cast into hell. Amazing, isn't it?"

"Yes, amazing. We were proud. I'm not sure if I'll ever be proud again."

6:15 A.M.

With the morning, the absolute flat calm of the sea had disappeared. A slight swell was growing, and it was beginning to worry Lightoller. Just watching the *Carpathia* picking up passengers in the distance was an act of torture. The air had gone down in the collapsible from a slow leak. It was now much lower in the water, and with the small waves, the icy brine was washing over the top of the little boat at regular intervals.

"All right, men, stand in the middle of the boat," Lightoller ordered. "Form two columns of absolutely straight lines."

The men struggled to the center of the overturned boat, each line positioned on a separate side of the small keel. They watched the water lap up the bottom of the boat and roll over their shoes to the opposite side.

"Now stand absolutely still," Lightoller called out.

"Mister Lightoller, Bride can't stand up," Nordstrom cried. "I think his feet are frozen."

"Then just hold him steady there. Don't even let him try to stand."

Morgan had been glum ever since Peter had died. He'd lowered Peter's body into the water himself to provide a spot for another man. It was the hardest thing he'd ever had to do in his entire life. Even though they were now in the light of day and the *Carpathia* was in sight bringing passengers aboard, he still couldn't decide which of last night's events haunted him more. The sight of Peter being lowered into the water sickened him. He also knew there was a murderer from the ship who most likely had gotten away unscathed and was more than likely someone he could never bring to justice. The only thing that even partially warmed his spirits was the thought that Margaret was already aboard the *Carpathia*.

"How many do you think went down?" Morgan asked Lightoller.

"That's hard to say, a thousand maybe."

The strangest sight of the day came to greet them five minutes later. A man who was bundled in a life preserver and a cook's uniform came paddling over in the direction of the small overturned boat. It seemed incredible.

Lightoller yelled over to the man. "Who are you?"

The cook stopped paddling. Cupping his hands to his face, he yelled back. "I'm Chief Baker Charles Joughin."

"How did you get here?" Lightoller shouted. "Did somebody throw you in?"

There was always a danger that someone in a boat might behave badly and endanger the other people. That was the only plausible explanation for a man still swimming at this hour.

"Nah," Joughin yelled, "I stepped off the *Titanic*'s stern as the old girl went under."

"Amazing," Morgan said. "How could anyone do that?"

Joughin swam over toward the barely floating boat. He tried to climb aboard, but one of the men at the other end of the boat pushed him back into the water.

"See here," Joughin said, "I been swimming all night."

"You'll tip us over," the sailor replied.

Joughin swam around the boat and saw one of the assistant cooks, a John Maynard. "Here, Johnny, how about a hand fer old Charlie?"

Maynard knelt down and extended his hand. "Here ya go mate, just hang on till we get ourselves picked up."

"How'd you manage to stay out there in the cold?" Maynard asked.

"I had myself almost a full bottle of brandy when I knew the ship was going down. I figured if I couldn't feel anything, then maybe nothing would hurt me."

The men closest to the man in the water all began to laugh. It seemed impossible to Morgan, impossible that he could ever laugh or smile at anything again. He did smile though. Hunter would have been proud.

7:30 A.M.

Boats No. 6 and No. 16 were tied up together. They were drifting, as the man in charge, Quartermaster Hichens had ordered. Hichens was a rather large man with muttonchop whiskers and a jowled look. His blouse was buttoned up all the way to his chin and his cap pulled down, revealing a small set of eyes that looked like marbles in a child's schoolyard game.

At least two of the women aboard the boats were outspoken critics of Hichens, Helen Candee and Molly Brown. They had tried to get the boats to go back for survivors after the *Titanic* had gone down, but Hichens had been afraid that the swimmers in the water would swamp them. There wasn't much more these two women could stomach from this man who said he was in charge but who to this point had shown his greatest proclivity in doing absolutely nothing.

They had spent the last hour only watching the *Carpathia* pick up people in the distance, a distance that Hichens seemed to have no desire to close. It was quite cold, and these women were more than impatient, they were downright mutinous. They were watching others shiver, others who like Hichens were doing nothing.

"Mr. Hichens, do you think that ship will ever come over here and rescue us?" Helen Candee asked. Mrs. Candee was an author and, as such, had become accustomed to making things happen and not waiting for them. Her furs were warmly pulled over her throat, and the broad-brimmed hat she wore was still in place.

"No, she is not going to pick us up," Hichens responded. "She is to pick up bodies."

"Did you hear that?" Candee asked Molly Brown. "They're picking up bodies, the man says."

Molly Brown was a colorful woman from Denver and one that could be counted on to say almost anything. Her husband had made his money in gold mining, and she showed it with a sable stole over a pink dress that sparkled like the stars. Her large hat looked like a small table at a Paris cafe, one with feathers and linens as a tablecloth.

"Nonsense!" Molly exploded. "They're picking up whoever comes their way and this idiot has us drifting with the tide."

"Maybe we should do something about it," Candee suggested.

"Dang right we should," Molly shouted. She pointed to a strong-looking man in boat No. 16 who was a stoker. The man was still grimy with coal dust. "You there, you climb into this boat. We're borrowing you."

The stoker looked over at Hichens. "Never mind him," Molly said. "You wanna get rescued before you have grandchildren, don't you?"

The man reached over and pulled the two boats together. Standing up, he stepped from boat No. 16 into boat No. 6.

Hichens got to his feet. "Here, here," the quartermaster said.

"Sit down and shut your face," Molly said.

A man on the bottom of the boat was barefoot and clad only in his pajamas. He'd been freezing through most of the night, with his teeth chattering so badly that they could be heard throughout the boat. Molly looked at the man and took her sable stole off. She bent down and wrapped it around the man's feet and up his legs.

"That ought to keep you warm till you start rowing." Reaching into her purse, she produced a knife and handed it over to the man. "Now here, you cut us loose from No. 16 there. We're gonna head over to that ship and get some hot soup in you and brandy in me."

She looked over at the rest of the women in the boat. "Ladies, I say we should all row. There ain't no sense in just sitting here, and the moving about will keep us warm."

Hichens got up from his seat. "Now stop this," he shouted, shaking his finger at Molly Brown. "What you're doing is nothing short of mutiny."

"Sit down, Hichens. If you interfere, I'm gonna have you tossed overboard. You ain't no good anyway, just taking up space like you do."

"That's right," one of the other women shouted. "We need to row."

The other women on the boat began to make noise and pass along their remarks. None of them were friendly to the quartermaster.

Hichens was visibly shaken. The idea of being ordered about by women passengers was one that was totally foreign to him. These were not mere suggestions, either. They were forceful words from a woman with a plan. His knees began to shake.

"Now you just sit yourself down, you no-account man," Molly yelled. "You made folks listen to you last night when we should have gone back for them men in the water. Every one of them would have been twice the man you are."

Hichens sank back to his blankets beside the tiller. Picking them up, he wrapped them around himself and began to mutter and curse. He then began to shout insults at Molly.

"I say," the stoker called out in disbelief, "don't you know that you are talking to a lady?"

"I know whom I am speaking to, and I am in command of this boat!"

"You're barely in command of your own behind," Molly roared back at the man, "and if ya don't stop your yammering I'm gonna give you a personal whuppin'."

The muttering died down to a series of barely discernible murmurs. It was plain to see the man was no longer in charge, no matter what he thought.

"Now, ladies," called out Molly, "let's all begin to row together."

11:00 A.M.

Morgan was one of the last men to leave what was left of collapsible boat B. He swung on to the rope ladder and scaled it like it was a tree and he was once again a boy. One of the *Carpathia*'s stewards was at the top with blankets. The man threw several of them on Morgan and turned him over to a woman who was one of the *Carpathia*'s passengers.

The woman had a tray of hot soup and coffee and sat him down on a bench, handing him a cup.

Morgan held the cup in his hands, shaking like a leaf. He could never remember a time when he'd been so cold. He held the cup to his lips and began to sip what he could only guess might be tomato soup. It was the best he'd ever tasted.

Looking around the deck, he could see hundreds of the *Titanic's* passengers and crew, all with blankets and many with steaming cups. He looked them over carefully, searching for Margaret and April.

Turning back to his cup, he didn't have to wait long. He heard the sound of Margaret's voice.

"Morgan!"

He looked up to see the woman as she practically ran to him. April was walking ever so slowly behind her.

Morgan got to his feet as Margaret ran into his arms. She began kissing him. "Here, now," Morgan said. "I don't want you getting wet and cold, too."

"I don't care. You're here. Praise God!"

Morgan held her tightly. He forced a smile at April over Margaret's shoulder. "It's good to see you, Mrs. Hastings." And then he caught what he thought was a genuine smile from the woman.

"We're both very glad to see you, Morgan," April said.

"It's a miracle," Margaret said, "an absolute miracle." Reaching up, she lifted herself on her toes and kissed him.

"I'm afraid I have some bad news," Morgan said.

It was one of the things he knew Margaret feared. He almost hated to tell her and spoil the joy she was feeling at the moment.

"Peter's gone," she said.

"Yes, I'm afraid so. He died on our boat during the night."

She clung tightly to him and began to sob, deep mournful groans.

"He was quite the sport, even in the end. The last words he spoke were about you."

Margaret leaned her head back and with the back of her hand, began to wipe the tears away. "Wh-wh-what did he say?" She almost blubbered out the words.

Morgan stroked the hair back from her eyes. He spoke the words softly, almost like a prayer in an empty chapel. "He said, 'Promise me that you'll love Margaret and that you'll name your first son Peter.' It would seem that Peter and I both had the same thing on our minds last night, Margaret, loving you." He held her close as she continued to cry.

2:00 P.M.

Both Margaret and her mother had gone down to the cabins for a nap, but Morgan couldn't sleep. His eyes were red and bloodshot, but his blood still ran cold. He had found Boxhall, and the two men had spent more than an hour talking about the disaster and going over the list of survivors. Delaney, Guggenheim, Hans, and Kelly had all gone down with the ship. The list of dignitaries who had perished was long.

Morgan was preoccupied, though, preoccupied at the sight of Kitty Webb. The woman sat on the deck between two well-dressed men, each of them fighting for her attention. Every hair seemed to be in place, and her ruby necklace and diamond tiara looked just as dazzling in the daylight as it did under the lamps of the dining room.

"Your mind seems to be elsewhere," Boxhall said.

"Yes." Morgan motioned with his chin to the far side of the deck.

Boxhall looked around. "I see. You still can't get Hunter out of your mind, can you?"

"No, and I suppose it's silly, given everything else that's happened."

"Not terribly silly. The matter is still unresolved."

Morgan shook his head, snickering at the idea. "With everything else that's unresolved, do you really think anyone's going to worry about an out-of-work actor that people think fell and hit his head?"

"No, I suppose not."

"I think it's just something I'll have to carry with me," Morgan said. "One of the many things a man carries about in life. You know when I came aboard the *Titanic* at Southampton, I thought so many things were important that don't mean a hill of beans to me any longer."

Boxhall nodded. "I can understand that."

"I was so concerned about proving myself and showing that I really belonged to my social class because of what I could accomplish and not because of who my parents were. None of that seems important now. The hand of God came down and showed no favors last night. The mighty were just as fragile as the weak."

"Who's to say who the mighty are."

"Exactly, no one but God. He shows His grace on whom he chooses, not on the people we think deserve to have it. I certainly don't deserve to be here and Peter," Morgan cast a glance out to the sea, "out there somewhere."

"I know what you mean," Boxhall said.

Morgan looked back at Kitty. The young woman saw him and gave him a smile. The two men were continuing to vie for her attention. Reaching into her bag, she pulled out a cigarette case. It was silver with gold trim on it. Opening it up, she took out a cigarette and drummed it on the lid. She leaned over to one of the men who fumbled for his lighter. Striking a flame, he held it under the end of the cigarette. She puffed it to life. Leaning back on her chair, she caught Morgan's gaze. She snapped the case shut and dropped it in her bag.

EPILOGUE

THREE MONTHS LATER—
NEWPORT, RHODE ISLAND

The house was a modest one, by Newport standards. A cobblestone drive swooped into a large manicured lawn and formed a horse-shoe that ended at the front door. Actually, there were two doors, two large, bright-green doors with brass knockers. Brass lamps hung on each side of the doors and shone in the bright sunshine of mid-July.

Morgan stepped out of the taxicab and watched the man pull his bags from the top rack. The motor was still running, and the machine seemed to shake and cough with the inactivity. It had run smoothly enough when on the road from the train station, but sitting still didn't agree with it.

"There you are, sir." The man set the two bags down. "Do you want me to carry them up to the house?"

"No, thank you." Morgan said. The two bags were relatively small, but Morgan had learned to travel light since the *Titanic*. Were the truth known, he had practically nothing left and had little time to shop. "I can take them from here," Morgan said.

He fished in his pocket and produced the coins to pay the man, with more besides.

The man tipped his hat. "Thank you, sir."

Morgan picked up the bags and stood looking at the house. He continued to stare as the taxicab sputtered off in the direction of the front gate. This was the home of his childhood. It had none of the memories of school: no homework, no late nights by the lamp, no report cards, just play. Technically, Lilly was still an employee. His Uncle John had finally consigned all of his business affairs to him, and that carried the house at Newport along with it. As far as Morgan was concerned, she could have the place as long as she wanted. He would be happy with the flat in Manhattan.

Morgan walked up to the doors, set down the bags, and lifted the brass knocker. He pounded the door twice with it. *What will I say to Lilly?* he wondered. She had been in New York to greet him when he came in on the *Carpathia*. Like many of the others there, she hadn't known if he had survived the disaster until she got there and read the final list of survivors. Rostron had permitted little in the way of radio traffic. He had finally allowed the list to be sent after making certain that it was only the *Carpathia* that was carrying the living.

Morgan had finished his first two and a half months at the *Herald*. His experience on the *Titanic* had done one thing for him; it had taken him off the section of the paper devoted to social events and placed him on the crime beat. It was a subject he warmed to, perhaps because he knew that crime wasn't just an activity of the poor, or perhaps it was because he knew full well that not all criminals were punished.

The door opened slowly, and Lilly greeted him by opening her arms as well. "Morgan, I hoped it was you."

Morgan hugged her. "You knew I was coming, didn't you?"

"Yes, I got your wire. I just wasn't sure when."

Morgan thought the woman was still beautiful. Her gray hair was pushed back in a sweep and piled on top of her head. She wore a pretty blue dress, with the customary summer short sleeves and a piece of white lace buttoned around her throat. Lilly's high cheekbones and blue eyes had stood the test of time very well.

"Where shall I put these?" Morgan held up the two bags.

"Just put them on the armoire, dear. James can take them up later." James was the handyman of the place and served as an occasional butler when need be. It wasn't often, since the house had few social gatherings after his parents died. The man's wife, June, was the cook, and his three, almost-grown children, helped to keep the gardens in bloom.

Morgan followed her into the parlor. Everything was just as he had remembered, including the worn sofa with its carefully located antimacassars, one placed in the spot where he had drilled a hole in the arm with the blade of his pocketknife. He hadn't been malicious. He wanted to see if the thing would cut. It did, and he became the worse for wear because of it.

"Please, sit down," Lilly said. "I can have June bring you some cookies and milk, if you like."

Morgan smiled. He sat beside the damaged arm. He'd have to remember not to finger the antimacassar. "I'm afraid I've got beyond the stage of cookies and milk."

Lilly smiled. "Yes, I suppose you have." She continued to look at him, almost as if he were still the boy in knee-high socks and shorts. "You have grown into a fine young man. Tell me, are you enjoying your work?"

"Yes, I am. I find it exciting."

Lilly nodded. "I'm glad." She shifted through several letters sitting on the table in front of her. "I have a letter you might be interested in reading. It's from your Margaret. She was so very nice to write to me."

Morgan's eyes brightened.

Lilly picked up the pink envelope and opened it. She pulled out several sheets of pink stationery. "This is a dear girl you're going to marry. I'm still not sure why you're both waiting until next June."

"It might take us that long before we're both ready for another cruise," Morgan replied. He bowed his head slightly and shook it slowly. "Besides, that will give me more time to get settled."

"Are you afraid people will think it too sudden?"

"What makes you think that?"

Lilly shifted through the letter and pulled out the second page. "Margaret seems to think you want to protect her from people talking. She thinks it's just like you to do that, think of her family rather than of your-self."

"Well, it is soon after Peter's death."

"Something which neither you nor Margaret are responsible for in any way."

"I know. I suppose it takes some time to put it out of my mind." Morgan shuffled his feet nervously. Lilly had always been able to see through him, and time hadn't changed that in the least.

"That's something you should never do, Morgan. Tragedy is that which brings meaning to joy. It's all a part of God's plan in making you the man you are." Lilly tapped on the envelope. "This is a sweet girl, Morgan. I wouldn't wait too long. Don't let time pass you by."

"Speaking of that," Morgan said, "I have something for you." He fumbled in his coat pocket and took out the old photograph. Given the sinking of the *Titanic*, he was glad he'd carried the thing in his pocket. It was a little the worse for wear, but still in relatively good shape.

"A photograph?" Lilly asked.

"Yes, an old one of you." Morgan passed the picture over to her.

Lilly took it and stared. He watched her as she studied the image. It was almost as if she were not looking at a mere picture. Rather, it was as if she were looking back in time, at another life, another person. "Where did you get this?"

Morgan waited for her to pass the photograph back, but she seemed to want to hang onto it. "I got it in England, from the man in the picture. It has your words written on the back."

Lilly turned it over and read the words. "Yes, I did love George."

"Do you still love him?"

She looked up at him, the trace of a tear in the corner of her eye. Taking a handkerchief, she dabbed her eye. "Yes, I suppose I'll always love him. I was a silly girl who should have known better, but a girl in love nonetheless."

"Who was he?"

Lilly shook her head. "Oh, you don't want to know that."

"Yes, I do. You see the man was killed right before my eyes."

Lilly's eyes began to tear up faster. She dabbed them and then tried to shake the thought out of her mind. "I-I-I haven't seen him in over twenty-six years," she stammered. "We wrote after that, but when you were born I asked him not to write me again."

Morgan nodded at the photograph. "Well, it's obvious the man never stopped thinking about and loving you. He was carrying that until the day he died."

Lilly shook her head. "I never would have thought."

"Who was he?" Morgan asked again.

"He was a man in the diplomatic service. He spoke twelve languages fluently."

"But who was he to you?"

"The man I loved." She began to weep. "Please don't ask me any more."

Lilly had been sitting on the love seat next to the sofa, and Morgan got up and took a seat next to hers. He put his arm around her. "We've never had secrets from one another and I wouldn't want to start now," he said.

Lilly looked up at him with tear-soaked eyes. "If you only knew."

"Knew what?"

"We've had secrets in this house since the day you were born, things you should never know."

Morgan placed his hands on Lilly's shoulders, turning her to face him. "Secrets about this, about George Sinclair?"

Lilly nodded. "Yes, terrible secrets."

"Then tell me, tell me now."

"I-I-I can't. I promised the Fairfields I would never say a word about it."

"Lilly, you can't mean that. My parents have been dead for over twenty years."

Lilly wrung the handkerchief in her hands. Her face was riveted to the floor. "No, I'm afraid they haven't."

"What do you mean?"

Lilly handed the photograph back to Morgan. "This man, George Sinclair, was your father."

The words struck Morgan like a sledgehammer. He sank back into the seat, unable to speak, barely able to breathe. His mind tumbled over and over.

"Oh, Morgan, please forgive me." She began to hold him. "I know I was foolish to ever say anything. I promised, and now you know why."

Morgan held onto her for what seemed like the longest time. There were no tears for him, only shock and dismay. Finally, he pushed her away. "What of my mother? How did she come to know this man?"

Lilly held onto his arms. Her face was bright red, with tears staining her cheeks. "Don't you see, Morgan? I am your mother."

It took Lilly the rest of the afternoon to describe the events that had led up to his birth. Morgan listened in absolute silence as they both strolled through the garden. What she pictured for him was a well-to-do couple that couldn't have children of their own and a housekeeper who had begun and then ended a love affair. The people he'd thought of as his parents were no less heroic. In a way, they were all the more so. They'd kept Lilly on as a nursemaid to her own child, an act of mercy in anybody's book, and they had both drowned trying to save a small child that wasn't their own.

He did finally break down and tell her the rest of his story, how he came to be in possession of the photograph and some of what George's final mission had been. In a way, it brought them even closer. It certainly went a long way in explaining the constant devotion he'd felt from her letters while he was being schooled in England. Not many boys had their nurses write several letters to them each week.

"At the time I was overcome with shame," Lilly said. "I never even told George in my letters that I was carrying his child. The poor man never knew. He certainly didn't know that it was his own son that held him when he lay dying. I know the Lord has forgiven me," Lilly said. "I only hope you can."

Morgan wrapped his arms around her and held her closely. "I forgive you, Mother." He used the word for the first time that he could remember and felt strangely warmed by it. "God's grace is a mysterious thing," Morgan said. "It finds us in the most unusual places. It found you in the garden, and it found me on the *Titanic*."